After a long prayer by one young man, Percy read from the Bible and gave a sermon. I still thrilled to the sound of his beautiful voice, his determined words, and his ardent faith. Percy was so sure, so confident, and compared to his, my own faith was full of doubts and unanswered questions.

It was late when everyone left. Then Percy put on his heavy jacket and handed Sophia her shawl. It was his week with her, and now they would leave me and go to her part of the house. Always as he left with her, my heart broke in two.

The wall between our rooms was not thick enough to deaden all sounds, and sometimes I could hear them talking. When he was there with her, they talked and laughed together; she was his wife and I was utterly alone. When he was with me, I was his wife, and I wondered what Sophia could hear on her side of the wall.

The situation lent itself to madness, and now when Sophia's laughter rang out, I could not endure it. Pushing a chair in front of me to lean on, I struggled over to the bed and got in without undressing. I cupped my hands over my ears and gnashed my teeth until I fell asleep.

NO BED IN DESERET

NICKOLAE GERSTNER

JUANITA B. ANDERSON

POPHAM PRESS
An Imprint of Ace Books

ace books
A Division of Charter Communications Inc.
A GROSSET & DUNLAP COMPANY
51 Madison Avenue
New York, New York 10010

NO BED IN DESERET

A Popham Press Original

First Printing: February 1981
Published simultaneously in Canada

2 4 6 8 0 9 7 5 3 1
Manufactured in the United States of America

To Jo-Ann
Olive's Great-grand-daughter

Chapter 1

I watched Pa, hoping to detect some sign of anger. I wanted him to shout and pound the table with his fist the way he usually did when he was about to give in, but he continued to take deep puffs on his pipe.

We had finished the evening meal, and Pa was sitting in the sturdy chair that had taken so much space on the wagon when we made the long journey from Ohio to Iowa. His huge frame always seemed to mold into that chair, and now his long legs were stretched out, his eyes were half-closed, and he smoked his pipe with slow deliberation.

I had braced myself, then told him that Percival Terry was coming to see him. "Please Pa, for my sake, don't send him away," I begged, clasping my hands under my apron. "He really must talk to you."

Pa's voice was much too calm. "Olive, understand that I've told you before and now tell you again. You can never marry Dr. Terry. I forbid it, and I don't want the man in this house."

I dug my nails into my palms, but that didn't release the agony that welled up inside me. I wanted to scream that he was being unreasonable, but I didn't dare. My last, thin hope was to convince him that I was grown up and knew what I was doing.

I struggled to keep my voice steady. "Pa, why can't you realize how much Percy and I love each other? We belong together, and we would never let our lives be affected by the wrong other people do.''

He shook his head, a sad gesture, and did not answer. I was his older daughter, his pet, the one who was always picked to persuade him when the family wanted a favor, but now when it was the most important thing in my life, he wouldn't even listen to me.

Ted was bent over the fireplace, poking at the blaze. He was nineteen and already a man. I wanted him to help me persuade Pa to talk to Percy, but suddenly Ted dropped the poker, jerked on his buckskin jacket and mumbled something about checking the beaver trap.

I adored Ted, and his fun and friendship had helped me fight off the loneliness that engulfed me during the dreary months that followed after we settled in the desolate town of Kanesville, Iowa. I wanted his support again, but he bounded out the door, avoiding any more involvement in the battle that had raged all winter.

Dorothy would be no help either. She sat, eyes downcast, helping Daniel print his name on his slate. She and I were as close as sisters can be. Born hardly a year apart, we slept side by side and shared every secret and every hope, but Dorothy was too loving and gentle to take a stand in a conflict. She stared at the slate and never looked up.

Little George wasn't feeling well and had climbed up to the loft, and only Joseph making happy noises in his cradle seemed unaware of the tension.

Desperate, I turned to my mother. ''Ma, you and Pa both know that Percy is a good man. You liked him—you know you did—until you found out about his religion. Please, oh please listen to reason and ask Pa to talk to him.''

Ma finished putting bowls in the cupboard, then pulled herself up as tall as her tiny frame would allow, a bad sign. "You are only seventeen, and what you are feeling now will not last forever. It is a sin, a plain sin, the way those people live."

"But *they* are not important! What really matters is that Percy and I love each other. He will never love anyone but me."

In one explosive movement, Pa rose from his chair and grabbed my arm. "Olive, no daughter of mine will ever belong to a man's stable of wives. He's a Mormon, and he believes in polygamy—he admitted it right here in this room—and I will not let you marry him!"

"But he has promised never to choose another wife, and—"

Pa didn't let me continue. "And those folks are thieves! I've heard more than one story about them carrying off what's not rightly theirs."

It was hopeless, and my despair gave way to rage. "You've always taught us to give a man his just due and not condemn anyone, but now you are listening to lies and rumors," I shouted. "But you can't really believe that a man like Percy would ever steal." I jerked my arm free. "I am going down to the road to wait for Percy, and I'll tell him that my father is too unfair to even talk to him."

As I rushed outside, tears blurred my vision. I ran a few steps and leaned against the barn, biting my hand to muffle a scream.

I was unaware of Dorothy's approach until I felt my shawl being draped around my shoulders. "Olive, it's too cold for you to be out without this," she murmured.

I pulled the shawl around me, but Dorothy lingered.

"May . . . may I stay with you?" she asked.

There was such concern in her voice that I turned toward her, and in a moment we were in each other's arms.

"Olive, I know how bad you feel, but if Pa did give his consent, you would be heading west soon. Maybe we'd never see each other again." Dorothy's voice rose to a wail, and tears rolled down her cheeks.

I loved my family. The thought of leaving them was anguish, but I couldn't keep Percy out of my mind for ten minutes a day. Life without him seemed impossible, but it was all so hard to explain.

"Dorothy, I don't want to leave you behind, but no matter what Pa says, I have to go with Percy. But you and I won't be separated forever. We'll be together again someday, I just know it."

I kissed her, and her damp cheek felt ice cold. "My goodness, Dorothy, you're colder than I am! You'd better go back in the house, and you can tell Ma and Pa that I'm all right."

Dorothy was reluctant, but I insisted. Then I headed for the road.

It was March, and for nearly a week the days had been warming, but suddenly winter was making a final stand. It was bitter cold again, and I was glad even though I knew that spring could not hold off forever.

I looked up, and in the fading light, I had a last glimpse of the bluffs spotted white with covered wagons. For months immigrants had poured in from the East and set up camp in Kanesville, waiting out the winter before continuing the long haul west. With the coming of the spring thaw, the first trains would pull for the Missouri River—the *Great Mo*. It was almost time, and excitement seethed all around me. Townspeople, immigrants—everyone seemed to feel the power of the great surge west, but I was in torment. Percy's wagon train would be one of the first to roll, and if he headed west without me, it might be years before I saw him again.

When I reached the road, I saw Percy coming at the earliest moment I could expect him. He walked swiftly, head up and arms swinging. I felt fresh pain, knowing that all his confidence and determination would be wasted. Pa would not even talk to him.

When he reached me, we embraced, and I felt his lips, his warm breath on my forehead. I didn't speak, afraid that a single word would start a rush of tears.

"Olive, dearest, you should have waited in the house." Before I could stop him, he took off his muffler and bound it snug around my neck. He was tender, as if I were a baby in a bunting.

He was a tall man, lean and clean-shaven, and a lock of dark hair usually fell across his forehead. His deep blue eyes added a look of gentleness to his fine features, and he was, without doubt, the handsomest man I had ever seen. When I looked at him, I knew again that Ma and Pa were wrong. I could never love any other man the way I loved Percy. He was special—he was mine—and there wasn't another like him in all the world.

"Is your father expecting me?" he asked.

I shook my head. "Percy, it's hopeless. He won't even talk to you."

Percy remained confident. "He will have to talk to me because God wants you to be my wife."

He began taking long strides toward the house, and I hurried after him. "Please believe me. You can't talk to him now."

Pa hated the Mormons for their polygamy, and he had just called them thieves. The tension was high, and it was a dangerous time for him and Percy to encounter each other.

But Percy was determined. "Olive, I promise that this time it will be different. I won't get angry no matter what he says, and I'll try not to make him angry. I'll answer all his objections. I will make him see that it is right for us to marry."

Percy walked so fast I could hardly keep up with him, but I couldn't let him knock on the door. I tugged his sleeve.

"Listen to me," I pleaded. "Pa and I were fighting. If you go to him now, he'll either turn you away or there'll be a terrible argument. This isn't the time."

Percy stopped. His beautiful confidence seemed to give way, and his shoulders sagged. "If I can't talk to your father now, when can I talk to him? Yesterday, Brother Benson put out word that our wagon train is to begin getting ready to leave. We'll be on our way soon."

I felt such utter despair I couldn't even cry. "Percy, I know we're running out of time, but there is nothing . . . nothing we can do."

Percy caught his breath sharply. He stood quiet, and after a few moments his confidence seemed to return. "Maybe we are both forgetting that the will of God makes its own time."

He put a comforting arm around me. "If I can't talk to your father now, I will be patient and wait for guidance."

We huddled together, but a sharp wind whipped my apron and blew my skirts against my legs. We couldn't stay outdoors much longer.

I turned my face toward his and when I spoke, my breath lingered in white puffs. "Let's go to our little house," I said.

"We shouldn't," he answered, "not after dark."

He hesitated. "But maybe this one time it would be all right."

Our little house was a wooden structure, the abandoned home of a trapper, and more of a shed than a cabin. We'd discovered it one day as we wandered along the deserted iciness of the river's edge, so eager to be alone that we were braving the hard winter's cold.

That first day Percy gathered kindling and started a fire in the circle of unmortared bricks the trapper had used for a fireplace. We had huddled together and held our hands toward the blaze. I had just passed my seventeenth birthday; Percy was twenty-two, but we had giggled like children.

The shed became our hideaway. Percy brought a heavy blanket for us to sit on, and he stacked a load of firewood in the corner. It was the only place where we could be alone, but Percy insisted we meet there only during the innocence of daylight. Never before had we been there at night.

We headed to the path that led down to the river, threading our way in darkness. We found the shed, but inside there was no light at all. I listened as Percy struck again and again at the flint box. When the light flared, it illuminated his face, and he smiled at me.

In a few minutes a fire was blazing, and we wrapped ourselves in the blanket and sat on the ground, pulling as near to the flames as we could.

"You're still shivering," Percy said, putting his arm under my shawl and pressing me close to him.

He pressed his face to mine, and the fine bristle of his whiskers rubbed against my cheek. "You might take a chill," he said. "It was reckless to come here tonight, but I wanted to be with you."

"And I wanted to be with you, Percy."

He opened his coat, undid the buttons of his shirt, then pressed me tight against the warmth of his body. "Let me warm you," he said.

I slipped my arms under the shirt, and I could feel the

strength, the firmness of his body. He began kissing me, and a cozy, beautiful warmth flooded through me. All I was aware of was Percy, his very being, the taste of his mouth on mine, the touch of his hand on my breast.

I had responded to his kisses before, and I had felt a strange pleasure at the light touch of his hand on the bodice of my dress. We had spent many precious hours here, sitting close to the fire just as we were now, talking, kissing, laughing. We had become familiar and comfortable with each other, but now everything seemed different. The joy was gone; our love was doomed to separation.

He was usually very gentle, very tender, but now his kisses had an energy that left me struggling for breath. He loosened the neckline of my dress and kissed the curve of my shoulder. He had never disarranged my clothing before, and I was startled, but nothing in me offered resistance. I was in his arms where I belonged.

He spoke, but his voice was muffled, and at first I could not understand. Then meaning came. He wanted to love me and make me his own.

I opened my eyes, trying to sort out the confusion of hopes and fears that ran through my mind. Suddenly I felt shy, even frightened. I knew that what he asked was wrong, but I did not want to refuse him. If I couldn't belong to him in marriage, then I would belong to him in a love that would last forever, whether we were together or apart.

As he began undoing the buttons of my dress, I felt safe and loved, but suddenly—violently—Percy groaned and jerked away. He covered his face with his hands. "God forgive me," he cried. "How could I try to lead you into sin?"

I was startled out of my beautiful haven and thrust

back into the world where pain existed. And Percy was in pain, stricken with shame because he had wanted to love me.

I had not refused him, and I shuddered, thinking of what he would think of me now. At first I was too shaken to speak, but when I caught hold of myself, I told him I was sorry. "Percy, I shouldn't have let you think I would—"

"No, dearest," he interrupted. "It was all my responsibility. It was wrong of me to ask you, and I beg you to forgive me."

Finally he looked up, and even in the soft glow of the fire, his expression was grave. "Olive, I promise that until we are married, this will never happen again."

He got up and began banking the fire. I felt weak and dizzy, but I forced myself to rearrange my clothes and refold the blanket. I knew it was the last time we would ever be together in the dismal shed that had housed our love.

Chapter 2

I felt as if Percy had always been the center of my world; it was almost impossible to remember life before I knew him, yet it was only five months since we first met.

Ted had met some of the Mormons camped in Kanesville, and later he had invited Dorothy and me to attend one of their services: "They are happy, friendly folks," he told us, "and there are many fellows and girls our age."

During the summer my family had moved from Ohio to Kanesville, a town that consisted of little more than a few log houses. It was a lonesome place. I missed my friends and the young men who had been so eager to court me, and it hurt to remember all our gay parties and dances, the apple-parings and corn-huskings. I was eager to meet new people, but when Dorothy and I promised Ted we would attend the Mormon service with him, he had something else to tell us:

"I've heard weird rumors about those folks though. People in town claim many Mormon men have two wives. I've even heard that some of the men have four or six wives."

Dorothy and I laughed. "Teddy," I cried, "even you have to be smart enough to know that a man can have only one wife."

Ted grinned. "I've always figured that one would

probably be more than enough, but just remember—
I've warned you."

The following Sunday, I put on my favorite calico, a
golden brown that matched my eyes and accented my
hair which I preferred to call gold instead of red.

Dorothy dressed up too, wearing a blue calico that
looked pretty against her blond hair. I wasn't as tall and
slender as Dorothy, but as she, Ted, and I walked
along, I held my head high, making the most of my
medium height.

The Mormon church was a long, log house, and on
one side a log had been left out and panes of glass set in,
one after the other, the length of the building. The small
sign in front read, *Church of Jesus Christ of the Latter
Day Saints*.

I read the sign aloud, and Ted said, "I guess that's
their real name, but everyone calls them Mormons."

We went inside, and to me it was just another church
service until Percy stood up to preach. I had never seen
him before, and I could hardly believe anyone was that
good looking. When I could take my eyes off him, I
looked at Dorothy. She was leaning forward in the pew,
her eyes shining, and I knew there wasn't a girl in the
room whom he hadn't enchanted.

Suddenly in mid-sentence, Percy stopped speaking.
I turned back, and he was staring straight at me. Our
eyes met, and I'm certain I blushed red as Christmas.
Then Percy caught himself and resumed preaching,
smoothly, as if nothing had happened. He had a strong,
sincere voice, and soon I was caught by the power of his
faith and the fervency of his sermon.

After the service, Percy broke away from the group
of people who quickly surrounded him, and hurried
over to us. Ted introduced us, and then Percy took my
hand. "Olive Harriet Banks," he said, repeating my

name. "You are so beautiful, I thought an angel had come to hear me preach."

My heart was pounding, but I smiled and tipped my head to one side. "Do all the ministers in your church flatter the ladies?" I asked.

Percy laughed. "If the ladies are as lovely as you are, I hope so," he said. "But I'm not a minister. I'm a physician, but all the men in my church are priests. We serve the church in whatever way we are needed."

People were pressing close, eager to shake Percy's hand.

"Will you attend our dance with me three weeks from Saturday?" Percy whispered before we were separated.

I nodded, and for a moment we looked at each other. A glow, a warm happiness washed over me, and in some wonderful, magical way, I knew Percy could feel it too.

Walking home, all I could think about was Percy. I was thrilled that he had asked me to the dance, and that evening he appeared at the door, asking if he could talk to my father.

Pa welcomed him with a hearty handshake. "Edward and the girls have been telling me that you preach a mighty fine sermon, sir. Someday I'll hear you myself."

Ma greeted Percy with a sweet smile, then said, "Dr. Terry, don't count on preaching a sermon to Mr. Banks. He's a God-fearing, Bible-reading man, but the only time I can get him inside a church is when we baptize a baby."

Pa was unabashed. "Well, Becky, we have six children, so that's six times already."

Percy threw back his head and laughed. "Mr. Banks," he said when he could speak, "I hope you won't hold my church-going strongly in my disfavor, because I've come to ask your permission to call on your daughter Olive.''

I know I blushed, but I didn't care. The only thing that mattered was that Percy wanted to court me. We had only known each other a few hours, but the great feeling that had caught me had caught him too.

Pa told Percy to pull up a chair. ''It's not my permission you need,'' he said. ''Olive is a level-headed girl. If she wants you to come around, it'll suit me.''

I turned away to hide another blush, but I was proud, knowing that my father meant what he said. He allowed us to choose our own friends, just the way he encouraged us to be independent in our thinking. He was firm and he knew his own mind, but we were allowed to disagree with him.

Pa took down the seldom touched jug that held his little supply of corn whiskey. ''Will you have a sip with me?'' he asked.

Percy shook his head. ''The tenets of my church do not permit the drinking of spirits nor the smoking of tobacco.''

Pa poured a tiny measure into his glass. ''Didn't know that. But I guess I never heard of your church until we came west to Iowa.''

They were both relaxed, confident men, and they quickly fell into easy conversation. Percy shared many of Pa's views about what was wrong in Washington, and I could tell that he was rapidly gaining Pa's respect. I pretended to concentrate on some needlework, but they didn't exchange a word I didn't hear.

Before he left, Percy and I went for a walk. We didn't say much to each other, but there was a wonderful feeling, almost a secret understanding, that bound us together better than any words ever could.

Percy called almost every evening. He was sweet and respectful to my mother; he and Pa had many serious conversations; he engaged in fun and foolery with Dorothy, Ted and me, and he knew games and stories that delighted Daniel and George. Everyone liked him, and I was madly, wildly in love. He was the sweetest, most wonderful man in the world.

One morning I sang all the time I was kneading the bread dough, and suddenly Ma put her hands on her hips and sighed. "Olive, happiness like yours just can't last."

I threw my doughy arms around her and gave her a kiss. "Ma, Percy loves me. He told me he did, and I love him too. How can I ever be anything but happy?"

It was Saturday, and that evening Percy took me to the dance at his church. We arrived early, and Percy led me onto the floor as soon as the fiddles struck up a tune. We circled, bowed and whirled, and when we were separated, his gaze followed me until the crier's "Swing your partners" brought us together again.

I didn't mind the cracks between the rough logs of the floor because my feet hardly seemed to touch the ground. There was a great happiness and cheer all around me, and almost everyone danced, even the gray haired men and women.

I was in love and having a wonderful time, but as the evening wore on, something baffled me. Perhaps I wouldn't have noticed it if it hadn't been for Ted's wild story about Mormon men having more than one wife, but I became aware that many of the men arrived accompanied by more than one woman. Little groups consisting of several women remained together, and the man danced with them one at a time.

It can't be true. A man can't have more than one wife.

Later Percy and I went over to a table where a woman was serving cranberry punch and cake. As she handed me a glass of punch, she winked at Percy.

"You two look mighty pretty dancing together," she said.

Laughing, Percy answered, "I don't know about me, but Miss Banks always looks pretty."

He turned to me. "This is Mrs. Isaac Dodson Terry, one of my father's wives."

I stood there, not really comprehending, and Percy continued. "My mother is Pa's first wife, but she's not here tonight."

I couldn't answer or pretend I wasn't stunned. *This couldn't be real.* Dizziness washed over me, and my hand shook so much I had to set the punch on the table.

Percy put his arm around me. "Let's go outside," he said.

He got my shawl, we left the dance and began wandering aimlessly.

"You've never heard of plural marriage before, have you, Olive?" he asked.

I shook my head. "Percy, why . . . why didn't you tell me?" I asked brokenly.

"I wanted you to know me first. I wanted you to know my people so that you could understand."

"Understand?" I gasped. "How can I ever understand why your father has two wives?"

"My father has four wives," Percy said. "They are all fine women, and we have one large, devoted family. Not one of us has ever harmed anyone, yet we've been persecuted right across the country."

We continued walking; I could hardly think, but Percy talked in a steady voice.

"One night when I was small, I was awakened by a shouting mob. I rushed to the window and saw our

people running. There were gunshots. Men, women
and little children fell before my eyes. My parents
herded us out of the house, but as we ran for safety, my
own little sister was shot in the back of the head . . . ."

His voice trembled. "We escaped from New York
and moved to Missouri, but when I was sixteen, we
were forced to flee again, and we headed for Nauvoo,
Illinois. When trouble came there, I wanted to stay and
fight, but my father wanted me to go to Philadelphia
and prepare for medical school the way we'd always
planned.

"My family and the rest of the Saints moved on to
Iowa but there were many deaths. They'd driven us
out in winter; food was scarce and tents and wagons
were the only shelter. My family fared better than most
because there's money, but the terrible suffering . . ."
His voice faded.

I shook my head to clear it. "But your father's
wives,'" I begged. "How does any of this explain
them?"

He took my hands in his. I tried to pull back, but his
grip was firm. "Many of our men were killed, and their
wives and daughters were left without a man to protect
them. Then our prophet, Joseph Smith, had a heavenly
revelation telling him to direct our leaders to marry
these women and give them a home and protection.
They are happy as plural wives. It is the Saints' way of
life."

Revulsion engulfed me. "It could never be my way
of life. I could never share my husband with another
woman."

He tried to take me in his arms, but I held back. "I
don't want you to be a plural wife," he said. "I want
you to be my wife, my only wife. I think I've wanted to
marry you almost from the first moment I saw you."

I began crying, an unexpected rush of tears, and this time I didn't resist when Percy took me in his arms. "Percy, I could never marry a man who believes in . . . in polygamy."

"I do believe in plural marriage for other men," he said, "but I don't believe in it for me—or for us. With you for my wife, I could never want anyone else. Don't you know that? Don't you know how much I love you?"

"If you love me," I managed between sobs, "you'll join another church."

"No," Percy answered, wiping my tears with his handkerchief. "My church is the one true church of God. That's why we are persecuted. Long before we practiced plural marriage, we were hated because we are God's chosen, and because our great faith and joy attract the many young people who join us."

"I could never join a church that approves of plural marriage," I blurted.

Percy's lips brushed my forehead. His voice was tender: "I'm not asking you to join my church, but I am asking you to marry me. I love you, and I want you at my side for the rest of my life. No one else. Just you."

Beautiful words, the words I'd expected and longed for. I looked up at him, my thoughts a throbbing conflict of love and despair. "I . . . I can't . . . ."

Percy put his hands on my shoulders and stared deep into my eyes. "Olive, you love me, you know you do. We belong together for time and eternity, and I promise—I swear to you—that you will be the only wife I will ever want."

He kissed me, and the fierce warmth of his lips on mine blotted out every thought. At last I pulled away, struggling to catch my breath. "Percy, I do love you," I gasped, "more than anything, but . . . ."

He kissed me again, and I felt as if I could lose myself forever in the strength and love of his embrace. "You and you only, Olive. I love you and there can never be anyone else."

I felt weak. I put my arms around his neck and clung to him for support.

"Marry me, Olive. Promise . . . promise that you'll be my wife."

Percy! He was more important to me than anything else in the world. The Mormons didn't matter. Polygamy didn't matter. The only thing that mattered was that we loved each other. Neither of us could ever love anyone else. Percy was right—we belonged together forever.

My voice was almost a cry. "I'll marry you, Percy. I'll marry you."

From that moment on, I let my love for Percy blot out every worry and concern. I loved him, and I would trust him too.

But my confidence in Percy's love didn't convince Pa. That same evening Pa went into town, and he came home aghast at the rumors he'd heard. He didn't mention them though, until the following afternoon when Percy arrived, invited by Ma, to sit down with us at her heavy-laden Sunday table.

Pa hardly ate, but he waited until dinner was over and Ma, Dorothy, and I were cleaning up before he questioned Percy.

"Sir, in town last night I heard serious charges laid against your people," he began, his voice bristling. "I put those charges to you now, so that you can tell me if they are true."

Percy lost none of his confidence. "Mr. Banks, my people are honorable, and our church does not condone anything that is wrong in the sight of God."

Suddenly Pa's voice thundered. "Is it true that your people believe in polygamy—that your men marry as many women as they want?"

Percy shook his head. "A man is responsible for all his wives and families. We condemn anyone's taking more wives than he can properly support and care for."

Pa slumped in his chair. "I had heard Edward and the girls talking, but until last night I thought it was nonsense beneath a man's notice."

Ma was stunned too. "But polygamy is illegal. Surely a man of your character could never be persuaded to believe in it."

"Mrs. Banks," he said gently, "I believe in it for other people. Not for me and not for Olive."

He made them all the promises he had made to me. Pa listened to every word, but his expression was stony.

"You can't understand our solutions until you understand our problems," Percy said. He sounded sincere and forceful, his preaching voice, and he told Pa and Ma of the bloody history of his people.

"Our children have been murdered, our houses and barns burned to the ground. Our crops have been destroyed and our stock stolen, leaving us to starve."

"And this is the life you want my daughter to share?" Pa intoned.

"No!" Percy shouted. "I want your daughter to come with me to Deseret, a new land in the Utah territory. Brother Brigham Young founded it for us, and there we will be free from persecution."

Percy was ardent. "With all my heart, I believe she'll be happy there. If I didn't, I wouldn't want her to go."

Pa's voice got louder and louder. They were arguing now, violently, and neither man would give an inch.

"You can believe anyhing you want," Pa said at

last, "but you can't marry my daughter. And you can't see her again, not until you come to your senses."

"But Mr. Banks," Percy said, "you told me that Olive was level-headed and could make up her own mind. Why can't she decide whether or not she still wants to see me?"

Pa looked startled, and suddenly he pounded the table with his fist. "Those are my words, and I'll live by them. Olive can see you if she still wants to, but not in this house. And she can't marry you. I want you both to understand that."

From then on, Pa tried to dissuade me from seeing Percy, but he never insisted. I loved my father and it hurt me to go against him, but I couldn't give Percy up. He was no longer welcome at home, but through the winter, we managed to be together.

His church was a place where people could come in out of the cold and visit with each other and plan for the long journey ahead. Percy and I spent many hours there, and the more I saw of the Mormons, the more I liked them. Cheerfulness was a way of life, and they seemed to be devoted to each other.

Polygamy was a thorn, a pain every time it came up, but Percy was always ready to reassure me. If I cringed when someone was introduced as a second wife, Percy would whisper in my ear, "You and you only, Olive. I'll love you forever."

He took me to meet his family, and occasionally I joined them for prayer and singing. I was treated with warmth and consideration, but Percy and I needed to be alone with each other. That's why our little house meant so much to us.

We were cautious, making certain no one saw us there, but our meetings were innocent and beautiful until we were made desperate by Pa's absolute refusal to talk to Percy. Then I had been willing to let Percy love me, and I was in awe of the great faith that had kept him from doing something he thought was wrong.

That night I had been afraid that Percy would blame me because no faith of mine had made me refuse him, but again and again he said, ''I'm a man and it is my duty—my responsibility—to protect you.''

Then Percy had held a heavy stick to the remains of the fire, igniting it to use as a torch to light our way home.

We walked in silence, but as we aproached my house, Percy said, ''You are meant to be my wife. Someday your father will have to give his consent, but we cannot take matters into our own hands. We must wait on the word of the Lord.''

Chapter 3

I entered the house, expecting to find Ma and Pa concerned because of my long absence, but their worries were for my four-year-old brother George.

When we'd gathered for supper, he hadn't felt well. At Ma's coaxing, he'd swallowed a few bites, but then he had climbed up to his tiny bed in the loft. Now he was downstairs in the large room that served as both kitchen and parlor. He was lying on the cot, and Ma and Pa hovered over him.

I peered over Ma's shoulder. George's face looked flushed and dry. His eyes were half-open, his breath caught in little moans, and he was tossing and turning.

I reached to take Ma's hand. "What's wrong with him?" I whispered.

"I don't know," she murmured, clinging to me. "We heard him crying and Pa brought him downstairs. I gave him a litle water. He swallowed it and lay back. I thought he was just going back to sleep, but a fever's caught hold of him."

She touched his forehead. "Now he's as hot as the poker."

"I haven't heard of any diphtheria in these parts," Pa said, "and it doesn't look like the scarlet fever. If we bathe the heat out of him, I think he'll be all right in the morning."

Pa's words sounded reassuring, but when I saw the grim fear in his expression, a chill ran through me.

George was special, a gay-hearted, loving little boy who delighted us all. Caring for him was my favorite responsibility.

Nothing can happen to him, I told myself.

But I knew it took a great deal to worry Pa. He had a natural confidence, and one sensed he felt he could handle any situation. For him to be badly frightened, he had to suspect that George's illness was more than a single night's misery.

Ma and Pa began covering his little body with damp cloths, and I helped, dipping and wringing. They tried to hold him still, but his arms and legs thrashed aimlessly.

Toward morning, Ma told me to go to bed. "I'll need you later," she said, "so you'd better be getting some rest."

I slipped into bed alongside Dorothy. I lay motionless, but my mind was in turmoil. I really ached for George, and I felt my parents' suffering. There could be no sleep for them.

When I finally convinced myself that George would be all right, I had a bleak vision of saying my last good-bye to Percy. From George to Percy, from Percy to George—I had no peace, and light was streaming through the window before I fell asleep.

I didn't sleep long, but when I awakened, my mind was momentarily blank. I was only aware of the quiet, so eerie because our tiny house usually echoed with the bustle and noise of eight people.

George! Everything came flooding back to me, and with a cry, I jumped up and rushed into the big room.

Ma was still at George's side, but she wasn't bathing him any longer. Her head bowed, and her hands lay limp in her lap. She looked tiny and helpless.

I knelt by the cot and looked down at my little

brother. He lay quiet, eyes closed, and his chest heaved sharply as he struggled to breathe.

Ma looked up, and her eyes were ringed black with worry and lack of sleep. Her voice was hollow. "Any minute now your Pa will be back with the doctor. I hope . . . I hope they're in time."

An ugly terror washed through me, and I felt dizzy, almost nauseous. "Ma, he'll be all right. I just know it," I cried.

Behind me Dorothy sobbed, and I turned to see her bury her face in her hands.

I struggled to my feet, and through the window I could see Ted and Daniel standing near the barn. They weren't doing anything, just waiting.

It was a day of endless waiting.

I dressed, and when Joseph fussed, I picked him up and changed his bottom cloth. It was a relief to be doing something that even momentarily distracted me.

As the day wore on, Dorothy prepared our meals. Hardly making a sound, she fixed soup, then urged Ma to take some.

Ma took the bowl Dorothy handed her, then raised the spoon to her lips. She stopped, and for over a minute she held the spoon in mid-air. Then she cried out, a sound that tore through me. The spoon and bowl clattered to the floor. Ma bent over, her body rent with deep sobs.

The tears I'd held in check all day came flooding, and I couldn't comfort Ma because of my own grief. I had never seen death, but what was happening to George needed no explanation.

Dorothy wrapped her arms around Ma. "It can't be much longer. Pa and the doctor will have to get here soon."

The three of us joined in prayer, and just as the sound of our *amens* faded away, we heard Pa's wagon.

Dorothy clapped her hands. "I knew it," she cried.

We all scrambled to our feet and rushed to the door. Pa had reined the horses; he sat on the high seat, making no move to climb down. He was all alone.

"Henry," Ma cried, "where is the doctor?"

"I couldn't find him," Pa said brokenly. "I was told he has sick kin of his own over in Omaha. He took the ferry across the river yesterday morning. I've been at the ferry station most of the day, but there's no sign of him."

"But that other doctor," Ma pleaded.

Pa shook his head. "He took the stagecoach back east three days ago."

"Is the little one any better?" Pa asked. Hope glimmered in his eyes, but all hope faded when he looked at Ma.

Abruptly, Pa turned to me. "Get your shawl, girl," he said. "We'll go for Dr. Terry."

I snatched up my shawl and climbed up and sat beside Pa on the high seat. He clicked to the horses. "Mike! Polly! Let's go!"

All day long I had thought of Percy. I had wanted to send for him, but at any moment we had expected Pa to arrive with another doctor. Then Percy would not have been needed, and it was not the day for a bitter encounter.

The horses were tired. Pa urged them on, but dusk was falling when we reached the Mormon encampment. We hurried, stopping at each tent and asking at every wagon, and finally I found Aaron Terry, Percy's younger brother.

"Percy's tending a farmer who just about went

through his own foot, chopping wood,'' Aaron told me. ''Seems he'd been out in the cold so long, his feet were numb, and—''

''Where does the farmer live?'' I cried. ''My little brother is dying, and I have to find Percy!''

''We'll be grateful for your assistance,'' Pa added.

Aaron snapped to attention. ''I'll go for him,'' he said. ''The place is beyond Mosquito Road, but I can find it. I'll get him to your place as fast as I can.''

Aaron saddled a horse, and we watched him gallop off. Then we got back in the wagon, and the weary team, Mike and Polly, trudged slowly back to the house.

At home, George still lived but just barely. He was burning up with fever, and all day long Ma had been able to get him to swallow only a few drops of water.

I sat at Dorothy's side, and we clung to each other, our hope growing weaker with every minute.

When Percy pounded on the door, Pa let him in. Percy didn't speak, not even to me, and with one quick stride he was at George's bedside. He lifted a limp little arm.

''You should have called me sooner,'' he said.

He opened his satchel, and Pa hastened to rearrange the candles to give him more light.

Percy examined George, then paused. ''That drug,'' he muttered.

He took off his coat, then turned to Pa. ''There's a new drug that I brought with me from the East. The boy's very weak, but he has a chance if I can get the drug into him. I'll need your help.''

Pa stood waiting, arms at his sides, ready to obey any instructions that might help his son.

Percy picked up a thin, rubber tube. ''I have to get this down his throat, and I want you to hold his head.''

With a whimper, Dorothy rushed into the bedroom. Ted stayed with me on the far side of the room, but he turned his head away. Hours earlier he had taken Daniel and Joseph to stay at a neighbor's, so it was only Ma and I who watched transfixed as Percy went to work.

With Pa holding George's head up off the pillow, Percy slowly worked the tube down his throat. George gagged, a terrible sound, and for a pain-wracked moment I thought he had died. But he continued to breathe, and Percy continued to work.

It took a long time—a breath-holding eternity—for Percy to ease the drug through the tube and into George's fevered body. Then he removed the tube and lay his hand on George's forehead. "Now we'll just have to wait and pray," he said.

Standing at George's side, Percy led us in prayer. Then he settled in Pa's big chair, and once again we waited.

Walking on tiptoe, Pa tended the fire. The candles flickered. I tried to keep my eyes open, but the day had been an unceasing agony, and I was exhausted. I dozed, then struggled to come awake. Ma, Pa, and Percy were like three sentries, keeping guard at George's side.

I couldn't remain alert. I was sinking . . . sinking.

With the crowing of the cock, I came awake. The long night was over.

Suddenly a voice rang clear in the silence of the room. "Mama, Mama, I'm thirsty."

George was awake and talking. His face was no longer flushed; he was breathing in deep, steady pulls.

With a cry of joy, Ma rushed to get him some water; I could hear Pa's husky sobs.

Percy knelt and intoned a prayer. "We thank Thee for the deliverance of this dear child from the shadow of death. We pledge ourselves to lie forever in Thy service.''

Pa knelt and prayed with Percy; then he got slowly to his feet. His head was down; his movements were jerky.

He took my hand and led me to Percy's side. ''Doctor, do you promise that my daughter will be your only wife?''

Percy's voice was firm. ''I love Olive. I will cherish and protect her forever, and I will never choose any wife but her.''

As the first rays of daylight shown into the room Pa put my hand in the hand of Percival Terry.

Percy's God had spoken.

Chapter 4

At dawn on April 30, 1854, Percy and I stood side by side at the altar of the Mormon church, and we said the words that forever bound us as one. Then my family pressed close to congratulate us and say good-bye.

I'd said my vows filled with a breathtaking joy, but my wedding day was also the day our wagon train started the long roll to Deseret. I looked forward to the trip—our wedding trip—and I was certain that happiness awaited me in the new land, but parting with my family was agony.

Tears ran down Dorothy's cheeks. "Olive, Olive," she chanted.

Pa hugged me so tight I thought I'd crack in two. Holding baby Joseph, Ma looked tinier than ever, and as she kissed me, her chest heaved in deep sobs. Daniel stood wide-eyed, and George, completely well now but still fragile, put his thin arms around my neck.

"When I get to be a big man, I'll come and fetch you back home, so I will," he said.

Ted, grinning but unaccustomedly speechless, shook hands with Percy, then grabbed me in a quick, violent hug.

It was my last look at all their dear faces, but I saw them through a mist of tears.

Murmuring words of comfort, Percy led me to our wagon: "You'll come back someday, Olive. I promise if your father doesn't come out west, someday you'll come back and see your family again.''

Percy handed me up to the high seat, then took his place beside me. As he snapped the reins, I waved my last farewell. Our six oxen plodded, the white drilling billowed behind us, the wagon lurched, and we were on our way to Deseret.

We'd had to rush to get ready, and on a single trip to the trading post we bought a bedstead, stove, table, chairs, and even four panes of window glass.

Percy had told me not to worry about money. "I can afford everything we need, and I'll buy you a pony to ride when you get tired of the wagon.''

Pa made me a rocking chair; Ma gave us a box of preserves and jams, and Dorothy sewed constantly to finish a wool-filled comforter for our wedding present.

I worked hard getting ready but sometimes I felt as if I were dreaming. Even when I watched Percy and the other men struggling to get the wagons across the Missour River, it was hard to believe we were really married and on our way.

As the last wagon touched the western shore, the bugle sounded, signaling us to move on. We traveled another five miles before we made camp, and the long day ended with a prayer meeting.

As we walked back from the meeting, Percy's arm encircled my waist. It was twilight. The air was fragrant with a sudden rush of spring, and we were surrounded by the feel and sounds of excitement.

We passed a small stand of trees, and Percy pulled me into their shadows. He kissed me the way he had that night in the deserted cabin. All the feelings I'd known then flooded over me, and my legs grew unsteady. I clung to him for support.

"I love you so much I can hardly stand it,'' I whispered.

He kissed me again, and when he released me, my eyes remained closed.

"Let's get to our wagon," he said.

My legs still felt unsteady, and when he put his arm around me, I leaned heavily against him.

On the way to our wagon, we passed the corral.

"Those horses look just like Mike and Polly," I said, pointing dreamily toward two huge bays that stood out even in the deepening shadows.

"We have better things to think about than horses," Percy told me.

Inside our wagon it was already dark. Percy silently undressed me, and I heard his breathing quicken as he explored the moldings of my body. His hands, his lips claimed every inch of me. A delicious tingling soared through me, and little sounds issued from my lips. It seemed natural to arch my back.

Then he stroked by legs and spread them apart. I gasped when his body entered mine, but I loved him and wanted to please.

"Olive, you are really my wife now," he said, his voice a half-groan.

I felt a confusion of pain and joy. Every thought in my head disappeared except one. "I belong to Percy now. I belong to him."

He fell asleep soon after, his head resting on my breasts. I lay at the brink, not awake, but unable to fall asleep. My body throbbed with new sensations, and fleeting images of the day's events kept coming to me, keeping me close to consciousness. As in a dream I saw myself standing at Percy's side, saying my vows. Again I saw my mother's face, tear-stained but smiling.

I opened my eyes and turned gently against Percy to get more comfortable. When I closed my eyes again, the wagons loomed up, pulling for the river. Then I envisioned Percy and me walking together through the twilight. We passed Pa's horses, Mike and Polly, together in the corral. *Pa's horses . . . .*

I heard a horse whinny, a loud sound and real. It brought me truly awake, and I lay there startled. *Could I really have seen Pa's horses with our wagon train?* It was impossible; I'd only been dreaming.

But I was troubled. Mike and Polly were Pa's only team. He couldn't get along without them.

After a while I told myself that I had to put the horses out of my mind, but the harder I tried to fall asleep, the more awake I became.

Eventually I realized I wouldn't be able to wait until morning to take another look at that team.

"Percy," I murmured. "Percy."

His body, heavy against mine, didn't move. I wanted to awaken him and ask him to go with me to the corral, but I thought of how foolish I'd feel if the horses weren't my father's. On the first night we spent together, I didn't want him to think me a silly woman who wouldn't let him sleep because I couldn't tell my dreams from reality.

Gently I eased my body away from his. I dressed, took my shawl and climbed out of the wagon.

I ran to the corral hoping, expecting, to be mistaken, but Mike and Polly were clearly visible in the moonlight. When I'd seen them earlier, all I'd really been aware of was Percy and how much I loved him. I had been preoccupied, but now I recognized Pa's horses beyond all doubt. I knew Pa hadn't sold them. They'd been taken—stolen—and Pa didn't have the money to replace them.

I recognized other horses I knew from Kanesville, horses that didn't belong with our wagon train. As I tried to make some sense out of it, I recalled ugly rumors: *Those Mormons steal and claim they are only taking back what's been stolen from them.*

As I stood there, Mike nickered; he knew me. I moved closer and stroked his neck. "You can't stay here," I whispered. "You have to go home to Pa."

All the horses had been hobbled to keep them from straying, and I struggled to untie the ropes that bound Mike's and Polly's front and back feet. The coarse hemp cut my hands, but the knots held tight. I pulled, tugged, and almost despaired, but at last the knots loosened and the ropes slipped down. My fingers bled as I tied the horses together and led them to our wagon.

I wanted to awaken Percy, but I knew he wouldn't let me take the horses back alone. He would take them himself—I was certain he would—but they were my responsibility. I hesitated, wanting to tell him, yet somehow afraid to, but I didn't have time for indecision. I saddled Brigham, the pony Percy had bought me for a wedding gift, and as I eased myself onto him, my body was filled with strange throbbings because Percy had made me his own.

I rode slowly, staying close to a stand of trees to avoid being seen by the guards. I held the reins with one hand, and with the other I clutched the rope that bound Mike and Polly.

When I was clear of the wagon train, I fastened my shawl as tight as I could against the sharp wind. I urged Brig to a lope, and Mike and Polly came trotting briskly behind us.

We were five miles from the river, and I strained in the moonlight to see the dirt road. To all sides eerie shadows loomed up. I was cold and frightened, but I was determined that in the morning Pa's horses would be home again.

They will be, I told myself, *if only the ferry is on this side.*

Approaching the river, I saw a small light at the ferry station. Then I cried with relief when I saw, gleaming in the moonlight, the ferry riding the ripples from its mooring to a tree on the near bank. But two men on the deck of the ferry pulled on a rope, bending forward and backward rhythmically.

"Wait, please wait," I shouted.

I dismounted, then dragged Mike and Polly to the water's edge. "Please, I want you to take these horses across for me."

One of the men leaned over the stern. He stared at me through the murky light, then with a leap over the water, he landed beside me. "Y'goin' that way?"

"No, I have to go back, but I want to send them home to my father."

The man chewed on his wad of tobacco and spat a stream of juice through his beard. "Where'd you get them?"

"They belong to my father, Henry Banks. They pulled our wagon all the way from Ohio to Kanesville, and somebody in the Mormon wagon train took them . . . by mistake. Please, oh please, take them across and head them home."

He called to the man standing on the boat. "I heard them varmints have a mind to steal, and this brave girl is trying to save her Pa's horses. What'ya say? Can we get them across for her?"

"Bring them on," the other man answered.

The man reached for the rope in my hand. "Why d'you want to go on with them weird folk for?"

"They're good people," I murmured, "and my husband is the finest man on earth."

He shook his hed. "Well, it's your bed you're making."

"I didn't bring any money," I blurted, "but if you take them to my father, he'll—"

"S'all right," he interrupted. "We have to be across before dawn anyways."

I touched his arm. "I can't thank you enough, and all you have to do is take them up to the road and head them east."

A lump formed in my throat as I gave each horse a farewell pat.

The men pulled the boat closer, loaded the horses, then moved out into the river. They waved to me, but when I waved back, a fresh grief washed over me. In my heart I was really saying a second good-bye to my home and family across the water.

Then I ran up the bank, caught Brigham, and pulled myself into the saddle. Brig seemed to sense my anxiety. He flattened his body to the road and ran hard, but soon the eastern sky began to brighten.

When we approached the camp, I brought Brig to a halt, and slid off his back. He was drenched in sweat and nervous from the long run. I patted and soothed him. "We've made it, Brig. We're back."

Holding the reins, I started walking. When I heard the harsh voice of a guard, I was much too frightened to act afraid. I took a deep breath, waved, and called out a greeting.

The guard approached with his rifle pointed right at me. He peered at my face. "Who are you and what are you up to?" he demanded.

"I'm Mrs. Percival Dodson Terry," I said with all the dignity I could manage. "And this is my pony, Brigham. We're out for an early morning ride."

"The pony's awful worked up, and I didn't see you leaving camp," he said, staring at me.

I swallowed hard, not knowing what would happen to me if the truth were known. I was new with these people, and I didn't want to be branded a troublemaker or even a horse thief. My grip tightened on the reins, but then the guard said, "Brother Terry shouldn't ought to have let you go out alone."

I forced a smile and started walking, hoping my legs wouldn't buckle under me.

"I'm Stephen Bradford," the guard said. "You're new with the Saints, so tonight I'll send one of my wives to your wagon to meet you."

I cringed, still unnerved at the mention of plural wives.

At the wagon I took care of Brig, but as I climbed over the front wheel, Percy's hand reached out to me.

"Olive, where in the world have you been?"

The concern in his voice shattered what was left of my self-control. With a cry I threw myself into his arms.

He hugged me close. "What is it, dearest? Tell me what's wrong."

When I lifted my face to his, his lips touched the tears that ran down my cheeks. "Pa must have his horses back by now, so everything is all right," I gasped. Then my whole body trembled, and I sobbed with relief.

Percy's strong hands gripped my shoulders, and he held me at arm's length. "Olive, what are you talking about?"

"Last night I saw Mike and Polly in the corral," I managed between sobs. "You were sleeping, so . . . so I rode Brig and took them back to the river myself. The ferrymen took them across."

Percy groaned. "Olive, it is right for you to love your father, but would he have wanted you to do anything so dangerous? You could have been hurt, maybe killed. My God, I could have lost you."

He gathered me in his arms, and in the security of his embrace, I asked the question that had tormented me all night.

"Percy, why were my father's horses with this

wagon train? Why are there other horses in the corral that belong to people back in Kanesville?''

"My little wife," Percy murmured, "don't you remember the things I've told you about what my people have endured?''

"Of course I remember," I said, responding to the hurt in his voice. "Your people have suffered terribly—but the horses?''

"Only the hand of God has preserved us from total destruction, but in Deseret our people have founded a new land dedicated to love, hard work, and religion. But, Olive, we would never get there—most of my people are poor and would starve along the way—if we did not obey the Bible's command to suck the milk of the gentiles. And we must take back the things they have stolen from us. Brother Edwards has just recovered a cow that was taken from him back in Nauvoo, the same night two of his sons were killed.''

"But Pa bought Polly back in Ohio, and he's had Mike ever since I can remember. It was not the same as taking back something that's been stolen.''

Percy's voice throbbed with emotion. "Dearest, I'm sorry about your father's horses. I really am, but please understand that my people must claim their right to stay alive by taking what God intends for them to have.''

He was a good man, devoted to his religion with a conviction and passion that left me spellbound. Sometimes I felt humble just listening to him, but this time he could not convince me. No one had the right to steal Mike and Polly, but Pa had them back. There was nothing I could do about the other stolen horses, and I didn't want to argue with my husband.

Utterly exhausted, I lay my head on his chest. It was a comfort to rest in his arms.

I felt his hand at my bosom, loosening the buttons of

my dress. Last night we had been together in the dark, but now he wanted to see me.

"You are mine," he said gently. "You belong to me."

I helped him take off my clothes, and I shivered, even as I felt the warmth of his hands. Then I gave myself totally to answering his demands.

The camp was noisy and the wagons were beginning to roll before I could cover myself and fall asleep.

Chapter 5

It was afternoon before I dressed and joined Aaron Terry on the high seat. He was driving our wagon while Percy helped herd animals alongside the train.

Aaron was a bushy-haired, lanky fellow of seventeen who didn't resemble Percy in any way. They had the same father, but it startled me to remember that they were born of different mothers.

"Good morning, Aaron," I said.

"It used to be morning," he said quietly.

I blushed, realizing how late I was getting up after my first night as Percy's wife. Aaron was trying hard not to grin, and it wasn't Pa's horses I was thinking about when a silly giggle escaped me. Then Aaron laughed aloud, and his laughter was as intense as everything else about him.

I could sense he liked me, and I was glad. He seemed so determined, so fierce in his loyalties, I knew if he were my friend now, he'd be my friend forever. The miles between me and my family were increasing with every turn of the wheels, and I needed to be liked by the Terrys, especially the ones close in age to Ted and Dorothy.

When Percy saw me, he rode up alongside the wagon.

"Did my little brother manage to keep the wagon steady enough for you to sleep?" he asked cheerfully.

Now it was Aaron's turn to blush, but he said, "I can do a better job of it than you can."

The two brother bantered and teased each other, but Percy's eyes were on me. His expression shown with pride and possession.

That evening I fixed supper for the three of us, but we weren't long at our meal when a man approached, calling to Percy. I couldn't hear their conversation, but when the man left, Percy's expression was somber.

"There's a special meeting being called. I must finish quickly and get over there."

Aaron left with Percy, and I cleaned the dishes. I was almost finished when, without a sound, a woman appeared at my side. She was long and lean, and only her full bosom persuaded me that she was not a youth masquerading in his sister's dress.

"I'm Linnie, and this here's Uriah," she said, referring to the husky child she carried.

I smiled and held out my hand. "I'm Olive, and I'm married to Dr. Percival Terry."

"I reckon I know that," she said. "My husband told me he talked t'you this mornin'. Said he promised you he'd send one of us over t'meet you." Then she added flatly, without smiling, "I'm glad t'was me, Olive."

The guard, Stephen Bradford, had told me he would send one of his wives, so here was Linnie.

Her densely curled, dark hair accented the thin, whiteness of her face. Her plain features were dotted with freckles, and just looking at her a person could tell she would cherish a kind word or act of affection. I held out my hand to her. "Linnie, I too am very glad it was you," I said.

Linnie was four years older than I, and Uriah was her only child. She told me she'd seen Percy and me together, buying furnishings at the trading post. "You looked so happy together, it pleasured my heart," she said. "Me, I'm a second wife, so I never had none o'that." She wasn't complaining, only stating facts.

Our conversation was interrupted when Percy came running to the wagon. He pulled himself over the high seat, and I hurried after him.

"What is it, Percy? What's wrong?"

Without answering, he dug to get at a strongbox that was buried beneath a stack of boxes. He took out several gold pieces and dropped them into his draw-string purse.

He grabbed me in a quick hug. "Olive, we'll handle this somehow," he said. Then he bolted over the side of the wagon.

Shaking, I climbed down and sunk to my knees.

"Something's fierce wrong," Linnie said.

"Linnie, last night I took my father's horses back to the ferry. They'd been taken from him, and he had to have them back. Now I'm sure I've been found out."

Linnie gasped. "T'was a brave thing t'do."

"What . . . what will they do to me?" I asked.

"I guess they'll punish you, Olive. I don't see how they can do more t'you than that."

There was no conversation now, but she made no move to leave until we saw Percy approaching. For an instant her bony hand closed over mine. Then she pickēd up Uriah and hurried away.

Percy was carrying a heavy wooden rod, but he extended his free hand to me and pulled me to my feet. "I'm really sorry, but it's not as bad as it could have been."

"I know this is about Pa's horses. I can't imagine how they found out I took them, but maybe if I could explain how Mike and Polly pulled our wagon all the way from Ohio—"

"I told them you took the horses. When we were asked if anyone knew anything about them, I had to speak up. I am a priest of the church, and it was impossible for me to lie. I've paid the community, and believe me, if you hadn't taken them back, I would gladly have paid your father."

I shrugged. "Well then, isn't it all settled?"

Percy sighed. "You endangered the wagon train. If something had happened and you hadn't been able to get back, no one would have had any idea where you were. In their loyalty, the brothers and sisters would have stayed to help me search for you, and precious days could have been lost."

"Percy, I didn't mean to endanger anyone."

He nodded. "They know that, so we can stay with the wagon train."

"Stay with the wagon train?" I echoed, stunned.

Percy grimaced. "It was suggested that we be sent back as a warning to everyone that the interests and safety of the community must come first. But I have standing in the church, and finally it was agreed that punishing you would be enough. I persuaded them against a public punishment. You are my wife, and I promised to deal with you myself."

I looked at the rod in his hand and gasped. "Percy, surely you don't intend to use that on me."

He looked desperate. "Olive, you know I don't really want to hurt you."

Disbelieving, I stared at him, and then, in a voice choked with emotion, he said, "We must get this over with."

We climbd into the wagon, and he began undoing the buttons of my dress. I shook my head. I couldn't believe that my gentle Percy was going to beat me no matter what he'd promised.

Together we struggled with the sleeves, then my dress fell around my feet. Percy's eyes refused to meet mine as he began undoing my corset and underthings.

I was naked, but even when he forced me to lie face down on the bed, I couldn't believe he would hurt me.

The first blow landed across my buttocks and thighs. I gasped and tried to raise myself, but the rod came down swiftly, again and again, and I could not get up. It was over quickly, but the burning pain was nothing to the agony of my humiliation and anger.

Percy sank to his knees and began kissing my stinging flesh. He was crying. "Please forgive me," he groaned.

I turned toward him, and in a moment we were in each other's arms. His tears mingled with mine.

I couldn't feel pain or shame or anger. I was caught in my overpowering love for him, and I ran my hands through his beautiful hair and kissed his brow.

He pulled off his clothes, and we lay together, sharing an ecstasy that blended us together and washed away all unpleasantness and sorrow.

Chapter 6

The next morning we passed a settlement, and the people cheerfully waved us on our way. Larkspur and verbena spotted the prairie with color; jackrabbits bounded into view, and above the rattle of the wagons we could hear the call of a meadowlark.

I sat next to Percy on the high seat. We rarely spoke, but I felt a closeness and love that crowded out resentment. Nothing could come between us.

It was a beautiful day, and during the days that followed, Percy and I were rarely out of each other's sight. Occasionally, he tended someone who was ill or he attended a meeting of the leaders of the company, but before he left, he always kissed me as though he would be gone a year.

Linnie Bradford often came to visit me, but then days passed with no sign of her. When the leaders declared a day of rest to check over the wagons and refresh the stock, I finished my chores early, then hurried to Linnie's wagon to check on her.

Sister Phoebe, Stepehn Bradford's first wife, was busy airing the bedding, and she barely answered my greeting. I realized—without really knowing how— that she disliked me because I was Linnie's friend.

Linnie lay on a blanket near her wagon. She was trying to amuse Uriah, but she looked pale and sick.

"What is it, Linnie? What's wrong?" I asked, kneeling beside her.

"It's my stomach," she groaned. "Everything I eat comes up."

A glance at Sister Phoebe convinced me she would not be quick to do anything for her husband's second wife. I was amazed by Mormon households where the wives revered each other as dear sisters, but that was obviously not the case here.

"Linnie," I said, "let me look after Uriah, and later I'll bring you some chicken soup."

Linnie nodded, grateful, and I held out my hand to Uriah. "Come with Aunt Olive," I coaxed.

He raised his arms, asking to be lifted, and bending my knees, I caught him under the arms and hoisted him up.

Though close to the same age, Uriah was much larger than my brother George. His tightly-curled red hair encircled his head like a flaming halo, and he was liberally sprinkled with freckles. He did not like to walk, but he was an alert little person, full of giggles and appetite.

I lugged him part of the way, but then I had to set him on his feet. I held his hand and tugged, but our progress was slow.

At my wagon I gave Uriah a big spoon. "Here, Uriah. You can dig with this," I said.

I reached into the chicken crate and caught a hen by the leg. She squawked furiously, and I shuddered. I'd never killed anything and I couldn't bring myself to do it. Amid flying feathers, I shoved the noisy thing back into the crate.

I called to Uriah, and together we went in search of someone to kill a hen for me.

We were only two wagons behind Father Terry's, and I asked one of his wives where Aaron was. She pointed toward a clump of heavy brush.

"He said he was going to gather kindling."

It was far, but I wouldn't feel so embarrassed asking Aaron. Uriah begged to be carried, and staggering under his weight, I trudged toward the brush.

Aaron was not difficult to find. He was with a dark-haired girl whose ringing laughter called my attention to them.

Aaron had his arms about her waist, trying to kiss her. She swung her head one way and then the other teasing him. I saw the loving, longing look on Aaron's face, and lugging Uriah, I hurried away.

Percy was waiting at the wagon. He threw his arms around the two of us and kissed me. "I thought you were probably with Linnie," he said, tickling Uriah under the chin.

"I'm taking care of Uriah because Linnie is ill. I'd like to make her some chicken soup, but with Uriah to look after, I can't clean a chicken."

Percy said he would do it for me, and I sighed inwardly. My weakness had not been revealed.

When the soup was ready, I fed Uriah and then took some to Linnie. Percy came with me, riding Uriah on his shoulders.

I wanted Percy to help Linnie, but she insisted she was no ways sick enough to need a doctor. She did manage to hold down a little soup, and then I returned Uriah to her care.

It was a starlit night, and holding hands, Percy and I walked back to our wagon. We enjoyed the dewy air, the fragrances and sounds of the prairie, and most especially, we enjoyed each other. Percy lifted my hand to his lips and kissed it. His touch was gentle, but it stirred a throbbing between my legs.

That night we lay together for a lingering time of closeness and love, and long after he fell asleep, I still held him in my arms. Suddenly I thought of Aaron. I wondered if he and the dark-haired girl loved each other the way Percy and I did. As I fell asleep, I smiled. *Maybe there will be a wedding on the wagon train before we ever get to Deseret.*

Two days later we caught up with another wagon train. Like us, they were bound for Deseret, and that night the two companies joined for a dance. The young men prepared the dance circle by wetting and packing the ground, and Brother Benson opened the festivities with prayer.

Excited, I heard the fiddles tuning up. Jew's harps sounded, and one man accompanied with his clarinet. The dancers took their places, and the caller shouted, "Swing your partner and promenade!"

Happy and smiling, Percy and I swung each other with carefree abandon. When the first dance ended, I fell against Percy, laughing and struggling for breath. He led me to the edge of the circle, and I saw Aaron staring straight ahead, an almost transfixed look on his face. I followed the line of his gaze, and I saw the dark-haired girl. She was with another young man, but she was laughing and sparkling for him the way she had for Aaron.

"Who is the girl in the red skirt?" I asked.

"Seems to me her name is Sophia," Percy answered. "She's traveling with her father, Brother Matthew Coles. I think his only wife died before we left Iowa."

The band struck up "Oh, Susanna," and Percy and I were off again. I caught a glimpse of Aaron, smiling rapturously now, dancing with Sophia; her red skirt twirled brightly as they went.

At last we all bid each other good night, and Percy and I returned to our wagon. Exhausted, we fell into bed.

"I'm too tired to move," Percy said with a groan.

I yawned and snuggled close to him.

Moments later Percy said, "You know, dearest, I'm not as tired as I thought."

I giggled as he pulled me into his embrace.

One afternoon in July, as we jolted and creaked along, our scouts came galloping from far across the plain, yelling as they came. I could feel Percy go tense, and fear washed over me. Even before we could hear the words, we knew that the furious haste meant Indians.

Quickly the lead wagon circled, and the other wagons followed into place.

"Get the pouch of bullets."

As he spoke, Percy reached for his rifle. He sounded calm, but I went numb with terror. I picked up the pouch, but my hands were shaking when I handed it to him.

He told me to tend the oxen, then he hurried away to join the line of men that was forming.

I scrambled to the ground and ran around to stay with the lead animals. I didn't dare unyoke them, but I tried to keep them calm so that they wouldn't stampede and pull our wagon away from the circle.

Men herded terrified, bawling animals into the center of the circle. Everyone seemed to be shouting; women gathered groups of crying children, and the snorting, bawling, whinnying of the animals continued to rise in a deafening roar.

Suddenly a howl of shrieking, yipping, and whooping drowned out the din inside the circle. My muscles tensed, and my breath held.

Hundreds of Indians rode furiously, yelping, their feathered headdresses billowing on the wind, their faces painted in a devil display of red, green, and black.

I screamed out, "Percy!"

A volley of shots splintered the whooping.

The fighting continued; it seemed like forever, but suddenly the Indians reined their horses and whirled, and with one, long, quivering howl, they galloped back across the prairie. The sharp odor of gunpowder spread across our encampment.

It was over, and I slumped to the ground and sobbed until Percy returned and lifted me in his arms. "They're gone, Olive. They're too smart to stay and fight guns, and thank God, we're well armed."

I was still clinging to him when Father Terry came and told us that we would remain where we were for the rest of the day: "That'll give them coyotes a chance to spread the word that we have guns."

He turned to Percy. "Son, you'd better get your medical kit and come with me. Several men are wounded, and I was told that Brother Dawson's oldest boy is real bad."

A hush fell over the entire wagon train, and I waited in the eerie silence until Percy returned. He looked haggard, and his voice was edged in pain: "The Dawson boy was only nineteen. An arrow hit him in the back of the neck. There really was nothing anyone could have done."

Then he told me about the two men who'd been wounded: "Brother Hammond will recover, but I'm very concerned about Brother Coles. He lost a great deal of blood. The wagon train can't stop and wait for his wounds to heal, but traveling will be hard on him."

That night Percy and I lay together, grateful for each other's safety, but it was a long time before I could fall asleep.

The following morning the entire company gathered at a deeply dug grave and put young Roger Dawson to his rest. Later I would remember that moment and wish it had been my funeral out there on the lonely prairie.

Chapter 7

The Indian attack left everyone anxious, and night and day scouts rode in circles far out on the prairie. The night guard was doubled, and Percy slept with his rifle. But there was no more trouble, and after a while, I began to enjoy the journey again.

We had left the prairie and were traveling through clumps of sagebrush and prickly pear. Sometimes the jolting of the wagon got tiresome, and then Percy walked beside the leaders, and I rode Brig up and down beside the train.

"Don't go farther than the first wagon and come right back," Percy would call.

He looked after me with care and tenderness. He would never let anything hurt me.

One night we camped near a river. Father Terry instructed the company to fill every barrel, keg, and pot, because we were coming to a long stretch of desolate country where there was no water fit to use. The terrain was bleak now, and along the road lay the carcasses of oxen and horses—bleached bones, sometimes swollen bodies with swarms of flies and an odor that made me press my handkerchief to my nose.

Every evening Percy checked Brother Matthew Coles. "There's not much I can do for him," Percy told me, "and he's getting worse."

On a broiling afternoon, Brother Coles died. I put on my sunbonnet and joined the entire company at the spot where the men had dug a deep hole in the sandy ground. Wrapped in a blanket, Matthew Coles was lowered into the earth as Brother Benson read from the Bible.

Then everyone turned to Sophia Coles and offered words of sympathy. She wore her red skirt, only now she wasn't twitching it around her ankles. For the first time I saw her when she wasn't flirting. She stood quietly, and untended tears rolled down her cheeks.

I knew how I would feel if it were my father, and my own tears were flowing when in my turn, I pressed her hand and told her I was sorry.

That night Percy said, "Brother Benson has called a meeting to decide what to do with Sophia Coles."

I shrugged. "What is there to decide? She'll go on with the train until we get to Deseret."

"She's alone now, and she's only sixteen. Brother Benson thinks someone has to be responsible for her."

When Percy left, I got out my little sewing kit and set about doing the mending. It was dusk, and I had to squint in the lantern light, but I felt matronly and proud as I stitched a big slit in Percy's favorite shirt. The shirt was deep blue, a color that nearly matched his eyes, and I sewed with infinite care. For my husband, every stitch had to be perfect.

When Percy returned, the lantern cast an eerie light on his face and he looked strange.

"Olive, there's something . . . something we have to talk over."

He sounded odd, as if it were an effort for him to speak. I shivered, even though the wagon was still warm from the heat of the day.

"What is it? What's happened?" I asked.

"Sit down first," he said, easing himself past the packing boxes to sit on the bed.

When I sat down beside him, he took my hand and

kissed it. "Olive, I love you, and I don't want to hurt you." He was so solemn, so anguished, it had to be serious.

With a rush of panic, I remembered the stagecoach that had passed the wagon train late that afternoon. The driver had stopped and spoken to the men in the lead wagons.

Maybe he'd delivered a message for me from home—a message of tragedy.

Suddenly faces swam before my eyes—Ma, Pa, Dorothy and my brothers—I could see them all. Pain sliced through me and I caught my breath, wondering which one I had lost.

"Percy, tell me," I groaned.

"At the meeting tonight we had a discussion . . . ."

A wonderful relief washed over me. There had been no sad report from home.

"There were seven of us, and it took a long time."

I sighed. "Oh, yes, about Sophia. Did you decide what to do with her?"

His voice was muffled. "It was decided—decided—that *I* should be responsible for her."

I smiled. "Percy, you really had me worried. I thought it was something serious, but being responsible for Sophia won't be so bad. She can drive her own oxen. Her wagon can be right behind ours, and you can watch out for her."

Percy shook his head, and his arm crept around my shoulders. "You don't understand, Olive. Pa and the others have said I must marry Sophia."

"Marry her!"

"Yes, as a second wife. The leaders of the Church all have plural wives. You know that."

"Of course I know that, but you said it would be different with us." My words sounded wild, as though

I screamed into an empty barrel. "Percy, tell me that you refused them. Tell me that you said you could never marry anyone but me."

Terrified, I waited for Percy's answer. His body slumped, and he buried his face in his hands. "Olive, I did tell you that it would be different with us—but now I have no choice."

I leaped to my feet. "My God, you can't go back on your word. You promised me, you promised my father that—"

"I promised your father I would never choose another wife—and I never will. Sophia was chosen for me."

"But you can't consent to it, Percy. It's impossible. You've told me—you've shown me—that you love me the way I love you."

"Of course, Olive," he said, reaching his hand toward me. "You'll always have the first place in my heart. I promise you that. No one can ever take your place."

His hand dropped to his side. "But I must marry her."

He began using his pulpit voice, preaching to me: "Sophia is only sixteen and she tends to be wayward. No one wants to take the responsibility for that kind of girl, so we agreed it was best she be married. Married women settle down. Then it turned on *who* should marry her. I'm young, I have money, and only one wife. They all agreed it should be me."

The pain in my chest was unbearable, and each breath was a struggle. "Percy, don't you know that your brother is in love with Sophia? If she must have a husband, let it be Aaron."

"We discussed Aaron," Percy said, still preaching. "But Pa will need Aaron when we get to Deseret. And

Aaron isn't ready for marriage. He's just a boy, and he has no money of his own. Most of my money I inherited from my mother's father, but Aaron's mother—''

"Give him *your* money," I screamed. "Give him everything we have. *You* help your father when we get to Deseret. Do anything, Percy, anything, but don't marry another woman!''

I was begging, pleading, but Percy could only shake his head. "I'm a doctor and lay minister—a leader—and I must accept the demands made on me by the priesthood. This is a demand, and I had to consent.''

In the confinement of the wagon, I couldn't walk or pace, but I wrung my hands together in despair. "Percy, tell them that I will be responsible for Sophia. I will look after her day and night. I will make certain that—''

Percy threw up his hands. "Please, please, dearest, be sensible. You can't be responsible for her. You're only a woman.''

My whole body was shaking, trembling, but I struggled to gain control of my mind. "Percy, there is still a long time before we get to Deseret. We'll come up with another plan, a better plan, so that you won't feel obliged to marry this girl.''

He raised his head and dared to look at me. "We are not to wait until we reach Deseret. The church leaders have decided I must marry her tomorrow.''

My world fell, clattering and breaking into a million pieces. I went to bed that night with my clothes on, too sick to think. I felt conscious of pain—a grinding aching pain. When Percy tried to put his arms around me, I rolled over against the side of the wagon.

Chapter 8

At the sound of the trumpet Percy rose and began to dress. "Olive, dear," he called, "you must hurry and get ready. My father will perform the ceremony before we break camp."

"I want nothing to do with it," I said dully, not moving. "Leave me alone."

"You must go. You are part of the ceremony," he said, slipping into his preaching tone. "You will stand next to me, and Sophia will be married to me through you."

I, the first wife, had to bow my head in consent to a second wife's being married to my husband.

I put on my shoes and smoothed my clothes without interest, without caring, and Percy put out his own breakfast. When he asked me if I wanted something to eat, I did not answer.

I looked out of the wagon toward the western horizon. In the distance I could see the purple mountains reflecting the new light of dawn. I wanted to run toward them—run until I died—but the wagon train loomed all around me. The scouts were out there, and they would ride me down.

Desperately the thought formed that if I withheld my consent, Percy could not marry Sophia. But I remembered all too clearly what had happened when the leaders of the wagon train learned I had returned my father's horses. I was judged disobedient and a threat to the wagon train. My punishment had been private because Percy had pleaded for me, but would he plead for me now?

If a public punishment were ordered, Percy could not oppose it. I would be marked and humiliated, and in the end I would be forced to obey. There was no holding back; there was no escape.

Percy reached to help me down over the wheel of the wagon, but I spurned his touch. I eased myself down and hurried ahead of him to the place where Father Terry and several of the company were gathered. My legs felt like sticks, my knees stiff and unbending, and each step stabbed with a jerk of agony.

Sophia stood with her eyes downcast. Her hands twisted nervously, and her obvious pain gave me grim solace. I wasn't the only unhappy one.

Erect and calm, Percy stood at my right side, and one of the assembly nudged Sophia into position at my left. Father Terry began to speak, and the holy words that had bound Percy and me together now tore us apart and laid open my heart to a scalding, unbelievable pain.

Percy's elbow touched me each time I had to answer, but I couldn't hear my own voice as my lips formed the word *yes*. Then Father Terry raised his voice.

"Sister Olive, take Sister Sophia's hand and place it in your husband's."

A horrible ordeal, an evil, wicked dream.

When it was over, Percy bent to kiss me before he kissed his new bride. I pulled away, escaping the touch of his lips, and then I turned and raced to our wagon. I threw myself on the bed, and soon the wagon was jolting beneath me. I couldn't cry. I couldn't think. I could only suffer, a hot quivering that wracked my body and tortured my soul.

When we stopped at noon, Percy brought me a plate of food, but at the sight of it a wave of nausea rose in my throat. I groaned and turned away.

The day's travel finally ended. I could hear musical instruments being tuned up, and the sounds of laughter and shouting drifted into the wagon. They were as voices from another world. In death I could not feel more completely cut off from life.

Suddenly Linnie's thin hand was smoothing my brow. "Don't take on so, Olive," she said. "It's the will o'God, and you can't turn the will o'God. You feel bad, 'course you feel bad. S'hard to share someone you love so much."

The sound of her voice comforted me, but I felt totally empty and couldn't answer her.

"I brung my Bible, Olive. I want t'read you what it says."

She read slowly, with many hesitations: *"Now the Lord said to Abram, I will make of you a great nation. I will make your descendants as the dust of the earth, so that if one can count the dust of the earth, your descendants also can be counted.*

"See, Olive, Abraham had many wives; that's how there can be many descendants. Jacob had two wives, Leah and Rachel, and great King David had a whole lot o'wives. It's all in the Bible, and it must be the will o'the Lord!"

She spoke so emphatically that I turned to look at her. Tears covered her face, and when our eyes met, she let out a cry and threw herself at me.

"Olive, I know how you feel, and I know how Sophia feels too, 'cause I'm a second wife. I ain't never been special to Stephen, not special the way you are t'Percy, but Sister Phoebe hates me anyways. I got the

two o'them bossin me 'most all the time. Not as I mind
that so much, but sometimes . . . sometimes I get a
loneliness inside me that's killing.''

We wrapped our arms around each other, and I could
feel the sobs that trembled through her body.

"My sister Lottie was a powerful comfort to me,"
she gasped between wails. "I love her better'n anyone,
'cept maybe Uriah, but she's away back in Ioway. I
expect I ain't never going t' see her again.''

Her tears washed away the hardness inside me, and I
could talk. "You'll see her again. Truly, I just know
that someday you will. And, Linnie, I'm sorry that
you're a second wife, and I'm convinced plural marriage is wrong, no matter what it says in the Bible.''

I sighed. "I can't understand how Percy can believe
plural marriage is right. But he's so sure, so positive. He has no doubts about anything, and yet . . .
yet. . . .'' I shook my head, fighting my own doubts
and anguish.

"A woman's got t'be married, Olive, 'cause she kin
only get into the highest heaven as the rightful property
of her husband. I reckon everyone in the church knows
that.''

I wrung my hands. "If a woman prays and tries to be
good, surely God will not deny her any blessings of
heaven because she didn't marry.''

Linnie shook her head. "That's what the church
teaches, so I don't know how else it can be.''

"I expect men mean more to the Lord than women
do," she added, "but I can't keep from hopin' my new
baby will be a girl.''

I attempted a smile. "So that's what has been wrong
with you these past weeks.''

She nodded. "She should get here in the middle of
winter.''

"In the middle of winter," I echoed.

I felt a fresh rush of agony. *My own baby might be born in early spring.*

I suspected I was carrying Percy's child. I'd been happy, counting the days until I could be certain, but a baby would tie me to Percy even more tightly than my vows.

If I couldn't be Percy's only wife, I wanted to return to my family. When my mind was clear enough to let me think, I was convinced I could find a way to go home.

I'll take money from Percy' strong box. I'll sneak off on Brig. I'll hide out until I come to an East-bound stage coach.

Perhaps I wouldn't make it; I might die trying, but anything would be better than sharing Percy with another woman. And a glimmer of hope told me that if I could make it back to Iowa, Percy might return and claim me for his one and only wife. *He would have to give up Sophia, and even his religion to get me back.*

But if I were with child, there was no escape. I'd never be able to make it back, and I wouldn't want to. Pa had warned me—begged me—not to marry Percy. He would take me back; I never doubted that, but could I ask him to raise Percy's child? It was a struggle for him to support his own children, and I had no right to add to his burdens.

Suddenly I heard footsteps. I caught my breath, waiting, but it wasn't Percy. He never came to me that night.

Through the long hours, Linnie and I talked, and her presence kept me sane. Without her, I would have been tormented to madness by visions of Percy and Sophia together in her wagon.

At dawn Linnie left, and I dragged myself to my feet.

I washed, splashing my face again and again with our precious water. What did it matter to me if we ran out of water crossing the desert?

I gagged trying to eat bread, but I managed to wash it down with a dipper of milk. Then I moved the front canvas and looked out.

Aaron had already taken his place on the high seat. He must have known I was right behind him, but he never turned or acknowledged my presence. I climbed out and sat beside him, but he didn't speak and neither did I.

In the weeks of traveling together, Aaron and I had become good friends, but now we could not comfort each other. Our mutual grief was an embarrassment, and though side by side, we suffered alone.

Ahead of us Sophia's wagon marked our way, and at a bend in the road I caught a glimpse of her sitting beside Percy on the high seat. I saw Aaron's hands tighten on the reins; his knuckles went white, and a grinding sound issued from his throat. As for me, I hurt so much already that I could not tell whether seeing them together caused me more pain.

That evening Percy came to my wagon and insisted that I join him and Sophia for the evening meal. "That's how it must be, Olive," he said. "Sophia will cook for the three of us; then it will be your turn."

As we walked toward Sophia's wagon, Percy talked to me of the road ahead and of the progress the wagon train was making. He mentioned things we had always fallen into conversation about, but I did not respond. I had nothing left to say to him.

Chapter 9

On September 28, the scouts galloped into camp: "We're just five days from Great Salt Lake Valley!" they shouted.

A roar went up throughout the train. People hugged each other; men tossed their hats in the air, and women cried. Spontaneous dancing broke out, although the only music was the joy that issued from almost every mouth in the company.

Percy came running to where I stood at my wagon, and he danced a wild jig in front of me. I laughed in spite of myself, but when he threw his arms around me, my laughter faded. My body went rigid, and locked my arms tight at my sides.

He released me abruptly. As he backed away, our eyes met, and I saw the joy drain out of his face. "Olive, you can't go on this way," he said, shaking his head. "Where is the sweet, affectionate girl I married?"

"Perhaps she's over there," I said, pointing toward Sophia's wagon. Then I turned back to my chores, unmindful of the celebration going on around me.

His head bowed, Percy walked away. He and Sophia had been married five weeks, and he did not know about the baby. Moments flashed when I wanted to throw my arms around his neck and tell him. I wanted him to laugh and kiss me and tell he was glad to have our firstborn on the way, but the barrier between us was insurmountable.

He spent every other week with Sophia, and during her week, Aaron drove my wagon. Aaron and I talked to each other now, but the lighthearted friendliness was gone, and the subject that haunted us both was never mentioned.

During the week Percy spent with me, another brother drove Sophia's wagon. At least Aaron was spared the agony of sitting beside the girl he loved while knowing he had lost her forever.

I hated the week Percy spent with Sophia, but the week he spent with me was even worse. His looks, his voice, his many kindnesses were exactly the same, but now—instead of bringing me pleasure—everything about him brought me pain.

During my week I prepared the foods Percy liked, and I poured silent love into everything I did for him, but I would not share his bed. The first time I refused him was the night he returned to my wagon after he had married Sophia.

Earlier that evening I had served dinner, and Percy had praised my cooking.

"Isn't this the best stew you've ever tasted?" he said to Sophia.

"Oh, yes, Percy, it is," she answered quickly.

I saw the new wonder in Sophia's eyes. Eagerly, she echoed everything he said. I understood, and a bitter hate settled all through me. How dare she fall in love with my husband!

When Percy returned from taking Sophia back to her wagon, he began a lively stream of talk, frequently mentioning my family and the good times he'd had with them. But mention of my family stirred my anger. When they knew about Sophia, they would suffer; what

Percy had done to me, he had done to them also.

I cleared a small place on the floor and covered it with a blanket. When Percy realized what I was doing, he came up behind me and slipped his arm around my waist.

"Olive, dearest," he said, his breath warm on my neck, "don't you know there's room for two on the bed?"

"Yes," I said, jerking away, "but not room for three." Sudden tears filled my eyes. "Percy, tell me that you and Sophia . . . that you haven't . . . ."

Percy remained calm. "Sophia is now my second wife," he began, and his preaching voice boomed through the wagon. "The true purpose of marriage is the procreation of children. It would have been wrong for me not to give Sophia the opportunity to conceive and bring—"

His sermon ended abruptly when I picked up the skillet and threw it at him. There was an ugly noise when it hit his shoulder, and I saw him wince in pain. I expected him to come at me, to hit me, and I intended to fight back, but Percy only looked at me, a hurt, sad expression on his face. He left me alone, and breathing hard, I lay down on the blanket.

Soon he got into bed. "I still love you, Olive," he said softly. "I love you more than anything in the world."

The next day I rode my pony up and down the wagon train. "I don't understand it, Brig. If he loves me, how can he hurt me so much?"

Brig loped along; the saddle creaked, and the odor of horseflesh, leather and sagebrush swirled about me. "It would be easy to die, Brig, much easier than living like this."

In my unhappiness I felt alienated from the other

people in the company, yet there were moments when I responded to the great spirit of the people with whom I traveled. Regardless of hardship and fatigue, the men called cheerfully to each other as they worked to get the wagons through mud and over rocks. The women went about smiling, and children ran beside the wagons, shouting in glee. And now, five days before the end of our long journey, the company rejoiced, but I could not join in.

It was the last day of Percy's week with me, and when he returned to the wagon for the evening meal, his cheerfulness had returned, but he made no attempt to touch me again.

When we finished eating, Sophia returned to her wagon. Then Percy came up behind me, and spoke in a voice filled with tenderness: "Will you go to the dance with me tonight?"

His voice was pleading. "We haven't danced together in a long time."

I started to refuse, but suddenly I felt dizzy. A lightheaded happiness washed through me. "Of course I'll go with you," I answered, almost wildly. "We'll dance and dance and dance."

I hurried to get ready, but just as I finished brushing my hair, Sophia returned. She was wearing her red skirt, and her heels were clicking as if she could already hear music. She took a metal mirror out of her pocket, and as she studied her reflection, she said dreamily, "I was so happy when Percy asked me to go to the dance. Does he like to dance, Sister Olive?"

Percy had asked Sophia, too. My wild happiness died. I no longer wanted to go, but something inside me refused to let Sophia have Percy all to herself. We walked to the dance, Sophia on Percy's left side and I on his right.

The men with the fiddles, clarinet and Jew's harps

were already tuning up, and folks were coming from all around the circle. Father Terry prayed, and then the caller took his place: "Claim your partners," he yelled.

Percy nodded to Sophia, took me by the hand and led me on to the dance floor to join three other couples to dance the quadrille. The lightheaded feeling returned, stronger this time, and nothing seemed real except that Percy and I were dancing together. How wonderful it was, smiling at him at last, my feet flying my body swaying.

"Swing your partners," the caller yelled.

Percy's arms went about me, and my body trembled. God, how I yearned for him.

The dance ended, and as we left the floor, I whispered, "I'm going to have a baby."

At that moment someone slapped Percy on the back and shouted a greeting. My precious message was lost and so was the moment for delivering it.

Percy kissed my hand. Then he left me and went to dance with Sophia. The warmth of having been his for a moment turned to ice.

Soon Percy came to claim another dance with me, but I refused. I couldn't endure his touch or his tenderness.

That night when Percy returned from taking Sophia to her wagon, I was already on my blanket, pretending I was sound asleep. I heard Percy undressing, then he called, "Olive, I love you more than anything else in the world. Don't you still love me a little?"

I caught my breath, but did not answer.

Suddenly Percy caught my arm and pulled me up. "You belong to me, Olive. It's a sin for you to refuse me, and I'm not going to let you sin anymore."

I jerked my arm free. "Percy," I said, keeping my voice calm, "I want to sleep."

I turned my back on him, but he spun me around and

pressed his mouth against mine. Physically I struggled with him; mentally I struggled with the part of me that wanted to sway into the mold of his arms.

He kissed me again and pulled off my nightdress. "It's wrong to lust after a woman," he groaned. "Sex is only intended to give issue unto future generations, but it's torture for me not to have you. Sophia tries to please me, but nothing is the same, and I—"

I clawed at him. "How dare you tell me about sleeping with her!"

I kicked him, then scratched at his eyes. When he raised his arm to protect himself, I grabbed his hand and sunk my teeth into it. Blood oozed into my mouth, and Percy had to force me to let go.

He pushed me on to the bed, but in a wild fury, I struggled up again. Still biting and clawing, I threw myself at him. The wagon was shaking violently.

Percy pinned me to the bed and held my hands fast above my head. He pressed one leg against my legs, and I could not move. He kissed me again with an urgency that left me breathless.

He came down, fitting his body between my legs. He was caressing me, and even as I tried to push him away, he kissed my breasts. I felt the sting of his teeth.

"I don't belong to you," I sobbed.

He forced himself into my body. I tried to stiffen, but I couldn't fight him and I couldn't fight the desire that spread across my groin.

"No, I won't," I gasped, but an ecstasy ran through me, and I began to respond. Every touch was a soothing fire.

Hours later I awakened cradled in Percy's arms. For a moment I was snug, comfortable, but with a jolt, I remembered that after all my struggles, I had responded to his love. Joyfully, I had answered every caress, but tomorrow night it would be Sophia who spread her legs to him. I shuddered. For the first time, I was truly a plural wife, and shame overcame me. I hated myself and wanted to die.

I pulled on my clothes, and before Percy was awake enough to stop me, I climbed out of the wagon. I ran away from the train, toward the barrenness of the desert.

I could hear Percy calling. I knew he would saddle Brig and come after me, but he'd never catch me. I'd run forever, run until I died. A sob escaped me when I thought of the poor baby who would die with me, but there was no way for me to go on living.

The wild country was full of huge rocks and steep grades, but every time I fell, I dragged myself to my feet and started running again.

Suddenly I lost my footing and fell over the edge of a chasm. I landed in a bed of plants that I could not see in the darkness. I tried to get up again, but when I moved, an agonizing pain shot through my right leg. I screamed and then I must have fainted.

When I regained consciousness, my moment of madness had passed. I wanted to live, and I wanted my baby.

Chapter 10

The plants beneath me shifted precariously, and I realized I might be near the edge of a cliff. Slowly I felt about me, trying to find something to cling to, but everything I touched came loose in my hand. Brittle twigs pierced through my clothing, and each movement brought a new agony to my leg. I tried to scream, but all I could manage were low wails.

"Oh, please, God," I prayed, "let Percy find me. And please let my baby be all right. Punish me, but don't let anything happen to my baby."

I was in total darkness; there was no way to measure the passage of time. The desert chill settled through me. I shivered and my teeth chattered, but perhaps it was the cold that kept me conscious and kept my thoughts so amazingly clear.

I finally realized that I had to adjust to the fact that Percy now had two wives. I was a victim, but so was Sophia. If she loved Percy, that love had been learned in a bed she had been forced to share—*and that bed I would never share again*.

For the sake of my child, I would be a good wife to Percy in all other ways. God help me, I still loved him, but I would tell him—*I would make him understand*—that if he ever forced me into his bed again, I would kill him!

After a while, I couldn't think anymore. My eyes

closed, and I began to sink into a warm world of perfect comfort. Then I heard voices.

"Olive! Olive! Olive!"

Over and over my name echoed around me, and at last I responded: "Here I am."

At first my voice was barely a whisper, but it brought me back from that other world.

As the sky lightened, I could see that I was on a ledge, amidst a clump of hemlocks and dwarf oaks. If I fell, I would be lost in a canyon below. I began screaming, and finally a man looked over the edge above me.

"Over here! She's over here! We'll need plenty of rope and some strong men."

Moments later Percy looked down at me. "Be brave, dearest," he called. "We will get you to safety."

I could hear Percy arguing, but the other men wouldn't let him descend. Instead, they lowered two young men who braced themselves against the fragile trees.

The first one who reached me grabbed me under the arms. The other lifted my legs. Firey stabs coursed through me, and with one shrill cry, I fainted again.

When I came to, I lay on a blanket on the ground, and Percy was examining me. His fingers felt along my leg. "It's broken," he muttered.

Then he began giving instructions: "One of you run back to my second wagon and bring the bolt of muslin that's stored under the seat. And someone cut two strong poles about three feet long."

When he had the poles to use as splints, Percy set my leg. As he worked, coarse hands stroked my own, and I tried to endure the pain by concentrating on the beads of sweat that stood on Percy's forehead.

After my leg was set, Percy eased my body onto a stretcher the men had made from a blanket and two long poles. Then he walked beside me, holding my hand, as the men carried me back to camp.

It was still another ordeal to be lifted into our wagon, and I sobbed with relief when I was finally on the bed. Sophia was hovering close, offering me water. I could hear Linnie too, but it was Percy whose gentleness and kindness truly moved my heart.

He put compresses on my cuts and bruises. He murmured words of love, and he did everything he could to make me comfortable.

The wagon train was already behind schedule, and I could hear Aaron taking his place on the high seat. He poked his head through the canvas opening.

"Olive," he called softly. "I'm sorry. I'm sorry for what happened to you. I'm sorry for everything."

Our eyes met, and then I glanced toward Sophia who had her back to us. "I'm sorry too, Aaron."

With the first jolt of the wagon, fresh pain seared through my leg. Sophia was with me, and from time to time she bathed my forehead; I didn't have the strength to resist her gentle ministrations.

"Sister Olive," she whispered. "Percy is walking with the lead oxen. He's easing them over the rough spots to help keep the wagon steady. Can I tell him it's helping? Can I tell him you don't feel the jolting too bad?" Her voice quivered.

I reached out my hand, and she took it. "Thank him for me, Sister Sophia. Tell him . . . tell him . . . ." My voice drifted off and my mind wandered. I patted the small, hard bulge on my belly and fell into a deep sleep.

That evening Percy knelt by my side, and I let him hold my hand. "Percy," I murmured, "I want to tell you . . . I want to tell you that I accept . . . accept the way things are. But what happened last night must never happen again."

I squeezed his hand tightly. "If it happens again, Percy, I promise you that I will—"

With a sob, Percy buried his face on the bed. "What happened was all my fault, Olive, and it'll never happen again. I love you and I'll wait for you. Forever if need be, but I'll never force you . . . I'll never demand . . . ."

His voice trailed off, and I closed my eyes.

A few minutes later Percy said, "Olive, when you were unconscious, you kept saying, 'My baby, my baby.' Why didn't you tell me you were with child?"

In spite of the pain he caused me, I reacted to the hurt in his voice. "Percy, I did tell you. I told you at the dance, but you didn't hear me."

I pushed myself up on my elbows. "Is the baby hurt? Will he be all right?"

"Yes," Percy said, easing me back on the pillow. "I think the baby is still all right, but you will have to lie very quiet."

Although Percy was due to spend that night with Sophia, he remained with me, sleeping on the blanket on the floor. "I love you, Olive," he told me before he went to sleep. "I'm glad about the baby. I hope it's a boy, and I hope you'll call him after me."

Chapter 11

The next day we reached the summit of Big Mountain, and lying motionless on my bed, I listened as the company went wild with joy at their first glimpse of the valley. My mind drifted, and I envisioned a valley of my own. It was beautiful, and Percy and I entered hand-in-hand and alone.

My dream was interrupted when Linnie appeared. "We're almost there, Olive! We kin see the valley shimmerin' in the sun, just like heaven's goin' t'look," she cried, struggling past the furnishings and boxes to sit by me.

"The downside of Big Mountain looks plumb straight down, and the men are puttin' new leather on the brakes of some of the wagons. And they're goin' to walk by the leaders t'steady them."

Before we started the descent, Percy tied everything down. "Hold tight to this," he said, handing me a rope that he'd fastened taut to either side of the wagon. "It'll keep you from slipping too much. And don't worry. I'll be out by the leaders, and I'll get you down safely."

When the wagon started to roll, everything around me lunged forward, as far as the ropes would allow. I clung to my rope, the only person in the whole company who rode down Big Mountain.

That night we camped beside Big Canyon Creek, and at nine o'clock the next morning we reached the foot of Little Mountain.

Linnie came to my wagon. "Little Mountain's shorter than Big Mountain, but it's steeper. The men goin' t'take the wagons over, one at a time, with two teams on each wagon."

Soon I was clinging to my rope as our wagon tilted and swayed across Little Mountain. It was dark before the last wagon descended, and the scouts had already ridden in to report that we were only ten miles from Salt Lake City.

The next morning Percy looped up the drilling so I could see out as we traveled through Emigration Canyon, the last miles of our journey. Late that afternoon, October 2, 1854, we entered Salt Lake City.

A crowd had gathered at Big Field to welcome us, and folks rushed around inquiring about relatives. I watched people laugh and cry as they greeted each other. Some embraced, others slapped each other's backs, and children ran unrestrained and happy through the meadow grasses.

Soon women were bringing out bedding, lopping it over wagon wheels to air. Other bathed their children.

I lay in the wagon, surrounded by life, activity and joy. This was the day we'd all yearned for, yet inside I felt empty. The future held nothing for me.

Suddenly I became conscious of a man standing near the wagon, staring at me. His tall figure cast a black shadow from the setting sun. Long, dark hair made him look like an Indian, and a fringed buckskin jacket swung from his broad shoulders. His eyes, bare slits in his leathery face, grilled me from above his heavy whiskers. I couldn't look away. His gaze held me paralyzed, like a snake.

Linnie's voice calling to me broke the spell.

"Who . . . who is that man?" I gasped, as Linnie ran up to the side of the wagon.

"He's Porter Rockwell, a Danite, and he scares everyone."

"A Danite?" I questioned.

"Yes, a destroying angel," Linnie explained. "Back in Missouri and Illinois when the robbers attacked us, some of our men mobilized to fight back— t'pay 'em back in like measure. They called themselves Sons of Dan, and after a while we called 'em Danites."

Spellbound, I turned to look again, but the man had vanished.

When Linnie and I parted, I clung to her hand, dreading the added loneliness I faced without her.

Percy went with the other men to get assignments of ground for each family, and when he returned, he leaned against the wagon. He looked weary, and it seemed like an effort for him to speak.

"Each man has been given a lot in town, and forty acres out in the valley," he said slowly, talking to me through the open drilling.

He shook his head. "Eventually I may have to do some farming because Brother Brigham doesn't think I'll find profit enough in doctoring. He says that homemade poultices, wild herbs and the laying-on of hands are the Saints' favorite remedies."

He attempted a smile. "I guess you'll have to wait a while longer before you're really a doctor's wife."

I gritted my teeth. *Didn't he know that as long as he kept Sophia, I could never think of myself as his wife?*

When he yoked the oxen to our wagon, Sophia followed him around, staying so close I wondered how he kept from stepping on her.

When both wagons were ready to move, Percy said, "We'll get to our city lot tonight, and in the morning we'll start building."

I didn't answer, but I was determined that when Percy began building, it would be two houses, not one.

Chapter 12

It was my first morning in Deseret, and I wanted to write a letter to my family. By leaning over and squirming, I managed to reach the box that contained paper, pen and ink; I used a medical book as a writing table.

I threw back the drilling where Percy had loosened it. White mountains stood bold against an intensely blue sky. The morning air was cool and fragrant, and I could hear birds chirping.

I sighed and began my letter: *My Dearest Family, We have arrived in Deseret, and it is beautiful*.

I wrote that I missed them, each and every one, and prayed for their welfare. I asked about our neighbors, the farm and the crops, and I enjoined them to let me know if the horses, Mike and Polly, were all right.

Writing about our journey, I described the prairie and the thrill of watching the mountains slowly rise in the distance. With tears in my eyes I reported the Indian attack and the deaths the Saints had suffered. I had to tell that I had broken my leg, but I assured them that it was healing well. Then I let them know they would be grandparents, aunt, and uncles in the spring.

There was something else to tell. Again and again I dipped the pen in the ink, but I could not touch it to the paper. I could not bring myself to tell them about Sophia. My beloved family must never share the agony of knowing that my Percy had married a second wife.

I sealed the letter and for a moment held it close to my heart. *How far away they were*.

When Percy came, he promised to take the letter to the tithing house. "I'll be sent out with the first messengers going back East," he said.

Despite my unrelenting coolness, Percy was always loving and cheerful, but that day—our first day in Deseret—he was obviously downhearted.

"I'll have to take up farming even sooner than I thought," he said. "Our acreage has to be plowed now and winter wheat planted."

He shook his head. "I want to open a medical office. I've no doubt I'd have patients enough to keep us going, but every man is instructed to grow crops enough for his own family."

He looked at me, and in spite of everything, his wistful smile caught my heart. "And house-building will have to be postponed until after the planting is finished. It grieves me to see you cooped up in the wagon for so long, but there's nothing I can do about it for a while."

"Don't worry about me, Percy," I said, my voice kinder than I wanted it to be. "I'll be all right, and I know that eventually you'll get your practice started."

I remembered little George. "You're a good doctor and people will need you," I added.

He smiled. "I'll be a farmer by day and a doctor when needed. And I'll be a house-builder too, as soon as possible."

He touched my hand, and we shared a moment of tenderness, so rare now. He looked as if he wanted to kiss me, and perhaps I would have let him, but our moment was shattered by Sophia's voice.

"Percy, your dinner is ready," she called. "It's roast beef and jonnycake, your favorites."

She sounded eager and loving and I cringed. There could never be any tenderness for Percy and me.

It was several weeks before Percy was able to begin building, but on the morning the first mud bricks were delivered to our lot, I made my demand.

"Percy," I said when he came to my wagon, "there must be two houses, not one."

He shook his head. "Dearest, that's unreasonable. Perhaps someday we can have two houses, but now you are with child and your leg is broken. Winter is almost here, and . . . ."

In interrupted, and the determination in my soul sounded in my voice: "Percy, I will never live in the house where you and Sophia share a bed."

He grimaced. "All right, Olive," he said hesitantly. "There can be only one house, but it will be divided into two rooms with a permanent wall between them."

Snow already covered the ground when Percy and several other men left for the mountains to cut timber for the floors, rafters and doors. During the three days he was gone, Sophia brought my meals. She tried to be sociable.

"It'll be nice when we get the house ready," she ventured.

"Yes, it will, and thank you for the food," I said briskly.

I had not been out of the wagon since I was lifted in with my leg in splints. My belly was beginning to swell with child, and there was no position in which I was comfortable. I was cross and unhappy, and Sophia was the last person in the world I wanted to talk to.

But she made still another attempt at conversation. "I hope the hoecake turned out all right, Sister Olive. I tried my best."

I tasted it. It wasn't done in the center, and the flavor was strange, but Sophia was watching me, so obviously hopeful.

She was a year younger than I—exactly Dorothy's age—and unexpectedly, something in me gave way to a warmer feeling. "Sister Sophia, this hoecake is just fine," I said. "Perhaps you'll bring me another piece later."

She smiled, and a little of her sparkle returned. "Oh, I hope Percy gets home soon, so I can give him some."

I caught my breath. How could I be friends with this beautiful girl who'd fallen so madly in love with the man I loved?

Of course the question that was still unanswered—the question that for months I had not allowed myself to ask—was, *Had Percy fallen in love with Sophia?*

I watched for signs and symptoms of that love, and the day after Percy returned, we argued because he wanted to give her my window glass.

The walls of mud bricks were going up, and Percy told me, "We're ready to put the glass panes in. Two of them will go in your end of the house, the other two in Sophia's end."

Percy had bought that glass for me, and now he wanted to give half to Sophia.

"But the glass is mine. It all belongs to me," I cried.

Percy stared at me. "Olive, there are four pieces of glass. Are you so selfish that you won't share with Sophia? Do you want her to live in a place without a window?"

He loved Sophia, and he thought I was selfish.

"She can have a window made of pig bladder, the way most people do. I won't let her have what belongs to me." In my anger, I tried to pull myself up to stand on my splinted leg.

Percy grabbed me and eased me back on the bed. "Olive, does that glass really mean so much to you?"

Unexpected tears gushed down my cheeks. I sobbed, realizing it wasn't the glass I was arguing about; it was

Percy himself. I didn't want to share *him*. My head fell back on the pillow. All my energy drained away, and I sighed.

When Percy unpacked the glass, he found one of the panes broken in two.

"Sophia can have the bigger window," I said, no longer caring.

Without answering, Percy left the wagon, but when he set the glass, two panes went into the wall of my room.

At least he still loves me more than he loves her.

When the house was liveable, Percy carried me in. A cot was in one corner opposite the big bed. The cook stove was in place, and the table and chairs were in the center of the room. After having been confined to the wagon, that single room seemed enormous.

Two days after we moved in, Percy took the splints off my leg. He assured me the leg was fine, but I had difficulty walking. Both legs felt weak, and dizziness accompanied every attempt to stand.

But Percy was persistent. "We must get you back on your feet," he said. Each day he and Sophia walked me around the room until I was finally able to walk a little on my own.

Christmas came, a desolate time because it was my first Christmas away from my family. My mind was full of them—Pa, Ma, Ted, Dorothy, and the boys—and I envisioned them together. I could hear their voices, and I could smell the Christmas fragrances of pine mingled with Ma's holiday cooking.

A Christmas Eve service was held at the wardhouse, but I couldn't walk well enough to attend. Percy was to preach, and he left with Sophia clinging to his arm. When they were gone, I cried bitterly for no reason and for every reason.

I must have cried myself to sleep, because late that

evening I awakened to the clatter of hooves, happy shouts, and laughter. Smiling, Percy led more than a dozen young men and women into the house.

"We decided to conclude our meeting here, so that you wouldn't be left out," he said.

Back in Ohio—before we moved to Iowa—I had attended many parties, and our own home had always been open to all my friends. As people bounded through the door, greeting me with smiles and gentle concerns for my condition, I felt a warm rush of feeling. It was almost as if I had returned to those happy Ohio days.

We had only two chairs, but everyone found a place on the floor, crowding close to the fireplace. A chubby, red-faced young man began singing a Christmas carol. He had a lovely, tenor voice, but after a chorus or two, he insisted we all join in. Someone had carried in a poke of apples, and as we sang, several fellows stuck the apples on sticks and began roasting them over the flames.

At the conclusion of a song, a thin youth rose to his feet. We all bowed our heads as he led us in prayer. Then Percy read from the Book of Luke, and afterward he talked about the beauty of the Christmas message in the life of a Mormon.

I still thrilled to the sound of his beautiful voice, his determined words and his ardent faith. Percy was so sure, so confident, but my own faith was full of doubts and unanswered questions.

When Percy finished, the sizzling apples were passed around. A girl produced a big plate of hoecake and a cup of honey, and we ate to the sounds of laughter and cheerful conversation. It was Christmas, and I was surrounded by friends. For a moment, I forgot the heavy stone in my heart.

I couldn't sit on the floor, and a gentle-mannered girl had pulled the other chair close to sit by me. When Percy turned around looking for a place, Sophia quickly made room for him next to her. Her red skirt was bunched around her, her dark hair was tied with a scarlet ribbon, and when she looked at him, adoration shown in her face. Watching her, I was suddenly all alone again. The desolate, empty feeling returned, and it took an effort to turn my attention back to our little celebration.

After everyone left, Percy put on his heavy jacket and handed Sophia her shawl. It was his week with her, and they were going to her part of the house.

"Olive," Percy called, "good night and Merry Christmas."

I could never get used to it; the pain was always fresh when they went off together. I watched in silent agony as they went out the door, Percy bracing against the hard wind.

I was disposing of apple cores and dusting up crumbs when I heard Percy and Sophia laughing. A shudder ran through me, and suddenly my weak legs were inadequate to my support. I grasped the table to keep from falling, and I stifled a scream.

The wall between our rooms was not thick enough to deaden all sounds, and sometimes I could hear them talking. When he was there with her, they talked and laughed; she was his wife, and I was utterly alone. When he was with me, I measured every word, wondering what Sophia could hear on her side of the wall.

The situation lent itself to madness, and when Sophia's laughter rang out again, I could not endure it. Pushing a chair in front of me, I struggled over to the bed. Without undressing, I climbed in and pulled the quilt over my head. I cupped my hands over my ears, but I couldn't hide from my thoughts.

I struggled against it, but I could see Sophia stepping out of her red skirt, loosening her camisole and offering herself to him. He had said she tried to please, so she would be smiling. My own husband would take her into his arms. He would caress her, stroke her body the way he used to stroke mine. She would kiss him, touch him, and he would gasp in pleasure.

I groaned, and on my first Christmas in Deseret, I gnashed my teeth until I fell asleep.

Chapter 13

My walking improved, and by spring I was able to do my own cooking and cleaning. I moved awkwardly, my body bulky, and I felt ashamed when I watched Sophia, her waist tiny, her movements light and graceful.

One day Sophia brought me some potatoes to cook, and while she was with me, a sudden wave of faintness engulfed me.

She grabbed my arm. "Oh, let me help you," she cried.

"Thank you," I whispered, fighting the dizziness. "You are always very kind to me."

"You're nice to me too," she said quickly.

She helped me walk to the bed, then she peeled the potatoes and put them in the pot on the stove. Afterward she took her metal mirror out of her pocket and gazed into it.

"Do you know, Sister Olive," she began dreamily, "before the elders told me I must marry Percy, I was always sure I would be a first wife."

"I'm not sorry about Percy," she continued, smoothing her hair with her hand, "but there were those who really did admire me."

I thought of poor Aaron. "Sister Sophia," I said softly, "did you like any young man especially?"

"All of them," she giggled. Still gazing into her mirror, she did a bit of a dance step around the room.

I laughed, but my heart ached for her. She was pretty, and she wanted to be admired. Allowed to do her own choosing, maybe she would have married Aaron; maybe it would have been another of the men who so quickly responded to her charms.

She had neither chose nor been chosen, yet—I had to admit it—she was beautifully free of malice. There were times when I truly wished I could be like her.

Percy was absolutely convinced plural marriage had the blessings of God; Sophia was sweet and eager to be loved. If I could only accept their points of view, life would be so much better—*but I could not.* I had told Percy before we married that I could never share a husband. I searched my soul—during the long, lonely nights I prayed for guidance—and my convictions remained the same.

The following morning I felt well enough to walk out to Brig's shelter. He wasn't there, and I hurried to Sophia's house and had her rouse Percy.

"Brig's missing!" I cried.

Percy rechecked Brig's shelter, then went to search for him. I waited anxiously, but Percy returned without my beloved pony.

"The neighbors have animals missing too," he told us. "We're convinced the Lamanite Indians have stolen them."

I cried, but soon my sorrow took another direction. My labor had started.

At my request, Percy went for Linnie, and she came, carrying her own second baby.

"I was sure t'was goin' t'be a girl," she said, "and I was planning t'name her Lottie Olive, for you and my sister, but Nathan here fit into my heart the moment I saw him."

I smiled at the chubby baby she held up for me to

admire, but my smile froze as a great pull tore across my middle.

When it passed, Linnie stooped and kissed my forehead. "Take it easy, Olive," she murmured. "Nathan and me, we just been through this, and it won't be as bad as you're thinking."

Sophia brought me hot broth, and she kept asking if she could do anything else. The midwife arrived; everyone waited, and I tried, but it proved to be a long, hard trial that lasted two days.

Percy never left me. He instructed the midwife on every move, and my baby came at last.

Later Percy smiled as he bent over the small form cradled in my arm. "He's beautiful, like his mother, and you're going to call him . . . ?" Hopeful, he looked at me.

I could no longer be a real wife to Percy, but my baby was his first-born son. Tears filled my eyes. "His name is Percival Dodson," I said.

My recovery was slow, and without complaining, Sophia did all the washing, smoothing, cooking, and cleaning. Her eagerness to care for the baby touched me, but I tended to all his needs myself, refusing even to let her hold him. Percy was no longer my own, and I would not share the small bundle in the cradle. I called him Val, because Percival seemed too big a name for one so small.

It was an afternoon in May when Percy burst through the door holding something out to me. I was still weak, but when I realized what he had in his hand, I flew across the room and grabbed it. It was my first letter from home.

It was from Dorothy, and it was dated January 17, 1855. The first sentence brought heartbreak.

Three weeks after you left, George died of diptheria.

She told me that Ma and Pa still grieved, but that everyone was well.

I sobbed at the news of my dear, little brother's death, but when I could attend to the rest of the letter, I read that Ted knew a sweet girl and wanted to get married. Again, many trains of immigrants were camped on the Kanesville bluffs, waiting until the spring thaw when they could continue on West.

She closed by saying they all sent their love. Then in a postscript that was blurred and hard to read, she added, *I miss you every single day.*

When I could hold back the tears, I read the letter again and again until I knew every word by heart. Then I began writing an answer. I told them that I would never forget our precious little brother. How I wished I could have been with them in their time of grief.

Then I described our new house, the garden and our acreage outside the city. I assured them my leg had mended and that I was walking as well as ever, and I used a whole page to describe little Val.

I made no mention of Sophia.

The next morning when Percy took my letter to post it at the tithing house, I stood at the window and watched him saddle his horse.

We had been allowed to marry because George had lived, but now George was dead.

I felt eerie, as if I were lost in a strange dream.

Late that afternoon Percy returned, and to my utter astonishment, he was accompanied by an Indian squaw who had a sickly-looking child tied to her back.

"She's been indentured to me by the court," Percy explained. "She was captured and brought in by the Utes for sale, and Brother Brigham's men bought her.

"Bought her!" I exclaimed. "For a slave?" My father's deep hatred of slavery had been instilled into me, and I recoiled.

"She's not a slave," Percy said. "She is to work for her keep, but we do not own her, and the court will take back any Indian who is mistreated."

"But how could Brother Brigham's men buy her?"

"There's been a great deal of fighting, raiding, and killing between the tribes. The Indians have learned that the Saints can't bear to see women and children killed, so they bring their captives here to sell. The Saints buy them to save them, and the law about their care was passed some time ago."

"What . . . what's her name?" I asked.

"It's unpronounceable, but she answers to Leah. She'll be a great help to you and Sophia, but first she has to get rested. From what I've heard, her tribe lives in the Wyoming territory, nearly two hundred miles from here."

The odor of the woman sickened me. "Sophia can have her," I said with finality.

Percy shook his head. "She won't be in the house. I've purchased a tent for her to live in, and she'll work in the garden. When cold weather comes, I'll see that she has a house of her own."

Although I didn't want Leah, in a few months I wondered how I could have gotten along without her. She was a tireless worker, and our garden grew green and lush under her capable hands.

Neither Sophia's cooking nor mine pleased her, and she indicated that she wanted to prepare her own food. She dug a hole in front of her tent, lined it with rocks and with the daily rations I gave her, she cooked flat cakes and savory-smelling stews for herself and her child.

He was named Shokup, after a chief of the Shoshoni, and he thrived along with the garden. His arms and legs filled out quickly, and he became more energetic, running and shouting, and throwing rocks at the gulls. He

showed a keen interest whenever I brought Val out of
the house, but I couldn't bear him near my baby. I
discouraged his smelly presence with harsh words,
spoken loudly so that Leah would hear.

She would come quickly, grab Shokup by the arm
and drag him away. She never looked at me, and her
face showed no feeling. Her brown skin was smooth,
and her black eyes remained veiled behind heavy
lashes.

I tried to compensate for my gruffness with Shokup
by giving Leah gifts—a calico dress, a wooden doll
from the tithing house, a large helping of jerky from our
limited supply.

Leah discouraged any help in the garden. She wanted
to tend it herself, and I was relieved because —if she
had needed help—it would have had to come from me.
Sophia, for all her eagerness to please, was not very
strong and gardening exhausted her. Percy hated anything related to farming, and during our early months in
Deseret he found working in the fields unbearable.

"I'm a doctor, not a farmer," he would say when he
came home sore and weary after a long day's labor.

His only patients were local people, and he treated
them in their homes or at our house. Often it would be a
knock late at night that would summon him, and he
tended many injuries and set many bones right at our
own table.

He wanted an office, a place devoted to his practice
of medicine. "That's how it is in the East, and that's
what I want here," he told me. "I want all modern
equipment, the best that can be ordered from New
York. I want people to realize that practicing medicine
isn't something you do as a favor for your neighbors."

Although many families thanked him with small
gifts, he was rarely paid cash for his medical help. He

had to work in the fields until Brother Brigham asked him to become one of his assistants. Percy was proud and pleased to accept, and from then on, he spent several days a week at the Beehive, Brother Brigham's home and office. He was paid well, and from his salary, he was able to pay two of his brothers to tend our acreage.

The new assignment made Percy much happier, and his closeness to Brother Brigham made our house a source of early news for the neighborhood. Whenever there were rumors of trouble, we were sure to have people tapping at our door, asking what Percy had heard.

That summer Chief Walker of the Utahs led war parties against new settlements in central Utah and down south at Provo. "The Nauvoo Legion will protect our people," Percy reported. "They are well armed, and they're moving from settlement to settlement to discourage Indian attacks."

Late that October, he spread the word that the long-awaited paper machine had reached Deseret. It had been shipped from England, brought up the Mississippi River, and hauled to Salt Lake City by four hundred oxen and forty huge wagons. Finally we would have good-quality paper for printing and writing.

Almost everyone turned out to see the huge machine, but as Percy, Sophia, and I walked to join the crowd, I was aware of the unholy picture we made. Carrying Val, I walked on Percy's right side; Sophia walked at his left. It pained me to take my place as a plural wife, and it pained me to see other little groups of husband plus wives. I smiled and greeted our neighbors, but my hatred of polygamy couldn't be shut out, even during an hour's recreation.

Supply wagons began arriving from California,

bringing luxuries we hadn't had before, and at Christmas Percy bought a woolen coat for Val, a new blanket for Leah, and leather shoes for Shokup. He was very generous with his wives, buying a length of blue silk for Sophia and green silk for me, plus fine linen for sets of drawers and chemises for the two of us. They were lovely gifts, but I felt no gratitude. As a favor to Sophia, I helped her finish the shirt she made for Percy, but I wouldn't give him a present.

It was my second Christmas in Deseret. I had managed to adjust, but a little of me died every time my mind tortured me with visions of Sophia and Percy in bed together.

Percy never made any demands on me after my leg was broken. Of course, when the splints came off my leg, Val's birth was only a few months away, but by Christmastime Val was learning to stand.

It had been over a year since Percy and I had lain together. I yearned for him terribly. There were moments when I wished he would force me, but then I'd feel ashamed. He didn't *need* to force me, because he had Sophia. With care and deliberation, I showed him little affection and no encouragement. If I wanted him, he would never know it.

Chapter 14

As the new year began, Sophia fell ill with a heavy cold followed by a persistent cough.

"It's nothing," she said when I tried to persuade her to stay in bed. "I'll be over it in no time."

Percy obtained dry mustard. "We'll mix it with hog fat and put it on her chest, and we'll get good doses of quinine down her to break that fever," he said.

But the weeks wore on, and Sophia remained weak and wracked with coughing. She was cheerful and uncomplaining though, and I felt no hardness of heart when I did everything I could for her.

It was hard winter now, and heavy snows banked against the house. Several times a day Leah lumbered in from the mudbrick house that had been built for her, lugging brush, cowchips, and wood. To my amazement she had no trouble learning to do the cleaning, washing, and smoothing, and she worked as diligently at the indoor chores as she had in her garden.

When examining the smoothing iron, the butter churn, or some other article that was strange to her, she would say, "*Imp-bar-bar? An-ne-ne-ah?*"

What is that? What is it called?

I learned a few words of Shoshoni; she knew a few words of English, and we managed to communicate.

After President Pierce appointed Brother Brigham to a second term as governor of the Utah territory, the Beehive was busier than ever. Percy never came home until late, and he spent every night with Sophia because she was so ill. I cooked, did the chores, cared for my baby, and tended Sophia, and by nightfall I was usually exhausted. I could fall asleep without dreaming that Percy's arms were around me.

It was cold and wet until the last week of March, then suddenly the sun shone, the days warmed, and we were into spring. Leah began digging in the garden, Shokup ran about and played, and Sophia felt strong enough to sit in her doorway.

"Spring conference is on April sixth," I said to her. "You must get well quickly so that you can attend."

She had lost weight; her skin had a wax-like pallor, but her smile was eager. "Oh, it would be wonderful to get dressed up and go and see everyone. I feel better just thinking about it."

On the bright spring morning of April 6, Sophia looked stronger than she had in months. I helped her get dressed, and she was overcome with excitement when she put on the new dress I'd made from her length of blue silk.

"It's so beautiful," she said, running her hands down her sides. "I can't thank you enough for making it for me. How did you ever find time to sew yours and mine too!"

I gave her a ribbon from the leftover silk to tie on her bonnet, then I went to get ready. I put on my own new dress, and I brushed my hair vigorously. I tried to straighten the curls that left to themselves would frame my face. I was nineteen, and I thought a smoother, less girlish look was more appropriate.

At the last moment I put Val into his lace dress. His hair was darkening, but his eyes remained a bright, clear blue. "When you're a man, you'll look just like your father,'' I told him, ''but I pray to God that you'll have only one wife.''

Percy harnessed the carriage he'd purchased, and Sophia, Leah and Shokup climbed into the rear seat. I sat in front with Percy, holding Val in my arms. We drove down Main Street, past the hotel, the butchery, the blacksmith shop, and the new general store.

Temple block, some ten acres square, already had crowds of people. Wagons and carriages lined the streets outside the wall, and oxen, mules, and horses grazed farther away.

When we entered the Tabernacle, Leah and Shokup found a place to sit in the back, and Sophia and I moved up front on the women's side and sat with the other ladies of our ward. Looking very handsome in his black broadcloth coat, Percy went to join the men on their side.

''Here comes the orchestra,'' Sophia whispered, excited. She clapped her hands. ''Oh, it's so wonderful to be here!''

As the dignitaries filed on to the platform, the congregation rose. Brother Brigham, dressed in gray homespun, took the center chair on the platform. To his right was Brother Jedediah Grant, the Mayor of Salt Lake City, and to his left was Bishop Abraham O. Smoot. When all were assembled, the services opened with the hymn ''Come, Come Ye Saints.''

Brother Jedediah led us in a long, eloquent prayer. Val wiggled and tried to stand up, but when I didn't encourage him the way I usually did, he began to get noisy. He pulled at the strings of my bonnet and began talking in a language that only he could understand, but that everyone could hear.

''Shsssh, Val,'' I whispered. I tried to rock him in

my arms, but he twisted and squirmed, and I knew that in a minute he'd be bellowing. When Brother Jedediah ended his prayer, I slipped quietly down the aisle, lugging my little one-year-old with me.

For our noon meal we picnicked, everyone sharing and visiting with one another. Linnie and I managed to exchange a few words, comparing the progress of her Nathan and my Val, and then it was time to return to the meeting. Val had fallen asleep, so I took him back in.

On the way home, Sophia sat silent, her head down. It was such a contrast to her lively mood of the morning that I was afraid she was getting sick again.

"Sister Sophia, when we get home, you must go right to bed," I said. "I'll fix the evening meal and bring yours to you."

Later, when I brought a plate to her room, Sophia's eyes were red; she'd obviously been weeping. I lingered, willing to listen if she wanted to confide in me, but when she didn't speak, I left.

It was the first week Percy had spent with me in a long time, and he lingered at the fireplace, something obviously on his mind.

"Olive, you had gone outside before Brother Brigham read the list of missionaries being sent out," he said.

My hand pressed against the sudden pain in my side.

"I'm to go to France, along with several others. We're to be ready to leave in a week."

The pain in my side turned into a heavy weight that seemed to crush my entire body. I felt almost too burdened to breathe. "You . . . you . . . consented . . . without protest? You didn't tell him that Sophia was ill and that I had a young child?"

Our eyes met, and I held his gaze. "Can you really go away and leave us?"

He wavered. He looked uncertain and confused, and he reached out his hand to me. I would have taken it, but suddenly he caught himself. His expression changed, and he straightened as if he were about to begin a sermon.

"Olive, we do not make decisions when counsel is given. We obey. The sending of missionaries is one of our most deep-seated beliefs. Joseph Smith sent out missionaries as early as 1837, and men have gone out from the valley every year. Other wives are proud when their husbands are called because they realize they share in his contribution."

I shook my head in despair. "But I thought Brother Brigham needed you as an administrator, and you are certainly needed as a doctor. How can he possibly send you away?"

"Brother Brigham is directed by God, Who is blessing me with this opportunity to bring converts into His Church. I will be gone two years."

"*Two years!*" I echoed. "Percy, you can't!"

Percy was totally confident again. "Olive, Brother Brigham is directed by God, and I will obey him."

It was useless to argue. I sank on the bed and buried my face in my hands, weeping. I knew now what had caused Sophia's red eyes.

Time passed. I could not get control of myself; I could not stop the useless sobbing that shook my whole body. Then a touch, light and gentle, seemed to melt around my shoulders. As if fearing to really touch me, Percy had put his arm around me.

"We should not question the will of God," he said, "but maybe . . . maybe this one time you will let me comfort you."

Trembling. I turned to him and hid my face on his chest.

He hugged me and kissed my hair. It had been an agonizingly long time since I had allowed him to show me affection, yet his affection was what I wanted most in the world. I turned my face to his, and he kissed me, gently at first and then with passion.

I threw my arms around his neck and embraced him with the strength of all my pent-up feelings. His lips kissed away the tears that dampened my cheeks, and he murmured, "I love you."

We lay across the bed, finally in each other's arms. Fear, anger and longing boiled up inside me, and I wanted him with a desperation that left me weak-willed. "I love you, too, Percy. I'll always love you."

He began to undo my clothes, and I was willing. I unbuttoned his shirt and pressed my cheek against the warmth of his flesh.

Nothing mattered to me, nothing at all, except that I loved Percy and he loved me. His body was warm and hard against my own. I was ready to received him when I heard a noise in Sophia's room, a chair being dragged across the floor. I winced and visualized Sophia, red-eyed and heartbroken. *Sophia!*

I screamed and dug my nails deep into Percy's shoulders. "Go lie with Sophia!" I yelled. "Let her cry for you! I will not."

I snatched myself away from him and pulled the quilt about me to hide my nakedness.

My screams awakened Val. He began to cry and as his wails grew louder, I pulled on my nightdress. I picked him up and sat down in the rocker. I comforted my little son, knowing there could never be any comfort for me.

I was utterly obsessed with Percy. I loved him; I hated him. I wanted to lie with him; I never wanted him to touch me. The thoughts that pounded through my head were as contradictory as the man himself.

Percy was like two people. He was the tender, gentle man I loved, and he was an unreachable, unbending person who could hear only the voice of his church.

But if my other thoughts were violent and contradictory, one thought remained ever-present and unchanging: *Percy was going away.*

Chapter 15

At dawn I tucked Val into his cradle. I'd been up most of the night, and my entire body felt as stiff and unbending as my heart.

When Percy got up, he acted reserved and formal. "During this next week there will be much to do," he said crisply. "I will make arrangements with my brothers to have our acreage planted and harvested, and the crops will be divided between you and Sophia."

I didn't answer, and he continued. "You have Leah to do the garden and help in the house. You will be all right, but if any problem arises that you cannot handle, you must let my father know. He stands ready to help you, and you must obey him."

"The way his four wives do?" I asked bitterly.

"Yes," he answered sharply.

After breakfast Percy left, and I began getting his clothes ready for the journey that would take him so far away from me and our little son.

I heard Sophia's light rap. "May I come and stay with you for a while?" she asked, poking her head inside. Her face was puffy and awful. I hadn't been the only one to spend a miserable night.

"I'm busy getting Percy's clothes ready," I told her, "but you may come in if you wish."

Sophia seated herself at the table. Her shoulders drooped, and from time to time tears rolled down her cheeks.

I concentrated on my work with fierce determination. I would not sit and cry with Sophia. Let Percy travel to France on her tears, not mine.

After a while Sophia let out a wail and covered her face with her hands. "I'm sorry," she gasped, "but I can't stop crying."

I was too empty inside to console her. "You must find something to do and keep busy," I said briskly.

"Those dark blue stockings you're knitting for Percy," Sophia began, "will you have time to finish them before he leaves?"

Without answering I went to my knitting basket and examined the stockings. I had just started them, and with everything else I had to get ready for Percy, there would be no time to finish them before he left. I picked up the stockings, yarn and needles and dropped them in Sophia's lap.

She pounced on the stockings like a kitten with a plaything, and she began to knit slowly and tediously. In the days that followed, those needles clicked continuously. Her tears often dampened the woolen yarn; she was frequently pulling out a row or two of bad stitches, but the day before Percy's departure, the stockings were finished and packed with his other clothing.

On the morning of April 14, Percy harnessed the carriage and strapped his small leather trunk to the back. In the privacy of our own yard we said our stilted farewells. Percy bid good-bye to a trembling, tear-stained Sophia, kissing her on the cheek. Then he turned to kiss me. I was dry-eyed and calm. If I had thought there was any hope of changing his mind, I would have fallen on my knees and begged him to stay, but there was no hope. My dignity was my only comfort.

Percy's lips touched mine; then he said, "I'll write when I can. Pray for me, and if you find it in your heart, go and be baptized. It grieves me to go to the other end of the world to win converts when my own wife is not yet won."

Percy helped Sophia climb into the back of the carriage, then he handed me up to the driver's seat. I drove, and Val played on his father's lap.

Percy talked to Val who responded by repeating one of the few words he knew: "Pa . . . Pa . . . Papa . . . Papa!"

They made a bittersweet picture.

We reached the tithing house just as the stagecoach arrived. It pulled up, the horses sweating and tossing their heads, and the livery stable men came running with a fresh team.

Percy turned to Sophia and me and said his last adieus. Then he joined the group of men who stood talking and laughing near the stage. I could hear Sophia's muffled sobs, but I was too empty to cry.

The new driver took his place, and calling to the crowd, the men poured into the coach. The whip was laid to the horses, and they were on their way.

I handed Val to Sophia, and she hugged him to her. I reached to touch her hand; then I cracked the reins and we started home.

Chapter 16

It was late in May, a morning so exquisite it seemed almost a sin to be indoors. I went to draw water, and I remained at the well, enjoying the soothing warmth of the sun and the delightful fragrances of spring.

In the six weeks since Percy left, we had gone nowhere excepting church, and suddenly I decided we were going on a picnic. I ran into the house and quickly prepared a lunch. Then I hitched the team to the carriage and went to get the others.

Sophia did not need persuading, but it took me a little while to convince Leah to leave her garden. Shokup and Val both loved to ride in the carriage, and they were squealing with delight even before I had the team headed toward the mountain road.

Shokup and Val stayed in back with Leah, and Sophia rode in front with me.

"Sister Sophia, keep your shawl round you," I told her. "It's warm now, but it'll be much cooler when we get up in the woods."

Sophia seemed much better. Her skin had almost a glowing prettiness, but she was still troubled by coughing spells that sometimes gave way to fits of weeping for Percy.

A dull but constant ache never let me forget that I missed him too, but since he had left, my feelings for Sophia had improved. She was a sweet, loving girl. I had long ago responded to her affectionate ways, but while she was sleeping with Percy, I had to resent her. With Percy gone, my resentment slipped away, and she became truly dear to me—but that day my new, unburdened feeling for her was almost shattered.

We drove a long time and finally stopped at a pretty meadow along side a rushing mountain stream. I took care of the horses, and Sophia spread a blanket on the ground and unpacked our lunch.

After we ate, Leah indicated she wanted to go away. Gesturing, she pulled weeds out of the ground and waved toward the surrounding woods.

"Sister Sophia, I think Leah wants to go into the woods to gather herbs," I said.

Leah yelled to Shokup in Shoshoni. He ran along behind her, and they both disappeared into the brush.

With Val toddling along behind me, I went to the stream and filled a small pitcher with water. Val was eager to put his hand in the bubbling stream, but I cautioned him away.

"Cold, Val," I said, taking his hand. "It is very cold."

The water was icy run-off from melting snows, and I cautioned Sophia not to drink any until it had warmed a bit. "You don't want to irritate your cough," I explained.

Val was soon busy picking flowers and pretty weeds. He gave me a handful. "Aunt 'Ofa too," he said.

I laughed and handed Sophia her part of the bouquet, and Val toddled away to gather more. He lost his balance, fell forward and righted himself with his hands.

I stood with my hands on my hips, watching him. "He's getting so big, he'll outgrow his cradle before autumn," I said.

Sophia's voice was very soft. "Perhaps . . .

perhaps you'll let me take the cradle when Val out-grows it. I'll be needing it.''

Her meaning hit me sharply. I caught my breath and looked at her. ''Does Percy know?'' I asked stiffly.

She shook her head. ''I didn't know until after he was gone. It would have been wonderful to tell him, but I'm going to write it to him in a letter.''

I shuddered. *When I first knew I was carrying Val, I hadn't been able to tell Percy because of her.*

Suddenly the visions I struggled against loomed up, and I saw Sophia and Percy in bed together. He held her close, kissed her, and they shared a love that left them breathless and glowing with joy. Now she would have his baby.

I shook my head to clear it, but the food I'd just eaten threatened to come up. I was gagging, but somehow I pasted a shallow smile on my face. Forcing each word I said, ''Percy will be glad when he knows, Sister Sophia.''

She giggled. ''Oh, I think so too. If the baby is a boy, he'll be his second son, but Percy will still love him.'' She laid her hand on her belly. ''If it's a girl, I just know she'll be very pretty and go to lots of dances and parties.''

''If she looks like her mother, she'll be very pretty indeed,'' I said, struggling to hold my smile.

My words pleased Sophia, and it wasn't long before she took out her metal mirror and began smoothing her hair. She wearied easily though, and soon she curled up in a little ball and fell asleep on the blanket.

I sank to my knees, staring at her and hating. My every ugly feeling and thought was renewed, and with an overwhelming vengeance I wished Percy would come home so that I could cause him some measure of the pain he caused me. It was not as if I hadn't known he and Sophia shared a bed, but this evidence of it was more than I could stand.

I thought of Sophia's unborn child. If a son, he would be Val's brother and equally dear to Percy. Sophia would be the mother of Percy's son; I would share even that claim of being special.

The sun no longer warmed me; the pretty meadow faded from view, and I was in a cold, dark tunnel that went on forever. Time didn't exist in the tunnel, and I remained there hurting . . . hurting, but then, as if from another world, I heard screams. Leah was screaming.

Dazed, I jerked to my feet and looked around. Shokup was running wildly toward the stream, and Leah, screaming in Shoshoni, was running after him. Sophia jumped to her feet and grabbed my arm. "What is it, Sister Olive? What's wrong?"

"I don't know," I answered.

Shokup had run downstream and was crawling out on rocks that jettied into the water. He was reaching for an object coming toward him with the current. Leah, bellowing at an unbelievable pitch, waded into the water after him. Shokup caught something in the water, and Leah lifted it up. In her arms I saw the limp body of my son. She grabbed her own son too, and struggling against the flow, she carried them both to shore.

Too frightened to run, I moved toward them on stiff, unbending legs. Leah lowered Shokup to the ground, and groaning from exertion, she carried Val to the blanket.

Through a cloud of terror I reached for my son, but with one hard shove Leah knocked me away. She held Val in one arm and began forcing her breath into his mouth. With her free arm she ripped away his icy, wet clothes and pulled the blanket around him. With rhythmic motions she continued to force her life's breath into him. He shuddered slightly and started to whimper. *He lived*.

I don't remember untying the horses and harnessing them to the carriage, but I must have. Sophia drove home, though, and I sat in the back, clutching my now sleeping son, my one hand resting on his chest to make certain it still moved. Shokup huddled between Leah and me, and his mother talked to him, a long, soothing flow of the words of their tribe.

As we drew close to home, Sophia was overcome with coughing. She reined the horses, and we had to wait until she was able to continue. Val's accident had terrified her nearly as much as it had me, and I prayed that getting so upset would not make her ill again.

At home Leah grabbed her child and took him into their little house. Sophia stayed in my house with Val and me. "Please sleep in my bed tonight, Sister Sophia, and I'll sleep on the cot," I begged.

I coaxed some warm soup into Val, and I made Sophia drink a cup also. Then she collapsed on the bed, and I pulled my mother's quilt over her.

For hours I sat in the rocker with Val cradled in my arms. I counted his every breath; I noted every movement and sigh. Silent tears rolled down my cheeks. I was burdened with a guilt worse than anything I'd ever known before. While I had been occupied with thoughts of hate toward Sophia's child, my own child had almost drowned.

Leah and Shokup must have been returning just at the right moment to see Val topple into the stream. A wide bend in the stream had enabled Shokup to cut across the meadow and catch Val before he was lost in the waters below. Leah had been shouting to him. I didn't know whether she told him what to do, or whether that bright-eyed Indian boy acted on his own to save his little friend.

I smoothed Val's damp curls away from his forehead. How could I have been wicked enough to begrudge Sophia her child when I so dearly loved my own? I felt ashamed, but relieved too, relieved that I would not have to carry a burden of hate. I would love Sophia's child as she truly loved mine.

When I thought it was safe, I put Val in his cradle. I checked Sophia whose breathing sounded raspy again, and then I went and knocked on Leah's door.

When Leah opened it, I entered her house for the first time. It was tiny, with a dirt floor, a pig bladder window and a fireplace on one wall. Around the walls were pieces of bark and small branches from trees. I could not tell if they were intended for warmth or decoration. Shokup slept on a mat.

The room was filled with a tangy odor that came from a pot suspended above the glowing embers in the fireplace. Leah took two cups and filled them from the pot. She nodded to a spot near the hearth, and I went there and lowered myself to sit on my legs. She said some words in Shoshoni, inclined her head slighly, then handed me a cup.

"Thank you, Leah," I said, realizing the cup had been ceremoniously offered. Leah watched me as I put it to my lips. It tasted strange, but not bad, and it was soothing as it went down. I knew it was some mixture of her herbs, and I smiled and nodded my approval.

Leah took the other cup, squatted down, and began to drink. She was no cleaner than she'd been when she came to us. She smelled of the earth and of the sweat of her labors—but her odor no longer repelled me. It was simply a part of her, a part of an intelligent, hard-working, and loyal woman. I looked at Shokup, the child I had not wanted near my baby. He could have lost his own life trying to save Val. He was filled with the same wonder and joy as any white child, and my heart told me that Val could never have a better friend.

"Shokup is a wonderful and brave boy," I said slowly. Leah could not understand my words, but I knew she felt their meaning.

"Shokup," she said, and began talking. She held her hands above her head, obviously indicating height. Her hands showed me the width of the shoulders. I understood. She was describing Shokup's father.

So many things had made me cry that day that when the tears came, I didn't bother to wipe them away. I had never thought of Shokup's having a father; of Leah having a husband. But she did, and she wanted me to know how big he was. She was proud of him, and she missed him, missed him as I missed Percy who had once been my heart's delight.

Before I left, I held out my right hand to her. She stared at it, then grasped it painfully tight with her left hand. She looked at me and said something in Shoshoni. I could not understand, but I hoped she had said, "You are welcome."

Chapter 17

"I told you I'd be comin' t'see you, and here I am!"

I'd answered a knock at the door, and there she stood, Nathan in her arms and Uriah at her side.

"Linnie!" I hardly gave her a chance to put Nathan down before I threw my arms around her.

"Brother Dawson had business that took him this way, so he gave me and the boys a ride s'far as the tithing house road. We're s'pose t'meet him there at four o'clock t'ride home. Reckon that gives us the whole day together if you don't mind."

"Mind! I couldn't think of anything better to happen to me today."

I turned to the boys. "Surely you can't be Uriah," I said, offering my hand to the huge youngster who stood partly hidden behind his mother's skirts. He had grown so much that only the tightly curled, deep red hair convinced me he was truly the boy I had cared for on the way west.

I couldn't hear his whispered answer, but his mother said proudly, "I reckon Uriah is bigger'n some boys twice his age, and he's strong as he can be."

Although the same age, Nathan was a much larger child than Val. They were too young to really play together, but they were soon absorbed in each other's presence. Linnie and I talked, and it wasn't long before I found myself telling her about Val's accident.

"It happened over a month ago," I said after I'd

given her all the frightening details. "Thank God, Val is fine, but I still think about it every day."

"Remember, Olive, that God ain't mad at you or he'd have taken your baby. And if God ain't mad at you, you oughtn't be mad at yourself."

I cut some hoecake. "Linnie, Sister Sophia loves company, and I'll go invite her to join us."

I ran around to Sophia's door. "Sister Sophia," I called, "Linnie Bradford is here. Come visit with us."

When she opened her door, Sophia was wearing her red skirt.

"You're all dressed up," I said, surprised.

"Oh, I've decided to go to the next wardhouse dance, and I was trying on my skirt to see if it still fits—and it does. Look!" The skirt swayed and rustled as she twirled around.

I started to say it wouldn't be proper for her to attend the dance when Percy was away and she was expecting a child, but she looked too eager to disappoint. "The skirt still looks very pretty on you," I said. "But come—Linnie is waiting."

Later, after our midday meal, Val was too excited to rest, so I let him go outdoors with Uriah, who promised to watch the little ones. Sophia returned to her house, and Linnie, watching her go, shook her head.

"She's real sick, Olive. It's a pity, her being so pretty and lively and all."

"You're wrong, Linnie," I exclaimed. "Sophia was very sick right after Christmas, but excepting for coughing spells, she's much better."

"T'was a girl back home had the coughing sickness. When she was havin' a baby, we all thought she was well again. Her skin looked so pretty and nice, same as Sophia's, and she felt a heap better too. But after her baby come, she didn't last no time at all."

An agony went through me. "Sophia's cough will go away, and she'll be completely well. I know she will be," I said fiercely.

"Praise the Lord! I wish Sister Phoebe cared for me the way you care for her," Linnie said, a deep longing in her voice.

"I'm certain your sister Lottie loves you dearly, and you're the best friend . . . ."

I was interrupted by a sudden burst of screaming. We rushed outside and saw Leah standing in the middle of the garden, a brush broom in her hands, flailing frantically at a blackness that covered the ground. Crickets—thousands of huge, black crickets swarmed over everything.

Nathan and Val screamed in terror, but Uriah and Shokup were trying to help Leah ward off the new hordes that hovered in the air, emitting a whirring sound.

Linnie grabbed Nathan and Val and dragged them inside the house. I snatched up the hoe, and Sophia, who'd come running, picked up sticks. Together we began smashing and hitting the black, ugly things that now seemed to be everywhere.

Neighbors were shouting and yelling, dogs were barking, horses were whinnying. I could feel the horrible things crawling on my arms and legs.

"Water," I shouted. "We'll drown them!"

I ran to the corner of our property and turned on the stopcock to flood the land. Someone had opened the watergate at the corner of the ward, and water flowed in a river. Linnie was fighting alongside me now, and we all were trying to force the bugs under the water.

"It's no use," I sobbed. "For every one we kill, twenty more come."

"Remember the miracle of forty-eight, and look to heaven," Linnie shouted. "Them gulls will be here soon."

A favorite Mormon legend was the cricket attack of 1848. At that time God had worked a miracle and sent gulls in great flocks winging over the lake to the cricket-covered fields. The gulls had gulped crickets until their craws were full, an then they regurgitated all they had eaten and immediately began to eat more. The crickets had been consumed; the crops had been saved.

I stumbled to my knees in the water that gushed all around us. I scanned the sky. Not a gull in sight.

Linnie was praying. "God help us! Send the gulls! Help us!"

No gulls came. The water soaked into the ground; the sound of the crickets droned on.

Sophia was soaked and leaning over in a coughing spasm. My wet skirts dragging, I moved toward her, but Linnie reached her first. Together we supported her and helped her into the house. I undid her bodice, and we took off her red skirt. We put her on the bed, a collapsed form whose breath came in heavy, trembling gasps. Linnie's grim prediction was raw in my mind, and every cough caused a pain in my own chest. I should not have let her help, but during our frantic activity there had been no time for sense and caution.

Leah dragged in. "Gone," she said. "Bugs gone. Garden gone."

Linnie and I went out and surveyed what had once been a beautiful garden. Gone were the long, green rows of lettuce, young onions and radishes. The tomatoes, abundant and green on the vine, had disappeared. Only a stubble remained where the corn had been three feet high and beginning to ear. The beans, heavy in their pods, had been eaten away. There were no lacy carrot tops or lush potato vines. Our main food supply had been destroyed.

Linnie took my arm. "I'll share with you, Olive, much as I'm allowed to."

"You are always a friend when I need you," I said.

Inside the house I picked up Sophia's red skirt, washed it carefully and hung it to dry.

Leah brought her pot, and I recognized the odor of her herb tea. I put three cups on the table, and she filled them.

I collapsed into a chair and sipped my cup of the brew while Leah drank hers.

"D'you think it's all right t'drink this?" Linnie asked, picking up the cup I'd given her. "I s'pect it's a tea, and you know Mormons don't never take tea, coffee, or spirits."

I sighed. "It's not tea or coffee and it won't make you tipsy, so you may as well drink it."

Linnie put the cup to her lips, and in silence we drank the soothing liquid.

Suddenly Linnie jumped up. "Me and the boys are s'posed t'meet Brother Dawson at four!"

I looked at the clock on top of the clothes cupboard. "It's past four now, Linnie, but don't worry. I'll drive you home."

I made Leah understand that she must watch Sophia, and taking Val with me, I hitched the horses to the carriage.

"I never would a'thought you'd be hitchin' up a team," Linnie said, admiration in her voice.

I gave the cinch a final tug and climbed into the driver's seat. "Linnie, I'm beginning to think I can do anything I have to do."

We stopped and talked with almost everyone we

encountered and every conversation left us heavier hearted. The destruction had been widespread.

When we reached the Bradford house, Sister Phoebe stood in the doorway, her arms crossed, her expression indescribably negative. "Now you come, when it's too late to be of help to anyone," she said to Linnie.

Linnie scurried down out of the wagon, and her sons hurried after her. "Sister Phoebe, were we as bad hit as most folks?"

"Yes, but most folks were at their own homes, helping fight off them critters. You weren't here, and we have no garden left to talk bout." Sister Phoebe raised her arm, and I know she would have struck Linnie if I hadn't been there.

For Linnie's sake I held back the angry retort that sprang to my lips. "I'm sorry your garden was destroyed," I said calmly, "but our garden was ruined also. Linnie helped me, but she couldn't do any good—no one could, and it is no one's fault."

"Linnie never does any good," Sister Phoebe said.

It sickened me to hear Linnie abused in front of her sons and me. Although most Mormon first wives didn't treat the other wives so badly, Sister Phoebe wasn't the only one of her kind. I had to leave to keep from giving her a good tongue-lashing.

"I'm glad I saw you, Linnie, no matter what else happened today, and I'll see you again soon." Then I called goodbye to Uriah and Nathan, clicked to the horses and started home.

On the way I stopped at Father Terry's and he came out to the carriage to talk to me. "The whole territory's been hit," he said. "Hardly anything left at all. Brother Brigham's already sent word that we must report all supplies on hand and indicate whether there is anything left to be saved from the crops."

"What about the fields?" I asked. "Surely the crickets didn't . . . ."

"Gnawed everything right to the ground. Looks like there won't be enough grain on a whole acre to fill a half-sack. We got the plows ready and as soon as we've gathered what we can, we'll plant the leftover seed, but there's not much of it."

My mind whirled: *Percy had been sent away; Val had almost drowned. Linnie thought Sophia was going to die. The crops were ruined, and there would be no food in Deseret.*

"So many bad things have been happening," I murmured as I left Father Terry. "So many bad things."

I had told Sister Phoebe that what had happened was no one's fault. I believed that, yet I could not shake a puzzling, gnawing sense of guilt.

Chapter 18

At dawn Leah was in the garden, digging the tiny carrots and potatoes, salvaging everything edible before she prepared the ground to plant again.

In the days that followed I helped her as much as I could. Together we planted our tiny supply of leftover seeds. We nurtured them with painstaking care, but the sun was against us. The fierce heat of Utah in July baked the ground dry as soon as we watered, and we could not keep the seeds moist enough to germinate. The few plants that pushed up were spindly, and although we struggled to maintain everything that grew, by late August the garden was all but barren.

The shortage of food was already serious throughout the territory, and I rationed our daily portions with infinite care. I had no idea how long our meager supplies would have to last.

But my greatest worry was Sophia. I'd thought it would be improper for her to attend the wardhouse dance, but when the time came, I would have been grateful if she'd been strong enough to go. She continued to decline, and by September she as so weak, she could no longer leave her bed.

"I cough so much now," she gasped one day. "Do you think it will hurt my sweet baby?"

I swallowed hard. "Not if we take good care of you, but you must try to eat some of this cereal."

She looked ashen, and my own hand shook as I

spooned the cereal to her. I had to get help. The moment she fell asleep, I took Val out to Leah, and then I ran to a neighbor's house.

"Please go to my husband's father, Brother Terry, and tell him that Sophia is terribly ill. Ask him to come as soon as he can."

The family consisted of the man, his three wives and their many children. They had food shortages and problems of their own, but they promised to get word to Father Terry immediately.

Early that evening Father Terry came, accompanied by the ward bishop and several other men, all priests of the order of Melchizedek. Stephen Bradford, Linnie's husband who was now a high priest, was among them.

"Almighty God, send your angels to minister to this dear sister. Bring her back from the jaws of death and restore her to life and health." With bowed heads and sober faces they gathered around Sophia's bedside and prayed long and fervently.

The bishop and high priest annointed Sophia with olive oil, and they laid their hands on her head.

"Elder brother, Healer of the halt and the lame, Giver of sight to the blind, Thou who dost raise the dead unto life, raise our sister from her bed of sickness. Give her a healthy child and bless her to long life in your service."

Sophia lay, eyes closed, making no sign she knew the priests were there. I was not unmoved by their sincerity and prayers, but I needed help on earth as well as help from heaven.

"Father Terry," I called to him as they were leaving, "I need someone to cut a door in the wall between Sophia's room and my own."

"I'll send someone tomorrow," he said, "but be assured that the Lord will hear our prayers and break the stranglehold this sickness has on our poor sister.''

The next day Aaron came, carting lumber and carpenter's tools. ''Pa told me you needed a door,'' he said.

I brought him into my house and showed him where the door was to go. He marked the wall and soon was busy sawing. Val and Shokup watched his every move.

When the opening was made, I watched Aaron, wondering how he would react to the pale form on the bed in the other room. For long moments he stood with his back to me, looking toward her. Her pregnancy was concealed by the quilt I had tucked all around her. Her long black hair spilled over the pillow, and she looked like a sleeping child.

Aaron handed his hammer to Val. ''You can hold this for me until I need it,'' he said calmly.

He's gotten over her, I thought.

But two days later Aaron came back with venison from a fresh kill and a large bunch of wild mountain flowers. ''For her,'' he said as I took the flowers.

Before I could thank him, he hurried away. I arranged the flowers in a bowl and placed them by Sophia's bedside. ''Someone who thinks you are very pretty brought these,'' I said.

She smiled thinly, but her eyes barely opened. In spite of the prayers that had stormed the throne of heaven, she was not better.

On a bleak day in October, Sophia's son was born, a frail blue mite with no hair, no fingernails and no breath.

Linnie and the midwife did everything they could to bring him to life, but at last they wrapped him in the little blanket his mother had knitted for his coming and folded a corner over his face.

''Ought we to show him to her?'' the midwife asked.

I looked toward Sophia, but I could hardly see her for my tears. "No," I murmured, "but we must tell her that he was beautiful."

That night I went to bed, not to sleep, but to wrestle with the guilt that threatened to engulf me. Since Percy had married Sophia, my life had turned into one calamity after another. *I'd broken my leg; Brig had been stolen; I'd learned that my little brother had died.*

I tossed and turned, but I couldn't blot out my torment. *Percy was gone; we were threatened with starvation, and now Sophia's poor baby was dead.*

"It's all my fault," I moaned. "God is punishing me for my sins."

Suddenly my sins were clear in my mind—hate and resentment. I had hated Sophia: I'd hated Percy. I'd resented their marriage, and I had resented the Saints for practicing plural marriage. I thought plural marriage was wrong—I would always think so—but what I thought didn't matter any more. I was ready to do anything that would take away my burden of guilt.

Early the next morning I dressed in my good lindsey-woolsey, and with unsteady hands I tied my Sunday bonnet under my chin. I left Sophia in the care of Percy's mother and another of Father Terry's wives, and taking Val, I harnessed the team and went to see the ward bishop.

He was a kindly man, and his gentle invitation to come into his office helped sooth my anxieties.

"I must join the gathering," I began abruptly. "I must be baptized, endowed, and forgiven for my sins."

I sat rigid, clutching Val in my lap, and the bishop questioned me. "Do you know the Book of Mormon?"

"I read it when I first met Doctor Terry," I told him.

"Do you believe that this book was given on golden plates by the angel Moroni to Joseph Smith, and translated by him through inspiration in the light of Umin and Thumin?''

"Yes," I said nervously. "Dr. Terry explained that to me long ago.''

"Do you believe that the Church of Jesus Christ of the Latter Day Saints is the true church, restored through Joseph Smith?''

"I believe," I gasped.

He read to me from the book of doctrines and covenants, then he peered at me over his spectacles. "Are you ready for baptism?''

"Yes, I am," I said urgently.

"I will give you a recommend which you will present to the high priest at the endowment house tomorrow morning. Leave your child at home and go in faith and prayer. Also, provide yourself with proper garments.''

When I arrived home, Sophia was awake and asking for me. "My poor baby," she murmured, tears rolling from her eyes. "Did you see him?''

I held her hand. "He was beautiful." I sobbed. "The most beautiful baby I've ever seen.''

Sophia's voice sounded far away. "Sister Olive, promise me . . . please promise me that when Percy comes home, you will tell him that my baby was beautiful.''

My heart seemed to stop beating. "You will tell him yourself," I said hoarsely.

A smile flickered. "Do you think so, sister? Do you think I'll see Percy again?''

"I . . . I'm sure you will," I answered, forcing out each word.

"Oh, I want to see Percy again, more than anything," she murmured, "but . . . but I'll be gone before he gets back.''

She tried to push herself up on her elbows. "You've been really good to me, and I want you to have my red skirt."

I put my arms around her and eased her back on the pillow. "Percy loves you," I said firmly, "and you will be here to greet him when he gets home. And someday you will wear your red skirt."

Sophia's eyes opened wider, and she gazed at me. "Percy loves me," she repeated. "I'll see him again, and I'll wear my red skirt." There was a light, a hope in her eyes that burned through to my soul.

I clutched her hand. "Yes," I cried. "I promise that someday you'll see Percy again and wear your red skirt."

Sophia was too overcome to talk anymore, but I remained at her bedside long after she fell asleep. I had promised her that she would see Percy again, and now I had to keep her alive until he came home.

Chapter 19

"Sister Olive Harriet Banks Terry, I place my hands upon your head to give thee a patriarchal blessing. The Lord shall give thee power over disease, and the angels of the Lord shall be around thee and shall warn thee of dangers both seen and unseen."

Thus I was baptized, and for my endowment I put on the long, white underwear that must never be completely removed.

"Always leave an arm or a leg on when you bathe," I was told.

I was greatly moved spiritually by the beautiful ceremony, and I prayed that I would be gifted with the total confidence that Percy had in the truth of his religion.

In the days that followed I waited, yearning to be engulfed in the peace of the Lord, but when Sophia did not get better and we ate the last of our food, peace seemed distant and anxiety was ever-present.

As her coughing spells became more frequent, Sophia needed constant attention, and I realized I had to move Leah and Shokup into the house. However, I was determined that before they moved in with us, like it or not, they would both have a bath.

Leah, unknowing, helped me set up the big iron kettle in the yard, fill it with water, and keep a fire blazing beneath it. When the water was warm, we filled the round, wooden tub that I had dragged close to my fireplace.

Then I took a deep breath, caught hold of Shokup, stripped off his dirty clothes and dumped him into the water. He screamed and Leah started forward as though she'd tear him away from me, but I smiled and waved her back.

"It's all right, Leah. He likes it."

And after the first breathtaking surprise, he did like it. Soon he was splashing merrily.

Watching him, Leah came as near smiling as her habitually expressionless face would allow.

When Shokup had been properly soaked and scrubbed, I dried him and dressed him in the clean clothes I'd provided. I changed the water and then I motioned for Leah to undress.

She shook her head and backed away.

At last by smiling and coaxing, I succeeded in getting her to stand in the tub, but she clung determinedly to the filthy blanket she always had around her. Innocently, I held up the pretty cotton dress I'd made for her, and I showed her the new, red-striped blanket I'd bought for her at the tithing house.

Her interest in the new clothes made her relax her grip on the blanket, and with a sudden move, I pulled it away from her. Before she could do anything but howl with surprise, I had her dress off and was splashing and scrubbing. She wailed as if I were scalping her, but I had won the victory. She even let me scrub her long, heavy hair until it squeaked and smelled clean.

After she had put on her new clothes, I brushed her hair and gave her a red ribbon which she tied around her forehead. She looked pretty and much younger, but her manner indicated that she'd liked the old Leah better.

I heard Sophia's faint laughter. "You did it, Sister

Olive. You cleaned them up, and they look wonderful.''

I started to laugh with her, but then she lapsed into a coughing spell. When she could swallow, I held up her head and gave her medicine made of ginseng and jack-in-the-pulpit. Then I called Leah to her bedside, and in Leah's few words of English and my few words of Shoshoni, I explained that from now on she was to stay in Sophia's part of the house to help me nurse her.

Leah's solemn nod meant she understood. She immediately became a devoted assistant, but even with both of us caring for her, Sophia's condition did not improve.

One morning I stood at her bedside and studied her frail form. I had promised her that she would see Percy again. If that promise were to be fulfilled, Percy had to come home soon.

I bathed, put on my green silk dress, then carefully arranged my hair into dainty curls. I even sacrificed a small pinch of our precious flour to smooth on my face. I desperately needed a favor, and I'd heard that the man who could grant that favor was known to respond to a pretty face.

I realized it would be the last time I hitched the horses to the carriage. The following day Father Terry was to try to exchange them for food; if he could not, they had to be let out on the range to forage with the cattle and oxen.

I drove to Brigham Young's huge house, which was called the Beehive because of its many gabled windows, allegedly one for each of his twenty-nine wives. The sentry in front of the office let me pass, and I entered to find Brother Brigham seated at his big desk. Although not extremely tall, his frame was huge. When he spoke, his personality radiated through the room.

Rising to his feet with swift, restless energy, his steady blue eyes searched my face. I swallowed, feeling almost as if I were in the presence of God.

When Brother Brigham smiled, his face glowed with an ethereal light. "Sit down, little lady, and tell me who you are."

"I'm Olive Terry, first wife of Dr. Percival Dodson Terry, daughter-in-law of Isaac Dodson Terry and great-daughter-in-law of Percival Dodson Terry, one of the seventy."

"And what brings you here in your prettiest clothes?"

"Dr. Terry's second wife is seriously ill. I've come to ask you . . . I've come to ask . . . ."

For a moment I could not continue; then I blurted, "Oh, Brother Brigham, she's dying, and she wants to see her husband again."

A sob escaped me. "It's the only hope of her heart, but she won't live to see him if he doesn't come home soon. You are the leader of the gathering, the only person in the world who can tell Percy to come home now, before it's too late. Please, please, I beg you."

I threw myself on my knees before him. "Send for her husband. Let her see him before she dies."

Brother Brigham lifted me by the arms and stood me on trembling legs.

"Even if I send for Dr. Terry today, it will be months before he can get here. Do you think she will live that long?"

The anguish in my heart sounded in my voice. "Brother Brigham, if I can tell Sophia that Percy is on his way, I know she will manage to live until he gets home."

"God gives no man a burden greater than his strength, but it shall be as you request. I will send someone today to relieve Brother Terry, but it will be a long wait. Travel isn't easy, and this time of year . . . ."

His voice trailed off, and he stared out the window. I wondered if he were thinking of his own agonizing trips back and forth across the plains and mountains. At last he turned back to me, and again his smile illuminated his face.

"Meanwhile, little lady, do you have enough to eat?"

I hung my head. "My Indian woman goes into the woods and digs sego lily roots, and that's almost all she and I have eaten for days. What little else there is must be saved for Sophia and the children."

He scribbled on a piece of paper. "Take this to the tithing house," he said. "It will provide you with enough to help preserve life. Go as often as you need."

Impulsively, I snatched his hand and kissed it.

"Save your gratitude for God. He is the One who provides." Then he pulled me toward him and kissed me on the forehead.

I flushed, then mumbling my thanks and clutching his precious note, I left and hurried to the tithing house.

The clerk at the tithing house read the note and listened to my pleas. "Dr. Terry's second wife is very ill. Please give me something for a nourishing gruel for her."

I returned to my carriage carrying packages of cereal, flour, lard, potatoes and dried peaches. Tears streamed down my cheeks. The Lord had provided.

Driving home I calculated how long it would be before Percy could reach us. *One month by stage for his substitute to go to the western end of the railroad, several days more to New York, one month to cross the ocean by clipper ship, and an equal amount of time for Percy to travel home.*

I added an extra month to allow for delays. *Five months, Sophia had to remain alive for at least five months.*

Reaching home, I piled the food on the table and called to Leah. She looked at our bounty, her expression unruffled, but she touched each package firmly, as if making certain it really existed.

"You'll have something better than bitter sego lily roots to eat tonight," I promised her.

With a grunt of approval, Leah gathered the laundry and went outdoors to the washtub, and Shokup and Val tagged after her.

I'd started to take off my good dress when I heard a loud knocking. Quickly redoing my buttons, I opened the door.

Staring down at me, his eyes mean slits in his leathery face, was the avenging angel or Danite, Porter Rockwell. He was long-haired and wearing buckskin, just as when I'd seen him the day we arrived in Salt Lake City. Behind him stood another man, blacksuited, who gazed at me unblinking until I collected myself enough to be able to speak.

"My . . . my husband isn't here," I said. "He's in France on mission."

We did not come to see your husband," Porter Rockwell intoned. "We came to see you."

"Then won't you come in," I said, trying to disguise the raw fear I'd felt at the sight of them.

They entered, and with a commanding manner they began examining everything. They paid particular attention to the food on the table, and the second man said, "She's more than well fed, and she's wearing silk."

In spite of my fear I bristled. "What is your business with me?" I asked.

Without answering they sat down, and Porter Rockwell beckoned to me to sit also. When I perched on the edge of a chair, they drew their chairs close to me.

"I am Brother Sneed and this is Brother Rockwell. We are Danites, and we have come to talk to you about sin. Do you believe that some sins are so grievous, forgiveness can come only through the shedding of blood?"

I gasped. Then Brother Rockwell said, "There are sinners among us, unredeemed souls who do not belong to the gathering. They bring famine and illness upon us, but the word of God tells us how to deal with them."

Brother Sneed opened his Bible and read: "When we are gathered together with the power of our Lord Jesus Christ, we deliver such a one unto Satan for the destruction of the flesh."

He turned to another section. "In the book of Hebrew it says, 'And almost all things are by the law purged with blood; and without shedding of blood there is no remission.' "

He peered at me. "Y'see, when the soul is burdened with sin, relief comes only by the blood of the body smoking on the ground."

Suddenly Brother Rockwell pounded the table with his fist. "Sister Olive Terry, you are not baptised. You are not an endowed member of the gathering. Do you now know that your sins and lack of faith disgust heaven and help bring the current famine and punishments down on the Saints?"

I was almost too dumbfounded to be afraid. He was accusing me of causing the famine that now ravaged through the settlement. In amazement I realized that my own guilt feelings had accused me of exactly the same thing. Listening to his angry words, I suddenly knew that the accusations were ridiculous and unfounded whether he made them or whether I made them myself. As he listed my sins, my burden of guilt dropped away.

But they were saying that when my blood soaked into the ground, the Lord would send the Saints more food!

"And look at all the food you have," Brother Sneed said, indicating the table. "Sinners are not the ones going hungry."

I rose to my feet. "Brother Brigham instructed the tithing house to give us this food to keep us from starving. You have no right . . . ."

Something moved behind me. "She was baptized and endowed. She's a good Saint and a good person. Leave her alone."

For the first time since she had delivered her dead son, Sophia was out of bed. Holding the wall for support and panting for breath, she had come to my aid.

"Ye been baptized?" Brother Rockwell questioned.

"Yes, less than a month ago," I answered, putting a trembling arm around Sophia.

We clung to each other as they stared at us. "Get baptized for the dead, did you? Your folks that are gone?"

"No," I gasped, "but the ward bishop gave me a recommend."

"He did! He did!" Sophia echoed.

They rose and moved toward the door. "Then that will do for now," Brother Sneed said, "but remember, we know where you are."

Terrified, I still called after them, "It is for God to judge me, not you." Then I slammed the door.

Her blazing eyes and flushed cheeks told me how feverish Sophia was, but even after I'd helped her back to bed, she would not be quiet.

"They're terrible men, and they had no right to say such bad things to you."

"Don't talk and wear yourself out," I said, arranging the covers around her.

"They're terrible men just terrible," she repeated, "and I think . . . ."

"Sister Sophia, Percy is coming home."

Sophia stopped talking, her head dropped to the pillow and she stared at me.

I sat on the bed and took her hand in mine. "I went to see Brother Brigham this morning. I told him how much we want Percy here, and Brother Brigham agreed to send for him. His substitute will leave Salt Lake City today. In no time at all, Percy will be here."

The hope and joy that illuminated her face were a balm to my heart, and I held her hand until she fell asleep. Then, suddenly overcome by weeks of unabated hunger, I rushed to prepare some of the food that now stood between us and starvation.

I went to bed that night, not to sleep, not to toss and turn, but to lie in the quiet and think. When I obtained Brother Brigham's promise to call Percy home for Sophia's sake, I found a peace that baptism had not given me and the Danites could not take away. I was not sorry I'd been baptized. I was now one of the gathering of people whose fate I shared, but I realized that the peace I sought I could find only within myself.

For the first time that day I allowed myself to think of Percy in a personal way. A yearning tore through my body, and my loins ached when I remembered the times we lay together. I still loved him terribly. No day ever passed when I wasn't aware of that love, yet I'd found exquisite comfort in having him called home to answer the need of another woman. I could not understand, but I had to be thankful. I drifted into a slumber more tranquil than any I'd known for many months.

Chapter 20

Even with careful rationing, our new food supply soon dwindled away. I made weekly trips to the tithing house, Brother Brigham's slip of paper clutched tightly in my hand, but my allotments of food grew smaller and smaller—a half-pound of flour or cornmeal, a cup of lard, a handful of dried peaches.

By December our food crisis was compounded as the prolonged lack of rain developed into the worst drought in the history of the valley. Streams in the canyons fell lower each day, and irrigation ditches were no longer flowing.

Leah scoured the canyons for sego lily roots, but they were so bitter that in spite of my agonizing hunger I had trouble swallowing them. If Sophia succeeded in swallowing a bite, she wasn't able to keep it down.

"I must find more food for her, or she will not live to see Percy," I anguished.

I had tears in my eyes when I gave Val and Shokup their last cups of milk, but after an agony of soul-searching, I'd decided that the cow's thin carcass had to be used to provide meat and broth to keep Sophia breathing.

Father Terry butchered the cow for me, and I gave him some of the meat for his own hungry family. With Leah's help I soon had the rest of it cut and immersed in brine. I thought wryly that in all of Deseret the only thing in abundance was salt.

The odor of the cooking broth tantalized us all, but

summoning my will power, I saved every drop for Sophia. Every day I rationed the meat—two bites a piece for Leah and me, three bites each for the children.

Many people in the valley had been forced to let their Indians go; hopefully they found their way back to their own tribes, but this was uncertain. If I sent Leah and Shokup away, we would have more food, but they might starve. I decided that if there was food for my mouth, Leah would eat; for as long as I could feed my little Val, Shokup would have the same ration.

Val didn't look like a normal little boy. His arms were thin as wooden spoon handles, and his once chubby legs were no bigger than the iron poker by the fireplace. Shokup looked like a withered, miniature man. His brown cheeks sagged, and his black eyes grew bigger and bigger. He no longer begged his mother in Shoshoni for something to eat. He sat, listless and pathetic, making no effort to play.

Under her ever-present blanket, Leah's body was hidden, but her face looked pinched and her cheeks hollow. My own dresses hung like sacks, and day by day, I felt my strength ebbing.

January was an agony relieved only by the coming of the snows that replenished our water supply. Sophia was kept alive more by my frequent reminders that Percy would soon be home than by the broth I coaxed down her throat. Her cough was so bad and came so frequently, it not only tore *her* apart, it yanked at my own insides.

Late one night during the first week of February, Sophia's cough seemed worse than ever. "Oh, I want to see Percy again," she gasped between spasms.

"You will. I promise that you will," I said hoarsely.

In the darkness I lifted her to ease the strain, and there came a flood of warm wetness. In terror I ran to fetch the stub of candle I'd saved. With shaking hands I lit it, and holding it high over the bed, I saw the blood soaking into her pillow and gown. Sophia's eyes drifted shut; she made no sound or movement.

Leah stood at my side, chanting in Shoshoni. "You must go for Father Terry," I told her. "Run as fast as you can."

Leah left, and I peered at Sophia's white face. Her eyelashes moved.

"Thank God," I muttered.

I brought clean clothing and fresh blankets, and after I'd done what I could, I blew out the candle to save it.

Suddenly there was a bright light, I stared, and then I saw warm, steaming loaves of bread, pans of cooked meat, baskets of fresh apples and peaches, bowls of sugar, pitchers of white milk. I cried out in joy and rushed to gather the bounty in my arms, but only the cold, hard table came in my grasp.

The light was gone, and for frantic moments I searched for the food. There was no food. Then, from far away at the edge of the world, I could hear a woman weeping. "Please, God, let Percy come home before Sophia dies. Let me find food for my little Val, and for Leah and Shokup. Oh, God, I am so hungry."

Strange, my own cheeks were wet when Father Terry came bursting through the door. I relit the candle, and Father Terry laid his hand on Sophia's chest. "She's still living, and I've brought some opium."

Struggling to clear my mind, I filled a cup with water and Father Terry stirred the brown, sticky opium into it. I lifted Sophia's head and between us, we coaxed the liquid down her throat.

The next day Leah stood watch by Sophia's bed, and I tried to sleep so that I could stay with her through the night. Soon the days and nights merged into one long vigil, Leah and I taking turns with short snatches of rest for each of us.

With the end of February came the end of hope. Sophia would die and soon afterward we would all be dead.

At dawn's light I smoothed Sophia's blanket. "It's Tuesday," I said mechanically. "You must rest and get better, because Percy will soon be home."

She did not respond, but I'd said the same thing so many times that the words came automatically. "Percy is coming home, Sister Sophia. Percy is coming home."

Abruptly my strength gave way. I sank to my knees: I laid my head on Sophia's bed, and with a final gesture, I took her hand in mine. The world and reality were slipping away. I was sinking into an inescapable blackness.

"Olive, Olive, wake up dear, wake up."

Percy's voice was calling me. I opened my eyes, and Percy's face was close to my own, but I remembered the wonderful food and could not be fooled again.

"I know it's not really you, Percy," I murmured.

I closed my eyes and began to sink back into the blackness, but something was shaking me, and I could hear Sophia's voice.

"Oh, Percy, Sister Olive told me that I would see you again."

My eyes flickered open, and slowly recognition came. Percy was on his knees beside me, one arm around my shoulders, the other arm cradled around Sophia. With a sob I turned toward him and buried my head on his shoulder. The three of us cried together.

"They told me that you were ill, Sophia, but I didn't dream . . . ." He turned to me. "And Olive, you're so thin and pale. When is the last time you ate?"

"I . . . I don't remember."

Percy kissed me, then he leaned and kissed Sophia's blue-veined forehead. "When Wish Peterson came to relieve me at the mission, he told me about the food shortage in the settlement. I've brought some things."

At the doorway with his portmanteau was a huge trunk he told us the stage driver had delivered for him. He dragged the trunk into the room and sprang the lid. It was stuffed tight with packages and tins of food.

"Tomorrow I will take a good share to the tithing house, but now my own two wives must eat."

Val, newly awakened and apprehensive, stared at Percy who picked him up and held him close. "My little son," he groaned, "you don't weigh as much now as when I went away."

With Leah's help Percy prepared some food. Val and Shokup stood wide-eyed, staring at the open trunk, but neither they nor Leah and I could eat very much. Percy put a bowl of cereal into my hands, but it took me a long, long time to get it down.

From her bed near the doorway Sophia's eyes remained riveted on Percy, who was bounding with joy at being home. "God has visited you with many painful tribulations, Olive, but now He has sent me home to take care of you."

For months it had been a never-ending struggle to keep Sophia alive—to keep all of us alive—and there had been no one with whom I could share the agony. Now Percy was here; my burdens were lifted, and I had someone to lean on. I cried heavy tears I thought would never stop.

But if Percy's homecoming brought tears to me, it brought a joy and animation to Sophia that I had not believed possible. With Percy spooning food to her, she ate willingly for the first time in months. In two days she was sitting up in bed, and she clapped her hands when Percy held up one of the beautiful crocheted shawls he'd bought for us in Paris.

Percy and I often sat at Sophia's bedside and he talked of his journey to faraway France.

"Do you remember that when James Buchanan was Secretary of State, he conscripted five hundred of our young men into the army?" Percy began one evening. "Well, leave it to Brother Brigham to bring good out of evil. Buchanan took our men, but Brother Brigham took the money the government paid and outfitted his hungry, ragged followers with wagons, oxen, and food for the first wagon train of Mormons headed west."

As he talked, Percy held Val in the curve of his arm. "That money was the beginning of the emigration fund, but there's little left of the fund now. When I was in France, we won many converts and every day the missionaries in England and all the other countries are bringing new people to the gathering. But wagons, oxen, and mules have become too expensive."

Percy's voice swelled. "In Iowa City, handcarts are being built, and in their devotion, new members of the Church of Jesus Christ of the Latter Day Saints will *walk* across the plains, the deserts, and the mountains to come to Deseret."

I shuddered in horror of what these new Saints must endure, but Sophia's face remained a glow of happiness. If she noticed Percy's affectionate behavior to Val and thought of her own dead son, she gave no sign. She seemed happy just to be near Percy.

My own strength returned, and I was overcome with joy as I watched Sophia's miraculous recovery—but that joy was short-lived. On the fourth day after Percy returned, Sophia's new vitality ebbed away as quickly as it had come. All day she lay motionless, her breathing sometimes harsh, sometimes imperceptible. Percy sat at her bedside, holding her hand.

Toward evening I fixed her opium and prepared soup for her to drink afterward to take away the horrid taste.

As I came near the bed, she opened her eyes and smiled at Percy and me. Her eyes closed, her head rolled on the pillow, and a thin stream of blood trailed from the side of her mouth. Percy gathered her in his arms, and I brought cloths to mop the hemorrhage that now ran in rivulets across the pillow.

She died easily without a sound, without a cough, without a word, just the blood trickling across her small chin to run over Percy's coatsleeves and drip steadily on the bed.

I went numb, and my vision narrowed until all I could see was Sophia's lifeless form; all I could hear was Leah's mournful chant.

Time passed immeasurably, but eventually I became aware that two of Father Terry's wives were washing Sophia's body for burial.

Percy's mother brought out Sophia's blue silk dress, the sheen still like new because she'd worn it so little.

"No," I murmured, "don't put that on her."

I went to the cupboard and got out her red skirt. "She must wear this."

Mother Terry took the skirt from my hands and held it up. "Olive, this really isn't suitable. Her silk dress is . . . ."

I clenched my fists and screamed. "She must wear that skirt."

I saw the two women exchange glances, but when Sophia was placed in her rough-hewn coffin, she was wearing the skirt that had meant so much to her. Tears streamed down my cheeks. She had seen Percy again. In his company she had smiled and laughed and known life. And once again—and forever—she wore her red skirt. I had kept my promises.

At the door the next morning we found a beautiful wreath fashioned of everygreen and holly berries.

"A neighbor must have brought it," Percy said, but I was certain that it was Aaron who had brought a gift to the beautiful, lively girl who had laughed and flirted with him.

Our little funeral procession headed for the cemetery in the northeast corner of the city where many fresh graves testified to the famine and the suffering of the Saints. Sophia's grave, shallow in the frozen ground, had been dug next to the tiny grave of her baby.

A small group—Linnie and Stephen Bradford, Brother Brigham and several of his wives, Father Terry and his wives and a few friends and neighbors—listened to the ward bishop read from the Bible and the Book of Mormon. Then several men lowered Sophia into the ground, and as I watched, a strangely bitter wind chilled through me.

Returning home we were surrounded by people who—in spite of their own daily suffering—did everything they could to bring us comfort. But the next day Leah and Shokup returned to their own house, and gradually the neighbors stopped calling. Percy, Val and I were alone.

I spent the morning writing a letter to my parents:
Yesterday we buried Sophia, Percy's second wife. He married her on the journey to Deseret. She was one of the sweetest most loving people I ever knew.

I sealed my letter and turned my attention to Percy who sat quietly, his shoulders slumped, his eyes reddened. My own heart ached too, and when I tried to make conversation, words just wouldn't come.

Suddenly Percy jerked to his feet; his chair tipped

over, but ignoring it, he came and hugged me to him.
He buried his face on my shoulder, and I heard a stifled
sob. "Olive, Olive, I mourn for Sophia. She was a dear
child. I cared for her, and it hurts when I think of her
dead baby, my second son, but Olive, my awful, empty
feeling is for you. I've never stopped loving you and
wanting you . . . ."

He turned his face toward mine, and our eyes met.

"Percy, I love you too. I don't know how to stop
loving you, but—"

"The church will never again ask me to take another
wife. There will never again be anyone but you."

Together we sank onto the bed. Percy leaned against
me, his arms about my waist, his face buried in my
skirts. My tears fell with his, and I clung to him. Then
he raised his face to mine, and we shared a tender,
tear-washed kiss.

All the yearning in my body welled up, and I wanted
to be his again. He carressed me, and his touch was an
ecstatic, glowing warmth. I was ready to submit. I
wanted to love him with all the passion in me, but then I
shivered. I felt cold, as if chilled by the strangely bitter
wind that had blown across Sophia's grave. I pulled
away, and with a start I realized I could not let him love
me.

Chapter 21

In early spring, mule-drawn supply trains from California broke their way through the snows of the High Sierras, manned by brave, young Mormons who had survived every threat in order to bring us food, seed, and hope. The food had to be tightly rationed, but the seed held the promise of better things to come, and soon the valley stirred with new life. Farmers took to their fields; women spread their washing on the zigzag pole fences, and the herdsmen whistled as they drove the milk cows out to range every day. People visited each other again, and for the first time in months I saw neighbors who lived but a lot or two away from us.

As soon as the ground warmed, Leah was out in the garden, planting, watering, and weeding. In May we harvested our first green edibles, and as the weeks passed the bins and shelves in our storeroom gradually filled up with food. The cattle and horses on the range had perished, but when new animals were brought in, Percy bought a beautiful span of bay horses, four oxen, several pigs, and a milk cow.

But the end of the famine marked the beginning of still another threat to the Saints. One Thursday evening in July, Percy returned from his administrative job at the Beehive carrying a sheaf of newspaper clippings.

"Brother Brigham asked me to read these and report to him," he said gravely. "They've just come from the East, and it looks like real trouble for Deseret."

"What do they say?" I asked.

"They're attacking us for something that is none of their business. Listen to this, 'Slavery and polygamy are the two abominable evils that beset our country. Both must be destroyed without delay.' "

Percy's blue eyes flashed with anger. "They can't leave us alone. You'd think all the commotion about slavery in the South would be enough for them to rant about, but they've got to attack our church, too."

"Slavery *is* wrong," I said; I didn't add that polygamy was wrong too.

Impatiently, he perused more of the clippings. "They even go so far as to say Deseret is disloyal to the federal government. Rumors are getting stronger that the President will dispatch troops to subdue us. It doesn't make sense. We're no threat to them, but they hate us because we're God's chosen people."

"Percy, don't you think that if the church reversed its stand on polygamy, the government would leave—"

"We were harassed and despised long before Joseph Smith's revelation on celestial marriage. And plural marriage is the will of God, and the will of God does not bow to a whim of the government in Washington. You're a baptized Saint now and should understand that."

When I didn't answer, Percy added, "But, Olive, I am afraid there are other things about our religion you still don't understand."

His tone held reproach, and I knew what he was thinking. It had been five months since he had returned from France, five months since we had laid Sophia into her grave, but I still could not share his bed.

"If you really understood our religion, you would no longer resent Sophia," Percy continued, his voice filled with pain, "or do you even envy her the blessed sleep that is now hers?"

I shuddered. "I've told you I don't resent Sophia, but if she had lived, you and I would never have been husband and wife again. It seems wrong to take advantage of the fact that she's dead . . . ."

I could not explain, and Percy could not understand, but every one of our conversations ended the same way. No matter what we talked about, eventually our attention turned to the fact that I could not let him love me. I wanted him; I yearned for him, but something within me refused to let go.

Over and over Percy told me that he would wait for me. "Forever, if need be," he once said.

I knew he could marry again and put another woman into the bed I spurned, but with tears in his eyes he promised that he'd never choose another wife.

Now forgetting the newspaper clippings, we stared at each other in silent longing until I turned away and put his dinner on the table.

The following weeks we heard that Brigham Young was calling up the Nauvoo Legion, which had been renamed the Mormon Battalion. Every able-bodied man between eighteen and forty-five would drill and train, and every man would be well armed.

"Today Brother Brigham ordered me to send to California for percussion lock rifles," Percy told me one evening.

My chest felt tight. "If we fight, will you have to go?"

"I'll go if Brother Brigham thinks I should, but I'd go as a doctor, not a soldier."

That night I tossed and turned and thought of Percy all alone in what had once been Sophia's house. If there was a war with the federal government, we'd be sepa-

rated again, and it was so very long since we'd really
been together.

Early the next afternoon I was looking out my window when I saw Percy riding home in the carriage.

"You're home early," I called to him from the
doorway.

"I have to go back," he answered. "I just came
home now because of him."

He pointed up the street. I strained my neck and was
shocked to see an Indian brave in full feathered headdress riding down the street on a large white horse
followed by a pony.

"A band of Shoshoni have ridden into town.
They've brought many horses, and they're exchanging
them for their women and children who were kid-
napped and sold to us."

Suddenly Leah cried out and came running past me,
her arms held over her head. The brave galloped to her
and dismounted at her side. They placed their hands on
each other's shoulders and stared at each other.

A lump formed in my throat. "He's her husband," I
whispered.

"That's right," Percy answered, "and he's one of
their chiefs. He'll take Leah and Shokup with him
now."

I went inside, leaving Leah to greet her brave pri-
vately, but a few minutes later she hurried to her own
house. I followed to help her get her few possessions
together.

I folded Shokup's clothing while Leah gathered her
own things. She gave little display of emotion, but I
could feel her excitement. She was talking in Shoshoni,
but suddenly she stopped, put her hands on her hips and
giggled, actually giggled. With one finger she poked
me in the ribs.

"He say, 'Long time no woman.' "

I threw my arms around her. "I'm happy for you, Leah. I really am."

My hug startled, but did not displease her. She giggled again, and then said, "I find Shokup."

Shokup was playing with some older Indian boys, and with a new spring in her step, Leah hurried off in search of him.

Returning to the front of the house, I could see how tall and muscular Leah's husband was. He stood proud and still, not looking around.

"Hello," I said, waving and smiling. "Leah's gone to get Shokup."

I didn't expect him to understand me, but the joy I felt for Leah encompassed him too. I meant to be friendly, but friendly he was not. With a slow, almost imperceptible movement he inclined his head toward me. He looked at me and through me. He in no way acknowledged that a white woman stood in his line of vision.

Leah and Shokup appeared, and though I had learned only a few words of Shoshoni, I understood Leah's joy as she presented her son to his father.

Beneath his flowing headdress, the tall brave's expression hardly changed, yet his look of pride was unmistakable. He lifted Shokup and placed him on the pony, holding him as if he were as fragile as a pane of window glass.

Hurrying inside the house, I put bread, meat, and cornmeal into a poke. I snatched a half-bolt of cotton material and some ribbon from my trunk, then I took my humble offerings to Leah.

As Shokup and Val said good-bye, we said our own farewells. She held out her right hand to me as I had once held out my hand to her. I grasped her hand tightly. "You are my friend, Leah."

"No," she said sternly. "Leah no your friend."

She patted her chest. "Letakoni. Letakoni your friend."

She'd answered to Leah so faithfully that I'd forgotten it was not her true, Indian name, but it was Letakoni, not Leah, who rode off in triumph astride her husband's mount, her arms wrapped snugly around his waist. A happy, smiling Shokup who never looked back followed them on the pony.

I was truly happy for her, but I'd grown so dependent on her consistent, loyal help that I dreaded life without her. Percy had returned to the Beehive, and with my feet dragging, I went to survey the garden. Leah had dropped her hoe in the middle of a row of squash. I picked it up, and with my back to the burning sun I finished that row and the other rows yet to be done.

During our evening meal Val kept asking about Shokup. "Can he come play with me like Uriah and Nathan do?"

"No, Percival," his father told him. "Shokup was a decent-acting boy while he was here, but once he's back with his own people, he'll go savage. Believe me, you'd never want anything to do with him again."

"Just remember the good times you and Shokup had together," I said.

Percy leaned back in his chair and clasped his hands behind his head. "You know," he began slowly, "it's surprising that he came back for Leah after all this time. You wouldn't think heathen savages would know much about family loyalty."

I remembered Leah's happy giggle. "Percy, I'm positive he's deeply attached to Leah. Marriage must mean something very important to the Shoshoni, and I'm sure that no matter what happens, they remain loyal to each other."

Later, after Val and Percy were in bed, I filled the

big, wooden tub with water and floated garden flowers on top so I could enjoy their fragrance while I soaked. I ached from unaccustomed work in the garden, and the long bath soothed my body. Relaxing, I slipped into a dreamy, half-asleep mood. Softly, in the quiet of my mind, I could hear my own voice echoing: ". . . no matter what happens, they remain loyal to each other . . . no matter what happens they remain loyal . . . ."

I opened my eyes, realizing I wanted to be loyal to Percy. No matter what had happened, we were married. I loved him, and he needed me.

I climbed out of the tub and patted myself dry. Running to Percy's bed, my feet hardly seemed to touch the floor.

He was asleep, but he awakened to the awareness that my body was caressing his. With a moan of pleasure he took me in his arms and began kissing me. His lips searched my neck, my shoulders, my breasts. The longing that had for so long been unfulfilled enveloped us both. At last we collapsed in each other's arms, struggling for breath, but joyful. As I fell asleep snug in Percy's embrace, I thought of Leah. She, too, was happy tonight.

Chapter 22

I awakened to a renewal of Percy's embrace. "I love you, Olive," he murmured between kisses, "and I thank God that you've come to a right way of thinking about our marriage."

Joyfully, I responded to his love, but within my heart beat a determinination never to look back. In any reminiscences, I would be sure to catch a glimpse of Sophia or hear the swish of her red skirt. I could lose myself in the totalness of my love for Percy only if I pretended that the past had never been and that all time began with today and tomorrow.

For the first time since he'd returned to his job at the Beehive, Percy was late leaving home. "I hate to go and leave you," he said, giving me a final embrace. "You're my wife who came back to me—the only wife I will ever want."

"Don't worry," I said, smiling at him, "I'll be waiting and loving you when you get home."

In the weeks that followed, Percy and I renewed the vibrant relationship that had been ours in the early days of our marriage. We talked endlessly, and we made love with a new rapture. Percy's laugh rang out frequently, and I laughed with him. Occasionally dark memories came, but I turned from them abruptly and told myself that this was the way our life had always been.

Percy's love for me approached devotion. He fussed

over me, doing things few husbands did for their wives; he brought me little gifts purchased at the tithing house, and he used his few precious hours of leisure to tend to my work in the garden.

"Percy, leave the garden chores for me," I called to him one evening. "You don't even have time to work our acreage, so what will the neighbors think when they see you doing my work?"

Percy laughed and continued working. "No one will see me, and I want to make you happy."

I was deeply touched, and my heart overflowed with love for him.

Statements and rumors from Washington convinced us that the federal government would send troops to Deseret, and somehow this threat to our very existence drew Percy and me even closer together. Our time with each other and with Val was doubly precious, because no one knew how long these days of peace and plenty would last.

On the twenty-eighth day of November, Percy and I went to the cemetery, and as Percy intoned a prayer, I arranged autumn flowers on Sophia's grave. It would have been her twentieth birthday. I knew that in her kind and loving heart, she would rejoice for the happiness that Percy and I were learning to share.

Riding home from the cemetery, Percy said, "We will never forget dear little Sophia, but you and I have a beautiful future ahead of us. No matter what happens when the federal troops come, I know Deseret will survive and go on forever. You and I will go on forever too, in this world and then the next."

He put his arm around me, and I snuggled closer to him on the driver's seat. "We must go to the temple to be sealed to each other for time and eternity. That will be enough kingdom for me in the hereafter."

"For time and eternity, Percy," I echoed, "we'll always be together."

In December, we stood before the high priest and repeated our marriage vows and were sealed according to the rites and laws of the Mormon church. Together we knelt in solemn ecstasy as the priest raised his hand over our heads.

"Brother Terry, Sister Terry, you are bound for all time and for all eternity. Amen."

A great joy swelled within me, and I told myself that this was truly a new beginning for our marriage. My love for Percy was deeper than ever, and I was certain that none of the pain or grief from the past would ever mar our future.

On the way home from the temple, I told Percy the news I'd been saving for just this moment.

"Percy, I have something very important to tell you," I said, squeezing his arm. "Next summer we're going to have another child."

"That's wonderful," Percy answered, "and Brother Brigham will be glad to hear it. He's urging a larger population these days."

I was certain that nothing could hurt our love, but several months later I received an answer to the letter I'd written home the day after Sophia's funeral. Pa had dictated the letter, but even through the mediumship of Dorothy's handwriting, I could hear him storm.

"Olive, you should have written to us as soon as Percival Terry married another woman. He broke every promise he made to us, he's a liar, and he does no way deserve to have you. We grieve with you for that poor, young girl you told us about, but her being so sweet makes no excuse for him.

"You didn't write it that way, but we know you don't want to stay with a man who has no respect for you or marriage. In the spring I plan to sell off some stock as we've been doing well lately. I will use the money to come and fetch you and my grandson, and while I'm gone, your brother Ted will work the farm alone. I'll ride the train west as far as I can, and then take the stagecoach to Salt Lake City. Look for my coming by early summer.''

Pa was coming to Deseret to bring me and Val home to Iowa. Tears scalded my cheeks as I thought about the love and sacrifice it would require of the whole family for him to make the trip.

In spite of all my resolves never to look back, I remembered the agonies I'd endured while Percy was married to Sophia. There had been countless times when I had wished I could return to my family, but now everything was different. I was Percy's one and only wife; I loved him and wanted to stay with him forever.

I caught my breath. As much as I yearned to see my father, I could not return with him, and it would be wrong for him to come.

Percy had brought me the letter from the tithing house, then gone outside to unhitch the team. When he returned, my look and manner startled him.

''Olive, dear, is there bad news from your family?'' he asked, putting his arm around me.

I shook my head. ''Percy, no one is ill or dead, but . . . but my father is coming to Deseret to take me and Val back to Iowa.''

''What?'' he exclaimed.

''Pa says . . . he says . . . .''

When I could not continue, Percy snatched the letter and read it himself.

''This is absolutely too much to endure,'' he said angrily after he'd finished. ''Our own government calls us traitors, and now people I thought were our friends call us liars, simply because we practice our religion.''

"Percy, believe me, my father is not a man to interfere with anyone's religion. But he's concerned about my welfare, and—''

"You don't understand, Olive,'' Percy stormed. "I read that last autumn Stephen A. Douglas made a speech in Springfield, Illinois, attacking us, saying we're disloyal and not to be trusted. When a person of his stature speaks against us, people like your father accept his words as fact.''

"Percy, you're the one who doesn't understand,'' I said, my voice rising. "My father isn't upset because he listened to a speech. He's upset because I told him about Sophia. You married her after you promised him you would never practice plural marriage. You . . . you misled him.''

Percy's voice thundered. "How can you say that? I promised your father never to choose another wife. I never did, and I never will. The church leaders chose Sophia for me. Why didn't you explain *that* to your father?''

"I did,'' I shouted back. "But Pa's concerned with the truth of the situation, not the words, and you did lie to him.''

Percy stopped short. "You . . . you believe that I'm a liar?''

The hurt in Percy's voice wrung my heart, but I hurt too, the way I always did when Percy tried to justify his marriage to Sophia.

"Percy, can't you see that from my father's point of view, you did lie to him?'' I tried to sound calm; I wanted to soothe both of us, but Percy's answer was angry and arrogant.

"If he really dares come to Deseret to take my wife and child—''

"He must not come," I interrupted. "The trip would be a tremendous hardship for him and the rest of the family, and it would be pointless. I'll never go back to Iowa. I belong here in Deseret with you. I . . . I love you." My voice faded. We both were still angry, but the battle was over.

I picked up Val who cowered near the doorway, frightened by our angry voices, and Percy took another look at Pa's letter.

"It's already the middle of March, and he says he'll be here by early summer. Even if you send a letter tomorrow, there's no certainty it would reach him before he left."

Percy paced the room. "We can send a telegram with the stagecoach driver. The driver will carry it east to the nearest telegraph office—Denver, I think—and telegraph for us from there."

"Good," I said eagerly, "and I'll send my family a long letter and explain everything—"

"What explanation will you give?" Percy said solemnly.

I did not answer. The past had loomed between us again, as insurmountable as ever.

For the remainder of the evening we barely spoke to each other, and Percy went to bed early. When I slipped in beside him, I thought he was asleep, but he was keenly alert and wanting me.

Our need for each other had not been curtailed even though my body was beginning to thicken with child. Percy was always careful with me, gentle and tender, but this time he was different. He discharged the rest of his anger in my body. I responded with an angry passion of my own. The next morning the impression of his teeth was still clearly visible on my shoulder, and it was many days before my other bruises lightened away.

That afternoon I went with Percy to the stagecoach station, and we made arrangements to have a telegram sent. Then I wrote Pa a letter telling him that Percy would never again take another wife and that I would never leave him.

"Pa, don't come for me," I wrote. "I'm totally happy here with Percy."

Chapter 23

On a rainy Monday evening in April, Percy returned from the Beehive looking so despondent that I knew something serious was wrong.

"Are the federal troops on the way?" I asked, gripping the edge of the table.

Percy slumped into his chair. "No, but we must move as soon as possible. Brother Brigham is sending us to a new settlement down south on Hobble Creek."

As long as Percy and I were together, I didn't care where we lived, but I preferred not to move before my baby was born. "Can we stay here until after the baby comes?" I asked.

He shook his head. "I don't think so. The settlement is small, but the few people there have sent complaints because there is no doctor in the vicinity."

"But, Percy, that's wonderful!" I exclaimed. "If they're wanting a doctor, you'll finally be able to establish the kind of practice you've always wanted. You can start an office, and . . . ."

He covered his face with his hands. "It won't be like that. There aren't many people and most of them are poor. There'll be no money for a real office and good equipment, and I'll even have to do my own farming to enable us to get along."

His yearnings for a formal medical practice had been softened by his relationship with Brother Brigham.

He'd been proud to work so close to the center of things, but this new assignment was a painful letdown.

Sharing his hurt, I said, "Percy, perhaps we'll like the Hobble Creek area even more than Salt Lake City." I put my arms around him. "If we're together, everything will be all right."

Finally Percy smiled, but as the days passed and we made preparations to move, it was clear that he was still downhearted. With obvious sadness, he arranged for the sale of our house and land, and my own days became a blend of trying to cheer him up and getting the packing done.

For myself, I had only two real regrets. I hated to move so far away from Linnie, and I hated to leave my glass window, which was one of the few in the settlement.

The day before we left, Linnie came to say good-bye. Tears rolled down her cheeks even as she told me she was determined not to cry.

"It's hard as sayin' good-bye t'my sister Lottie, back in Ioway. I haven't seen her since she walked behind my wagon, weepin' and wavin', and my heart still hurts when I think of her."

"Linnie, I promise that some day I'll come to visit you. And I'll write to you too, and you must answer my letters."

"I wasn't good at schoolin' and writin' is hard for me, but I'll answer. I'll answer."

My own cheeks were wet as I hugged her good-bye, and I stood at the doorway waving until she was out of sight.

Early the next morning I looked out my glass window for the last time. The dawn streamed through, flooding the house with a beautiful light, and outdoors I could see spring blossoms. Sighing with resignation, I turned away and called to Val who was watching two of

Percy's younger brothers hitch the oxen to our wagon.

"It's time to go now, Val," I called cheerfully. "You, Papa, and I will have a new house."

Percy, Val and I traveled in the carriage, and Percy's brothers followed with the wagon which was soon far behind us, the oxen plodding along as the boy drivers dozed on the high seat.

The settlement on Hobble Creek, located about ten miles south of Provo, consisted of about a hundred buildings squatting among the bunchgrass, sagebrush and greasewood bushes. Our first view was discouraging, and the hardpacked soil didn't show promise of allowing green things to grow. Percy pointed to a sign nailed to a tree. It read, *This Is Springville*.

We stopped at the tithing house which was flanked by a blacksmith shop and a store. Percy took Val inside with him, and I waited in the carriage.

When Percy returned, he said, "There's a place for us just beyond the town on Union Bench. It was abandoned by a Hickory Saint."

"A Hickory Saint?" I questioned.

Percy sounded scornful. "That's a person who never took our religion seriously and who left when the first testing came. Well, it's his loss and our gain if the place is half as good as the clerk in the tithing house claims."

I watched eagerly for the first glimpse of our new home, and Val, catching my excitement, jumped up and down between Percy and me.

"Are we there, Mama? Are we there?" he repeated.

The horses trotted up a road that was hardly more than a track through the bushes. Then, as we came around a curve in the road, I saw it—a small square house made of logs and mudbricks with a lean-to on one side, set against a grove of cedars. The lone window looked white in the slanting rays of the sun.

"The window is pig bladder," I groaned. I'd known

it would be, but seeing it was a fresh disappointment.

"We'll get glass when we can," Percy said. "It comes in on the supply wagons occasionally."

I nodded, but inwardly I doubted that glass would ever come to this faraway place.

A smokehouse stood in the yard, and nearby was a large, walled corral. A short distance away we could see a similar house, but homes in the area were few. Somehow the place felt even more desolate than it looked, and only Val was still excited as we pushed open the front door.

The inside was dirty and showed evidence of a hasty departure. I wandered around aimlessly for a few minutes, staring at what was now our home. I noticed an old broom with a broken handle propped in one corner. Almost automatically I picked it up and began sweeping away the heavy dust that covered everything.

"It's not taking you long to start settling in."

In the doorway stood a man and woman. "We be your neighbors," the woman said, pushing back her straggly hair and smoothing her apron with her big, red hands. "Brother and Sister Potter, and we're glad to welcome you."

Percy stepped forward. "We're Brother and Sister Terry, from the city. It's nice of you to come," he said. "Perhaps you can tell us where we can find a family that will take us in for a few nights—until our wagon gets here."

"Why, you'll lay-by with us," Sister Potter said. "I saw you drive up an hour ago, and I just stopped to neat the house before I come over. Supper'll be ready in no time, so you come right on."

Brother Potter spoke up: "All of our young 'uns are growed and gone, so there's room a'plenty and we'll be right glad to have you."

Percy drove the carriage near the house and put the horses in the corral before we went to the Potters'. I was weary, but Sister Potter's company was soothing and friendly.

Two days later our wagon arrived, and Sister Potter lent her strong back and arms to help me unpack and arrange our things. Brother Potter took a whole day from his fields to help Percy get his plow set up and his seed bag filled, and other neighbors came and helped their new doctor get an irrigation ditch dug.

Sister Potter helped me plant the garden. "It's sore-sad for you to be doin't the stoopin' when you be in the family way," she said.

I missed Leah, but with Sister Potter's help, the garden was finally planted in long, hopeful rows.

Percy's services as a doctor were sorely needed. Few days passed when there wasn't a bone to set, a wound to suture or a fever to tend, but grateful as they were, his patients could give him little in tangible payment. Even time was precious. The ground was so alien to crop-growing that all the men slaved long hours in the fields. He was assisted by appreciative families, but Percy still had to work part of our land himself.

"It was different in Salt Lake City," he said one evening. "There I worked directly for Brother Brigham, and what I did was important. Here I spend most of my time breaking my back in the fields, and the people hereabouts think of doctoring as little more than a skill that's handy to have around—like Brother Hodson's being able to mend wagon wheels."

"That's not true," I cried. "The people here truly appreciate what you do for them. They'd pay you if they could, but the crops have been poor for everyone. I'm certain, really certain, that next year things will be better."

"My cheerful, hopeful Olive, you're like a good medicine," he said, giving me a winsome smile. "You are the best wife a man could have, and I couldn't get along without you."

He put his arms around me, and when I felt his lips on mine, I forgot all the hard work and drudgery of life in Springville. I was Percy's wife, his only wife; we were together, and life was beautiful.

On the evening of August the seventh, a sweltering day, Percy took charge, giving orders to Sister Potter who midwifed my baby into the world. The heat and pain seemed endless, but at last it was over and I heard my baby's first cry.

"It's a girl," Percy told me.

He covered her with olive oil, a precious ointment obtained from the priesthood, then he wrapped her in a soft muslin cloth and laid her in my arms.

He kissed me. "We'll call her Olive for you, and Eugenia for the Empress of France."

He touched the baby's cheek. "She's beautiful, like her mother, and someday she'll be a fine Mormon wife to a good Mormon man."

At his words a new pain tore through me, a pain worse than anything I'd experienced giving birth. My arms tightened protectively around the innocent bundle in my arms, and I made a silent vow: *My daughter will never share a husband the way I had to share her father. She will be a first wife, and an only wife, no matter what I have to do to make it so.*

Chapter 24

Olive Eugenia was a lovely baby with downy blond hair and alert blue eyes. In the cool of the morning on her seventh day of life, I sat with her in the big rocker, gently moving to and fro. It was Monday, and Percy had several patients to visit.

"Before I leave, there is something I must give you," he said, taking a letter from his pocket. "This is from Linnie. It came two weeks ago, but I didn't give it to you because I didn't want you upset right before the baby was born."

He pulled his chair close to the rocker and put his hand on my knee. "Olive, I'm sure that she's writing to tell you that the federal government has dispatched troops under General Albert Johnston—twenty-six hundred men with seven hundred supply wagons and two thousand oxen. They say they are coming to restore order and to support civil authority in the entire territory of Utah. The Saints in Salt Lake City are preparing for war."

"But *why*, Percy? Why should the government fight us?"

Percy's voice rang with bitterness. "We are God's chosen, Olive. We're different, and folks can't tolerate anyone who's different."

"What . . . what do you think will happen?"

"They'd like to kill us all, but if I know Brother Brigham, we'll fight to the last man."

I tucked my baby in her cradle and tore open Linnie's letter.

"Dear Olive," she wrote. "I got to write and tell you that some men come the day of the picnic in Big Cottonwoood Canyon to tell Brother Brigham the soldiers was coming to do us mischief. We look to Brother Brigham to protect us. He keeps saying that we are united and all is well. My heart hurt when you moved so far off, but now I am being thankful that you are a good piece away from the trouble. Love, Linnie."

I handed the letter to Percy. "It *is* better for you and the children to be here now," he said after he read it, "but I should be in Salt Lake City, assisting Brother Brigham. Instead I'm trying to grow crops in this dry, worthless ground."

I'd hoped that he'd grown more content in our new surroundings, but he still hated being away from the Beehive, and he despised farming. But personal concerns seemed far away when our precious Deseret would soon be under seige.

"If there's any important news today, I'll come home early," Percy said before he kissed me good-bye. Val followed him out to the corral as he usually did, eager to watch him hitch up the team.

That afternoon I took my baby outdoors for the first time and walked down the road to join a cluster of neighbor women and children who stood huddled together speaking in whispers, although only the sagebrush and meadowlarks could overhear. An older woman scolded me for being up and about so soon after my confinement.

"I'm quite well," I told her, "and I must know what's going on."

It was the first wife of the ward bishop who spoke: "A messenger rode through Springville early this

morning bound for Carson Valley and then San Bernar-
dino, California. Brother Brigham has ordered the
folks in those settlements to return to Deseret, and he's
declared martial law."

"We're at war, just like in Nauvoo," Sister Potter
said, her kind face lined with grief.

"But this time our men will fight until we win,"
someone answered, brave words in an unsteady voice.

The ward bishop's wife continued: "There's a captain, Van Fliet or something like that is his name, who
went right into the city and told Brother Brigham to
assign a place for the federal troops to camp."

Sister Potter clapped her hands. "But our Brother
Brigham sent him packing, he did. Said *no* troops will
enter the city as long as a single Mormon man and gun
survive."

The little children clung to their mothers' skirts as
Val clung to mine, feeling the stark fear of the grown-
ups. Suddenly the fierce heat, the dust, and the terror
were more than I could bear, and I swayed. Sister Potter
put a strong arm around me, and another woman took
little Olive from my arms.

"We'd best get her and the baby back to the house,"
Sister Potter said.

I leaned heavily against her as we walked, but even
when I was home and lying on my bed, I could not rest.
I knew that when the fighting began, doctors would be
needed. In Springville the children and I were safe, but
what would happen to Percy?

Two days later he received a personal letter from
Brother Brigham, ordering him back to Salt Lake City.

"The Mormon Battalion is prepared to fight at Echo
Canyon," Percy said, trying to reassure me. "They'll
fight guerrilla fashion—sniping, burning, stealing
oxen, mules, and horses—and the federal troops will

never come near the valley. I'm to set up a field hospital to treat our wounded, but don't worry. I'll be safe.''

The next morning Percy bent to kiss our little daughter as she lay in her cradle. He embraced me, then he picked up Val who wrapped his arms tightly around Percy's neck, tears rolling down his thin cheeks.

Val had survived the long months of near starvation, but he had never really filled out again, nor recaptured the joy and energy of a little child. He was a subdued little person, so obedient it worried me, but he adored his father. He could not understand the meaning of war, but he did know that Percy was going away.

"Can I go with you, Papa?" Val begged. "I'll be good if you let me go."

"You are too little to come with me," his father said gently. "When you are a man, it will be your turn to stand up for Deseret."

Brother Potter drove Percy to the tithing house to catch the stage. I stood in the doorway with Val's hand in mine. We waved good-bye until the carriage was long out of sight and the dust had settled. More than a year would pass before we saw Percy again.

In the days that followed, Val was desperately lonely for his father and quieter than ever. Trying to interest and arouse him helped to relieve my own heartache, but it was little Ollie who cheered us both. She was a quick baby, soon full of smiles. Val, his face sober, his voice solemn, would lean over her cradle and talk to her. She would respond with a happy face and waving arms.

Late in September I saw Sister Potter striding up the path. She walked thrust forward, as if into a raging wind, and I knew she was bringing bad news.

Inside, she scooped off her sunbonnet, plopped into a chair and put her hands on her knees. "There's a terrible news being spread all over the valley," she said. "It's so bad, a body can't really believe it."

I swallowed and waited.

"They're saying it happened over in Mountain Meadows . . . a massacre . . . one hundred and forty people killed and scalped . . . every person on a wagon train bound for California dead, except about seventeen babies."

I felt the blood drain from my face; I lowered myself to a chair. "Horrible, horrible," I murmured.

Suddenly Sister Potter burst into deep sobs. She buried her face in her workworn hands. "The worst thing . . . the worst thing is that they're saying it wasn't Injuns who done it. They're saying it was Mormons, some of our people who went plumb crazy because them immigrants boasted in Cedar City that they was the ones what killed our prophet, Joseph Smith, back in Illinois."

"Mormons?" I gasped.

"Mormons," she repeated. "And they're saying the ones a'done it will be brought to justice. But justice can't bring those dead folks back or take lovin' care of them little orphans."

I shook my head, stunned and disbelieving. For years I'd lived among the Mormons; I'd joined their number, and I knew they were kind, hard-working, and deeply religious. Surely if Mormons were responsible, it was a few—only a few—on whom guilt rested.

"I'm trying hard to believe that it wasn't our folks," Sister Potter managed between sobs. "But if it was—if it was really Mormons a'doing the killing—it'll put a black mark on us and our children and their children until God calls the last man on earth home to heaven."

It was nearly time for me to nurse Ollie, and I felt my breasts grow heavy as they filled with milk. "The mothers of those little ones . . . were . . . were they killed too?"

"They were all killed, all killed," Sister Potter said

with a new burst of weeping. "I heard that Mormon women are tending the babies until they can be sent back East to relations, but them mothers are as murdered as the fathers."

My heart felt as if my own children had been left alone in the world and helpless. I joined Sister Potter in tears, and Val, not understanding, but saddened by our grief, came and cried with us. But I knew that if Sister Potter's story were true, no tears could ever wash away the stain of blood in Mountain Meadows.

For months afterward a gloom enveloped the whole area, a gloom worse than anything occasioned by the coming of the federal troops. Winter came on. War continued to wage between the Mormons and the federal government.

Usually letters from Percy came a few days apart, but occasionally weeks would pass before one got through. I'd go through torment, not knowing whether the mails were delayed or whether Percy was wounded or dead.

In February, Percy wrote, "Our men are holding them at bay, and we're not giving them an easy time. We've scorched the earth all around them, and many of their supply wagons have gone up in smoke. I heard that Alfred Cummings, the governor President Buchanan has appointed to usurp Brother Brigham's office, is with the federal troops. We plan to force them to spend the rest of the winter holed up on Green River."

The war continued, waged in strange fashion. The guerrilla fighters harassed the federal troops encamped in makeshift shelters on the Green River, stealing their animals and burning their supply wagons. But when the troops were in danger of starving, the Saints sent wagons of food for which the soldiers gladly paid.

Thomas E. Kane, who sympathized with the Mormons, was sent by the government to help bring peace to our agonized land, but the Saints in Salt Lake City, finding no security in Kane's efforts, moved en masse to the south, leaving only a few men who would burn the city to the ground if federal troops moved closer.

It was springtime now. Little Ollie took her first steps, and I began teaching four-year-old Val to read. He learned with a quickness of mind that delighted me, and I was sorry there was not yet a school in our part of the district.

Brother Potter plowed our fields and helped with the planting, but the spring rains were sparse, and the grain came up spindly. The days lengthened; the sun got hotter, and the ground got drier. The crops would be poor.

Without Percy the days were long and the nights were lonely. Throughout the settlement I could sense a feeling of desperate determination. War was anguish, but we were ready to endure forever. Then in late summer word reached us that a compromise between Brother Brigham Young and Governor Alfred Cummings had brought the fighting to a halt. The federal troops marched through Salt Lake City molesting nothing, and went on forty miles to Cedar Valley, where they established Fort Floyd.

Although the government still referred to us as rebels and traitors, President Buchanan issued a pardon to all Mormons. Amid a feeling of jubilation we heard that people who had fled the city were returning. The war was over. Every day I caught myself staring down the road, watching for Percy who would soon be coming home.

Chapter 25

"Mama! Mama! Come quick!"

It was early afternoon on the last day of August. From out near the corral Val was calling me with an excitement in his voice that could mean only one thing.

I caught my breath, smoothed my hair with my hand, and rushed outside. Val was already running to his father, who was approaching on foot. I paused long enough to scoop up Ollie so that she could join in the reunion; then I rushed down the road.

Dropping his portmanteau, Percy ran to gather us all in his arms. Amid tearful rejoicing, we hugged and kissed. Even after a year of separation, Val clung to his father with all his strength, but Ollie was indignant at being embraced by a stranger.

"You were hardly a handful when I went away," Percy said, hoisting our chubby, radiant little girl into the air. "And Percival, I think you're a good bit taller, but you still need to gain weight."

As Percy studied the children, I studied him. His mustache and trim beard were gone; he was clean-shaven, and his face looked thin and boyish. His once well-fitted coat hung loose, and there was a weariness in his every movement.

Silently I renewed every promise I'd ever made to love and care for him. I was certain that heaven could offer me no greater joy than to be forever at his side, to cook and clean for him, to raise his children, and in my devotion to help him forget the hard, bitter year of war.

"I rode into town on a supply wagon," Percy said as we made our way back to the house. "If I'd waited until evening, I could have gotten a ride home, but walking was worth it. I'm here sooner."

We weren't long inside when there was a soft knock at the door. "I'm not wanting to be a bother," Sister Potter said when I opened it, "but I came to tell you not to do any cooking for your evening meal. Pa and I will bring some good vittles over to you later, so you can be using all your time to welcome Brother Terry home."

As always, I was touched by her thoughtfulness, and Percy was also. "They're good people," he said, stretching out on the bed, "and it's good to be home."

He said he wanted to rest for only a few minutes, but he immediately fell into a deep sleep. I eased a pillow under his head, and Val helped me take off his father's shoes. In sleep, Percy looked handsome and beautifully peaceful. He was as happy to be home as we were to have him, and I prayed that the discontent he'd known before he went away would be gone. Perhaps farming wouldn't seem so tedious to him now; perhaps his medical practice would grow. Perhaps, after these long years, we could be happy and together.

For nearly a week after Percy's homecoming everything was joy and pleasure. In bed at night I responded eagerly to his love and passion. During the day my heart was grateful as I watched Percy spending long, happy hours with his children.

It delighted Percy to write words on a slate for Val to identify. "He's not five years old yet," Percy said. "It's amazing how much you've been able to teach him."

Ollie adored having Percy pay attention to her, but he

had to do it from a prescribed distance. If he came too close, she screeched and ran from him, but if he neglected her, she soon let him know that she was nearby.

It was a beautiful time, but it ended abruptly on the day Percy returned to work in the fields. When he came in for the midday meal, he didn't talk much, but that evening when he sat down to supper, he said, "Things are even worse than I remembered them. There's not enough water, and there'll be very little harvest again this year."

I put the food on the table, wishing there was something I could do to ease the despair in his voice.

"I'm beginning to understand that Hickory Saint who left this place," he continued.

I stopped ladling soup into bowls and put my arm around him. "Percy, if you're still unhappy here, why don't you tell . . . I mean, ask Brother Brigham if you can return to the city?"

Percy sighed. "Brother Brigham assigned me to this territory, and I won't complain to him."

"But you've said yourself that he's never lived here and doesn't know how difficult it is to coax a crop out of this dry, rocky ground. He has no right to expect you to stay," I said, my voice rising.

"He does have the right," Percy said firmly. "He's the one person who enables Deseret to survive, and only the people really close to him can know the agony he goes through every day. And in addition to all his other responsibilities, now the federal government is always putting requests on him for one thing and another."

I smoothed his dark hair, noting the gray strands that lined his temple.

"When I was in the city, Brigham's son contracted to furnish telegraph poles for the new lines being built, but later he found he couldn't produce the poles at the agreed-upon price. The line supervisors said they would pay more, but when Brother Brigham heard about it, he insisted that the poles be delivered at the original price.

"Olive, that's the kind of man he is, and every last Saint knows it. I'll stay here forever if that's what he thinks is right for me, but I wish . . . I wish he'd call me back to the Beehive so that I could be a real help to him again." The longing in his voice tore through my heart.

Just then Ollie decided to show her approval of Percy for the first time. She toddled over and tugged his shirt, demanding that he lift her up. He hoisted her to his lap, and she stared at him, her little chin thrust out defiantly as her appraisal was by no means over.

He laughed; his gloomy mood was broken. From then on I made a constant effort to keep him cheerful, but often as not my efforts failed.

Although the fighting was now over, we soon found that the silent war with the government was unabated. Percy was in charge of the tithing house, and as the months went by, he was frequently angered and frustrated by the interference and snooping of government officials.

"They're not Mormons. They're gentiles, and they have no constitutional right to check our books and tell us how to run things," he said one evening after he'd arrived home in a rage.

"I think Governor Cummings is trying to be fair, but there are others in office who hate us. They'll continue to cause trouble, and I see no end to the threat against Deseret, against our very lives."

Percy had been home for over a year, and—if anything—the situation had worsened. Once he appealed to the mayor, Lorenzo Johnson, and to the ward bishop, and although they tried diligently, they were unable to do anything. The leaders of the church and community stood helpless under the grievous rule of outsiders.

I tried to be cheerful and encouraging, but there were moments when my own thoughts were bleak. I worried about the future of my children. If the government never left us alone, what would happen to them?

And my heart ached for Percy. Even in this sparsely settled country, Percy had many patients now—people who paid him in the fruits of the fields—so he spent less time farming. That helped—he was happier caring for people and doing work that meant something to him— but even after he'd been home two years, his attitude toward Springville hadn't changed. He still hated it. Sadly, I wondered if there would ever be a time and place where he would find contentment.

But in spite of our problems, I was willing to be happy—there was so much we did have—and soon I was blessed with a new source of joy. Letters from home began arriving regularly and frequently, carried by the pony express. The express started out in St. Joseph, Missouri, and there were relay stations where horses and riders were changed, horses every ten miles, riders about every seventy-five. At first I could hardly believe that I was receiving letters that had been written only two weeks earlier. I wrote home oftener too, always stressing how much I loved Percy and how happy we were together.

The rapid exchange of letters had a strange effect on me. In the past letters had included only news of some importance—births, deaths and reports on the harvest. Now day-by-day details of life were included. Dorothy described furniture she and her new husband bought;

she was making a fashionable dress she thought I would admire. Ma's rose bush bloomed out-of-season, and almost everyone in town came to see it.

I wrote about little things too: Val's ability to read, Ollie's spirited antics. My family was close to me again; they shared my life and I shared theirs. It was wonderful, but it brought a homesickness worse than any I'd ever known. I yearned to see my people, and I wanted to show them my children.

In October, we gathered what harvest we had. The vegetables from the garden had barely fed us during the summer, and only the root vegetables remained to be stored for winter use. Even with the contributions squeezed by grateful patients from their own inadequate harvests, the grain sacks barely filled one end of the storeroom. It would be a long, lean winter, and my awareness of Percy's dejection ate into my soul.

That November—the November of 1860—Abraham Lincoln was elected President of the United States. Percy didn't hide his bitterness. "He's the man who suggested the territory of Utah be divided and each part governed by one of the adjoining states. He's like all the rest who refuse statehood to us. They know that if we were a state, we'd run our own business."

With Lincoln's election, there came the fulfillment of another of Joseph Smith's prophecies. We were at the wardhouse attending a harvest dance when we heard the news. The fiddler stopped in the middle of a dance, and with Percy's arms still around me, I watched the ward bishop mount the platform.

"We have just heard that the state of South Carolina has seceded from the union," he intoned.

Although we in Utah did not feel involved in the slavery conflict, everyone gasped.

"Joseph Smith predicted there would be a great

trouble for the nation,'' Percy whispered to me, ''and he said it would start in South Carolina.''

All around us we heard people murmuring the same thing. ''Joseph Smith predicted it,'' and ''Our beloved prophet said it would be so.''

The ward bishop held up his hand for attention: ''We ask God to grant His mercy to our nation in these troubled times. We pray that peace will prevail throughout the land, but if there must be war, let it be between the South and the North. Let them turn their faces and guns away from us, so that we, Thy people, can live in peace and harmony as Thou ordains.''

Heads were bowed, but a cheer echoed through the assembly. If the government were conducting a big war in the East, surely we would be left alone.

Chapter 26

In April of 1861, I heard that fighting had actually started between the South and the North. I listened to the reports, grateful that my relatives in Iowa were far from the battlefields. However, President Lincoln's war seemed remote, and not nearly as important to us as the heavy rains that fell that spring, finally filling our irrigation ditches.

"Isn't this wonderful," I said, listening to the rain thunder against our roof. "With all this water our crops will be good."

Percy sighed. "I don't think anything here will ever be good."

It was early morning, and the downpour had kept Percy home. He sat with his hands clasped behind his head, his expression as dark and cloudy as the skies outside. Percy still enjoyed his children; occasionally there were light moments between the two of us, but he suffered from a growing despondency that nothing seemed to relieve.

In May, I knew I was with child again. I was delighted and Percy seemed pleased. Val had just turned seven, and Ollie would be four in August. It had been a long time since we had welcomed a new baby, but Percy's lack of joy reached even into our bed. He was seldom happy, and we were seldom together.

Percy's depression was creating a poison that effected us all. I prayed that something wonderful would happen, something that would enable us to move to an important place where he could establish a big medical practice, the one thing he really wanted to do.

The answer to my prayers came on a beautiful afternoon in June when Percy returned from the tithing house looking more cheerful than he had in months. He lingered outdoors to play with Val and Ollie. When he came in, he grabbed me, swung me around and kissed me soundly.

"Percy, something good happened today," I said, laughing.

"It certainly did," he answered, showing me a letter. "Today this came from Brother Brigham addressed to me personally. He plans to visit this part of the territory within a month. From the sound of it, I'm convinced his visit will bring a new assignment for me."

A burden lifted from my heart. "Oh, Percy, I hope so," I said.

Throughout the settlement preparations for Brother Brigham's visit began immediately. Men took time from their fields to bring fresh boughs for the summer meeting place, and two men headed for Provo to buy flags and bunting for decorations.

I went about my tasks—even the back-breaking work in the garden—bubbling with hope that Brother Brigham's visit would truly be a turning point for Percy. It was important that the visit be successful, and I was as eager as anyone when I attended a planning meeting of the wives.

"Everyone's got to bring the best they got," one of the mayor's wives said.

"We got a young pig. He's right little, but he'll make a platterful," Sister James volunteered.

The woman next to me spoke up. "I'll make a butter

duck, a big one with clove eyes and fuzzy wings, and I'll have him on a bed of sieved butter.''

Before I could volunteer, the ward bishop's first wife said, ''Sister Terry, something about your baking is tastier than most, so I expect you'll want to bring lots of bread and rolls.''

''You should see how fast she works,'' Sister Potter chortled. ''She gets her dough kneaded and rising in the crock in the time 'takes most folks to measure off the flour.''

I laughed. ''I'll bring a full basket of bread and rolls if that is what's wanted,'' I assured them.

On a hot day in July, we heard that Brother Brigham and his entourage had arrived in Provo. They'd be in Springville in a day or two. Excitement seethed.

Early the next morning, Sister Potter came running. ''Best you do your baking. I'm gatherin' dried cow chips to do mine. It's better'n brush, 'cause it don't burn so hot. I'm aiming to have the most delicious cake on the table. I got some fresh saleratus so's it got to raise good.''

Messengers left for Provo; each hour one would ride back to keep us informed as to how far away our guests were. When they drew close, everyone gathered at the summer meeting place. Then word came that they were only ten miles away. Percy drove out in the carriage to meet them with the mayor and bishop seated at his sides, the horses brushed until their coats shone like grease in the sun.

Men and women marched out on the dusty road. They carried flags and signs: *Bless Brother Brigham, The Lion of the Lord, the Gathering of Zion.*

The rest of us waited, dressed in our best, and I inspected the tables that gleamed with scoured dishes, knives, and forks. The food boxes were ready to be unpacked and the milk jugs bobbed in the creek where they'd keep cool. The flowers on the tables drooped in the heat, but I hoped no one would notice when all the food came out.

Suddenly a great cheer went up. The first carriage was in sight. Val stood on a bench and I held Ollie high. Straining, we got our first look at Brother Brigham. He sat alone in his carriage, his portly body bowing first to one side and then the other. He smiled joyously and saluted his people.

There was a moment of milling excitement, punctuated with calls of welcome:

"Glad to have you, Brother Brigham."

"Mighty fine of you to come, Brother Brigham."

The crowd surged back, making way for the illustrious visitors who arrived in a long stream of carriages. As the women hurried to unpack the food, men took places at the tables. I noted that Brother Brigham had the bishop on one side of him and Percy on the other.

Silence fell as Brother Brigham raised one of his big hands: "We'll pray now," he said, "giving thanks to God for all the blessings He gives us."

Heads bowed, but ears strained to hear the words Brother Brigham spoke to the Lord:

"We feel grateful for all the tribulations that have caused us to be united, for all the hardships that have made us strong, for Thy deliverance from the hands of our enemies, for the showing of Thy will. Bless these good people assembled here today and give us all grace in abundance. Amen."

As the men ate, the women poured milk into pewter and tin cups and saw that all the plates and bowls kept moving. I bustled with the other women, serving and refilling bowls and plates, but my attention was really on Percy whose face was illuminated and happy as he talked to Brother Brigham.

When Brother Brigham and the men finished, they left the table with grunts of satisfaction and went to lounge in the shade. Then we cleared away the dirty dishes and prepared to serve the women who traveled with Brother Brigham's party. They could not eat with the men, but they were our special guests and were served attentively before the rest of us ate.

Following dinner, there was a meeting. Percy sat on the front bench on the men's side, his smiling face raised to the platform where Brother Brigham talked.

When the service was over, fiddles, Jew's harps, horns, and clarinets appeared, and "Oh, Susanna, Rosin' the Bow" and "She'll be Comin' Round the Mountain" set feet to tapping. Benches were moved aside, and a double quadrille formed.

I saw a young girl in a full-skirted pink dress and fashionable bonnet being escorted to the table where Percy and Brother Brigham were seated. Percy rose; I saw him talking to the girl, and I wondered who she was.

A few minutes later Percy appeared at my side. "Would you like to dance, Olive?" he asked, holding out his hand to me.

I put Ollie in the care of another woman, and hurried to join Percy in a new quadrille that was forming. I didn't remove the apron that concealed my waistline that was beginning to thicken as I was nearly three months with child. Percy was happier than he'd been in so long that my own happiness swelled. I danced with joyful abandon.

Later I sat on a bench emptying the dirt that had collected in my shoes. When I looked up, I saw Percy dancing with the girl in the pink dress. I was still wondering who she was when a young man with Brother Brigham's party invited me to dance.

"I'd be honored to have a dance with just about the

prettiest woman I've ever seen," he said, "if there's no one who'll be minding my asking you."

"My husband is already dancing," I answered, extending my hand.

Away we went, bowing and swaying with the others. I enjoyed it, but dancing was only a thrill when Percy was my partner.

Soon the sun sent long shadows across the ground, and at last the visitors left to return to Provo for the night. Riding home in the carriage, I listened eagerly as Percy told me the news: "I'm to be in charge of a new emigration to a town in California called San Francisco. If the place keeps growing the way they say it has in the last ten years, it will be an important city before long. They'll need doctors, not farmers. I'll finally get my chance to establish the kind of medical practice I've always wanted."

I listened enraptured, sharing Percy's new self-confidence and pride. I willingly ignored my own fears about making the trip with a new baby coming. I'd manage somehow. If Percy were content, nothing could go wrong.

That night I fell into bed exhausted but supremely happy, and Percy showed his happiness by loving me with a fresh exuberance.

"Olive, you're the true love of my life," he said, "and no one can ever mean as much to me as you do."

In spite of my weariness, it was a joy to respond to his words and his caresses. Until recently his despondency had been a wedge between us even in bed, but now there was nothing that could keep us apart. As my body arched toward his, I shared his passion and was filled with a beautiful hope for the future.

"I love you, Olive," he groaned as his body exploded into mine. "I love you."

He rolled over, still holding me close. I lay against him, my cheek resting on his chest. My breath came in long, deep pulls. I knew an ecstasy so exquisite I wished the moment could endure forever, just Percy and me together with our love.

Gently, Percy rubbed the back of my neck, running his hand down to the small of my back. I floated in a beautiful glass bubble.

"It will be wonderful when we're all together in San Francisco," Percy said, his voice caressingly soft and deep. "You would be the one to go with me now if it wasn't for the new baby coming, but I'll come back for you and the children as soon as I get well established. And in San Francisco you'll have a separate house, and I promise you that it will have glass windows."

I opened my eyes. A tight band of pressure began to enclose my chest. Suddenly, vividly, I could see a living, breathing Sophia dancing in Percy's arms, but before the vision passed, her red skirt faded to pink.

"This time we won't have the problems we had before," Percy said, his voice still caressingly soft, his hand still stroking my back. "You're a Mormon now, and God will grant you special graces to enable you to be happy as a plural wife. You know how precious you are to me, more precious than any other wife will ever be, and I think you will like Emily. She's Brother Brigham's own niece, and he ordered me to marry her so that she can gain her right place in heaven. Olive, I know that this time you will understand."

He continued, a soft, melodious flow of words. I lay not moving, my body still entwined with his, my cheek still resting on his chest. The bubble had burst, and its crystal fragments were falling all around me. There was nothing left but pain.

Chapter 27

The next morning I behaved as if I were still alive, but deep inside I was dead, a vital part of me had stopped living. But I dressed, stirred the oatmeal that had thickened on the stove all night and then set bowls on the table. I did not become ill until I heard the voice.

"Last night when I told you that Brother Brigham had instructed me to marry his niece, you didn't say anything. I hope that means you understand and have no objections."

A buzzing noise started inside my head, and suddenly the sight and smell of the oatmeal made my stomach churn.

"Olive dear, I never told you this," the voice continued, "but I've always believed I was assigned to Springville because I was one of the few leaders in the church who had only one wife. I was not a good example to the Saints in Salt Lake City, because it seemed that I did not make a proper effort to practice the principle of celestial marriage. One day Brother Brigham even mentioned to me that I should add more wives and children to my kingdom in heaven, but I couldn't. I had promised you never to choose another wife, and an honorable man keeps his promises. However, now Brother Brigham has chosen for me. I must obey him, but, Olive, I hope you realize that my word to you has not been broken. I . . . ."

I rushed toward the door, my hands clasped over my

mouth, I reached the edge of the garden before I doubled over, retching.

Someone who looked like Percy came to help me, but when he touched me, the buzzing in my head got louder. I pulled away and staggered back to the house, managing to reach the bed before I collapsed.

The buzzing in my head turned to thunder, but it could not blot out the voice. "Olive, don't worry about the children. I'll take care of them while you rest. So much excitement yesterday was very fatiguing, and with the new baby coming . . . ." I pulled the coverlet over my ears.

I stayed in bed that day and the next day too. It was afternoon of the third day before I could remain up for longer than a few minutes. Then I cleaned myself, changed my clothes and began to move about. Gradually I noticed something strange about the house. Nothing had changed, yet everything looked different, shabbier somehow and ugly; the pig bladder window was hideous.

"Olive dear, you haven't eaten, and I'm worried about you," the voice said. It was Percy's voice, Percy talking and talking forever. I could not silence him, but I could pretend I did not hear. No matter what he said, I would never answer.

An adorable little girl with bouncy, gold curls stood with her hands on her hips. "Mama, you finally got up," she said. "I'm glad."

She ran to me and wrapped her arms around my skirts. I picked her up, and her warm cheek pressed tight against mine. *Ollie, Ollie, my little girl.* I began to tremble; tears misted my eyes, but I would not let them fall. I would not let Percy see me cry.

"Are you feeling better, Olive?" Percy asked.

"Ollie, Mama is going to warm the soup," I said, putting her down.

"I'm really sorry, but I have to leave for Salt Lake City in less than two weeks. There's a great deal to be arranged before then. If you're strong enough, we should talk things over."

"Ollie, is Val outside? Will you go call him for Mama?"

"Olive dear, do you feel well enough to talk?"

"Ollie, I will go with you."

"Olive, I asked you a question. Didn't you hear . . . ."

I closed the door behind me. With a true feeling of wonder, I looked around. The corral, the smokehouse, the lean-to, the sagebrush, and the hard, dry earth—everything was familiar, yet I felt as if I were seeing it all for the first time.

This is a horrible place, desolate and ugly. How did I ever manage to be happy here?

My knees started to shake. I called to Val, and the three of us went back in the house. I heated a pot of soup, then carefully filled three bowls. "Here, children," I said, calling them.

My legs were still unsteady, and it felt good to sit down. Slowly, I downed a few spoonfuls of soup, the first food I'd eaten in two days.

Later Percy served himself. He kept talking to me, but it was getting easier not to hear what he said.

The following morning Percy left early. "I have much to do today, and I probably won't return until late. Will you be all right, Olive?"

I stood at the dresser, counting strokes as I brushed my hair. "Eighteen, nineteen . . . ."

"Olive, will you be all right?" His voice seemed unnecessarily loud.

"Twenty, twenty-one, twenty-two . . . ."

"Olive!"

"Twenty-three, twenty-four, twenty-five . . . ."
The door slammed.

The children and I ate our evening meal earlier than usual, and I was already in bed when I heard him come in.

As the days went by, Percy talked to me, explaining the various arrangements he had made, but he stopped asking me questions.

"Brother Potter will work our fields in return for one-half the harvest. He'll work the oxen for their keep, but you can use them whenever you want. I'm sorry that I have to take the horses, but it's necessary. Oh, my God, Olive, I wish you'd look at me. I wish I knew if you could understand what I'm saying."

I can understand, Percy, but if I answered you—if I told you that what you're doing is wrong—you would preach at me and preach at me. You couldn't convince me, and I won't give you the chance to comfort yourself.

The evening before Percy left, the ward bishop visited us soon after the children went to bed. I was sitting in the rocker, my hands idle, and it was Percy who answered the door.

"Olive dear, it's the bishop," Percy said, leading him into the room.

"Good evening, Sister Terry," the bishop said with a courteous nod.

I smiled in his direction and continued rocking.

Taking a seat at the table, the bishop said, "It's best you don't travel in your condition, so you can send your consent to Brother Terry's marriage through me."

He took out paper and an envelope, and Percy hurried to bring him pen and ink.

"I'm explaining to the bishop in Salt Lake City that I have talked to you and you have stated your consent."

He peered at me over his glasses, waiting.

Again I smiled, rocking back and forth.

"Ah . . . Sister Terry has been ill," Percy said, his voice less steady than usual. "Hasn't really been herself lately."

The bishop sounded concerned. "But you know, don't you, Sister Terry, that if a wife withholds consent to her husband's celestial marriage, she is damned by God to spend all eternity in hell? You *do* give your consent?"

"Bishop, he can do whatever he wants to do," I said aloud. "He can be loyal to me and stay here. He can marry another woman, desert me, our two children, and unborn baby, and go to San Francisco. I have no objections; I consent to anything he wants to do."

Percy stood right in front of me, and I wondered why his face looked so red. "I've diagnosed it as a nervous disorder, Bishop, resulting from her pregnant condition. I've prescribed draughts for her."

The bishop looked at me again, then slowly began to write.

After the bishop tucked his letter into the envelope, Percy said, "Olive, don't you think the bishop would like some milk and hoecake?"

I folded my hands in my lap.

"But, Olive dear, you stay right where you are and rest. I will get it for him."

The bishop rose to leave, courtesouly declining any refreshment. "Here is your letter, Brother Terry. Sister Terry, I hope you feel better soon."

"Thank you, Bishop," I said, "but I feel perfectly well right now."

His departure seemed hasty.

It was getting dark. Percy lit a candle and set it on the table. Then he pulled his chair close to my rocker. He sat leaning forward, his elbows propped on his knees, his head down and supported by his hands.

I could not bear to have him so close. I stood up, intending to get ready for bed, but he grabbed my arm.

"Olive, I want you to know—you *must* know and believe—that I love you. You're beautiful and loving. You work at my side when there is work to be done. You're always cheerful and uncomplaining. You are the best wife I could ever have. You have a mind of your own, there's no denying that, but in every other way, you are perfect."

I stood motionless, staring straight ahead, not trying to free my arm. Abruptly, he released me. I prepared for bed, and I did not try to comfort him when I heard his anguished moan.

I slept but little, and in darkness I arose. As the first rays of light touched the room, they seemed to illuminate Percy who lay asleep, one arm over his head, his dark hair tousled on the pillow. I stared at him, wondering how it was possible for him to look so near when in reality, he was separated from me by a gulf no time or space could ever bridge. Oh God, how could he look so handsome? I forced myself to turn away. *How could he do what he would do today?*

As I began preparing breakfast for the children and me, Percy got up and finished his packing.

"Don't feel bad about my laundry," he said. "You haven't been feeling well, and I can have my shirts and things done in Salt Lake City."

Will Emily, wife number three, do them? Will she be your devoted slave also, like Sophia and me?

Val was awake now and upset by Percy's obvious preparations to leave. "Are you going to that north and south war, Pa?" he asked, his voice heavy with grief.

Percy sat on the edge of the bed and lifted Val to his

lap. "No, Percival, but I must go to a place beyond the mountains and find a new home for all of us. It will be better for us there."

"It's better for me with you here, Pa," Val said, nuzzling close.

I had to pull my attention from Percy and the small boy so like him. I was determined to keep control, no matter what agonies were taking place within me, but the son's grief and the father's tenderness were more than I could endure.

I rushed outside, and with a fierce energy I began feeding and watering the chickens and barnyard animals. I would not think; I would only work.

In the back of my mind I knew when Percy was hitching the team to the wagon. I caught sight of his trunk, the same trunk that had bounced precariously, strapped to the side of our wagon as we traveled west.

Val and Ollie were both sobbing, and they ran to me and tugged my skirts.

"Mama, ask Pa not to go," Val begged.

I knelt and put my arms around them. "Don't cry, dears. I will take care of you, and I promise everything will be all right. And later when our chores are done, we'll walk down to the tithing house, and I will buy you sugar sticks."

They were losing their father, and I was promising them sugar sticks.

Percy's shadow fell across us. He knelt at my side and his arms encircled me and our son and daughter. "Every day I will ask God in prayer to take care of my dearest family," he said, husky-voiced.

Val began a final, frantic pleading. "Don't go, Pa. Please don't go!"

"I have to go, Percival. Maybe for a long time, but I'll come back as soon as I can."

I had neither moved nor spoken since Percy embraced me, but I didn't resist when he lifted me to my feet. Then he put his hands on my shouders and kissed me.

These are the last moments. Don't weaken now.

As his lips pressed hard against mine, I stood as if unaware, but I was almost overwhelmed with a sense of his warmth, his life, his very being.

"There's a pouch with a thousand dollars in gold in the hiding place in back of the cupboard. It should provide you with everything you want until I get back. Take care of yourself and the children. I'll write to you as often as I can." His words and sentences sounded disconnected.

He hugged Val, gathered Ollie in his arms for a moment, then turned toward the carriage.

"Percy," I said softly.

He turned abruptly in response to the first word I'd spoken to him since that night in bed.

"What you are doing is terribly wrong, but I will love you until I die."

Percy opened his mouth. "Olive, you must understand . . . ."

Our eyes met, and I stared through to his soul. His voice failed, he turned pale. When he climbed into the carriage, he looked as if he were going to be ill.

Chapter 28

Before the carriage was out of sight, I turned my back to the road and picked up the hoe. Val was crying uncontrollably, but instead of comforting him, I insisted that he help me.

"Come, Val, you must work in the garden." My own voice sounded unfamiliar.

A sobbing Val and wailing Ollie followed me.

In the garden I began swinging the hoe, whacking at the ground with an unseeing frenzy. Val bent to firm the dirt around the roots of the growing plants, but after a moment he plopped on the ground and buried his face in his hands. I kept swinging and whacking, not caring whether I hit weeds or our carefully nurtured vegetables.

Suddenly I felt a stabbing pain in my back. I was bent forward when it hit, and it was torture to straighten up.

"Val, Val, please help me," I gasped.

Val scrambled to his feet and tried to help, but he was too little. I held his hand until the pain subsided. Then, counting every step, I went into the house and eased myself on to the bed.

Val stayed right at my side. "Are you sick, Mama?"

New tears coursed down his cheeks. His father had left him, and now he was worried about me.

"It's a little pain in my back. That's all. I'll be all right in a few minutes." I tried to sound reassuring. My little boy had to feel he still had one parent who could love and care for him.

Gently, without shaking the bed, Val climbed up to lie beside me. He pressed his little body close to mine, and I could feel him tremble with deep sobs.

"I'm sorry, Val. I'm sorry." I had no other comfort for him or for me.

The room grew hot as the sun moved overhead. I heard the rocking chair squeak against the floorboards as Ollie rode hard, playing a lonely game of pony express. I closed my eyes.

Hours later I awakened and found Val curled up in a ball, sound asleep at my side. I moved carefully, checking, but the pain in my back was gone.

Percy had abandoned me, the agony in my mind and heart was unrelieved, but my little ones still had to eat. I had to get to my breadmaking. I got up without awakening Val, but the first thing that held my attention was the empty rocker.

"Ollie," I called. "Ollie, where are you?"

When she didn't answer, I began searching. It took only a minute to determine she wasn't in the house; then I went outside and checked the yard and garden.

"Ollie! Ollie!" As I got farther from the house, my cries became louder and louder.

"She has to be here someplace," I told myself, searching through the bunchgrass and cedars.

When I didn't find her, I hurried down the road to the Potter house. "My Ollie, she's wandered off and I can't find her."

Sister Potter reached for her sunbonnet. "Don't fret yourself, honey. She ain't gallivanted far. We'll find her in no time."

But we didn't find her. From out in the fields, Brother Potter saw us searching and came to help.

Sister James, another neighbor, joined us, then went to get others. Soon the canyon and fields were dotted with neighbors.

"Ollie! Ollie!" Her name was shouted in all directions, but Ollie didn't answer.

Brother Potter and another man went to search near the creek. "See if we can find a trace of her down there," he said.

My mind whirled. If Ollie had fallen into the creek, there would have been no little Shokup to pull her out.

I heard murmurings. "Indians seen in the territory. Been known to carry off young 'uns."

"Sister Potter! Sister Potter," I gasped.

She hurried toward me and put a protective arm around my shoulders

"I . . . I must go home. Val . . . all alone. When you find her . . . when you find her . . . ."

"I'll go home with you now. When they find her, Pa will bring her to you, jes' you wait."

We walked in deepening shadows. It would be dark soon, time for the bears, the wolves, and the mountain lions to prowl for food. I shuddered. Was it possible that I would lose Percy and my precious Ollie on the same day? I would have fainted if it hadn't been for Sister Potter's strong, steady voice.

"I was planning to sit with you this evenin'. With Brother Terry a-going, I knew you'd be hurtin'. Wish I'd been early, before that muffin had a chance to lose herself."

Val was awake and frightened to be all alone in the growing darkness. I gathered him in my arms, but suddenly he jumped up. "A carriage is coming. I hear a carriage. It's Papa. He's coming back!"

He ran out the door, and Sister Potter and I scrambled behind him. Down the road came a carriage, careening widely as the horses galloped in haste. As it skidded to a halt, I recognized Brother Anderson who lived several miles from us. Behind him on the seat I caught a glimpse of blue gingham.

"Ollie!"

"This the little one you're hunting for, ma'am?"

Without answering, I mounted the carriage step and scooped Ollie into my arms. She was happy and unruffled, but I was overcome.

"Would have brought her to you sooner, but we didn't know where she belonged. Found her down near the tithing house."

"Mama, I went to get our sugar sticks, 'cause you and Val were sleeping."

As her father was leaving us, I had promised her sugar sticks. She had gone to get them.

The wound that festered within me could not be suppressed any longer. I sobbed, and as if from a distance I heard my sobs become ugly, piercing screams. Sister Potter took Ollie from me, and I cried aloud for my rescued daughter, for my lost husband, and for my son, heartbroken because the carriage had not brought his father back to him.

"There, there," Sister Potter comforted. "She's safe, and Brother Terry won't be gone for as long as you're thinking."

When I got control of myself, I was drained of energy, but the pain within me had known release. And Ollie was frightened at last, not be her adventure, but by my cries.

I was still shaking when I held out my hand to Brother Anderson who lingered at his carriage.

"I . . . I don't know how to thank you and Sister Potter and all the good people who helped me look for my child."

He clasped my hand in his big one. ''Well, Sister Terry, I reckon you know that for us Saints, it's our joy and responsibility to look out for each other.''

Then he took a letter from his pocket. ''We took her to the tithing house to find out who she was. The clerk recognized her, and he gave me this for you.''

I took the letter and stuffed it in my pocket. Then I turned to my children. I had my Ollie back and I had Val. In a few months I'd have a new baby. Deep inside I could never stop aching for Percy, but I still had life and love to give to my children.

Sister Potter insisted on fixing our dinner, and to my amazement I ate with appetite. She stayed with me late into the night, refusing to leave until the children were asleep and she was convinced I was all right.

''I'll be fine, Sister Potter, and I'm more grateful to you than I can say,'' I said, embracing her.

I stood in the doorway, watching the light of her lantern bob until it was out of sight.

I was weary, but the long afternoon nap left me unable to sleep. I lit a second candle to dispell the gloom, then checked the children. Even now there was a look of sadness on Val's face. I touched my cheek against the damp warmth of his forehead. I could not atone for the loss of his father's love, but I was determined that my love would surround and protect him.

Then I remembered the letter Brother Anderson had given me. I hadn't even checked to see whom it was from, but now I recognized Dorothy's handwriting.

Setting a candle close to the rocker, I sat down to read. I don't think I could have borne one more pain that day, but the letter overflowed with happiness. Dorothy was expecting her first baby.

''We've been waiting a long time,'' she wrote, ''and we are very happy. If it's a girl, I will name her for you, to have the comfort of calling someone *Olive* again. You wrote that your new baby is expected in December also. If you have a girl, maybe you will call her Dorothy.''

''I hope,'' she concluded, ''that someday I will see your children and you will see mine. It's been years now, Olive, but we still miss you very much. I pray that someday we will be together again.''

I read the letter three times before I folded it carefully and replaced it in the envelope.

I sat a long time, rocking slowly back and forth, thinking. Percy was gone. All hope of happiness here was lost forever. For me there could be no haven, no bed in Deseret.

''Dorothy,'' I said, my voice loud in the stillness, ''I'm coming home.''

Chapter 29

Percy had been gone only a few days when I wrote to Linnie. It was a long six weeks before I received her reply, but her first words made the wait worthwhile:

"Yes, I can come visit you in December," she wrote in big, round letters. "There's a woman here will mind Uriah and Nathan. Sister Phoebe is dead against it, but Stephen is on mission to the south seas, won't be back till summer after next. It is four years and more since I see you, and it is no sin for me to make the trip. And I have my own house now, a spell away from Sister Phoebe's place. I won't have to hear about it too much after I get back."

In those few words she had told me all the things I most desperately wanted to know. Her husband was away; she no longer lived within constant surveillance of wife number one, and she could follow her own mind.

In my letter I had asked her to come in December to be with me when my baby came. I truly needed her to help me face childbirth without Percy, but there was another, far more important reason why I wanted to see Linnie.

I had made up my mind to return to my people. At first I had considered traveling by stagecoach, but that was clearly impossible. Without a letter from Percy giving me permission to make the trip, the ward bishop and church leaders would never allow me to leave the

area. Even outside of Utah, there was no place along
the stagecoach route where I would be safe from detec-
tion. I'd heard too many rumors about runaway wives
who were brought back to Deseret after being discovered hundreds of miles away.

Under the best circumstances the trip by stagecoach
involved many risks. Percy knew this, but he would
realize that the greatest risk was that once I was in Iowa,
I would never return. Even if he didn't know my real
plans, he could never forget that my father had wanted
to come for me when he learned about Sophia. Now
Percy had married again; he'd gone away and left me
and our children. Percy knew how my family would
react to this, and I could get no letter of permission from
him.

No, there was only one way that I could return to my
family. I had to leave secretly and go back the way I had
come. I had to travel by wagon, a thousand miles over
steep hills, through waterless deserts, across rivers of
rushing water, through Indian territory and across
states involved in a war with each other.

I remembered all the agony of the trip seven years
ago. I stood in awe of all I would have to endure, and
this time I would have children to care for. Time and
again my mind pulled away from knowing it had to be
done, but I had no choice. My heart insisted that I take
my children and go back to the love and protection of
my parents and family. And from the first somehow I
knew—without really knowing—that Linnie would go
with me.

The rest of her letter reported the joining of the east
and west trunks of the transcontinental telegraph lines.
''We was all proud and excited when Brother Brigham
sent the first message from Salt Lake City to President
Lincoln away off in Washington. Brother Brigham said

us Saints was loyal to the federal government, making
no difference how bad the government treated us. It's
wonderful the way Brother Brigham knows how to
speak out for the gathering.''

The transcontinental telegraph. Word from home
could reach me in only one day. That was exciting, but
Brigham Young's message to the President meant nothing. Once I would have been greatly moved, but with a
shock I realized that my heart and mind had already
turned homeward. In my thoughts I no longer belonged
to the gathering, and I no longer belonged to Percy. I
was Olive Harriet Banks Terry. Where and how I
would spend my life was up to me and to God.

My baby wasn't due for several months. Linnie
wouldn't come until then, but meantime there was
much to do. As the days grew shorter, there were apples
to pare and dry, beans to pack in muslin bags, onions to
braid together and hang, and potatoes, turnips,
parsnips, and beets to store.

Brother Potter piled sacks of wheat, oats, barley and
Indian corn to the rafters of my lean-to, and I stored the
overflow beneath Val's bunk.

''Nobody ever expected so much crops,'' Brother
Potter said. ''Such a stack, it dazes me.''

When the harvest was gathered, I began making
garments for the children and myself from rolls of
goods obtained from Salt Lake City. As I sewed, I
disciplined my mind. I tried not to regret the past or
grieve for Percy. Ahead of me, as if down a long, dark
tunnel, was a warm, bright light, and there my family
waited for me and my little ones.

Before I laid my sewing away, I made myself a pair
of black muslin bloomers. News from the East reported
that the bloomer girl was the newest fashion, but it
wasn't fashion that motivated me. I remembered all the

awkward climbs, and the everyday struggles to get in and out over the high wheels of the wagon. No woman could ever wear trousers, but now that bloomers were acceptable, they would be a great traveling convenience.

November roared in with a cold, raw gale. Brother Potter came to butcher the pigs taking one for himself and leaving the other two hanging, all scalded, scraped and dressed, on a trestle in the backyard.

"Best to let 'em cool. I'll come by tomorrow or next day and take 'em down. Just keep your eye out for those Laminite Indians. Have your gun ready in case they come sneakin' around."

Several days later Sister Potter and Sister James helped me pack the salted meat.

"You clean the heads, and mix the cheese," Sister James said to me. "Takes a sight of stooping to pack the tubs, and I can do that better 'n you."

It was all grueling work. My large belly hampered my movements, and the blue veins on my legs swelled like puffed strands of rope. But I was grateful for the bounty. This food would keep us on our long journey back to Kanesville.

"No," I told myself. "It's not Kanesville anymore. They call it Council Bluffs now."

Two days after the meat was stored. I felt rested enough to take Val and Ollie to the tithing house. They were busy inspecting a crate of live chickens when the clerk handed me a letter.

I looked at the name of the sender: *Dr. P.D. Terry, Oriental Hotel, San Francisco.* I shoved the letter into my pocket. It was the third letter from Percy, and like the other two, it would go up in smoke unread. I sighed. There was nothing he could write that I would want to read.

On the fourth day of December, I began feeling twinges—my baby was ready to be born. The weekly stagecoach from Salt Lake City was due the next day. Linnie would be on it, but I worried that she wouldn't arrive in time. But my babies were slow in coming, and the following afternoon Linnie hustled through the door as my real labor was beginning.

She kissed me, laid aside her bonnet, and rolled up her sleeves. "Olive, it looks a mite like I got here just in time," she said.

She put the kettle on to heat, then turned to Val. "Hustle to the neighbors. What's their name, Olive—Potter?—and tell Sister Potter to hurry on over. And take your sister with you. Wait there until I send for you t'come back."

Val, wide-eyed, dashed out the door.

I walked to the cupboard and began pulling out the things I'd prepared for the birthing: pads made of clean straw covered with muslin, rags and an old quilt. Linnie came to take the load from me.

"Y'just keep walkin', Olive," she commanded. "The longer y'stay on your feet, the better."

I paced the room several times before Sister Potter came bustling in, wearing a heavy woolen bonnet and wrapped in a horse blanket.

"Sister Potter, this is my dear friend, Sister Bradford."

The words were barely out of my mouth when a pang cut its way down from my hips to my knees. I caught hold of Linnie's arm, bending to endure the hurt. A wave of nausea surged up, and I staggered toward the slop pail. Linnie and Sister Potter supported my pain-wracked body. When the torture passed, they led me to the bed.

"Better rest," Sister Potter said. "You're coming to the hard part."

I slept between pains, and I dreamed that Percy bent over me. His voice came tender and loving. "It will be better soon, Olive darling. Soon—soon."

When I awakened to another convulsion of agony, Linnie was arranging the bedclothes. "It won't be long now, Olive, so you better get straight on the bed."

She wiped my face with a wet cloth. "Y'been through this. Y'know how t'do it."

Her voice encouraged me as I fought the bearing-down misery. "Push, Olive, push."

In my searing agony I could smell the sour odor of Sister Potter's body.

"Percy!" I screamed. "Oh, Percy, Percy!" My voice came from somewhere out in the room.

With one last push, I summoned all my strength for a final, great expulsion from my body.

Sister Potter's cry filtered through a veil of utter exhaustion. "A boy! A fine, healthy boy!"

Linnie crooned over me, and I felt her rough, little hand smooth my brow. "It's over, Olive. It's over, and you done good."

I dropped into oblivion, scarcely conscious of the plaintive wails of my infant.

When I drifted back to awareness, I lay, eyes closed for a long time. There was no sound in the room, no singing of the kettle, no movement, no rustle. It felt so good to rest—just lie quietly and rest.

I opened my eyes. It was night, and on its nail in the corner, the lantern hung, its candle burning steadily. I could see Linnie asleep on Val's bunk.

By my side lay my new son. I took him in my arms and kissed his damp little head. My love was big enough to hold him too.

"I'll call him George," I whispered. "George—for the little brother who promised to come for me when he was big, and who didn't live to grow up."

Tears filled my eyes and rolled down on the pillow. I wept for the little brother, I wept for the new baby whose father was so far away, but most of all, I wept for myself. *So lonely—so terribly lonely—without Percy.*

Chapter 30

I'd hardly finished telling Linnie about my determination to return to Iowa when she threw her arms around me.

"Oh, Olive, let me go with you," she cried. "I come to this part o'the world a'thinkin' Deseret would be like heaven, but for me, it's more near t'hell."

She was perched on the edge of the bed where I lay propped up on pillows. It was late at night, and three-day-old George was a tiny, sleeping bundle at my side.

Suddenly Linnie's good, honest face was lined with pain. "Stephen don't care a hoot and holler 'bout me, never did, and Sister Phoebe is a plague t'me, same as them crickets you and me fought. Seems like it's forever that I've been dreamin' of goin' back and livin' near my sister Lottie. If I can go with you, my dreamin' can come true."

"Linnie dear," I said softly, "I've known right along that you would go with me."

Linnie agreed that our going would have to be kept an absolute secret. "We daren't tell anyone who's still a'breathin'," she said. "With Stephen away on mission and Percy a'leadin' a church emigration, we'd be counted unfaithful wives if'n folks found out."

The penalty for unfaithfulness was death. For a long moment neither of us spoke.

Many disgruntled Saints left the valley, some going

west, some going east, so we decided that one or two more white-topped wagons would go unnoticed.

"I'll get ready the minute I get home," Linnie said. "But you better be tellin' me what all I'll need."

"Can you get a heavy wagon and two teams of oxen, Linnie? We should have two wagons."

"I'll get hold o'one somehow."

"There must be food for five or six months."

"I'll plant early as I can, Olive. Maybe, if things go right, we'll have a passel o'green things."

"We mustn't plan on that, Linnie. Dry food is best, but we'll need barrels. Remember the alkali desert with its poisonous water? We'll need enough barrels to see us across with good water."

"I plumb forgot 'bout that."

I squeezed her hand. "Linnie, we mustn't forget anything. Our lives depend on our being properly equipped."

In the days that followed we tried to think of everything, because no word of our plan dared be written back and forth.

Linnie left a week before Christmas. Our last word of parting was a whisper, our arms about each other, our heads close together.

"See you in the spring, Olive."

"Yes, Linnie, in the spring."

After Linnie left, the weeks melted together in one long stretch of work. I used odd moments to make a patchwork quilt to take as a gift to my mother. I inspected and mended all our blankets, and I dragged out the drilling for the wagon, which had been stored since our trip from Salt Lake City four years ago.

"It's covered with funny spots, Mama," Val said when I unfolded it.

"That's mildew, Val," I told him. "I'll have to put patches under all the bad places."

My unending load of work was brightened by Val's eagerness to help and Ollie's sunny disposition. And George was a beautiful, easy-to-care-for baby, soon chubby and social like Ollie, but with quickly darkening hair and bright blue eyes that marked him as Percy Terry's child.

In April, Brother Potter came with the oxen to plow the ground for my garden. I followed along, hoeing out the furrows. When we finished, I said, "Brother Potter, when you get the plowing done at your place, I'd like to take the oxen to go visit Sister Bradford in the city."

"That's a right smart trip for a woman with three young uns," he said, shaking his head, "but the oxen can be ready when you want them."

In the middle of May, Brother Potter brought the oxen over. "They're lean. Been workin' hard. Better feed 'em some grain and fatten 'em up some."

I brought out oats, and the oxen ate greedily. Then Val helped me hitch them to the wagon, and we drove to the blacksmith shop.

While Brother Turner, the blacksmith, looked over the wagon, I said, "The tires should be reset, the spokes firmed up, and maybe the metal hounds should be replaced. The drilling is here, and I'll be grateful if you'll put it up. Oh, and the oxen need shoes."

Brother Turner said he'd have everything done in three or four days. Then his son drove us home.

"If you'll drop these grain sacks off at the grist mill and pick them up when you bring your wagon, it'll be a real help," I told the boy.

"Seems like you're taking a good load of grain," he commented, hoisting a sack.

"Too much is better than too little," I said, smiling. Already I had many sacks of grain that Brother Potter had taken to the mill for me last autumn.

That night I baked unleavened bread, and I managed a baking every night thereafter. When one batch was out of the oven, another was ready to go in. By morning there were many loaves wrapped in clean cloth and packed in wooden tubs. They would dry out, but they wouldn't spoil.

During the day, I worked in the garden, and Val helped.

"Could I make a scarecrow, Mama?"

I would not reap the harvest of all my labor, but everything must appear as usual. "Yes, Val, put him up. He'll tell the birds to stay away."

One evening Sister Potter came calling. I sat down to visit as though I hadn't a task in the world.

"The stagecoach runs once a week," she said. "Wouldn't that be better'n taking the wagon?"

I smiled pleasantly. "Oh, with three little ones, I think the wagon will be more comfortable."

Each moment she stayed seemed like a week, because not until she left could I continue my packing.

The wagon came back, its wheels sturdy, the black-streaked drilling stretched over the bows. The oxen went on a daily diet of grain, and each day as darkness fell I packed the wagon.

No bed and no cookstove would go, for I needed the room for the grain sacks and all the food I'd take. The rocker father had made would have to be left behind. Rolls of bedding, our clothes packed in bundles, a tub of salted meat, the ham and bacon, packages of jerky, sacks of dried fruit that I'd saved, potatoes, turnips, carrots, all a bit shriveled after the winter's storing but edible when soaked and cooked—everything went into the wagon.

"George shall have a cradle," I said, "right here, behind the seat."

I tied a blanket to either end of the bows, making a little, free-swinging hammock. I lined it with soft pads. "He'll be comfortable in that," I told myself.

I brought out the rifle, the horn of powder, the pouch of bullets, and the ramrod, and conceled them beneath the seat.

Everything was ready, but the night before we left, I was tormented with doubt. I tossed and turned on the bed, half-asleep, half-awake, overwhelmed and frightened by the thought of what I was undertaking.

I thought of Percy. I would never see him again, never until I died. Tears dampened my pillow as I remembered all the beautiful times we'd shared. *But I could not be a plural wife.* And Val might never again see his adored father. *But I wasn't separating them. They were already separated.*

My mind churned, and in those last hours I wavered. Maybe . . . maybe I should stay where I was. Unable to sleep, I arose long before the dawn and went outside. Everything was dark and misty, reflecting my desperation, and I slumped against the door, wishing . . . wishing I knew what to do.

Suddenly a light glowed in the garden as though the oncoming sun cast a gleam far ahead. The light grew brighter, becoming a sphere of unearthly brilliance that hurt my eyes. Frightened, I sunk to my knees. I wanted to cry out, but could not.

Gradually the light dimmed, and in the center of it—almost like a picture—my mother, father, Ted, Dorothy, and all the little ones appeared. Above them floated my little brother George, his arms outstretched, his face smiling. Spellbound, I saw him beckon, and his voice, so well remembered, called, "Come home, Olive. Come home."

The vision faded. Still on my knees, I stared into the

blackness, but now all I could see were the fragile beanpoles that stood like shabby sentinels, guarding the hard clay earth. I rubbed my eyes. The mist was lifting, and the air was warming to the new day.

A radiant happiness surged that washed away all indecision. I was going home.

Chapter 31

I hitched the four oxen to the wagon, and tied Midge, our milk cow, to the rear. I awakened Val and Ollie to a quick breakfast, and I put George in his hammock-cradle.

It was scarcely daylight when I led the oxen to the road, but Brother and Sister Potter arrived in time to see us off.

"I brung some sweetmeats for the young uns," Sister Potter said, "and here's a reticule for you, Sister Olive, made by m'two hands."

Brother Potter shoved his hand toward Val, "I whittled a mite o'scrub oak and filed a smidgen o'steel. It's piddling."

Val beamed. "A bowie! Oh, thank you."

As we drove away, tears dimmed my eyes. They were good people and good friends.

It was fifty-three miles to Salt Lake City, and that day we traveled over ten miles, reaching Provo early in the evening. We camped in a vacant field, and after helping Val tend the oxen and milk the cow, I built a fire and cooked porridge.

"I wish Papa were here to go on the trip with us," Val said.

I looked at him, feeling love and sorrow. "When we get to Salt Lake City, maybe we can stop and see Grandfather and Grandmother Terry before we go on to Aunt Linnie's. Would you like that?" I asked. Maybe a visit with his other relatives would keep him from yearning for Percy.

The more I thought about it, the more it seemed like a good idea. The Terrys now lived on the near side of Salt Lake City, far from Linnie. My stopping there was safe, and it would make my journey seem casual. Also, the Terrys had been good to me. Perhaps it was right to give them a final visit with their grandchildren.

Three days later we arrived at Father Terry's farm on the southern outskirts of Salt Lake City. In the large, sprawling house, he lived with his four wives and many children. Most Mormon men preferred a separate house for each wife, but the Terrys remained together, seeming happy and compatible.

The great joy with which we were greeted made me glad we had come. We were surrounded by eager faces, but Mother Terry's frequent references to Percy ripped my heart.

"Little Percival is much thinner than his father was, but that baby is him all over again. See those bright blue eyes? No one else in the family has eyes like my Percy's."

I smiled, hiding the hurt.

"Percy and Emily stayed with us for two days before they left for California. It worries my heart having him so far off, but in his last letter he sounded busy and more than happy. I guess San Francisco is a wonderful place."

My heart turned to stone.

We stayed with the Terrys two days, but on the first evening I heard something that almost shattered the courage I needed to head east. When we sat down to the evening meal, I asked Aaron's mother about him.

"Why, Aaron is fine as can be," she said, beaming. "He's got two little daughters now, right pretty things.

And when he gets back, he's going to marry Brother Baker's youngest girl.''

I winced, forever hating plural marriage, but my voice was calm. "Where is Aaron?"

"He's on patrol for the valley," Father Terry said. "The federal troops have pulled back now, but with the war in the East getting nasty, there's no telling who and what will be coming our way. Our men are patroling the entire area, and no one's coming in or out without them knowing about it."

I couldn't swallow the soup in my mouth, and suddenly the room was too warm. How could we escape if the valley was under constant surveillance?

I was jolted, but that night, before I fell into a deep, restful sleep, I remembered the beautiful vision. Truly, God was sending me home and had alerted me to this danger. Now it was up to me. Drowsy, I decided that if I were questioned by a scout, I'd say I was traveling between one town and another, going from home to visit my husband's family. In my mind I would map out all the towns in the area. No matter where I was, I could say we were in transit between nearby places. Better not say anything to Linnie . . . do all the talking myself. I fell asleep smiling at the thought of how convincing I'd be.

We visited with the Terrys another day, and after a warm farewell, we moved on across Salt Lake City. I had lived there through years of anguish, and only the final months before we moved to Springville had brought me any happiness. *Percy and I had been reconciled. We had loved each other*. With a deliberate effort, I jerked my attention from thoughts that could only bring me pain.

The oxen clopped on, past the sawmill on the south side of the city, through the familiar streets of Sugar

House Ward, past the sugar house standing tall and gaunt. We traveled on for four miles and then passed the twelve-foot-high wall of mud and stones that marked Temple Square.

As we passed the Bowery with its covered top of green, leafy boughs, I was overcome with a feeling of sadness. Then Val and Ollie called out excitedly as we drew near Brother Brigham's house. It faced South Temple Street and gleamed white in the midst of the slate-colored city. Continuing north, we went toward Ensign Peak, to the gray, mudbrick house where Linnie lived.

The first evening stars shimmered in the sky as we drove into the yard. Linnie came rushing to greet us, and with her came a boy and a young man.

"Olive, you're here. You're here!" Linnie cried. "I'm more'n glad."

I climbed down, George in the crook of my arm, and Linnie threw her arms around me. "I was scared you wouldn't come," she whispered.

I kissed her cheek. "Linnie, I said I'd come and here I am."

Linnie straightened, wiped her eyes on the hem of her apron, and smiled. "Here's my Nathan, Olive."

She pushed the boy forward. He was eight, only a few months older than Val, but he was a much larger child. He had a thin face like his mother, and his hair was dark. Like Val's, his babyhood had been a time of famine. He was a solemn youngster, in many ways similar to Val, and from the first, they were devoted friends.

With a start, I realized the young man had to be Uriah.

"But you can't be," I said aloud, looking at the tall, broad-chested youth who stood at Linnie's side. Only the tightly curled, deep red hair and liberal sprinkling of freckles brought to mind the child I remembered from long ago.

"Uriah, you remember Aunt Olive, don't you?" Linnie said, nudging him.

Blushing, he took the hand I extended.

"Uriah, I wouldn't have known you. You're all grown up."

"Yes'm. I had my thirteenth birthday already. I'll be fourteen come September."

Ollie and Val had climbed down from the wagon and had their part in the introductions.

Before we went into the house, Linnie took us in the back to see her wagon. "Got it from some folks who came to Deseret last year," she said. "It's in right good condition, and I got four oxen too, just like you said."

Her voice turned to a whisper. "If folks come around and see the wagon, I'm saying that when you leave, I'm headin' to Farmington to stay a spell with some relations of Stephen's."

Late that night we made our final plans. "We'd better not leave for another week, Linnie. It'll be the middle of June then, and we won't have to worry about running into deep snows in the mountains."

"D'you notice the size of my Uriah, Olive? He'll be a big help t'us."

I smiled. "I remember he was always big and strong, and now—why, when we first got here, I mistook him for a young man."

"He's a'most as strong as one, but you'll see that yourself, soon as we get going. He can help with the wagons and tendin' the oxen. Nathan and your Val will look after the cows and do the milkin'." Linnie sounded efficient and more spirited than she ever had before. I'd be able to rely on her during the hard months ahead.

We had only one disagreement. Linnie insisted on

taking a huge dresser that had come with her on the trip
west.

"It's big and heavy, Linnie. You mustn't overload
your wagon."

"T'was my mother's, Olive. I got t'take it."

I sighed, reluctant, but with Uriah's help, we lugged
the chest to the wagon.

The day before we left, Linnie picked all the lettuce
in her garden. "It's tiny," she aid, "but we might as
well eat it as leave it behind."

She added vinegar to the grease run-off from fresh
meat that sizzled in the skillet, then poured the mixture
over the lettuce crock. *Wilted lettuce*. It tasted delicious, and it would be a long time before we ate food like
that again.

That night the children slept in the wagons, and as
the sun dipped behind the mountains, I lay on Linnie's
bed without taking my clothes off. George snuggled
against me, and I nursed him until he released my
nipple and belched with satisfaction. I listened to him
coo until I fell into a deep, dreamless sleep.

I awakened at Linnie's touch. "It's been plumb dark
for hours, Olive. It's time to go."

Chapter 32

The grinds and squeaks of the wagon, and the clopping tred of the oxen shattered the middle-of-the-night stillness. In my anxiety, the sounds seemed deafening although in summer wagons moved at all hours, and ours would not draw attention. Clouds drifted across the face of the moon, plunging us into total darkness. I walked with the lead oxen, holding my lantern high.

Linnie's wagon followed close behind mine. She sat rigid on the driver's seat with Uriah at her side.

Linnie had told Uriah our real destination. "I kin trust him," she had explained earlier, "and he was right sure I wasn't doing all that fixin' just so's we could go on a little trip t'Farmington."

In the last days of getting ready, Uriah had secured barrels, piles of heavy chain, tools and a stout pole that could be slung under a wagon as a spare tongue. He was quick-witted, husky and loyal, and it was a comfort to know he was at Linnie's side, ready to help when we needed him.

I walked for the first two or three miles, taking large strides and hurrying the oxen with the goad. In the uncertain moonlight my lantern was needed, and walking eased my tensions. After many months of preparation, we were actually on our way, I kept swallowing, and I could hear the beat of my heart.

Finally we reached the northern side of the city and headed east. I goaded the oxen; we had to hurry.

Moonlight filtered through the clouds as we passed the walled cemetery. The pale headboards cast an eerie glow.

"Pray for us, Sister Sophia," I whispered, looking toward the slope where she and her baby rested. "Ask the Father to guide us safely home."

The road turned south to skirt Big Field where many families were camped. The white tops of the wagons mingled with the night mist that floated like a veil from the mountains to the lake.

We turned northeast, heading for Emigration Canyon four miles away. We had to get through the canyon and to the foot of Little Mountain before daybreak. Up a steady incline, the hardpacked road lay in gentle curves. On the first bench, or level ground above the city, I halted my wagon.

"Stop here, Linnie," I called. "The oxen need to rest."

Suddenly the moon escaped the clouds and shone brightly, giving me a final look at the valley. The city was below us, and far to the west a dim line marked the shore of the lake. The Jordan River and the irrigation canals were pale ribbons in the distance.

"Good-bye, good-bye," I murmured.

I felt grief, as though I stood again beside the dying Sophia, but then all the terror, misery and unhappiness disappeared, and all that remained was a deep, empty ache.

I sighed and turned back to the wagon. I had to ride now as the incline steepened, and the oxen weaved from side to side. Each time we stopped to rest the oxen, Uriah and I jumped down and put rocks behind the wagon wheels to keep them from slipping.

Our progress was slow, and I could see that morning wasn't far away. Rushing water cascading down the side of the road crossed our path at intervals as the road became a narrow shelf between the stream and a high wall of rock. I held my breath as we maneuvered through patches of snow and sharp turns in the road.

Dawn was breaking; I had to find a place to take the wagons off the road. Bushes, dark and threatening, clung to the side of the ravine below, but the slope was becoming more gradual. Far ahead the dark bulk of Little Mountain loomed against the brightening sky.

Hurry. We had to hurry.

Beyond us nestled a little valley with lots of trees and a gentle incline where we could get down. I signaled to Linnie and Uriah, then I awakened Val and Ollie.

"Put on your shoes," I told them. "You'll have to walk until we get the wagons down."

Uriah took my wagon down first and, holding George, I stood with the others and watched as the wagon swayed and rocked down the slope. Dwarf oak, mountain mahogany, balsam, and pine made a heavy cover, and in a few minutes, the wagon was completely hidden. Uriah bounded back, and as he led Linnie's wagon down, we all followed cautiously.

Val and Nathan staked and milked the cow, and Uriah dammed a small stream. "I'm makin' a pool for the oxen to drink better," he said.

We decided not to build a fire. There must be no sign of our presence in the little valley. Linnie brought out a crock of lettuce, Val and Nathan found some wild onions along the stream, and with the fresh bread and the morning's milk we had a good breakfast.

After we ate, we told Val and Nathan our real plans and then explained that we had to be very quiet throughout the day.

They listened wide-eyed as I stressed that we must not be found. "We're not sure, but we think they might take us back and not let us go," I finished.

"Would they kill us, Ma?"

"Oh no, Val," I said, unwilling to terrify them to keep them quiet. "No one would hurt us, but we want to go on, don't we? You want to meet your other grandparents, don't you?"

He nodded solemnly.

We needed a routine. "Uriah must sleep through the day, and you and I will take turns napping, Linnie, because the three of us must be awake through the night."

"What are we goin' t'do with the young uns, Olive?"

"George will sleep a good bit of the time, and when he's awake, Ollie will play with him. That'll keep her busy too."

"What if the baby cries, Olive? Takes on so's we can't stop him?"

In my medicine chest, along with the hartshorn, calomel, quinine, nitric, linseed oil, and ginseng root, was a bottle of laudanum. "I have sleeping liquid, Linnie, but I don't want to use it unless it's necessary."

Uriah went to sleep, and I insisted that Linnie rest too. Val and Nathan played quietly, and I devised a game to keep Ollie occupied. The morning stillness was broken only by the chirps of birds flitting among the trees, and the soft munch-munch of the oxen grazing on the tender green of the bushes.

Suddenly I became aware of his presence. He stood staring at us from under a shabby hat, his eyes squinting in his leathery face, his mouth lost in his long, bushy beard. He cradled a long rifle in his arms, his buckskin jacket bulged over the pistol he carried on one hip, and there was a big bowie knife stuck in his belt.

I jumped to my feet, irrationally thankful that I had not yet shed my skirts.

He stared at me, not speaking. He could be a hunter,

but he looked like a Danite, hell-bent on taking us back. I felt myself go numb with fear.

At last he unlocked his gaze from my face and looked around. "Good camp ya got here."

"It's pleasant," I replied, forcing myself to use the same friendly tone he'd used.

"Here long?"

"Just overnight. We'll be moving along just as soon as our men get back."

"Where they gone?"

I gripped my hands in the folds of my skirt, feeling the nails cut into my palms.

"They're taking a look at the road up the mountain. We're on our way to Echo Canyon Station."

He made no move to go. I wanted to ask him if he was hunting, but the words wouldn't form.

I heard George begin to cry. "I must tend my baby," I said, hurrying toward my wagon.

I climbed over the wheel and gathered George in my arms. Tubs of fresh bread were directly behind his hammock. I hesitated a moment, then took a loaf and climbed down. Nathan, Val, and Ollie had stopped their play and stood staring mutely at the stranger.

I handed him the bread. "Maybe you'll like this since you're far from town."

He rested his gun upright on the ground and bit into the loaf. He chewed slowly, emitting small grunts of pleasure.

"That's good bread, ma'am," he said, "and since you done me right, I'm gonna do you right. The road up that hill is about as steep as you'll find in these parts. Better take one wagon over at a time with all the oxen you got. After ya get over, it's 'bout five miles to Big Canyon Creek Station. Ya better stay clear o' that place. The feller runs it is a mean one. Got seventeen scalps hangin' in his house, they say."

"Thank you," I said, knowing my mention of men returning hadn't fooled him.

He lifted his gun and took another big bite of bread. "God guide ya," he said, plunging into the bushes.

I listened to the cracking of branches and the crunch of his big boots as he disappeared. Then I slumped down beside the children, my legs shaking.

As the sun climbed toward the zenith, I fed the children and settled Ollie down for a nap. I lay down beside her while George, wide awake and playful, sat up between us. I tried to rest but my nerves were taut, and the small sounds of the woods loomed large and threatening.

When the shadows began to lengthen, I awakened Linnie and Uriah. "We must go soon. There's a steep climb ahead, so all the oxen must be hitched to one wagon. It will take two trips to get over the mountain."

I turned to Uriah. "Can you add the extra pole to the wagon?"

"Yes'm, I kin do it," he said.

"Olive, what 'bout you?" Linnie asked. "Did you get any sleep at all?"

"Enough," I answered. My mind was alert, and I was anxious to get moving. I didn't need to sleep.

I helped Uriah add the extra pole to my wagon while Linnie hitched the oxen. We started off with Uriah holding the reins, and Ollie holding George and sitting with me on the high seat. Linnie, Nathan, and Val would wait in our hiding place until Uriah came back with the oxen. The wagon jolted as it lurched over rocks, and when we reached the sharp incline up the road, I asked Uriah to stop.

"I'll walk behind with the children," I said, "and you'd best walk beside the lead oxen. The wagon might tip."

I had removed my skirts, and with Ollie clinging to my bloomers and the baby in my arms, I struggled up the steep slope, slipping, almost falling.

"Mama, I don't like this," wailed Ollie.

"I know," I soothed, "but it'll be better when we get to the top. See, up we go!"

After a few flounders we reached the wagon on the high road. The oxen breathed audibly; their flanks quivered, and we could smell the heavy odor of their sweat.

In the wagon again, we continued our upward climb, and every time we stopped to rest the oxen, Uriah braced the wheels with rocks. It was dark when we reached the summit.

After we rested a few minutes, I helped Uriah chain the wheels, then cautiously we began our descent. The oxen pulled back on their yokes, and I held my breath as the wagon rumbled and rocked.

When we reached level terrain, we hid the wagon in a thick stand of trees, then Uriah started back with the oxen to get Linnie and the others. I watched him disappear into the blackness, then I lay down beside Ollie, aching with weariness.

A shriek of wind and the flapping of the drilling awakened me as a jagged streak of lightning slashed through the wagon. Thunder roared. Ollie screamed, and I took her in my arms.

Rain fell like bullets on the drilling, awakening George who squalled in panic. I picked him up, then sat nestling both children close.

I guessed it to be about midnight, late enough for Uriah to have started back with the second wagon. I shuddered, thinking of Linnie and the boys trying to make it up the mountain while this storm beat on them.

Suddenly water began splashing into the wagon where the drilling was patched for mildew. I put

George next to his sister and hugged them both. "Mama has to get some things moved," I said.

Struggling, I dragged sacks of grain out of the way and piled them as best I could. With rags and a pail, I mopped and wrung, mopped and wrung.

"It's all right, Ollie, hush, George. Mama's right here. Everything will be all right."

The wagon shifted. With a cry, I ran and jumped over the front wheel, landing full length in mud and water.

Scrambling to my feet, I felt about for rocks, frantically gathering all I could hold. I braced them as tightly as I could against the wheels, then I climbed back inside.

I shed my soaking clothes and began mopping and wringing again, as fast as I could.

Gradually the wind died down, and the rain became a drizzle. The drilling sagged above us, heavy with water, but it didn't break. Ollie quieted, and with George at my breast, I leaned wearily against the side of the wagon, letting the chill of the night creep over me.

I slept sitting up, and at dawn I went to peer up the road. *No sign of Linnie's wagon.*

As the day grew warm, I rinsed my muddy clothes in a nearby stream and hung them on a line strung across the wagon. Briskly, I turned sacks of grain so their damp sides would be exposed to the air. I fixed breakfast, then lunch for Ollie and me. I forced myself to remain active, but I could only concentrate on sounds from the road. Val, my precious first-born, Linnie and her two boys could all be dead or lost. Without oxen, I was stranded, helpless. I kept busy, but I truly did not know what to do.

Chapter 33

"Way down upon the Swanee River, far, far away
. . ." I sang loudly, ignoring the cramp around my
heart.

"More, Mama, more," Ollie begged.

I continued singing to entertain Ollie, but as the sun
moved into the western sky, I strained to hear the
rumble of a wagon. They would have reached me by
now unless overtaken by disaster.

Sick with grief and terror, I was still determined
never to go back. I'd stay in hiding for months, as long
as our food lasted. If Linnie's wagon never came,
eventually I'd hail the mail wagon that passed this way.
I'd tell the driver my predicament, and if—if he were a
Mormon . . . .

I heard something in the distance. Holding my breath
I listened. Nothing. Only a hawk wheeling leisurely
overhead. I swallowed hard, but despite Ollie's pleading I couldn't sing another note. Then I heard it again,
closer.

"Yoo-hoo, Olive, yoo-hoo!"

Joyfully, I ran to the road. Linnie's wagon minus its
drilling top was rolling and sliding down the mountain
with Linnie and Uriah stumbling along beside the lead
oxen. Val and Nathan sat on the high seat, shouting.

"We're here! We're here!"

As soon as Linnie's wagon was off the road and
concealed from view, we all started talking at once.

"Are you hurt?"

"Did it storm here?"

"Mama, the mud was so deep, we didn't think we'd ever get through."

"Olive, t'was a miracle happened," Linnie said with finality. "We was plumb played out fightin' the storm and tryin' t'get the wagon up on the road. The drillin' blew off and everythin' got soaked. Uriah was yellin' and proddin' the oxen t'get 'em up the steep place, and the boys and me was pushin' with all our might—and you know what happened? An angel came t'help us. Looked like an old man, but I knew he was an angel the minute he come."

As I helped her unhitch the oxen, Linnie continued: "The angel ran back and forth, first helpin' Uriah with the oxen, then coming t'help me and the boys push. We could never have made it without him, no chance. Most folks don't believe in angels, but when you see one like I did last night, then you got t'believe."

With a feeling of awe I looked at her. "Did . . . did the angel say anything to you?"

"Sure did," she said proudly. "Said to remember that the man at Big Canyon Creek Station was a mean one. And he said Big Mountain's longer, but it ain't so steep as Little Mountain. Told us to take both wagons over at the same time but to rest the oxen every little spell."

"Oh, Linnie," I said, clasping my hands, "a man came to our camp yesterday morning. I gave him a loaf of bread and . . . ."

I stopped abruptly, not wanting to put out the light in her eyes, but she'd been too enraptured to hear me.

"Now I know we're doin' the right thing," she said, "'cause no angel would be helpin' us if'n we were disobeyin' God. I feel a heap better, and I ain't never goin' t'be scared like I was before."

I smiled, and a feeling of peace washed over me. I had my vision; Linnie had her angel. Together we would make it back to Iowa.

Suddenly we heard the rattle of a wagon and the pounding of horses' hooves. Linnie, Val, and I scurried toward the road, crouching low behind the bushes.

A stagecoach with three teams of galloping horses rattled by, its roof covered with runks and mail sacks, its body swaying and bouncing. The horses slowed as they reached the steep grade up Little Mountain, but they didn't stop. Soon all we could see was a cloud of sand swirling in the air.

I took a deep breath. "That's good news. When we cross Big Mountain tonight, we won't have to worry about being seen by the stagecoach driver."

"Tonight?" Linnie gasped as we trudged back to camp. "Seems to me we're all tuckered out and needin' a rest."

I shook my head. "We have to get moving by sundown to make it past Big Canyon Creek Station before daylight."

"But my things are soppin' and the drillin's got t'be put back on the wagon," Linnie said anxiously.

"We'll get everything ready now and then rest. Tonight we're crossing Big Mountain."

My determination motivated everyone to action. We strung Linnie's clothes and bedding on lines inside the wagon, so that when we moved on, they could still hang. The drilling was a problem, though. Soaked, it was too heavy for us to lift over the bows.

"We'll have to spread it out to dry," I aid.

The boys helped us spread it out in a clearing where the sun could hit it. I restaked the oxen so they could have fresh clumps of grass, and then with Ollie resting nearby I sat with my back against a tree and nursed George until he fell asleep, his little mouth rimmed with milk, his tiny fists resting on my breast. With my baby still cradled in my arms, I dozed, suddenly too tired to drag myself back to the wagon.

When I awakened, the sun was behind the mountain and our small valley was in shadows. I moved quickly, getting the little ones settled on the wagon and then calling impatiently to Linnie and the boys. "We have to get the drilling up and move on."

The drilling was dry, but it took much muscle, patience, and puttering to get it over the bows. When we finally had it in place, we tied it down.

Linnie rejoiced. "Sure is a caution what women can do by themselves if they try hard enough. No man's goin' t'believe we done this."

"We believe it, Linnie," I told her.

That night our little wagon train crept past Big Creek Canyon Station after Uriah had inspected the area on foot, making sure our roadway was deserted. Using great caution, we made it safely. Linnie was grateful to her angel; I blessed that loaf of bread.

As we started up the grade at Big Mountain, memories took me back nine years when I'd ridden across in the wagon, my leg in splints. I had been miserable because Percy had just wedded another woman. I grimaced. *It's the same now as it was then.*

The road climbed at a steep angle. We rested the oxen frequently, and at every stop, Val and Nathan helped Linnie, Uriah, and me brace the wheels with rocks. When we finally reached the summit, the oxen were heaving, and all of us puffed and panted. The boys threw themselves on the ground, and Linnie and I slumped down on the side of the road. We couldn't rest long; the sky was already turning gray.

"We must find a place to camp for the day," I said.

We hid the wagons, and the day passed peacefully,

most of us sleeping as much as we could. At nightfall
we made our way down Big Mountain, struggling
against the steep drops and sharp turns. Then we followed a road that wound this way and that, through
streams and meadows, and in the hour before dawn, we
eased our way past another station. In the valley of the
Weber River we went off the road and hid in a nestling
of trees and bushes.

That night—and every night—we traveled, sometimes covering only a few miles. By day we camped,
hidden in the brush, behind rocks, down in a gully,
always out of sight of the road. One day we camped in a
small valley beside a salt spring that Val and Nathan
found interesting.

"Taste it, Mama. It's salty."

I laughed. "Not all the salt water in Utah is in the Salt
Lake, Val, so we have to make sure the oxen don't
drink from that stream."

It took us three days to cover the thirty miles through
Echo Canyon; then we struggled our way past Cache
Cave and Needle Rocks.

In the valley of the Bear River, we encountered a
new enemy. It was a drowsy afternoon. I was nursing
George when suddenly I heard Linnie screaming.

"Olive, there's snakes all 'round the oxen. Big ones,
a whole nest, and the cattle are bawlin' and yankin' on
the stakes. They goin' to run, Olive, what—"

"Take George," I commanded, thrusting my baby
into her arms.

I seized a shovel and dashed toward the oxen. As I
ran, I screamed for Uriah.

The snakes were clustered together, crawling, writhing, coiling and uncoiling, some almost under the feet
of the terrified cattle.

Using the shovel, I began to strike and chop at the

mass of writhing green and black. Uriah came running, the ox goad in his hand. As he hit and slashed, he tried to reassure me.

"They ain't rattlers, Aunt Olive. They're just mountain bird-eaters."

Most of the snakes were slithering away, but the wounded twisted and bled in the grass, driving the oxen further out of control. Throwing the shovel aside, I picked up a chopped snake and whipped it in the air, sending it flying over the stream. I picked up another, a big one, oozing blood, and it took both hands to send it sailing. I threw another, and then another, until the remainder managed to crawl off in the reeds and grass.

As the oxen eased their clamoring, I restaked them. Linnie, still clutching George, was gaping at me, and Uriah, his face twisted into a huge, silly grin, stared too.

"Snakes," Linnie said, wincing. "You was touching them bloody snakes."

Uriah broke into a nervous giggle. "Didn't think no woman could ever do that. Why, Ma don't even like choppin' heads off chickens."

Looking at Uriah, my mind caught a distant memory. I stood transfixed, suddenly seeing him the way he'd been years ago, a fat, husky little boy who didn't like to walk. I remembered carrying him, struggling under his weight, as I went from our wagon train to a distant clump of brush to get Aaron Terry to kill a chicken for me because I couldn't force myself to do it.

Could I really have been that helpless?

I burst out laughing and couldn't stop until tears ran down my cheeks.

Linnie and Uriah thought I'd been struck daft. They hovered around me until some of my self-control returned.

"Uriah," I said, struggling to speak, "when you were a little boy, I packed you in my arms for quite a distance to get a man to kill a hen for me."

Linnie and Uriah exchanged glances, not understanding why that struck me so funny.

I went off to wash myself and change my bloody clothes, still giggling over the memory of that long-ago afternoon, but suddenly my recollections weren't funny anymore. *That was the first time I ever saw Sophia*. She and Aaron had been hiding in the brush, kissing and hugging.

I sighed. She was so pretty and he had loved her so much. And she had loved him too; she's loved all the young men who were smitten with her beauty and charm.

"*All of them*," she had answered when I asked if she had liked any young man especially.

I found myself wondering if Aaron adored his wife the way he had adored the sweet, captivating Sophia. *But if he doesn't love his first wife that much, maybe he will love his second . . . or his third . . . .*

My heart turned to stone, but thinking about Aaron made me remember the Mormon patrol that was keeping the area under surveillance. With all the stresses and strains of traveling, it had all but slipped my mind, but we were finally getting close to Fort Bridger. I'd known right along that this was the area where we'd be in the greatest danger of being caught. There were fewer stations and less activity, a good place to keep check on people entering or leaving the territory.

I reviewed the story I'd tell if I were stopped: *I'm taking the children to visit my husband's family. They haven't ever seen George, and here he is, nearly seven months old already. Meant to come last month, before it got so hot, but I didn't get my garden in on time.*

Lucky my friend was able to come with me. That boy of hers can manage things much better than two women can.

I would be very convincing.

That night's travel was unusually rough, and by morning one of the wheels of Linnie's wagon threatened to give way. The tire was loose and the spokes rattled.

"We can't stop," I said, keeping my voice firm. "We have to move on to the next station to have this wheel repaired."

"But, Olive, what if'n we run on to a Mormon official or even a . . . a Danite?" Linnie's voice was hoarse with fear.

"Oh, we're not apt to run into anyone now," I said, "but we had better get moving."

The oxen, weary from the night's hard journey, plodded slowly. Linnie dozed on the high seat of her wagon, and only my anxiety kept me from sleeping too. I had reassured the others, but not myself. We were traveling in daylight, totally exposed and unprotected. Every inch we traveled might bring us closer to danger.

The air was hot and sticky; annoying insects circled the oxen, and we were an exhausted, disheveled band as we straggled into the station on the bank of Muddy Creek. In a lean-to next to the small log house, I could see a forge and anvil. I sighed with relief; the keeper was a blacksmith.

"The wheel's in mighty bad shape," he said, examining Linnie's wagon, "but I can fit it soon's I get 'round to it."

He inspected the wheels on my wagon. "They're dried out. Should soak 'em in the creek overnight or they'll crack 'most anytime."

"Can you fix the broken wagon now, so it will be ready before it gets dark?"

"Well," he drawled, "it's a hot day, and I wasn't planning—"

I interrupted. "I'll pay you well, but I want the job started immediately."

He shrugged. "Well, I guess," he said.

He's too lazy to be a Mormon, I told myself.

We left Linnie's wagon and took my wagon to the creek to soak the wheels. We moved it out into the water, on a bed of stones, then we unhitched the oxen and led them back to shore.

"Linnie, there are too many mosquitos here," I called, waving my arms around my head. "We'll have to take blankets and food and find a better place."

We moved upstream to a grassy meadow. In the shade of some aspens we laid our blankets on the ground and ate our noonday meal.

"You stay here with the children," I told Linnie, "and I'll go back to watch my wagon."

It was hot and muggy, and as I walked through waist-high grasses, I waved away the bugs that flew at my face. I was nearly to the creek before I looked up. Immediately before me was a man shouldering a rifle. His back was to me, and he faced my wagon. Instinctively, I knew he was a member of the Mormon patrol, but I couldn't take time to be afraid. I took a deep breath and forced myself to smile, all the details of my story vivid in my mind.

"Hello there," I called cheerfully.

He turned around.

My story was useless. He would never believe me.

Chapter 34

"Olive!" His voice was hoarse with wonder.

I stared at him, feeling even more stupid than shocked. I had rehearsed my story until it fell off my tongue with convincing ease, but it had never occurred to me that this could happen.

"I . . . I never expected to see *you*," I murmured.

He looked dazed. "Olive, is this *your* wagon?"

I sighed. "Yes, it's my wagon."

There was silence until I forced myself to speak. "Your father told me you were on patrol."

Aaron and I stared at each other. He was heavier now and handsome, no longer the lanky, winsome young man who had sat beside me on the high seat, driving this same wagon on the way west.

Suddenly we fell into a conversation as casual as if we'd run into each other at the tithing house.

"Heard you had a new baby last Christmas—boy, wasn't it?"

"That's right, little George. And you have two daughters. Your mother told me how pretty they are."

"The little one, Sophie, has golden red hair, about the color of yours."

I stood talking to Percy's brother, exchanging homey, family gossip, but my fingernails dug into my palms and my mind raced. *I couldn't let him take me back.*

He was asking me everyday questions, but I knew his

real questions were still unspoken. In desperation I led him to the point.

"Aaron, I'm sure you're wondering what I'm doing here."

His expression hardened. "Olive, you're more than a hundred miles from home and that wagon looks well stocked."

He suspected the truth, and it wouldn't help to deny it. "I'm taking the children to Iowa to visit my family for a while," I answered calmly.

"You're trying to cross the country with no man and just one wagon?" His voice rang with disbelief.

If I told him about Linnie, it would make things worse, not better. But I had to tell him something.

I turned and walked along the edge of the creek, kicking stones into the water like a carefree child. "My father and brother Ted are waiting for me at Fort Bridger. I expect to reach them before this time tomorrow."

"Why didn't they meet you in Springville?" he asked.

I shrugged. "Two men coming all that way to see me would have made the neighbors and everyone suspicious that they intended to take me home with them." I had never been a liar, but in my desperation, the only truth I knew was that I had to continue my journey.

Aaron shifted his rifle to his other arm. "How did you get this far?"

No man will ever believe we done this. Linnie's words echoed in my mind. She was right, and Aaron would never believe I had traveled a hundred miles without masculine assistance.

"There's an old man who lived in Springville for a while, Willy Ferguson, you may have heard of him. He's not a Mormon, and when I told him I would pay him to take me to Fort Bridger, he agreed.''

I had never heard of a Willy Ferguson. I made up the name as I stood there, but it convinced Aaron.

''We've been traveling for two weeks,'' I continued, ''and yesterday Mr. Ferguson asked me to pay him. I did, and this morning he's gone.''

''You shouldn't have paid him until his job was finished,'' Aaron said solemnly.

''You're right,'' I said, ''but it's just a few miles further and I can make a short distance like that on my own.''

Aaron's voice was harsh. ''Olive, I'm sure you don't have a letter of consent from Percy, so I have to take you back.''

I sat down on the ground, my legs straight in front of me, my hands folded in my lap. My future—maybe my life—was at stake, yet something in me refused to beg.

''Aaron, I will never go back willingly. If you force me—really drag me back against every effort of my own—I'll be judged an unfaithful wife and sentenced to death.''

''That's right,'' Aaron lashed out angrily. ''If anyone else had found you, you'd be in a lot worse trouble than you're in now.''

I didn't tell him that if anyone else had found me, I didn't think I'd be in any trouble at all. Instead, I stared up at him, unflinching. ''But *you* found me, Aaron, and you're the only person in the world who can really understand why I'm leaving.''

''Me?'' he gasped.

''Yes, you,'' I said, my own voice rising. ''You're the one who can understand how I feel about Percy getting married again, because you can remember how horrible it was for me—and for you—when Percy married Sophia.''

So many years later, but this was the first time the words had ever been spoken between us, the first time I'd ever acknowledged that I understood the depth of his feeling for Sophia. And he'd named a daughter Sophie, so that feeling wasn't completely dead.

Without speaking, Aaron sat down on the ground a short distance from me. His rifle rested across his lap and he looked out over the water. "She . . . she married . . . my own brother. I never thought of her . . . that way or . . . or coveted her again."

"But, Aaron," I said softly, "you never stopped loving her."

He turned toward me, his face flushed and the muscles in his neck taut. "You were so good to her when she was sick. Everyone talked about that, and you even had me cut a door in her wall so you could take better care of her."

"She was the sweetest, most truly loving person I ever knew," I told him.

Aaron's eyes glistened. "Did she . . . did she ever say anything about me?"

For the second time in two days I heard an echo of Sophia's girlish voice. *All of them!* She had loved all of the young men who courted her, yet years after she'd been put in her grave, Aaron still yearned to know if she had spoken his name.

His face twisted in pain, and I reached out to him. He was beyond my touch, but I had to say something soothing. "Aaron, when she was ill . . . feverish . . . she told me you had been . . . special to her."

He jumped up and grabbing my arm, he pulled me to my feet. His face was only inches away from mine. "Did she say she loved me?"

God forgive me, I could not look into those pleading eyes and say no. Slowly, in a steady voice, I said,

"Yes, Aaron. Sophia told me that she had loved you very much."

With a groan, he released my arm and turned away. I hurt for him. He still loved Sophia, and whether he had one wife or ten, it meant everything to him to think that she had loved him too.

But my concern for Aaron couldn't blot out the awareness of my own situation. If he tried to take me back, I'd struggle every mile of the way. There would be no doubt in anyone's mind that I had intended to leave Deseret forever. My heart hurt when I thought of my poor children—no father to care for them, and perhaps no mother—but facing death could be no worse than facing a life of unending anguish and loneliness. Tears smarted against my sunburned cheeks, and I was too overcome with weariness and despair to shoo away the gnats that swarmed about me.

Aaron began talking, his face suddenly as expressionless as the stones on the ground. "I'll be gone for at least two hours, Olive. I want you to wait here for me."

Taking great strides, he bounded to where his horse was tethered to a branch of a tree. He mounted swiftly and galloped off, without even glancing back in my direction.

I was stunned, but finally the truth dawned on me. I had answered the question that had tormented him all these years—I'd told him that Sophia had loved him—and in return he was giving me a chance to get away. Precious moments were lost as I stood dumbfounded, watching him disappear into the canyon.

The fatigue that wracked my body vanished, and I became a frenzy of movement and energy. I ran to unstake the oxen, and all alone, I led them into the water and hitched them to the wagon. My soaked skirts clung to my legs as I led the oxen and wagon to dry ground. Then I ran for Linnie, Uriah, and the children.

"We don't have a minute to lose," I shouted. "We must reach Fort Bridger today!"

Linnie, groggy with sleep, reacted slowly, and the children wailed from heat and discomfort. I felt cruel prodding them to action, but I had no choice. Aaron had let me go because he was distraught, but when he came to his senses, he'd come after us. We might have only two hours; we might have only two minutes. We had to make the most of it.

The children and Linnie rode in the wagon as we headed back to the station. The stationmaster had actually begun work on Linnie's wheel, but his slow movements and lack of interest made the job threaten to take forever.

"Please, please," I begged, "I'll pay you twice the amount I promised, but hurry. Please hurry."

I was drenched in sweat and too frantic to rest while he finished the job, but at last he declared the wheel ready to go.

"Can't say as how long it'll last, but it'll be good for a while, anyways."

"Thank you," I said, paying him.

"Olive," Linnie called, "we're needing our rest and so's the oxen. In a few hours it'll be sundown. If we wait—"

"We can't wait, Linnie," I said sternly. "We have to get to Fort Bridger." I didn't dare tell her about Aaron, but my manner alerted them to the fact that something serious was wrong. Without another complaint we headed for the road.

I walked with my lead oxen. They were tired and needed constant prodding to keep moving. Behind me Uriah struggled constantly to keep his oxen trudging. He was big and strong, but still only a boy. It was a cruel strain for him to work so hard after so little rest, but at any moment Aaron might appear to force us back. At Fort Bridger we'd be safe because Aaron believed my father and brother waited for me there. He wouldn't oppose my father or initiate a pursuit that might result in a battle in which the innocent mught be injured.

As I battled fatigue and heat, my mind wandered. Dazed, I kept envisioning Sophia, smiling, happy, clapping her hands in glee. I had asked her to intercede for us, to ask God to see us safely home, and she had heard. She was happy now, because it was Aaron's love for her that had blessed us on our way.

"Thank you, Sister Sophia," I murmured. "Thank you. We'll make it. We'll keep going and we'll make it."

George cried from hunger, but I couldn't stop to nurse him. "I'm sorry, George," I cried, running and stumbling in the dust of the road.

The sun sank behind the mountains. We trudged on in ever deepening shadows. By the last light of day, we saw the flag flying atop Fort Bridger.

"We made it," I cried, tears running down my cheeks. "We made it."

Little Ollie called to me, "Are we there, Mama? Is this Ioway?"

My heart stopped. How could I tell her that Fort Bridger marked only the beginning of our journey?

Chapter 35

I looked down at my endowment garment and wondered what to do. It had been over six years since I had
been baptized and endowed, and never once had I
completely removed the white underwear that sym-
bolized my acceptance into the Mormon Church. When
I bathed or changed clothes, I always kept an arm or leg
in one endowment garment until I had an arm or leg in
the fresh garment. But now the garment I had on was
dirty, and the others were soaking in the washtub,
together with my bloomers splotched with snake's
blood, my dresses, and other underthings soiled from
the mud and dust of travel.

When we arrived at Fort Bridger the previous night,
we had set up camp by a running stream where a natural
dam formed a sparkling blue pool amid a seclusion of
tall trees and thick brush. I wanted to bathe; I wanted to
rid myself of grime and tension, but if I wore my
endowment garment into the pool, I would not have a
clean one to don when I came out.

I sighed. Surely the God Who was big enough to
have made the world could not be small enough to mind
my taking a much needed bath and washing my clothes.
I removed the garment, tossed it into the tub, and
wrapped myself in a piece of toweling. Then I gathered
my good dress, my soaps and hairbrush, and after
checking to make certain I was unobserved, I climbed
out of the wagon and ran to the pool.

At first the water felt too cold, but after I splashed about for a few minutes, it was wonderfully refreshing.

George was asleep in his hammock-cradle, and Linnie had taken Ollie and the boys to the fort's general store. I had given each child a coin, and I knew that the wonder of shopping would keep them busy for quite a while. I was alone, and it was a rare and luxurious moment.

After a while I washed my hair, soaping it several times to get it truly clean. Then—reluctantly—I climbed out of the water. Quickly I dabbed myself with a towel, then I put on my dress. With nothing underneath, it clung to my still damp body, but I didn't care. No one could see me.

Tucking the skirt under me, I sat down on a large, flat rock that jettied over the water. With long, smooth strokes I brushed my hair that dried to form deep curls that hung below my shoulders. My weary feet dangled in the stream. I had walked so many miles—there were so many miles yet to go—but for these few minutes I wiggled my toes and felt the soothing waters wash over the blisters.

"Good afternoon, ma'am."

I jumped to my feet, but was immediately sorry I'd done so. My dress clung to my breasts, to my legs, to all of me, outlining my body as clearly as if I had nothing on at all, and before me stood a soldier in the uniform of the Union Army. I felt myself blush as I wondered how long he had been close by.

"I'm Sergeant Robert Madison. I'm sorry to disturb you, ma'am, but Captain Sellers sent me to speak to your husband."

I laid my arms across my body, discreetly trying to hide myself, but Sergeant Madison's gaze was clearly fastened to some point above and beyond me. To my increased embarrassment, he would not look my way. He already knew I was not fit to be seen.

"Go tell your captain my husband isn't with us," I said, trying to get rid of him quickly.

"Well, ma'am, then I'll speak to your father or any man who's with your party."

"There is no man. We have a young boy, that's all."

His eyes widened and he allowed himself to look directly at me. "You mean you're traveling *alone*?"

"No," I said. "I'm not alone. A friend and our children are with me."

He shifted the rifle he carried and cleared his throat. "Then I guess I'd better give *you* the message."

"Please do," I said sharply.

"Captain Sellers says—suggests—that you move down nearer the stockade. Tomorrow's the Fourth of July, and—"

"The Fourth of July!" I exclaimed. "Why, we've been traveling eighteen days and covered only a hundred and sixteen miles."

He smiled. "If you've come from Salt Lake City, I'd say you did well to make it over those roads in so little time."

Then he asked, "Are you going on East?"

When I hesitated, he spoke up quickly. "Ma'am, Captain Sellers didn't order me to ask questions, just to suggest that you move closer. There'll be celebrating tomorrow—a dress parade, and we're firing the cannon. All the Indians around will come in to watch, and some of them—the Arapajos especially—are terrible thieves. They'll steal everything you've got."

"Thank you for telling me," I said primly. "We'll move down before dark."

Stiff and correct, he turned on his heel and marched off toward the fort.

Even after he left, I felt weak and angry from embarrassment. My exposing myself had been the most ill-advised thing I'd ever done. My only comfort was the thought that with any luck, I'd never see Sergeant Madison again.

I rinsed my soaking clothes in the creek, hung them on lines strung in the sun, then hurried back to my wagon. The captain of the fort knew we were here, so we weren't as secluded as I had thought. I wouldn't leave the wagon again until I was respectably dressed.

When Linnie and the children returned, I told them we had to relocate. "But not until my clothes are dry," I added.

Later our little caravan moved to within sight of the stockade, and the moment we were situated, I sent Nathan and Val to find wood for the first fire we dared to build since we left Salt Lake City.

Linnie immediately set to work mixing a batter of pancakes. "They'll sure taste good for supper," she said.

"They will, Linnie," I told her. "And after we eat, I'm going to boil George's bottom cloths. Rinsing in cold water isn't enough. I've already had to dust burned flour on him because he looks so sore."

With an upside-down tub for a table, we all sat on the ground and enjoyed a hearty supper of Linnie's pancakes, the first hot food we'd eaten on the trip.

While we were eating, Linnie told me her bad news. "Olive, I talked t'the blacksmith, but he don't have a wheel t'fit my wagon. He's got t'build one for me, but he says tomorrow he's not goin' t'work."

"Oh, Linnie," I cried, "I planned for us to leave late tomorrow night after everyone's asleep."

"I figured that, Olive, but we daren't go without a new wheel for my wagon."

"That's true," I said, wiping my hands on a towel. "You mind the children, Linnie. I'll go talk to him."

I found the blacksmith hard at work, pounding out oxen half-shoes, his hammer ringing and clanging.

"I'm with the lady who needs a new wheel for her wagon," I told him when he paused to talk to me. "We're grateful for your willingness to make a wheel for us, and it would be wonderful if you could finish it in time for us to leave tomorrow night."

He shook his head, but I hurried on. "We're traveling with two very young children, my little girl and baby boy. So far, they've kept well, but you know how it is with little ones. Traveling is hard for them, and sickness comes fast. Every single day counts. Will you help us?"

He picked up his tongs and lifted the half-shoe into the fire of the forge. Pumping the bellows, he made the fire leap up, hot and blazing. I thought he was ignoring me, but when he turned around he said, "Well, since you put it that way, I guess I can do it. The wood's got to soak for a while, and maybe I can get the tire pounded out tonight. Ought to have it ready by tomorrow evening."

"Oh, thank you, sir. Thank you," I repeated. "I'll bring the wagon over first thing in the morning."

That night I lay down, finally unmindful of every noise and stirring of the wind. Until now my awareness of all the dangers we faced had made true sleep almost impossible for me. I'd learned to catch snatches of rest, but anxiously, always with my ears cocked, ready to return to alertness at any second. But encircled by the fort, we were safe from pursuing Mormons, from the Danites, from unfriendly Indians and from prowling bears and wolves. When I closed my eyes, I tumbled into a deep, untroubled sleep.

At dawn we were awakened by the bugle. Linnie quickly whipped together another batter of pancakes, and just as we began to eat, Sergeant Robert Madison appeared. He was wearing buckskin pants and a fringed jacket.

"Excuse me, ma'am. Captain Sellers agrees that it's best for a man to stay with your party today. The Indians are already here looking to be fed and not much escapes their eyes. If you don't mind, I'll just be your guest today."

When I answered him, I hoped I wasn't blushing too noticeably. "Sergeant Madison, under the circumstances, you're welcome to stay."

Then I added, "This is my friend, Mrs. Bradford, and I'm Olive Terry." It startled me to realize I hadn't called myself *Mrs. Percival Terry,* but Percy seemed so far away, so eternally separated from me that it seemed wrong to call myself by his name.

Linnie offered Sergeant Madison a plate of pancakes. "If you're goin' t'stay with us, you got t'eat with us," she said.

He laughed and accepted the plate. "Mighty kind of you, ma'am."

When Sergeant Madison joined us at our makeshift table, Val and Nathan scooted close to him.

"Tell us about the army," Val begged. "Are you going to fight Indians or are you going to fight in the north and south war?"

Sergeant Madison smiled at my young son. "To tell you the truth," he said slowly, "I won't fight anywhere if I can avoid it."

"Don't you *want* to fight?" Nathan sounded as shocked as Val looked.

The sergeant shrugged. "Well, boys, I figure we're

all going to die someday anyway, so why hurry it up by shooting guns at each other."

His answer startled me too. "Sergeant, if that's how you feel, why did you join the army?"

He looked cautiously at the children. "I was married, ma-am. Our boy would be four years old now, but there was a diphtheria epidemic. He and his mother were both lost."

His steady voice did not ask for sympathy, but my heart went out to him. "I'm very sorry, Sergeant," I said.

Her eyes glistening, Linnie heaped more pancakes on his plate.

"Afterward it seemed best for me to get away," he continued. "President Lincoln had just issued his call for volunteers, so—here I am until the end of the war."

Feeling his grief, my embarrassment faded, and I was able to really look at him. He appeared younger than thirty, and a lock of sandy colored hair hung down on his sun-scorched forehead. He smiled easily, but a faraway expression dominated his light blue eyes.

If he does fight, he'll be a good soldier, I thought.

Despite his size and ruggedness, he took an unembarrassed delight in playing with the children. Val and Nathan never left his side, and Ollie even let him hold her on his lap.

Uriah took Linnie's wagon to the blacksmith. When he returned, he told us that people were already gathering to watch the parade. Linnie and all the children were eager to join the crowd, but I wanted to stay with my wagon.

"I'll stay and watch your wagon, Aunt Olive," Uriah offered.

I gave him a quick hug. "No, you go with the others.

I've seen lots of parades, so I don't feel bad about missing this one.''

Before Val left, it pleased me to see him give Sergeant Madison a sugar stick obtained during yesterday's visit to the general store.

"I'll stay with your mother, Val," the sergeant said. "When you and young Nathan come back, you can tell us about all the festivities."

After I nursed George in the privacy of the wagon, Sergeant Madison asked if he could hold him. I handed George cautiously, he wasn't used to strangers, but it was becoming apparent that Sergeant Madison had a way with little ones.

"Babies this age sure are a splendor," he said, hoisting my smiling, cooing son into the air, "but they get big awful fast."

I sighed, thinking of the long journey still ahead of us. "They do indeed, Sergeant, and it hurts me to have George spend so much of his babyhood bouncing across country in a wagon."

"Where are you going, ma'am?" he asked.

This man was clearly no threat, and I answered honestly: "To my family in Council Bluffs, Iowa."

Neither of us spoke for a few minutes. Then Sergeant Madison asked, "Olive, *why* are you going?"

I had just finished hanging George's bottom cloths on a line strung between the wagon and a tree branch. With my hands on my hips, I stared at him. His question was direct, but not prying, and I yearned to talk to someone.

I sat down on the grass, a short distance from him. "I'm leaving my husband. He's a Mormon and believes in plural marriage. I don't," I said crisply.

Sergeant Madison nodded. "I had a hunch it was something like that. A woman like you—well, a person can tell you wouldn't be hightailing it without good reason.''

"My husband's a good man," I said slowly, "but according to his religion there isn't anything wrong with having . . . more than one wife."

"Olive, how many wives does he have?"

"One . . . other," I said brokenly. "There was another, but she died years ago."

Madison's voice was harsh. "That's a plain sin," he said, repeating the very words my mother had uttered so long ago. "Of course I knew the Mormons practiced polygamy, but—*my God*—a man married to a woman like you and lucky enough to have such sweet young ones and all . . . . They must be terrible people."

"No, Sergeant Madison, the Mormons are not terrible people," I said firmly. I had lived among the Mormons and I had loved them. They still deserved my loyalty and honesty.

"They are wonderful people, religious, hardworking, and eager to be happy. And many Mormon women accept plural marriage, but I cannot."

A group of Indians lounged nearby. They stared at us and were clearly interested in the wagon, but they never came too close, thanks to the sergeant's presence. I felt tremendously grateful to him, and to my amazement, I found myself telling him how I decided to return to my family after Percy left for California. I described our escape from Salt Lake City, and I felt an unexpected swell of pride as I explained how we traveled by night and hid by day.

He was easy to talk to. He showed an honest interest, but no pity, and he was calm until I told him of my encounter with Aaron.

"When you leave this fort, he can overtake you anytime," Sergeant Madison said, his voice rising.

"It's too dangerous for you to continue, but if—"

I interrupted. "Sergeant, I *must* continue."

He shook his head. "I wish I could help you."

I smiled. "You are helping me."

The cannon boomed. In Sergeant Madison's arms, George's whole body trembled; he puckered to cry.

"Big noise, huh?" Sergeant Madison said soothingly. He snuggled the baby closer to him and began a long stream of cheerful chatter.

George looked dubious, but even when the cannon sounded again, he did not cry.

"Boom! Boom!" Laughing, the sergeant imitated the noise of the cannon, and he coaxed a smile from the baby.

With a start I realized that this was the first time a man had ever held or played with George. His own father had yet to see him.

Sergeant Robert Madison had a good face, not handsome, but intelligent and cheerful. *But,* I thought, *his eyes are not as blue as Percy's.*

Suddenly I felt baffled, wondering why I was comparing this man to Percy.

Chapter 36

Taking advantage of our fire, I cooked a dinner of ham and vegetables, and while the dried fruit was soaking, I stirred up a hoecake. I expected a hungry, cheerful group to return from the parade, but when I caught sight of Linnie, tears were running down her cheeks.

"Linnie," I called, hurrying to her, "what happened? What's wrong?"

"He says I can no way take it with me, but I gotta even if he says I shouldn't."

I had no idea what she was talking about, but she broke into sobs and was unable to say another word.

Uriah kicked at the ground. "The blacksmith put the new wheel on our wagon, but he says the hull's a'breakin' under the weight of grandma's dresser. Says it's gotta come off, or the wagon won't last another fifty miles."

At Uriah's report, Linnie let out another deep sob.

I grieved for her, but it was no time to be tender. I put my hands on her shoulders and shook her. "Linnie, life is worth more than a dresser. It has to be left here, because we cannot risk your wagon breaking down."

"My poor dead mother—I'll walk, Olive, every step of the way. That'll make the load lighter."

"But the wagon is breaking under the dresser," I said sternly. "It has to be left behind."

247

I turned away to hide my own tears, shed not for the dresser but for Linnie.

Sergeant Madison spoke, coaxing Linnie almost the way he'd coaxed George. "Come on, Linnie. Don't cry. I'll go see Captain Sellers, and I bet you can leave your dresser with him. When the war is over, I'll be heading East, and I promise to bring it to you if I possibly can."

"S'mighty kind of you," Linnie said, sniffling.

Robert Madison went to see Captain Sellers who consented to the dresser's being stored in his quarters. "We can leave the dresser with Captain Sellers when we bring Linnie's wagon back here," he told us, "but we'd best wait until after dark when the Indians are gathered around their fires."

With Sergeant Madison still lounging near our wagon, I climbed inside and slept. I hadn't told him, but at night we would slip out of Fort Bridger and continue on our way.

Long after the bugle sounded taps, I climbed out of the wagon. Stars brightened the sky, and a breeze rippled the leaves on the trees. The rhythmic steps of the sentries thudded faintly.

Uriah and Linnie brought the oxen, and quietly we yoked them to the wagon. I checked the sleeping children; then we led the oxen up the slope from the fort and started down the long road.

We wound our way through a valley, along a stream where willows grew, forming a dark maze that bathed us in shadows. Well rested, the oxen stepped faster than usual, and I knew we were making good time.

At daybreak we came to a swift stream. I decided to ford it at once and not wait until dark. Uriah waded through, checking, and he declared it to be shallow with a solid bottom. We led the wagons through, and then, deep in the cottonwoods, we found a place to hide. Val and Nathan took the oxen to water them and stake them out in a clearing with bunchgrass.

Suddenly Val came running, breathless and almost incoherent. "Mama, we're near an Indian camp," he panted. "It's like a town of stick houses, and not far away there's a big pile of old wagons."

I froze for a moment, almost too frightened to think. "Get Uriah," I gasped. "He's over there in the bushes. Get the oxen. Hurry!"

Dragging at the hackamores of the oxen, Val and Nathan returned to our hiding place. Uriah came too, and we huddled everything together. We couldn't continue until protected by the black of night, and we couldn't recross the stream and put ourselves in view of any Indian who came to draw water.

"We'll have to stay here all day," I said, my voice a nervous whisper. "We must maintain absolute quiet, and we must trust in God to protect us."

Linnie looked ashen—I'm certain I did too—and Uriah giggled nervously.

Val's face was stark with fear, and a trembling Nathan put his arms around Linnie's waist. They were both trying to be brave, but our danger made me realize what young children they really were.

They were all so dear to me, and if they were massacred by the Indians—even if I died too—I would be responsible for their deaths. The journey to Iowa had first been my dream and my plan. They wouldn't be here if it wasn't for me, and now I had to do everything—everything—to see them to safety.

As quietly as we could, we gave the oxen and cow water from the barrels and plenty of grain. If they were

well fed, they'd be less apt to moo and stir around.
Then we sat on the ground, without attempting to fix
breakfast.

When Ollie and George awakened, her happy chatter
and his small wail made me know that today I had to get
the laudanum from the medicine chest.

It hurt me to give laudanum to such tiny children, but
our lives were threatened. The Indians might be
friendly, but Val's report of old wagons was ominous.
Tears running down my cheeks, I put a few drops of
laudanum in Ollie's cup of milk. Then I put the drug on
a bit of sugar that I gave to George after he nursed.

Time dragged, and the children remained alert and
noisier than usual.

"Ollie, you must be very, very quiet," I begged.

"Mama, it's hot in the wagon," she said fretfully.
"I want to get down."

"You must stay in the wagon," I said, fear making
my voice stern.

"No, no," she shouted.

She had chosen the worse possible time to display
her high spirits, and never had her voice sounded so
loud. Her tantrum was arousing George too, and his
playful gurgles soon became angry cries.

Desperate, I reached for the laudanum bottle again,
and this time I gave them each a larger dose than I had
before. Then I held them both, whispering and soothing, until their eyelids drooped and their heads lolled.

I put George in his cradle and eased Ollie onto her
sad little bed. Then I handed the gun and pouch out to
Linnie. I took a pan of beef jerky, then silently lowered
myself to the ground. The five of us—Linnie, Uriah,
the boys, and I—sat huddled together, sometimes
chewing the tough jerky, sometimes holding hands in
silent prayer.

Our day of terror passed slowly, minute by minute. The chirping of the birds came to a halt in the broiling heat of the day. Then all was quiet except for an occasional call or voice from the Indian village. One time, when an Indian voice sounded close, Val buried his face in my lap.

The boys wiggled in uncomfortable fear. Again and again I dried my wet face on my apron.

Suddenly we listened in fresh terror as we heard something cutting its way toward us through the bushes. Linnie thrust out her chin in solemn defiance and slipped her arms around her sons.

I gave Val a swift embrace, then stood up with the gun loaded and cocked in my hands.

A voice grew nearer with every crunch of underbrush. Listening, I thought I was losing my mind when I realized the voice was calling *me*.

"Olive! Olive!"

"Answer, Olive!" Linnie cried joyfully. "Maybe it's God!"

The call came again. "Ol-leeve!"

"I'm . . . I'm over here." I tried to shout, but my voice was faint.

"Over here!" Linnie yelled, and the boys, nearly out of their minds, echoed her call.

A crashing of brush, and then—before my unbelieving eyes—Robert Madison broke through.

"Whoa, Olive, don't shoot. It's me, Robert."

He took the gun out of my trembling hands. "Sure glad I wasn't an enemy, Olive. You'd have blown me from here back to Bridger." Even in my dazed state, I realized he sounded proud of me.

Following him was a troop of soldiers who led horses and carried rifles.

My quiet Val jumped for joy, and Nathan's usually

somber expression had been replaced with a huge grin. Uriah was giggling from relief just as earlier he'd giggled from anxiety, and Linnie looked almost as joyful as if she had truly found herself in the presence of God.

"When I realized you were gone, I got Captain Sellers's permission to lead a squad of ten men to find you and accompany you on your way," Robert said. Then he added, his voice low, "You *could* have told me you were going."

"How . . . how did you find us?" I asked.

"It wasn't easy," he answered, "because you covered more miles than I thought possible. When we came to the stream, I was ready to turn back until I saw your tracks leading into the water."

We urgently wanted to move on, and the soldiers helped hitch the oxen to the wagons. With Sergeant Madison beside me on the high seat, we headed back to the road.

I thanked God for sending the soldiers to rescue us. I wanted to thank Sergeant Madison too, but what words can hold the gratitude you feel toward the man who has saved your dearest ones from the threat of death?

Three soldiers rode ahead and three rode behind us, and a pair kept pace at either side. I felt secure even when I realized that the road lay directly through the Indian camp. As we passed, all the men, women, and children came out to stand motionless, watching us, but only the faces of the children revealed their interest. Sergeant Madison lifted a hand in greeting, and the Indians responded with the barest movement of their heads.

"We'll not return this way," he said, "so they won't know you've gone on alone."

"How far can you go with us?" I asked.

"It's about eighteen or twenty miles to the turn of the Black Forks. We'll leave you there. You'll be about twenty-five miles from Green River, and you should make that in a couple of days."

Green River marked the boundary of Deseret. After we crossed, we'd be in the Indian country called Wyoming. There'd be no further danger of the Danites finding us and taking us back. Then only the Indians and the desert would threaten us with death.

Chapter 37

When we came to the banks of the Black Fork River, we made camp.

"Sergeant Madison, we can eat supper here," I said, "but if your men are willing, I'd like to go on tonight. After the cattle eat and rest a while, I think they're good for another few miles."

He put his hands on his hips and laughed. "Olive, *you'll* be ready to continue, but us human folk and the animals need to sleep now and then."

Still grinning he said, "What do you say we leave at daybreak?"

I started to object, then realized he was right. Hard miles lay ahead, and we would travel better if we weren't tired.

But if we needed rest, my little ones needed to wake up. When Sergeant Madison joined the other soldiers, I sat in the wagon beside Ollie, holding George in my lap. I called them both by name, I patted their cheeks and finally shook them. Ollie sighed faintly; the baby barely moved, then they continued their deep, drugged slumber.

With tears in my eyes, I kissed my baby, tucked him in his hammock and went to help Linnie prepare supper. Soldiers helped the boys build a fire while we cooked ham and made pancakes. I poured and turned dozens of pancakes for the children and hungry soldiers, but I couldn't swallow anything. My babies were still sleeping; they'd gone all day without food. My anxiety grew worse with every minute.

After supper Val and Nathan went right to sleep, and Linnie and I cleaned up the supper things.

"It sure's been a wonder of a day," Linnie said, yawning. "First them Indians right next door to us, and then the soldiers coming t'save us." She yawned again. "A wonder of a day."

"You and Uriah go to bed," I said. "I'll finish up here."

She managed a few words of protest, but I shooed her and Uriah off to their wagon. Hastily, I finished cleaning up.

The soldiers had made camp a short distance from us. Their fire blazed, and I could hear their voices and laughter when I climbed into my wagon.

I picked up George and cradled him close. I put my nipple in his mouth and a trickle of milk flowed, but he didn't swallow. I waited, hoping his little gums would clamp down eagerly, but nothing happened. My tears were falling when I put him back in his hammock.

"Ollie, Ollie dear, you must wake up." I turned to my little girl, shaking her and becoming violent in my anxiety.

"Mama," she moaned.

I got a bowl of hasty pudding and a cup of milk and began spooning food to her. "Please, Ollie, please," I begged.

Her mouth opened in response to my coaxing, and sip by sip I got food into her. She was groggy, but awake.

I lifted George and tried again to get him to nurse. He still would not respond, and his little head rolled helplessly when I tried to sit him up. Desperate, I ran to Linnie's wagon, clutching George in my arms. The soldiers' fire no longer burned, and my cries shattered the night quiet.

"Linnie, my baby won't wake up. I'm afraid, Linnie—help me . . . help me . . . ."

Linnie's answer was immediate and alert. "Olive, let me get my candle lit so's I can have a look at him."

As I climbed into her wagon, she took my baby. She tried to awaken him, but in the flickering light of the candle, his face looked white and still. I pulled him back into my arms and pressed my ear to his chest. I couldn't hear a heartbeat.

"Get Sergeant Madison," I choked. "Run!"

Linnie jumped over the side of the wagon, but agonized moments passed before Sergeant Madison appeared.

"It's the laudanum," I cried. "I gave him too much and I killed him." Sobbing, I clung to my little son.

Robert Madison had to pry my arms loose to take George from me. Holding him, he pressed George's wrist between his fingers. "I get a pulse," he said, "but it's very weak. We had better put him in warm water."

Linnie called out, "The fire's smoldering. I'll get it blazing and set up the kettle."

When the water in the kettle was warm, Linnie poured it into the tub, and we immersed the baby, clothes and all. Robert held the baby in his big, sun-browned hands, and in contrast, George looked ghastly white. Linnie added warmer water, and the sergeant supported George with one arm and slowly massaged his chest. Suddenly George's face puckered, and one tiny hand raised in the water.

Robert let out a loud whoop, and Linnie shouted, "Praise the Lord!"

"I'll get his blankets and dry clothes," I said, joy swirling through me.

Later, holding the baby to my breast, his small mouth worked with only the barest tip of his nose and chin showing out of the blanket. My tears rolled down. I'd never give him laudanum again, no matter what happened.

Linnie and Sergeant Madison laughed aloud as they watched the baby nurse.

"Olive and me knew 'bout a warm soak for spasms, but we didn't think 'bout it for this," Linnie said.

I looked up at Robert. "I'll never forget that you saved my baby."

He patted George's blanket and smiled, but his voice sounded hollow. "It'll be a comfort remembering I helped this baby, because when my own boy sickened, there was nothing I could do for him."

With my free hand I touched his arm, my feelings too deep for words. Twice in one day this man had saved us from disaster, and I wished there was something I could do to ease his pain.

And Linnie too—joy rendered her plain face beautiful, and she hugged me. "Olive, if it ain't one thing bad, it's something worse, but God has his eye on us." She sighed. "I'm goin' t'say a big prayer of thanks first thing in the morning', but now I got t'get some sleep."

As she staggered toward her wagon, her voice grew fainter. "Hope . . . hope nothin' else happens before sun up."

Sergeant Madison chuckled. "She's a good woman." Then he added, "If you'll take no offense, I'd like to spend the night in your wagon. We can take turns watching George to make sure nothing goes wrong."

"There's not much room," I answered, "but you can clear a place behind his cradle."

I wanted to stay awake in case the children needed me, but the moment I settled down, I sank into a deep, exhausted sleep. The last thing I heard was Robert talking to the baby and soothing a fretful Ollie.

It was barely daybreak when Linnie called at my wagon: "How's that baby this mornin', Olive? Is he a'right?"

Yawning, I poked my head out the drilling, and Robert answered, holding George up for Linnie to see. "He's awake and hungry. He's going to be fine."

"Goodness . . . oh my . . . well . . ." Linnie stammered.

She was embarrassed because she realized Robert had spent the night in my wagon. She hurried off in dismay, but later, when we were fixing breakfast, she slipped her arm around my waist. "I know t'was all right for the Sergeant to stay in your wagon. He was just a'helpin' you, and way out here, folks will never find out 'bout it. And I'm your best friend. I'll never tell."

I hugged her, but didn't answer. Time was when I would have been horrified to spend a night with a man and no other adult, but I was no longer that childish. Robert was my friend; he had helped me. That was all, and I didn't care what anyone thought, not even Linnie.

The soldiers milked the cows and tended the oxen, so this one precious time Nathan and Val were allowed to sleep late. Whenever they awakened, they could eat breakfast on the trail.

I rode on the high seat beside Sergeant Madison, and little Olive sat between us or played in the wagon. George remained in my arms because I couldn't bear to put him down. Through the quiet of the morning we rode in comfortable silence, but as the sun moved overhead, we talked.

I told him about the man who found our camp and who came back later to help Linnie and the boys in the storm.

Robert chuckled. "Sounds exactly like old Bridger

himself. He's Brigham Young's mortal enemy, and he'd be glad to help women leave Salt Lake."

He paused a moment, then asked, "Olive, are you ever going *back* to Salt Lake?"

I sighed. "No, I'll never return to Deseret."

"Or to your husband?" he asked sharply.

I shook my head. "I . . . I don't know. He has another wife now, so marriage between us is impossible. But I still love him. I'll always love him . . . ." My voice faded.

"We'd better walk a ways," Robert said abruptly. "The jogging of the wagon gets very tiresome."

We walked by the leaders, and I let Robert carry George as we trudged along for a mile or so.

Two soldiers rode off to hunt, and in the later afternoon they caught up with us, carrying a large deer. It was the first fresh meat we'd had in a long time, and that night we all feasted. The bread was no longer fresh, but I spread it with our precious chokeberry jam to the delight of the soldiers and boys. The soldiers jerked the leftover meat, because fresh meat would spoil in the intense, daytime heat.

Late that night Robert Madison came to my wagon after I had lain down. "Tomorrow we'll reach the turn of Black Forks where my men and I have to turn back," he said.

I sat up and raised the drilling so we could talk, but he paced back and forth the length of the wagon. "I can't sleep worrying about you—all alone and traveling nearly a thousand miles across rough, dangerous country. I can't let you do it. You have to go back to the fort with us. I'll be discharged when the war is over, and then I'll see that you get home safely."

Before I could answer, he continued: "Your husband doesn't deserve you, running off like that with another woman, and maybe someday you'll change your mind about him. Believe me, Olive, it would be a joy to me to take care of you and your children—to marry you—but now the important thing is your safety." He stopped pacing and turned toward me, but his face was hidden in shadows.

I didn't know what to say. His offer of protection and marriage stirred me deeply. I was overwhelmed with gratitude, but there was no decision to make. "Oh, Robert, I have to continue, and with God's help, we'll make it through safely. And . . . and no matter what my husband has done, I could never marry anyone else."

I reached out my hand to him. "But God bless you, Robert, and thank you."

He took my hand in his, and I felt the warmth and strength of his grip. Then, without another word, he strode off.

Early the next morning, the men brought buckets and tubs of water from the river to fill our barrels and kegs. We'd carried small amounts of water in each receptacle to keep the staves damp, but now everything had to be rinsed and filled to the top. For the next two days we would travel through waterless country.

"Get to Green River in daylight," Robert said sternly, "because the fareman puts up at night. He'll charge you two dollars a wagon. Fill your barrels at Green River. You're heading into two hundred miles of desert, but there are stage stations and wells every twenty-five miles. Fill your barrels every chance you get so you won't be caught short on a dry stretch. And don't let your cattle touch the alkali water. It's poison."

Then the soldiers gathered around and sang for us: "*The Arkansas Traveler,*" "*Frog Went A-Courting,*"

and *"She'll be Comin' Round the Mountain."* The
boys grinned and Ollie clapped her hands. My own
hands were clenched together under my apron, and I
struggled to keep tears out of my eyes.

Then Sergeant Madison and his soldiers mounted,
and waving good-bye, they rode off. We watched until
the cloud of dust they raised disappeared in the morning
sunlight.

Linnie and I looked at each other, and my empty
feeling was reflected in her eyes.

I sighed. "The cattle are rested, maybe we should go
on a few miles."

With the oxen yoked, we drove into the morning sun,
headed for Green River. The land on either side of us
stretched far in an emptiness broken only by clumps of
sagebrush and rocks. I felt exposed traveling in daylight without an escort of soldiers.

When it was time to rest, we pulled the wagons
behind two large rocks.

"I'll get the wheels greased today," Linnie said.
"Usin' the tar will help lighten the wagon."

The oxen nibbled at the sagebrush, but it was evident
they didn't like it. I got out half-buckets of grain for
them.

I heard a horse approaching, and looking to the east,
I saw the swirl of dust it raised. I started to hide, then
paused. When I discerned the rider, I raised my hand
over my head, hurrying to within full view of the road.

Robert reined his horse and dismounted at my side.
"I put Private Radmaker in charge of the other troops.
I'm going on with you."

I was torn between joy for us and anxiety for him.
"Robert, you don't have the captain's permission to
continue with us. You'll be disobeying orders."

"I know," Robert said briskly, "but there are times

when a man can't obey orders. Sometimes a man has to think for himself.''

Suddenly from across the years, I could hear Percy's voice: *Olive, we do not make decisions when counsel is given. We obey.*

Tears misted my eyes, and I wondered what my life would have been like if Percy had ever thought for himself.

Chapter 38

"Tindy! It's Tindy!" Ollie shouted gleefully.

Tindy was her own name for Robert, and I could neither figure out why she called him that nor persuade her to call him anything more respectful.

Awakened by the commotion, Linnie, Uriah and the younger boys gathered around joyfully.

"Sergeant Madison, are you goin' the rest of the way with us?" Nathan's usually somber face shone with hope.

Robert rumpled his hair. "Yes, I am, Nathan," he answered. Then glancing at me, he said, "Providing, of course, your Aunt Olive will let me."

I winced, not wanting to be responsible for so heavy a decision, but Linnie answered, "Olive and me both bid you welcome t'travel with us a'far's we're goin'." Blushing slightly she added: "I'll make you up a bunk with Uriah here. You kin sleep with him."

She was telling him to stay away from my wagon, but though she was concerned, I was not. I had a good feeling about Robert, and I knew there were no hidden motives to his offer to come with us.

Robert agreed that we should continue to travel by night and hide by day. "But you don't want a soldier traveling with you," he said. He went behind my wagon to change his clothes, and when he reappeared, he was wearing a plain shirt, and buckskin pants.

The sun was descending the western sky, and Robert helped yoke the oxen, tied up the cow, then secured the drilling on both wagons. Everything was ready much quicker than usual, and we were all in a cheerful mood when we headed for the trail.

The road was rough, but with Robert holding the reins and whistling an army tune, the traveling seemed easy. Later he drove Linnie's wagon for a distance, allowing Uriah to get some unaccustomed rest.

Two mornings later we arrived at the Green River, the boundary between Deseret and the Wyoming territory. The fareman was a fierce-looking creature who was certain we were Saints abandoning the faith.

"Don't like to see Mormons a-hightailing it back East," he growled. "Y'know, Brother Brigham don't have much use for apostates." He stared at Robert. "And I think the men who run off should be tarred and feathered."

"Don't order out any tar for me," Robert responded cheerfully. "I'm on my way to Denver to handle some important mining deals. Thought I'd take two of my wives with me, but all my other wives are waiting for me back in Salt Lake City."

Suddenly Robert grinned from ear to ear. "I'm proud to tell you I have more than twenty children."

The fareman's manner changed to deference. He scurried down the slope to help Uriah guide Linnie's wagon onto the flatboat. We watched the boat slowly cross the river, and at last we saw Linnie's wagon swaying up the bank on the other side. When the flatboat returned, the fareman scurried around, doing everything he could for us. Robert had really impressed him.

As soon as we were clear of the river, we found a sheltered place and set up camp for the day. Robert built a fire while Linnie and I fixed breakfast, but all three of us kept breaking down and laughing, thinking about the fareman.

"Not twenty children," Linnie chortled. "He's got *more* than twenty children. I guess he's got more'n he can count."

"And, Linnie, they're all girls," Robert responded, "but I don't suppose any of them will ever make pancakes as good as yours."

"D'you really have a pack o'wives and more'n twenty children?" Uriah asked, his bright red hair almost standing on end.

Linnie howled and I laughed until I could hardly catch my breath.

"No, I don't, son," Robert said, patting poor Uriah on the shoulder. "Fact is, you folks are about all the family I have."

Robert seemed like family to all of us. Linnie and I both liked him; the children adored him. That's why I decided he had to go back.

After we ate, I asked him for his army shirt. I washed it in the tub, then hung it to dry. When the others settled down for their rest, I told Robert we had to talk.

"What's wrong?" he asked.

"You . . . you're what's wrong," I answered. "You can't risk everything coming with us. You have to go back to Fort Bridger."

"No, Olive," Robert began, "I've made up my mind—"

I didn't let him continue. "Robert, if you go on with us, you'll be one of those soldiers who leave the army during wartime."

"A deserter," Robert said softly.

"Well, aren't deserters . . . I mean, well, don't they punish them?"

"If they get caught, they get shot," Robert said flatly.

I shuddered. "I don't want that to happen to you. I won't travel another mile until you leave us and head back to the fort."

We stood exposed in sunlight, barren country all around us. His hands were on his hips; my arms were crossed in front of me.

Suddenly Robert's arms dropped to his sides. "I know you mean that, Olive, and there's no arguing with you."

"That's right," I said firmly.

I walked over and felt a sleeve of Robert's army shirt. It was still damp, and while we waited for the shirt to dry, I packed his saddlebag with food.

"You'd best leave while the others are sleeping," I said.

Robert's voice was low. "Say good-bye to them for me."

He left dressed like a soldier of the Union Army, but before he went, he drew several maps for me. "Take the road to Fort Steele and Fort Halleck. You'll be safer going that way," he said.

His horse was saddled, and he took the reins and began leading her to the road. Suddenly he grabbed me by the arm and pulled me along with him. When we were clear of the wagons, he turned and embraced me. Before I could protest, his lips were firm against mine. He held me tight, and I didn't think to struggle.

When he released me, my eyes were closed.

"Olive, you remind me of my wife," he said, lifting my chin so he could look at me. "You've got her kind of spirit, and I admire you more than I know how to say. Scares hell out of me thinking of you going so far alone, but if there's a woman on earth who can make it—if any *person* can get through with so little help—it's you."

Then he made me promise to write him as soon as I reached Council Bluffs. "I'll be thinking of you every minute," he said, "and waiting to hear that you're safe."

He mounted his horse, rode a short distance then turned to wave good-bye. I waved vigorously, but Robert had all but disappeared behind a mist of tears. He had defied orders to help me, a woman he'd met by chance and to whom he owed nothing. He was a true friend, and from my heart I wished him well. I knew that when he reached the fort, he might be in trouble for having been gone so long, but I smiled, knowing he was man enough to take any punishment meted out to him.

When I heard Linnie stirring, I went to tell her that Robert had returned to Fort Bridger. She was clearly exasperated.

"Olive, he was a powerful help to us, and if'n you'd called me a'fore he left, I'd a'helped you talk him into stayin'. I'd a'made him more o'those pancakes he hankers for, and . . . well, tell the truth, it ain't none o'my business where he sleeps."

My spirits lifted. "Oh, Linnie," I said, laughing, "he didn't leave because he couldn't sleep in my wagon. He left because I didn't want him shot as a deserter. He was risking his life to come with us."

Linnie sighed. "Well, I guess that's true," she agreed, "and sure would be a hateful thing for a man like him t'be shot."

Later I told Val and Nathan, and it broke my heart to see their sad faces. But at least they could understand *why* I had sent Robert back. Ollie could not understand,

and she could not be consoled for the loss of her Tindy.

Uriah was brave: "If the Sergeant ain't here to help me, I better get hustlin' right now," he said briskly.

As darkness spread over the land, our mournful little group took to the long road east. The oxen seemed sluggish, and we crawled along, covering only a few miles before it was time to hide again.

The boys staked the oxen and milked the cow, we ate breakfast and then settled down to rest. I lay in the wagon alongside Ollie, with George at my breast still nursing.

In minutes I fell sound asleep. I awakened to an unfamiliar sound, and looking up, I caught a glimpse of a tall figure walked just outside my wagon. Easing free of George, I closed my bodice.

"Robert!" I called eagerly.

I jumped over the front wheel of the wagon. I spun around, and with a knife thrust of fear, I found myself surrounded by three Indian braves.

Chapter 39

A shred of sanity warned me I didn't dare panic everyone, and I struggled against the wild screams that rose in my throat. I gasped and my legs trembled, but I managed to remain standing and reasonably silent.

The Indians drew away from me, but after a few moments, one inched forward. Gingerly, he lifted the drilling and peered into the wagon, I grew faint, thinking of Ollie and George asleep inside, but I was grateful that Val was out of sight, resting on the ground a short distance away with Uriah and Nathan.

"What do you want?" I asked, knowing they couldn't understand, but hoping my voice sounded firm enough to threaten them.

The Indian at the wagon turned to me, and suddenly his face changed. He seemed startled. I didn't know what he was looking at until he reached over and touched my hair. Gently, he pulled a few strands between his fingers, eyeing them strangely.

At his touch I panicked, and I had to fight down another scream when I realized what intrigued him.

It's the color. He'd probably never seen red-gold hair before. As he stroked the top of my hair, I stood rigid, unable to breathe. Then he said something to his companions that set one of them giggling, a youthful sound.

I looked at them again—really looked at them—and I realized they were quite young. Small splashes of paint brightened their foreheads and cheeks, but their faces were the faces of boys, not men. They were about fifteen years old, sixteen at most. One held a stone-headed hatchet; another had a small spear. I could see no other weapons, and I began to have hope.

They know we are traveling without men. I felt certain they had observed us for a long time, they knew we were only two women and a few children, no threat to them, and they had come to investigate.

I heard a trembling voice behind me. "Don't be a'feared, Olive. I'm comin'."

The ox-goad shook in her hands, her face was whiter than death, but Linnie was marching to my aid.

"Drop the goad, Linnie," I said sharply.

It was impossible for us to fight our way out of this. We had to cooperate . . . and hope.

The goad hit the ground, and the Indian closest to Linnie picked it up.

"*Imp-bar-ar,*" he said.

Suddenly I had a mental picture of Leah quizzically examining a metal spoon, the smoothing iron, a candle holder—the dozen of things that were strange to her.

"*Imp-bar-ar,*" she would say. *What is this?*

These young Indians spoke Shoshoni. They belonged to the same tribe as Leah.

I struggled to remember that afternoon, so many years ago, when Percy had come home with Leah trudging behind him, little Shokup tied to her back. She'd been completely exhausted, and they had both been close to starvation. Percy had explained that they'd been brought to Salt Lake City from the Wyoming territory, nearly two hundred miles away. Now we were in the Wyoming territory, her country, confronting her people.

I took a deep breath, then calmly touched the ox-goad the young Indian still clutched in his hand. "Ox-goad," I said.

I pointed to where the oxen were staked, then nodding, I swung my hand, demonstrating the use of the goad as I had demonstrated the use of so many things to Leah.

He pondered a moment, then swung the goad in the direction of the oxen. He smiled. He had understood.

I heard a familiar hissing sound, and I knew it was Uriah trying to get my attention, but the Indians heard him too. Two of them crept behind some huge rocks, and after a terrifying moment of squawls and hollers, they returned, dragging a shrieking, fighting Uriah between them. He was almost a match for them, and the third Indian raised his hatchet.

Linnie lunged toward her boy, but I caught her skirt and held her back. "Shut up, Uriah," I ordered. "Stop fighting or we'll all be killed."

It was a moment before Uriah gave up the struggle, but at last he lay on the ground, limp and quiet. Linnie jerked away from me and ran to kneel at his side.

"I'm all right, Ma," I heard him murmur, "and we better do like Olive says."

George began crying and Ollie peered out of the wagon. I expected her to start screaming, but she didn't.

"Where did these Indians come from, Mama?" she asked cheerfully.

"They're Indian friends," I said, forcing myself to smile.

My smile froze when I realized that the Indian who had studied my hair was now looking at Uriah's rich red curls that shown brilliant in the sunlight. The Indian was clearly fascinated.

"Stay 'way from me," Uriah blurted out.

Linnie folded up like a flag when the wind stops blowing. She had fainted, and I knew her thoughts had been the same as mine. *That Indian is thinking Uriah's hair would make an elegant scalp.*

Blackness threatened to engulf me too, but I was determined against it. I wasn't ready to give up.

Making no attempt to assist Linnie, I folded my hands in front of me and stood perfectly erect. In a loud, steady voice I said, *"Ar-ver bar Letakoni? Ar' ver bar Shokup?"*

All three Indians wheeled and looked at me, and I smiled. *"Ar-ver bar Letakoni? Ar-ver bar Shokup?"* I repeated. *Where is Letakoni? Where is Shokup?*

They began a rapid talking among themselves, and although I listened intently, I could not understand.

The tallest of the Indians rushed up to me, and with his face close to mine, he spoke long and earnestly. I understood a few words, not enough to get his meaning, but I acted as if I did.

"Od-ah, ar-ver bar, Letakoni?" I intoned slowly.

He reared like a startled deer. Then the three of them huddled, talking too rapidly for me to understand a word.

They seemed to be arguing, and the two taller, older Indians pointed their fingers at the third. He was probably not yet grown to his full height, and in comparison to his two lean tribesmen, he looked almost plump. There was still a roundness to his face, but his expression was wary. He did not like what he was being told.

He began an easy run toward the brush, but after a few strides, he stopped and looked back. The tall Indian shouted, sounding angry, and then his tribe brother began running again and soon disappeared.

I didn't know what was happening, but I was determined not to act frightened. With all the stateliness I could manage, I walked to the keg on the back of my wagon and drew a dipper of water. I carried it to Linnie who was sitting up but moaning.

"Here, Linnie, drink this," I said, "and then move out of the sun. But don't go where they can't see you."

Exposing my breast so the Indians would know my intent, I climbed in my wagon and picked up George. I sat where they could see me and nursed my baby.

I studied them, and soon realized they were as nervous as we were. There were only two of them now, against three of us, and glancing down I could see the rifle a short distance from my feet. I could put the baby in his cradle, then snatch up the rifle. If I shot straight, I could kill one before either could do anything . . . and there would be three of us to take care of the survivor.

But they were boys. They hadn't really harmed us, and I didn't want to kill them.

Everytime Uriah moved or spoke, the Indians were ready to pounce on him. His movements were cautious though, and he spoke only once.

"I made Val and Nate go aways from here and hide," he said softly. "Told them if anything happened, they was t'head to the Green River."

I was afraid to answer—I didn't want them to think we were plotting—but I yearned to tell him he was the most unselfish boy I had ever known.

As the sun inched its way into the western sky, the Indians seemed restless. They were waiting for something, but I dared not think what.

Suddenly I had an inspiration. Tucking George into his cradle, I picked up the tin tub. I held it so it mirrored the rays of the sun, then I flashed it in their direction. They whooped and covered their eyes. They were alarmed, but then I laughed and held the tub out to them. One strode over and took it out of my hand. He examined it solemnly, then he held it up so it would reflect the sun in the tall Indian's eyes. Then, unexpectedly, he giggled.

The tension eased. Moving slowly, I got bread and venison jerky to offer them, but they were busy playing with the tub. They were no longer watching Uriah. Their attention was completely diverted, and I guess mine was too. I didn't hear the other Indians approaching.

It was a man's voice, deep and authoritative. Everyone jumped. I gathered my little ones to me, Linnie moaned painfully, and the tub clattered to the ground.

An Indian chief walked boldly into our midst, and a short distance away I saw several other Indians on horseback. He spoke to the two youths who seemed to nearly dance in fear. Our own danger had increased, but we were no more terrified than they.

Suddenly the two young Indians shot off, running as if pursued by a herd of buffalo. Then, slowly, the Indian chief turned around and inspected us for the first time.

I blinked, not really believing, but it was true. He was Leah's husband.

We stared at each other. His expression barely changed, but I knew he recognized me.

"Letakoni," I said, pointing at him cautiously.

He gave a barely perceptible nod, then slowly walked around examining our wagons. Then, with an expansive wave of his arms, he spoke, I tried, but could not understand him.

He strode toward his horse and the other Indians. He was leaving.

"Wait! Wait!" I shouted. I scrambled to the back of the wagon and started searching frantically. I found what I wanted, folded neatly and wrapped in an old sheet. I jumped out of the wagon, almost falling on my face, but I chased after him.

When he turned to me, I held out the patchwork quilt I'd made for my mother.

"For Letakoni," I said.

He stared for a moment, then accepted my offering. Moments later he and the other Indians rode off.

I sunk to my knees, sobbing, overcome by the fear and tension I'd held so tight within me.

"Let's get out of here," Linnie gasped.

I couldn't speak for a long time, but when I did, I assured her we didn't have to leave. "They won't be back, Linnie," I managed between sobs. "I'm sure of it. And we'd best stay here all night. I'm tired . . . too tired to travel a single mile."

Val and Nathan appeared, tearstained and trembling. Their ordeal had been long and painful too.

It was Linnie who finally fixed something for us to eat. "You have to keep up your strength," she said, urging me to swallow a few bites.

We all huddled together, still shaken, and only Ollie seemed unaffected by what had happened.

"Where did the Indians go?" she asked brightly.

"T'where they come from, I expect," Linnie declared, "and if they was t'have stayed one minute more, I think I'd o'plain died."

"Linnie, they were Shoshoni, and the chief was Leah's husband. You remember, the Indian woman who worked for me in Salt Lake City."

They all gasped. "Did he know you, Aunt Olive?" Nathan asked. "Is that why they didn't kill us?"

"He knew me," I said, "but I don't know that they ever intended to kill us."

"Them two was more scared of him than I was o'them," Uriah said triumphantly.

I nodded. "I think so, Uriah, and I think they'll be in

deep trouble when they get back to their village. There
were only three of them; they weren't well armed, and
even though we're only two women and a boy, *we
might have killed them.*"

"D'you think they was just boys gettin' into more
mischief than they could handle?" Linnie asked.

"It looks that way now, Linnie," I said. "When I
talked to them in Shoshoni and mentioned Letakoni and
Shokup, they didn't know what to do, so they sent for
help."

"S'pect they could of killed us and no one would of
knowed," Uriah said thoughtfully.

"They didn't, Uriah," I answered. "Thank God,
they didn't."

We all agreed it was time to try and get some sleep,
and my whole body ached with weariness when I
climbed into the wagon and snuggled close to my
children.

At daybreak I arose, well rested and planning to
leave early, even though it meant abandoning our shelter of darkness.

As I went to call Linnie and Uriah, I saw a large
covered bowl near the front wheel of my wagon. It was
made of baked clay and decorated with colored paint-
ings of flowers atop slender, curling stems.

Lifting the lid, I caught a fragrance that brought back
memories of long ago. The bowl was filled with the
kind of herbs Leah had used to make the tea I had
learned to like. I was momentarily bewildered, then I
realized the bowl was a gift from Leah. One of her
tribesmen had delivered it while we slept.

I closed my eyes, and warm memories of her friendship and loyalty washed over me. Joyfully, I realized
she was alive and back with her people, and in my heart
I felt she was happy. I would use the herbs to make tea,

and I would cherish the bowl forever. Then, returning to the moment, I realized that the bowl had to be hidden in my wagon. I didn't want the others to know we had had another Indian visitor during the night.

A short time later we all assembled to eat a cold, nervous breakfast.

"They could be watching us this minute," Linnie said, glancing furtively toward some of the giant rocks that dotted the country.

"Leah's husband is a gentleman—an Indian gentleman—and neither he nor his people will harm us," I insisted.

Linnie and the boys were determined to move on as quickly as possible, and they yoked the oxen and tended Midge faster than I had ever seen them do it before. We pushed on, and the oxen, fresh after a restful night, moved at a good pace.

We were approaching a sharp bend in the trail when Linnie cried out, "I knew they was watching us!"

I looked back. Beyond her wagon, on a rise of ground, were two Indians on horseback. I knew immediately that one Indian was Leah's husband, but the other . . . .

I held my hand above my eyes to shield them from the sunlight. The second Indian was smaller, a youth.

"Val, Val, wake up," I called urgently.

Val had fallen back to sleep in our wagon. Still drowsy, he crawled out to join me on the high seat.

"Climb down," I urged.

Without halting the oxen, I followed Val to the ground.

"Wave," I told Val, pointing toward the Indians. "It's Shokup, and he saved your life when you were a baby."

Waving, Val and I walked backward to keep pace

with the oxen. I knew they would not come closer, but Shokup's arm was above his head. He was waving to us.

The oxen started around a bend in the road that descended into a gully. In a moment Shokup and his father would be lost from view. Val and I waved wildly, and so did Shokup. Then, in the last second before they disappeared from view, Leah's husband raised his hand in salute.

Chapter 40

That day I traveled with an easy heart—if danger had lain ahead, Leah's husband would have known and warned me—but our progress was agonizingly slow. The road rose and fell in twists and turns, and it was pockmarked with rocks and chuckholes. By afternoon the oxen had slowed to a crawl, and we made camp behind a formation of huge boulders and strange, unearthly rocks.

I dipped water from the barrels for the oxen while Val milked the cow.

"Not much milk this time," he told me.

"Did you strip her dry, Val?" I asked, examining the half-empty pail.

He shrugged. "Just like I always do," he said.

The long trip was beginning to tell on Midge.

Later, when I nursed George, he fussed. He'd suck a few seconds, then release the nipple and cry. For weeks my own supply of milk had been diminishing. Like Midge, I was succumbing to the hardships of the trip.

I took a tin cup, filled it from Midge's pail and held it to George's lips. Coaxing patiently, I got him to sip. If my milk failed, at least Midge still had enough for one small baby.

We didn't dare stay in camp too long, because in this waterless country every mile counted. As night fell, we pushed on. We inched our way, wearing from the struggle, but the first rays of light revealed that the terrain hadn't changed at all. The land we crossed was still barren and rocky in all directions.

After we made camp, I tried again to nurse George, but he cried and squirmed, then sat up stiff and angry in my arms. I got a cup of Midge's milk and held it to his mouth, and this time he drank greedily. A constant trickle was lost down his chin, but his loud slurping assured me that most of the milk was going into my baby.

Leaning against the wagon wheel, I fell asleep holding George in my arms, but I awakened when the drilling on the wagon began to flap and crackle. I stood up, but could barely hold my balance against the force of the wind.

Linnie climbed down from her wagon and came toward me, her dress billowing. "The wind's terrible. Never saw it blow so hard," she cried out.

"Linnie," I shouted, "it's getting dark already. *My God,* we've slept all day!"

Here we had no boulders to guard us; we were so exposed we decided to go on.

"Maybe it'll be better down the road some," Linnie yelled.

"Don't see how it could get much worse," I answered.

Bracing ourselves against the wind, Linnie, Uriah and I yoked and chained the oxen. When we started, the wind pushed us along, and the oxen could hardly move fast enough to keep the wagons off their heels.

"Uriah, set the brakes and get by the leaders. I'll drive." The wind ripped the words from my mouth.

Suddenly the dark seemed ominous. It wasn't night descending. It was a sandstorm coming.

The wind blasted and roared, then sand pelted, filling my eyes, ears and throat. I didn't dare open the drilling to check Ollie and George, but I knew sand was blowing its way into the wagon.

We rocked on through clouds of grit. We could no longer see, and time was meaningless. I wasn't even certain we were still on the road. We could be lost and wandering the barren waste of desert. The wagon continued to lurch and jog, and I thought it would fall apart. But the wind pushed us onward. We couldn't stop or take refuge in a gully.

It seemed as if hours passed, but then the wind gave one final wail, then settled down, still blowing, but no longer on a rampage.

I checked the children. Ollie held George, and they were both coated with sand.

"I took care of George," Ollie said, "but I thought we were going to blow away. And I don't like this sandy stuff on me." She spit hard, trying to get the sand out of her mouth.

"You were a brave girl," I said, brushing her off, "and I'll get you some water."

The pitcher on the wagon had sloshed nearly empty, so climbing down, I went around to the back. I was eager to check Midge too, to see how she had endured the storm, but I couldn't see her familiar outline. I rushed to feel. The plank that supported two barrels of water had been torn away. My hands touched a broken strut. The barrels—and Midge—were gone.

With a cry, I ran to Linnie. "The cow's gone!"

Linnie hurried to my wagon to feel the struts that had held the plank. "She got so scared she yanked off the whole back," Linnie said.

"We've got to find her," I cried. "She's food for Ollie, and George has to have milk."

It was truly night now. The air was still heavy with grit, and we couldn't see anything. Anxiety tore

through me, but there was nothing I could do. I took a
little of Linnie's water for Ollie, than I climbed into my
wagon and waited for daylight.

With the first graying of the sky, Linnie and I un-
yoked and staked the oxen. Then we dipped water from
one of Linnie's barrels into buckets. "It may be two
days before we reach Almond Station," I said, "and
with my water gone, we have to ration every drop of
yours."

Linnie moaned pitifully. "Oh, Olive, it shames me
to be telling you this—but I only got one barrel o'water.
My wagon's been a'creakin' and a'groanin' so bad that
yesterday mornin' I emptied a barrel to lighten my
load." She burst into tears.

A wave of nausea swept over me. We were seven
human beings and eight oxen with less than a barrel of
water to last us for two days of travel over the desert. I
wanted to cry with Linnie, but somehow I knew I had
nothing to waste, not even tears.

We gave each ox a half bucket of water. They all
drank greedily, but they made no move to look for
food. They bunched together as close as their tethers
would allow and kept their heads down.

I looked around, trying to decide how to begin the
search for Midge and the barrels. The sun was rising, a
huge orange ball that rested in a brown, hazy sky. The
wind had ceased, not even a breeze stirred, but all
around everything looked an eerie, yellowish-brown.
We were still on the road, but there were no tracks, no
guidelines. The cow could be anywhere.

Linnie stayed at the wagons with George and Ollie,
and Uriah, Val, Nathan, and I began the search.

"We'll walk west, the way we came," I said briskly.
"We'll keep about fifteen to twenty feet apart, so we
can see over a wider area."

We began trudging, but I knew from the first it was hopeless. I should have given up right away, while we still had our strength, but I couldn't. My breasts were nearly dry, and without Midge, there was no food for George. He could starve and without my water barrels we could all die of thirst.

We plowed through deep sand, stepping around sagebrush and greasewood. We were hot and dry, and my voice croaked everytime I called out: "Midge! Midge!"

"I'm thirsty, Ma," Val said, his voice a whisper.

I laid a hand on his shoulder and looked down the road. Its emptiness numbed me. The boys flopped on the ground, and Uriah looked at me, his eyes haunted, his face grimy and streaked.

"We'll go back," I said.

One part of me cried out I was giving up too soon, but the other part, the saner part, told me our search was useless.

Suddenly Uriah cried out, "I see something down there."

He pointed, and we all looked, our thirst and fatigue forgotten.

We hurried in the direction of Uriah's find. A dark object lay on the sand, one of the missing barrels, and beside it, scattered all about, lay the staves of the second barrel. Uriah rolled the barrel over. It was empty, and I couldn't bare to look at Val and Nathan.

"She must a'got loose 'bout here," Uriah said.

We spread out, frantically calling and searching, but time passed, and we found no trace of her. It was midday. The water was wasted; the cow might never be found. We had to return to the wagons and head for Almond Station.

At the wagon Uriah and the boys each had a small

drink of water, and Linnie and I drank buttermilk from the churning keg. It was full of sand, and everyone else refused to touch it after the first sip. I gave George water, then let him try my empty breast. He screamed from hunger and heat, but there was nothing I could do for him.

To further lighten her load, we put Linnie's barrel of water in my wagon, carrying it so carefully it barely sloshed. Then we moved on, inching eastward through the blazing desert.

At night we watered the oxen, but this time each animal received only half the morning's ration. I didn't plan to water them again until we reached the station, because the remaining water had to be saved for us.

"We must go on," I told Uriah. "We don't dare stop for anything."

But at dawn we had to stop to rest the oxen. I looked all around, anxious for some sign of human habitation, but the road went up and down through an endless stretch of nothing.

The oxen were worn out, but after a short rest, we had to prod them on. They moved slowly and unwillingly. Close to midday, they stopped. Uriah and I shouted and goaded, but to no avail. They would not budge. Then, almost in unison, they gave a gutteral moan, an unearthly wail that tore through the desert stillness. I'd never heard such a sound before.

Oh, God, I prayed, *don't let it be their death call.*

Uriah and I took a small pan. The water was so low in the barrel it terrified me, but we gave a panful to each ox. Again Uriah prodded; the poor beasts dragged onward, but they stopped frequently.

At one stop Linnie came to my wagon. "I got t'have water, Olive," she said. "Nathan and Val too. They're crying."

"There's barely enough left for my babies, Linnie."

"Uriah and Nathan are *my* babies, Olive."

We looked at each other, then I said, "Get cups."

We poured the last of the water into a pitcher, then carefully I dribbled it into seven cups. Linnie took her cup and drank it slowly, holding each sip in her mouth before swallowing. Then she took two cups to her wagon for Val and Nathan.

I called Uriah, and his anguished eyes riveted on the cup of water I handed him. His lips were so swollen, he had difficulty swallowing. Then he croaked, "I'll get them oxen movin'."

Carefully I poured my share of water back in the pitcher, and I added the water from the children's cups. I'd make it last as long as I could.

The wagon wheels turned slowly. The sun beat down hot and stifling, and I could feel my tongue grow large in my mouth. Up ahead by the leaders, I saw Uriah stagger as he walked.

He staggered again and fell, face down. The oxen stopped, and I clambered over the wheel and ran to him. He opened his eyes. I helped him sit up, but his whole body shook.

"Come," I whispered, but the word had no sound.

Linnie came running, and together we got him to his feet and helped him into the wagon. I looked at the water in the pitcher and thought of Ollie and George. He had just started to cry, and Ollie, coated with dust and grime, was saying, "Please, Mama, I want some water."

I shuddered, but resolutely poured the remaining water into a cup and held it to Uriah's mouth. Drop by drop, he managed to swallow.

Linnie sat on the floor of the wagon, holding his head, and as he drank, she lifted her eyes to mine, her gratitude expressed without words.

Uriah was alive, but totally spent, so I walked by my

leaders, Val drove my wagon, and Linnie and Nathan managed to keep her wagon rolling behind us. I had to pull at the hackamores to keep the oxen moving. The sun boiled over me, and I could hear George and Ollie crying pitifully. My head swam and I could no longer see. I only knew that we must go on, to stop was death.

I squinted down the road, and in the distance I saw Almond Station. For one agonized moment I thought it was a mirage, but the two log houses and the high stockade were real. The oxen, seeing habitation or perhaps smelling water, hastened their gait. They were almost running, and I was clinging to their hackamores when we reached the wall. The lead oxen plunged toward an empty trough alongside a well. The oxen behind screamed, an inhuman sound of torture.

I lowered the bucket into the well, and Val and Nathan helped me pull it up. We gulped water by the handful, then unchained the wailing oxen.

Linnie came with her oxen as we lowered the bucket again. Ollie scampered down from the wagon to join us, and I gathered up George. I sprinkled water on his face to rouse him from a deep, faintlike sleep, then I held a cup of water to his lips. He sipped.

"Don't drink too much all at once," a man's voice said.

Swaying, I turned around. The world around me was beginning to shimmer in streaks of light and dark, and a heavily-bearded face swam before my eyes.

"You look like you need rest and something to eat," he said. "I'm John Sparks and I'll tend your beasts. You go on up to that far house. My wife will help you."

As I staggered toward the house, a woman opened the door. I thrust my baby toward her, and she took him from my arms as I sank to the ground.

Chapter 41

When I awakened, I was lying on a bed, a real bed, and a wet cloth covered my forehead. I was in a large, airy room, and Linnie, Nathan, Val and Ollie were crowded around a small table, spooning soup. Uriah lay on a bunk near the door. I tried to sit up, but my head fell back on the pillow.

"Reckon you'd better stay put for a while," Mrs. Sparks said, leaning over me with George in her arms. "I'll mind this little one. Don't have any milk for him—old Bessie died in June—but I'm cooking him some pap."

"Pap?" I murmured.

"Best baby food there is," she answered. "It's made from flour and sugar boiled in water. Babies like it, and it keeps."

She poured a little white mixture into a saucer. "What did I tell you," she said, lifting a spoonful to George's mouth. "He likes it fine."

Later Linnie brought me soup. "It's made from antelope meat, Olive—good as beef—and it'll get you going again in no time."

Grateful, I drank the soup, then sank back on the pillow, too weak to get up, too weak to thank Mrs. Sparks for her wonderful kindness.

I felt as if I would never be strong again, but three days later I was clean, rested, and eager to go on. Uriah had recovered too, and seemed as hungry and devoted as ever. The others were well, but I worried about George. He fussed a great deal, still not his usual self, but he ate pap greedily.

"I'll never forget you for teaching me how to make it," I told Mrs. Sparks. Then I added, "I never knew anyone who was so kind to strangers."

"Oh, it's not often we get a passel of women and children," she said. "We been here over a year, and mostly we just see the folks coming through on the stagecoach."

"We're grateful to you—more grateful than I can say."

"Well, we figure you must be getting away from something beyond human endurance to go gallivanting like this, all alone across the country with no man to protect you." She waited expectantly, inviting me to tell my story.

She was a round-faced, middle-aged woman full of bustle and good cheer. After all she'd done for us, she deserved to be told anything she wanted to know, but I couldn't face the anguish of telling her about Percy and our flight from Deseret.

"My friend and I are returning to our families in Iowa," I said. "That . . . that's all there is to it."

Linnie and I cleaned our wagons, getting sand out of our bedding, food boxes, and clothes, and Mr. Sparks went over everything with a blacksmith's sharp eye. He soaked the wheels and reset the tires, then he checked the oxen's shoes and took care of the metal hounds and brakes.

We bought two new barrels from him, and before we left, he filled all our barrels, kegs, and pots with water. Mrs. Sparks gave me a large jar of pap that I stored under the driver's seat.

They both insisted we didn't owe them anything

extra, but when I shook hands with Mrs. Sparks, I pressed a gold piece into her palm.

"You're wonderful, both of you," I said before I climbed on to the high seat. "And I'll remember you in my prayers."

"We'll be praying for you and yours," Mr. Sparks said solemnly. He shook his head. "You sure have a long way to go."

We waved good-bye, and with our backs to the sunset, we headed for Bitter Creek. Val and Nathan were in my wagon; I held George, and Ollie, wide awake and frisky, played in the wagon with a rag doll Mrs. Sparks had given her. When the moon came up, we could see the great rock buttes that spotted the desert to the north. We knew there were long miles of desert still to travel, but we tried to keep each other cheered up.

"I don't mind it at all now, Ma," Val said. "Traveling's not so hard when we got water."

"That's right," echoed Nathan. "Ain't nothing to it now."

As much as we could, we continued to travel at night and rest through the day. At every stage station we took on more water, sometimes getting it free, sometimes having to pay dearly for it. The ground we covered was white with alkali, and during the daytime we had to keep our faces coated with hog fat to protect us from the strange, stinging air.

One afternoon I was awakened by Nathan's frightened cries. "Two of Ma's oxen broke loose. Can't find 'em anywhere."

We all searched, and it wasn't long before Uriah spotted them, drinking at an alkali creek. We led them back to our wagon and gave them fresh water.

"Maybe the alkali won't hurt so bad if they drink a

lot o'fresh water too,'' Linnie said hopefully.

But by late afternoon the poor beasts could no longer stand on their legs. They sank to their knees and rolled on to their sides; less than an hour later they were dead.

''What are we goin' t'do?'' Linnie cried.

Our oxen were double-yoked, so I couldn't give her one of a team. ''Two oxen will have to pull your wagon, Linnie,'' I said. ''I'll take the kegs and as much of your load as I can. Val and Nathan can ride in my wagon when one of them isn't driving for you.''

Linnie stood looking at the dead beasts, the carcasses so much thinner now than when we left Salt Lake City, and tears splashed down her cheeks. She had not only lost power, she'd lost a substantial investment. She'd planned to sell all her oxen in Iowa to obtain money to live on.

I put my arm around her. ''When we get home, I'll give you an ox,'' I promised.

Linnie's wagon came along much slower now, and often I had to wait for her to catch up. The country was the most rugged we'd encountered, and during the day the heat shimmered, rising and falling in misty waves. At first Linnie succumbed to the mirages that appeared.

''Look, Olive, trees and water!''

''No, Linnie,'' I cried, tugging her sleeve. ''If we went toward it, the trees and water would disappear and we'd be lost in the desert.''

The sagebrush, sometimes a foot high, gave off a sickening odor of turpentine, and the oxen refused to eat it. The grain in Linnie's wagon soon disappeared, and the sacks in my wagon began to empty.

Despite the intense daytime heat, the nights were freezing cold and snow banks appeared as we climbed higher into the mountains. The strange country seemed to be a creation of Satan, and I remembered that when we traveled to Deseret, the land had become treacherous after we crossed the Great Divide. Now I hoped that when we crossed the Divide going eastward, our way would become easier.

George ate pap, but he didn't seem to thrive on it. He cried continually. I cleaned him, head to toe, with hog fat to soothe the hurt of the dry wind and heat, but nothing I did really comforted him. I worried about him constantly, and Ollie troubled me too. Her brave, cheerful manner deserted her. Day and night she huddled in the wagon, and her sad little moans broke my heart.

One night when Val was driving Linnie's wagon, I heard him scream. I dashed back, and in the dim light, I saw Linnie's wagon breaking apart. One of the wheels had broken. The rear axle snapped with a sharp crack, and as the bed crashed down, I shouted, "Jump, Val, jump!"

Bounding over the wheel, he sprawled in the dirt. He scrambled to his feet, stunned but unhurt.

Linnie wept over this added loss.

"Don't cry, Linnie," I said, putting my arm around her. "We've known all along that this would happen sooner or later."

"But, Olive, how are we goin' t'go on?" she sobbed.

I sighed. "Your oxen will be an extra team for my wagon, and I'll make room for your drilling, food, bedding, and clothes."

I looked down the long, dark road. "But you and I and the boys will have to walk most of the way. We can't risk my wagon breaking down from an overload."

Linnie dried her tears, and when they came again, as they did for many days, she hastened to wipe them away. ''I know it's the will o'God, Olive, but I can't hardly get over it.''

Now Uriah, Linnie, and I walked through the long nights, and until a late bedtime, Val and Nathan walked with us. The soles of our shoes wore even thinner, and I lined the insides with George's bottom cloths. But our feet throbbed almost beyond endurance, and during the day we took turns easing the agony by soaking them in the tub.

As we climbed higher into the mountains, the days grew cooler. In the distance we could see snow-capped peaks. One night our road descended between high walls of rock, and I knew we were traveling through Bridger Pass.

Day after day our road continued to rise and fall, but gradually I noticed that we were descending more than we were climbing. One morning when we made camp, I filled a bucket with water from a little creek. Something caught my eye. A leaf floated on the water, carried by the current, and it was drifting *east*.

''We've crossed the Divide!'' I shouted triumphantly. ''The way will begin getting easier, and we'll be coming to settlements soon.''

We built a fire, for once unmindful of smoke, and we had a breakfast of porridge coated with jam, delicious in the cold morning air. I brewed a pot of tea using Leah's herbs, and Linnie, the boys, and I all enjoyed it.

''Didn't know you had anything like this with you,'' Linnie said, sipping hers eagerly.

I didn't answer.

''Tastes like the stuff your Indian woman used to cook up. What was her name, Leah?''

''Yes,'' I agreed. ''It tastes just like the tea Leah used to make.''

In the days that followed we continued the long

descent, traveling through beautiful valleys filled with scrub oak, stunted fir, and pine. Rivers and creeks were plentiful now, so we carried less water, allowing us to take turns riding.

We arrived at Fort Halleck on August 20, a day of rejoicing because according to Robert's map, we had traveled more than two-thirds of the way to Denver. For the next two hundred miles, forage would be good, water would be plentiful, and it had been several years since there had been Indian attacks in the Colorado territory. We stayed in Fort Halleck for one day to have the wagon gone over, and we bought milk, eggs, and other supplies. Then we pushed on, joyful in the hope of reaching Denver by the first week in September.

Our joy was short-lived.

Chapter 42

The night after we left Fort Halleck, George became ill, throwing up his milk and running a high fever. We left the road early so that I could care for him, and we made camp near a bubbling stream.

All day long I sponged his hot body with the cool stream water, and I dribbled thin threads of water into his mouth. I gave him quinine too, but nothing seemed to help. From time to time his eyes opened, only to roll vacantly, and I was almost mindless with fear. Linnie stood by, ready to do anything she could.

Toward evening George seemed to be sleeping soundly. I felt we had to go on, but I refused to put him in his sad cradle. I held him snug in my arms, and Linnie and Uriah yoked the oxen and broke camp. They did everything they could to steady the wagon, but that night the jolting seemed worse than usual. At each bump George moaned in his sleep, plaintive little sounds that squeezed my heart. Finally I could stand it no longer.

"Stop, Uriah, stop," I called. "The jolting pains George, and I'm going to walk with him."

Gently, I eased myself to the ground, my precious bundle safe in my arms. "If I get too far behind, stop and wait for me."

As I trudged behind the wagon, the dust and sand from the wheels rose in a cloud around me. I slowed my pace, allowing the wagon to get far ahead. George ceased his moans, and bending my head close to his, I heard his deep, rhythmic breathing.

"He's better," I said aloud. I took a trembling breath, and my tenseness eased.

When dawn broke, my arms ached and I could hardly drag one foot after the other. Uriah and Linnie held up, waiting for me to come to the wagon.

"Do we camp, Olive?"

"Yes, Linnie," I gasped, almost too exhausted to answer. "You must look and find us a place."

She nodded, then reached to lift a corner of the blanket I had over George's face. "D'you think he's feelin' . . ."

Her voice hushed in mid-sentence, and her face contorted. As she looked up, our eyes met. I felt a sinking, grinding pain. With slow, careful movements, my suddenly cold hands moved the blanket away from my baby.

His dark lashes arced on his waxen cheeks, and thin, blue veins traced his temples. His small hands lay limp on the little chest that did not move.

Linnie burst into sobs. "Oh, Olive, Olive."

I stared at her, knowing but unable to respond. Then I kissed George's forehead, not feverish now, and I smoothed the blanket around him to make him more comfortable.

Uriah jumped down from the high seat. "Ma, the baby . . . he ain't . . . he ain't . . . ."

"He's dead," Linnie cried.

I staggered to a tree and sank to the ground. I sat on the grass, tenderly rocking my baby.

After a time I could hear Linnie's voice. "Uriah's fixin' a place for him, a right nice place where there's trees and all."

"Linnie, what is the name of the place?"

"Oh, Olive, I reckon there ain't no name. It's just a place.

I shook my head. "Never. Not for my George." I snuggled him closer still.

As if from a great ditance, I heard Linnie call: "Olive says we can no way bury him here. Reckon we'd better head for the next station, fast as we can get the oxen yoked."

With Uriah and Linnie tugging me along, I walked to the wagon, and they boosted me up. I sat on the high seat beside Linnie. Val sat to my other side, pressing close and sobbing.

I looked down at him. *He lost his father, and now he has lost his brother too, the only brother he can ever have.*

I patted the still blanket. Percy and I would never be together again. This was our last baby, a baby Percy had never even seen. Our baby—and now he was dead—dead.

Ollie's voice sounded closer to my ear. "Mama, is my baby brother really dead? Can't we do something to make him better?"

I couldn't answer. I couldn't utter the words that George was dead, and Ollie continued in a child-world of grief and hope.

"I'll help you take care of him. I'll sing pretty for him when you walk ahead of the wagon. Oh, Mama, I don't want him to be dead!"

Voices, more voices. Nathan whispering his sorrow, Val telling me he would take care of me forever.

We traveled through the day; night came on, and before dawn we were rolling again. Linnie encouraged me to lie down, but I would not let her take George from me.

"No, Linnie, no," I repeated when her voice became insistent. "He wants *me* to hold him."

When we reached the station, the keeper came to the wagon.

"We got a dead baby," Uriah said, "and we want to bury him."

"There ain't no graveyard here," the keeper answered.

"We can't carry him no farther," Linnie cried. "He's been dead two nights."

The keeper looked at me, at the bundle in my arms. "Well, there's lots of land 'round. One hole ain't gonna harm no one."

I lifted the blanket to look again at my son. His hands and face had turned a purplish-blue, and I caught the smell of death.

I turned to the keeper. "This place," I murmured, "does it have a name?"

He nodded. "S'called *Virginia Dale*."

"*Virginia Dale*," I repeated. "*Virginia Dale*."

My arms loosened, and I did not protest when Linnie took my baby.

Later we all stood in a circle around the little grave that Uriah had dug and lined with pine boughs and grass. I smiled. "He'll like it there," I said.

Linnie laid George to rest, then she clutched her Bible.

I am the resurrection and the life. He that believeth on me, though he were dead, yet shall he live.

She read for several minutes, then prayed: "God, thank you for havin' George with you. Take special care of him 'cause he was special t'us. And help Olive t'accept it. Amen."

We walked back to the wagon, my feet pounds of lead as I lifted one after the other. Uriah stayed by the grave, and in my mind, I could see him pushing in the sand, a shovelful at a time to cover the tiny form.

My empty arms ached, and I moved in a numb,

unfamiliar world. Ollie, clinging to my skirt, seemed far away, and Val, holding my hand, looked strange to me.

"I got a toothache, Ma. It hurts."

"I hurt too, Val—all over."

"I'll get you t'sleep now," Linnie said.

I let her lay me down in the wagon. Time passed, but I couldn't close my eyes. The gray-white above me came closer and closer, shutting off the air. I couldn't breathe. With a cry, I jumped up and hurried back to George.

The grave lay rounded and brown with fresh earth, and at the head of the small mound stood a rough wooden cross with his name scratched on it: *George Henry Terry.*

"Thought since we had a grave, might as well get it marked," a man's voice said behind me.

Turning, I faced the stationkeeper. I nodded to him, unable to speak, unable to thank him. He walked away, and I watched him disappear among the bushes. Then I threw myself on the mound of earth. I couldn't cry, but dry sobs wracked my body.

When I try to remember what happened then, everything seems misty. I recall snatches of strange conversations, but it's as if it all took place in a heavy fog.

It seemed that Percy was beside me, and together we were walking away from Sophia's grave.

"Percy, it was the baby," I told him. "When she lost it, she didn't want to live."

A woman pulled on me, begging me to come with her.

"No, I have to stay with Percy now. You see, wife number two has died. I am the only wife he has."

The woman cried out. "Come on, Olive, you got t'sleep."

"Yes, Percy," I heard my voice answer. "And you must sleep too. I know how tired you are."

The woman held my head and pried my teeth open with a spoon. "Take it, Olive, get it down."

A sharp, sweet liquid filled my mouth and trickled down my throat. I swallowed convulsively, and the woman laid me down.

"Percy, Percy, don't leave me."

"There, there. Go to sleep, Olive."

The sharp sting in my mouth slowly faded, and the gray-white above me drifted farther and farther away.

Chapter 43

Someone was crying.

I opened my eyes, but they drifted shut again. I felt as if I'd been asleep for a long time, but I didn't want to wake up. My bed seemed to be bouncing, jogging along, and there was a loud rumble that never ceased. But then I heard it again—soft, plaintive sobs.

A warm body crept close to me, and a hand brushed my face.

"My tooth hurts something awful, Ma. I can't hardly stand it."

"Oh, it's you, Val," I murmured, folding him in my arms.

"Please help me, Ma. It's hurt and hurt for two days."

"Val, go to the cupboard. On the lower shelf in the left-hand corner you'll find a cloth bag of cloves."

"Ma, there's no cupboard. We're in the wagon, traveling."

I sat up, startled and confused, trying to remember. Val's arm went about my neck and his tear-wet face pressed mine.

Linnie appeared. "You all right, Olive?"

"I don't know," I murmured. "Where are we?"

"We're goin' as hard as we can, Olive, headed for Denver t'where there's a doctor for you."

We're in a wagon, traveling, on our way to Denver.
I pulled the information into my mind, trying to under-

stand. Then Val sobbed, and his thin body convulsed in my arms.

"Get the bag of cloves, Linnie. It's here somewhere."

Linnie seemed doubtful, but she pulled and poked at the boxes. At last she straightened. "Here it is! You really did pack cloves. Why, I reckon you thought of everything."

She handed the bag to me, and I dumped some of the dried cloves into my palm, rubbing and crushing them into a powder. "Wet your finger, Val, and dip it in the powder. Now rub it on the place where it hurts. Rub and rub."

"Olive you're better! You're really better," Linnie said. She exhaled loudly, as though she had shed a great burden. "Reckon I kin go help Uriah now," she said.

Val stopped crying. "It feels better, Ma."

He sighed, a quivering sound, then he stretched out beside me. Another sigh trembled through him and he was asleep.

Ollie crept on to my lap. "I love you, Mama," she said determinedly, turning my face to make me look at her.

Clinging to her, I remembered the soft feel of George's body. A sharp ache nagged my heart, and at last the tears came flooding. Ollie cuddled closer, her small hand patting me the way she had often soothed her little brother. I buried my face in her tangled, gritty hair.

When at last I could speak, I said, "Wash your face and find the brush. I will fix your hair pretty and tie the red ribbon in it."

Val and Ollie were my children too. They were still alive, and they needed me.

As I brushed Ollie's hair, the tears continued to roll

down my cheeks; there were sobs I could not check, but I had returned to the world. I would go on living.

We drove into Denver in the early evening, the oxen barely moving, their feet sore and festering. We were all walking to lighten the load, and we gaped at the first town we'd seen since we left Salt Lake City.

Low, rambling buildings with leaning porches lined either side of the street, and signs marked the business establishments. I noted the blacksmith and the telegraph office, and Linnie and I stared wide-eyed into the window of a dress shop.

We camped on a pleasant knoll overlooking a broad expanse of the city. "We'll have to stay here at least two days," I told Linnie. "The oxen need time for their feet to heal."

Linnie and I smeared the oxen's feet with all the salves and ointments we had left, but in the morning there was no improvement.

"We'll just have to wait and see what happens," I said anxiously.

Then I cleaned up, smoothing my dress and arranging my hair as best I could. Taking Ollie with me, I headed for the telegraph office.

I sent a telegram to my parents: *In Denver with children. Will arrive Council Bluffs soon. Do not worry. Love, Olive.*

In June, I had written to them saying I planned a long visit with Linnie in Salt Lake City. I told them they would not hear from me for several months. My telegram would be a jolt, but I hadn't wanted them to know the truth and worry for long months until we arrived.

I started to pay, then told the operator I had decided to send a second telegram. "To Sergeant Robert Madison at Fort Bridger," I said.

Have arrived in Denver. Rested George at Virginia Dale. Expect to reach Iowa soon. God bless you, Olive.

As I wrote the message, I blinked back tears, remembering Robert's joyous smile when George had awakened from his long, laudanum sleep. The death of his own son was still an unhealed wound, a wound that would be rubbed raw by the news of George's death, but he had given my son the only fatherly affection he was ever to receive in his short life. Robert had earned the right to be told.

When I handed the message to the operator, he said, "Will that be all, Ma'am?"

For a quick moment I thought of sending a telegram to Percy—we were too far from Deseret to fear his knowing where we were—but then I shook my head. Percy had chosen not to be with me when our baby was born; he had never seen his son in life, and I would not send news of his death.

As Ollie and I climbed the low-grade embankment to our camp, I saw Linnie talking to a tall, reddish-haired man.

"Olive, this here's Mr. Bruce Mulhaney," she said when I drew close. "Sir, I want you t'meet my friend, Mrs. Percival Terry."

Smiling, Mr. Mulhaney turned to greet me. He was very handsome, and he made a courtly bow in my direction. "My great honor, Mrs. Terry," he said in a clipped, foreign speech.

Linnie piped up, "He's from England—that's why he talks that way."

"Mrs. Bradford is correct," Mr. Mulhaney said. "I have been explaining to your lovely friend that I am from England, and I am in the trading business. She tells me that you ladies are journeying alone, without benefit of male escort, and I usurp the privilege of offering you my assistance.''

Linnie smiled like a Utah farmer sighting rain clouds come to end a drought. "He's willin' t'trade us for the oxen, even though their hooves is so bad. Says he got some fancy mules that'll pull us to Ioway in no time."

Mr. Mulhaney nodded. "Ordinarily I would not consider a trade so distinctly disadvantageous to myself, but I hope I am gentleman enough to assist two ladies in distress."

He cleared his throat. "I will give you four healthy, intelligent mules complete with hull outfit and whippletrees, for your six, sadly crippled oxen and one hundred dollars."

I was so overwhelmed with his charm and manners that it took me a minute to collect myself. "Mr. Mulhaney," I said hesitantly, "we've never driven mules. I don't think—"

"Ah, Mrs. Terry, you have nothing to fear. A fragile lady like yourself will find mules much easier to handle than oxen, and I assure you that I shall teach you everything you need to know about them."

His sincere gaze met mine easily, but I was troubled. I did not look like a fragile lady, and not many people would think Linnie lovely, especially after our long months of drudgery on the road. I knew nothing about mules or what they sold for, but I had the distinct feeling that if we did business with Mr. Mulhaney, *he* would get the best of the bargain.

"No, Mr. Mulhaney," I said firmly. "I don't know enough about mules to make an intelligent trade. We'll just have to stick with what we have."

Ollie pulled her hand away from mine and walked toward the wagon. I followed her, but Mr. Mulhaney called me back. "I hate to see you in this predicament," he said solemnly. "Crippled oxen, no men to help you—it's really a tragedy, and I'll go one step further in order to help you. You may have the mules for your oxen. I will cancel the one-hundred-dollar fee."

On inspiration I said, "Would you give us the mules plus fifty dollars?"

He looked startled. "For a woman you drive a hard bargain," he said, "but let it be done your way. This evening I shall deliver the mules and fifty dollars and take your oxen."

"Mr. Mulhaney, you are truly kind," I said politely, "but I don't want your mules." In a lowered voice I added, "I daresay they're ready to die of old age."

His eyes widened and he stared at me. Then, with the barest nod, he stalked off.

Linnie was inconsolable. "He was so nice t'come 'round t'see if there was someways he could help us, and then you talked t'him so mean. Olive, that wasn't right, 'specially when he was so pretty and sounded so grand."

"How did he know we were alone?" I asked.

"Val and Nathan and me went to look in the stores—t'was all right 'cause Uriah stayed with the wagon. We went into Mr. Mulhaney's store—a real, nice tradin' place—and Mr. Mulhaney started talkin' t'me. Reckon I told him 'most everything."

I shook my head. "Oh, Linnie, that man is certain women have no brains at all. If he talks nice to one, he expects her to believe anything he says."

Watching him retreat down the hill, I felt a hot surge of anger. To Linnie's utter amazement, I said, "I can't tolerate that kind of man."

But even if I couldn't tolerate him, by the end of the

day I owed Mr. Bruce Mulhaney a debt of gratitude. He had given me an idea.

When I examined the oxen, their hooves seemed better, but only slightly. It promised to be days before they were able to travel again, but I was certain the animals weren't worthless. Mr. Mulhaney would not have been so eager to own them if he hadn't known the hooves would heal. Maybe I could trade the oxen after all, but not for mules—for horses.

Late that afternoon I marched into the blacksmith shop. The smith was just pulling his heavy, leather apron over his head, and his brawny, naked arms and bearded face were covered with soot and dust.

"I'm Mrs. Olive Terry," I said briskly. "I want to sell six sturdy oxen and buy four horses, and I would also like to trade a heavy wagon for a Conestoga. I need someone to assist me."

"I'm Bill Frazzle, and I reckon I could help you," he said, his apron still half-on and half-off, "but why don't your man do it?"

"That is none of your business," I said, holding my head erect. Mr. Frazzle was nothing like Mr. Mulhaney—he seemed like a simple, honest man—but if I was going to do business with him, I preferred to have him think of me as a competent person, not as a fragile lady in distress.

"Didn't mean no harm," he said quickly. "And there ain't no reason why I can't help you. Reckon I know all the dealers and traders around."

I allowed myself to smile. "Very well," I said, "I shall do business through you—but remember, I can tell a good bargain from a bad one." I really doubted that I could, but Mr. Frazzle was convinced.

"Reckon I know a good bargain too," he said. "I'll do all right by you, but it'll take a few days. And 'course I s'pect to be paid."

I ignored Aaron's caution not to pay a person for a service not yet performed. "Here is a gold piece," I said, removing one from my reticule. "I'll pay you now and trust that you will do everything as quickly as possible."

His eyes lit up at the sight of gold. "Sure will, ma'am," he said, "and first I better have a look at them oxen you're wanting to sell."

When Mr. Frazzle inspected the oxen, he assured us their hooves would heal in a week or two. "It's the sand and heat what's done it," he said. "Ain't no real hoof disease."

The following day Mr. Frazzle found a buyer for the oxen, and three days later Linnie and I were the owners of four beautiful bay horses and a Conestoga wagon. It didn't take long to transfer our belongings to the new wagon, but I couldn't hold back the tears when I untied George's hammock-cradle.

Linnie and the boys inspected the wagon, almost beside themselves with glee.

"We goin' t'get there in no time," Uriah cheered.

We drove out of Denver before the dawn broke, having decided to travel by day for the remainder of our journey. We headed for the Platte River, which we would follow almost all the way to the Missouri.

The horses traveled eagerly, their heads up, their brown sides swaying in rhythm. During the rugged part of our journey, they wouldn't have served as well as oxen, but now—as Linnie often said—they were a dream come true.

We rode through Julesburg, a sad little settlement at the junction of the North and South Platte rivers, and in less than a week we reached Fort Kearney.

As we continued on, we passed through several tiny towns where we bought food for us and grain for the horses. The roads were good; the late September days

were a blend of vivid colors and refreshing breezes.
When I could jerk my thoughts from the mound of earth
at Virginia Dale, traveling was pleasant.

"We're passin' lots o'houses," Linnie said one afternoon

"Yes, looks different than when we came this way
nine years ago."

Linnie nodded. "Weren't nothin' but buffalo 'round
here then."

As we neared our destination, our excitement began
to bubble fresh and eager as a mountain stream. We
stopped for only a few hours each night, and our meals
were fixed and eaten in a hurry. On the first Saturday in
October we set up our last camp on the western outskirts of Omaha. We were almost home.

Chapter 44

The boys gathered brush and kindling, and for hours our fire roared as we heated water for all of us to bathe in the tin tub. There were shouts and shivers as the brisk wind snapped against wet skin, but our mood was ecstatic.

In the morning Uriah brushed the horses until they gleamed. We dressed in our best clothes; Linnie and I perked up the ribbons on our hats, and Ollie's hair shone golden against a gay, red ribbon. The boys donned their white Sunday shirts, and although there wasn't a fit pair of shoes among the six of us, we looked beautiful.

Uriah was awarded the privilege of driving the last miles.

"We could never have made it without you," I told him, "and I want everyone to see you sitting in the driver's seat, bringing us home."

He giggled. "Never did no more than I had to, Aunt Olive, and never minded all the work." He set his black Sunday hat on his tightly curled red hair, grown long in our long months on the road. "My legs and shoulders ache most o'the time though," he added, "and I won't be mindin' stayin' in one place for a time."

I threw my arms around him and hugged tight. He giggled again, a childish habit, but his childhood had ended on the road home. He was barely fourteen, but he was a man.

We scrambled up to our places, Uriah clicked to the horses, and amid cheers and shouting, we began the end of our journey.

Driving through Omaha, we were overwhelmed.

"It ain't no town," Linnie said breathlessly. "It's a big city."

I looked at the impressive buildings and cobblestone streets. "It's hard to believe," I gasped. "When we came through in fifty-four, there were only a few houses and a trading post."

We drove slowly, looking at everything.

Suddenly Linnie shouted. Ahead of us was the Missouri River—the *Great Mo*—and close to the water I could read the sign: *Council Bluffs and Nebraska Ferry Co.* We drove toward it, and above the din of shouts and tearful cries, I could hear my heart beating.

We didn't have to wait for the ferry, and it carried us, the wagon, and horses over all at one time. We poured out of the wagon to stand at the rope railing, straining to see every rising detail of Council Bluffs.

"It don't even look like Kanesville anymore," Linnie said, wide-eyed. "S'no wonder they changed the name."

We began hugging each other, and Linnie and I fell into each other's arms, laughing and crying.

"Oh, Olive, I never thought as we really would make it, but here we are—here we are!"

As we neared the shore we began to sing:

Come, come ye Saints, no toil or labor fear,
But with joy wend your way,
Though hard to you this journey may appear,
Grace shall be as your day.

We were still singing as we drove off the boat. We were given instructions at the landing, but in our excitement we must have missed the turn we were told to take. We wound our way up one street and down another, looking for a landmark, anything familiar that would give us our bearings.

We reached a church crossing shortly after the Sunday morning service concluded. Uriah reined the horses while the congregation streamed past the wagon. I noted the families—children, a father and mother—one mother. Men and women walked together in pairs. I hugged Ollie to me. That's the way it would be for her. I had kept the promise I made on the day she was born.

We came to the road along Mosquito Creek. "Grandpa and Grandma can't be far from here," I said, swallowing hard.

I looked for the Mormon Church with its one long pane of glass, but there was no sign of it. I studied every log house, fearing I wouldn't recognize my old home.

Suddenly a noisy clanging sprang up behind me. Laughing uncontrollably, Val and Nathan were banging the tin washtub with big spoons.

"We're here," they shouted wildly. "We're here."

I started to hush them, then stopped. They had known few childish pleasures since we left Salt Lake City, and they were entitled to this one.

People poked their heads out of doors to see the commotion. The door to a weather-beaten log house opened, and a blond-haired woman looked up the street.

"Dorothy!" I screamed.

I jumped down before the wagon stopped rolling, and Dorothy and I fell into each other's arms.

"Oh, Olive, Olive," she chanted, hugging me hard. "We got your telegram, but it was hard to believe you were really coming."

Over her shoulder, I saw Ma and Pa running out of

the house. Ma was smiling and tears were coursing down her face, exactly as I had last seen her so many years ago.

I moved out of Dorothy's grasp and wrapped my arms about my mother. We cried together for a moment, then I lifted my head and reached a hand to Pa who crowded close, his tall frame looming over Ma. He was really as big and she was really as tiny as I remembered.

The others had followed me out of the wagon, and I took Ollie and Val by the hand. It was a proud moment when I showed my family my . . . living children.

We made our way into the house, talking, laughing, crying.

There was a flurry of introductions.

"This is Mrs. Linnie Bradford and her sons, Uriah and Nathan. They plan to stay with her sister, Mrs. Lottie—"

"Holson," Linnie finished. "My sister's last name is Holson. You must know her, 'cause she don't live far from here."

Dorothy came forward holding a dignified, well-dressed man by the arm. "Olive, this is Caleb."

I gave him my hand, and he bent to kiss me on the cheek.

"Dorothy's sister is *my* sister," he said, smiling.

The family had gathered for Sunday dinner, and my brother Ted's wife was there too. She was Deborah, a sweet-faced woman, obviously far along with child. Two little children, Anthony and Elaine, clung to her skirts.

Two boys waited for their turn to greet me. "I'm Daniel," one said, thrusting his hand toward me. "I helped load your wagon. Couldn't do much at the age of six, but I was always glad I helped."

I kissed him and turned to the smaller boy. "Now let's see. You're Joseph, the fat baby who sat on Ma's arm and waved bye-bye."

Dorothy lingered at my side, her arm around my waist. "Olive Ann is asleep in her cradle, but where's George?"

I looked up, and when our eyes met, I didn't have to tell her. Mother hovered close, and we all hugged each other in grief, but then I forced myself to smile.

"Dorothy, I want to see *your* baby," I said.

When I looked at the chubby form, snug and beautiful in her cradle, I fought against a vision of the desolate grave in Virginia Dale. But if I shed tears, they were tears of joy for my sister and Caleb who were so thrilled with the baby they had awaited for so long.

Everyone was talking at once, but the room fell quiet when I asked, "Where is Ted?"

There was a solemn pause, then my father straightened to his full height and said proudly, "Your brother Edward is a lieutenant in the Union Army. He is fighting in Tennessee."

Deborah sniffled, and Ma wrapped an arm around her. "He will come home safe and well."

Then Ma clapped her hands, looking almost like a little girl. "If Olive is still here when Edward gets home, we'll have all our children together. Oh, then we'll praise the Lord and gave a big party."

"Percy has moved to California, and the children and I will remain in Iowa," I said softly, grateful for the chance to mention Percy before I was asked about him.

No one spoke, but I could feel the sympathy that welled up around me.

In the confusion, I hadn't seen Daniel leave, but he reappeared at the doorway, leading a tall woman whose surprisingly ample bosom accented her thinness. Dark, tightly curled hair framed a face that was almost a mirror reflection of Linnie's. She and Linnie cried out in unison, then embraced each other, both crying too violently to speak.

I swiped Nathan's hair away from his face. "She's your Aunt Lottie," I told him.

"Linnie," her sister managed between sobs. "I didn't never expect to see you again, not 'til we run into each other in heaven."

Linnie pulled Lottie in my direction. "Years ago Olive promised me I'd be seeing you again someday, and on this side o'the raptures. And 'twas Olive herself what made it come true. When she first said we could hightail it home alone, with no man t'help or nothin', I thought it weren't really possible. But she did it—she did it! She stood up t'Indians, t'the desert an' t'every devil-made thing there is—and here we are!"

Her words astounded everyone. "Does she mean you traveled alone?" my father asked, placing his hands on my shoulders. "You weren't with a train? Only you two women and the children coming all that way?" His voice trembled.

I nodded, and then everyone began questioning us about the trip. I answered, talking slowly, remembering, but as I told of the things we had endured—even George's death—it all seemed detached and unreal. It was as if I were talking about a long, vivid dream—a nightmare from which I had finally awakened.

Lottie was too overjoyed to be impatient, but she yearned to take Linnie, Uriah, and Nathan home to meet her family. Before they left, Linnie and I silently embraced. We had shared something that could never be put into words.

Soon my mother was herding us to crowd around the

table. Daniel and Joseph wedged Val between them, and Ollie sat enthroned on Aunt Dorothy's lap.

Before we ate, Pa led us in prayer. His voice boomed when he thanked God for our homecoming, and then he asked for divine guidance and protection for Ted. "Don't let those Southern varmints or any pestilence harm him," he intoned loudly.

Then—to my great surprise—he prayed for "our President Lincoln."

Protect him as he does Thy work and leads our country out of jeopardy.

To the Mormons, Abraham Lincoln was not a hero. He had advocated dividing the Utah territory like a pie to be devoured by the neighboring states—a death warrant to Deseret. And he was perpetually making severe demands on Brigham Young, demands that Brother Brigham felt honor bound to meet. But I could read in the faces of my family that to them Lincoln was indeed a man of quality. Startled, I wondered if I would ever learn to admire him.

Pa concluded with a thundering amen. Then the bowls and platters began their journey around the table.

Ma's homemade bread, the fried chicken, the mounds of white, mashed potatoes, and the freshly baked pie were all delicious, but I could eat very little. My throat—all my insides ached—full to bursting with a gladness that dripped with unshed tears.

Deborah, Dorothy, and Caleb stayed until long after dark, but finally they had to go home.

"There's plenty of room, and you and your children are welcome to live with us," Caleb said in parting. "And if you ever need anything, stop in at the bank. I'm usually there."

Daniel and Joseph climbed up to the loft; Val and

Ollie were tucked in bed, and then Ma, Pa and I gathered close together around the fire.

While I was gone, my mother's rich, brown hair had blended with gray. Lines on her face counted the passing years, but she was as gay and energetic as ever. Pa's hair was a flawless white—only his dense eyebrows were still red—but he seemed to have lost none of his strength or fighting spirit.

They waited quietly, knowing I had something more to tell. It was painful to think about it, to remember, but in a faltering voice I told them that Percy had married again and had settled in San Francisco with his new wife.

"You didn't want me to marry him, and maybe . . . maybe you were right," I sighed, "but I loved him so much, I could never have gotten over it. He made promises he didn't keep, but he is really convinced that plural marriage has the blessings of God. He doesn't think he's done anything wrong."

Before either of them could say anything, I continued: "And in many ways, Percy was a wonderful husband. He was kind and generous, and he was a thoughtful father too."

Ma pulled herself to her tallest. "If he was so thoughtful, how could he go off and leave you and those little ones?" she snorted.

I shook my head; it was a question I could not answer.

"I'd like to get my hands on him someday," Pa said, rubbing his hands together.

Suddenly Ma was all bustle and business. "Olive, after everything you've come through, you need rest."

I didn't protest, and she hustled me off to share a bed with Val. I eased myself onto the smooth, comfortable mattress, expecting to fall asleep at once, but from deep beneath the quilt, I heard Val's quiet sobs.

"Val," I murmured, "there's nothing to cry about now."

"Ma, you told them we were going to stay here, but that can't be right," he said, his voice quivering. "Someday Pa will go home to get us, and we have to be there."

I opened my eyes and stared into the darkness, trying to form an answer. "Val, Pa won't go back home. He has a new home in California." I wished the truth were not so painful.

Val's voice pitched louder and louder. "He will come back, Ma. I heard him say so. Someday he'll come back to get all of us."

I stroked his shoulder. "It takes years and years to get a medical practice going, and he can't come until that's done."

"But what about when he *does* come, Mama?"

"Val, they're talking about putting a railroad clear across the continent. When that's built, distances won't be so far. Your father can come clear to Council Bluffs quicker than we went from home to Salt Lake City."

"Will he come all the way *here* to get us, Ma?"

"We'll plan on it," I said.

Comforted, Val drifted off to sleep.

Exhaustion engulfed me, and I sank deeper into the feather bed. Reality inched farther and farther away, but I couldn't let go and fall asleep. I had lied to Val. Percy would never come to Council Bluffs . . . never. I would never see him again.

I was too weary to open my eyes. I couldn't fight the visions of Percy that suddenly loomed up to torment me. I saw him smiling, standing in the doorway of this very house, inviting me to attend a dance. I saw him sitting at the fireplace, nodding solemnly as he listened to Pa. I felt the real pressure of his arms around me, and I sighed aloud when his lips brushed my forehead. Then I saw him, portmanteau in hand, walking . . . running towards us. My children gathered around me, Val, Ollie, and George. Percy swept us into his arms.

"I've come for you," he said. "I've come for you at last."

Chapter 45

The next morning I awakened to a new day and a new life that I was eager to begin at once. With Caleb's assistance, I sold the horses and Conestoga for an excellent price. Linnie was delighted with her share of the money, and I still had enough to get a tiny house for Ollie, Val and me. My parents wanted me to remain with them; Caleb and Dorothy tried to persuade me to move into their house, but much as I loved them all, I was determined to live independently.

The house was less than a mile from my parents, a cabin really, that consisted of a kitchen and sitting room with lovely glass windows on two walls. Ollie and I shared the bedroom and Val helped me arrange comfortable sleeping quarters for him in the attic. His window was the size of a handkerchief, but it was real glass, not pig bladder, and on a sunny day, it let in a happy stream of light.

Our yard was big enough for a vegetable garden, and the following spring, Pa helped us get one started. Despite my protests, Caleb and Dorothy gave us a cow, claiming she wasn't good enough to sell. We dubbed her Midge II and sheltered her in a lean-to behind the house.

Our money was limited, and to earn a little extra, I began baking bread and rolls for my neighbors. Linnie was working too.

"I'm takin' in sewin'," she told me, "and Lottie learned me how t'do the fancy stuff."

She and her boys had their own place, a house rented from Mr. Willis, the blacksmith who had hired Uriah as a helper.

With Uriah's wages and her own earnings, Linnie managed quite well, but my little reserve of money was dwindling. I decided to expand my baking business. One morning in August, I went ot the hotels and restaurants in Council Bluffs, a basket of rolls and bread under my arm. When I returned home, I had several orders, steady customers if I could keep them supplied.

It took time to work out a routine. Life seemed hectic for over a year, but by our third Christmas in Iowa, I was operating an efficient business and making enough money to meet our needs.

Flour and sugar were delivered to my house in barrels, and my father and brothers insisted on keeping my woodshed filled. Every afternoon I mixed large bowls of dough and I baked through the night. On the journey home I had learned to sleep at will, and while one batch of bread was in the oven and another was waiting to go in, I would rest.

Fresh and delicious, my bread and rolls were delivered first thing in the morning. On weekends and during the summer, Val made the deliveries, driving a wagon borrowed from my father and pulled by old Polly. Mike had died two years before I returned to Iowa, but Polly trudged on, an aged horse now, but still able to earn her keep.

When Val was in school, my brother Daniel made deliveries for me.

"Daniel, I'll pay you a half-dollar each week," I'd told him when he first offered to drive for me.

He shook his head, refusing to accept money until I made it clear that he wouldn't drive for me unless he did.

Ollie, Val, Nathan, and Joseph attended the same school, and the three boys maintained an enthusiastic friendship. Ollie was the delight of her Aunt Dorothy and Uncle Caleb, and she spent many afternoons at their home, playing little mother to her cousin. My children seemed to be growing up healthy and happy even without a father, but when I allowed myself to admit it, I fought a deep yearning and loneliness living without a husband.

I tried not to think about Percy, but when I did, I was filled with a deep, bitter ache. That February—the February of 1865—I received a letter from him, addressed to me in Iowa and sent from San Francisco. I was sure he had gotten my address from the Potters, our loyal Springville neighbors. I had written to them shortly after we reached Iowa to thank them for their wonderful kindnesses and to let then know that Baby George slept the blessed sleep at Virginia Dale and that Val, Ollie, and I were alive and well.

I hadn't seen Percy since the summer of 1861, nearly four years earlier, and when his letter was delivered, I held it in my hand for a long time. I studied his handwriting, and my fingers fumbled with the seal. Suddenly I caught my breath sharply, rushed to the potbellied stove, and tossed the letter in on the roaring flames. Then, unable to support myself, I sank to a chair and cried for long minutes.

My reaction startled and shamed me. I had thought I could suffer no new pain because of Percy, but part of me still loved him and cherished the memory of our better days together.

"But I can't melt like summer snow simply because I receive a letter from him," I told myself sternly. "If another letter comes, I'll throw it away without tears. Eventually he will stop writing."

The next letter from Percy arrived the first day in April. Without wincing, I marched to the stove and fed it to the flames. It was easier to put the second letter out of my mind because there was something else to think about. Throughout Council Bluffs and across the entire North, a tense eagerness was growing. *Our* armies were fighting deep in Southern territory, and hushed whispers and bold shouts expressed the hope that the long, bloodsoaked war would soon be over.

As Monday, the tenth of April dawned, and word broke through that General Lee had surrendered at Appomattox. Flags and festivities sprang up all over, and that evening my family gathered at my parents' home for prayer and jubilation.

"Just as soon as Ted gets home, we'll have a lovely party," Ma said, clasping her hands. "We'll invite everyone to rejoice with us because all our children are safe and together at last."

"Ma, if you're really planning to invite a crowd, you had better have the party at my house," Dorothy said. "There's not room here for many more than we are now."

"Maybe so," Ma said, "but I'll do the cooking, and it will be a real feast."

Ma was serious about her party. She immediately began making plans, but that Friday, President Lincoln was shot. We all went into stunned mourning, and party-making was postponed until after the black and purple bunting came down.

I had come to admire President Lincoln, and with real sorrow I draped my own door with death ribbon. But our national grief did not keep my family from rejoicing when Ted came home to stay. He arrived on a rainy day in late April, and when I greeted him, the banter and fun were instantly renewed. He was still the adored older brother of my girlhood.

He seized my shoulders. "Sis, you haven't grown an inch up or out, and what did you do with all those years? You're not a day older!"

"You've grown both up and out," I teased, "but you're a handsome creature even if your flattery is more than I can believe."

One Saturday, two weeks after Ted came home, my brother Joseph bounded through my side door: "Olive, Ma sent me to tell you there's a soldier at the house asking for you. Says he's a friend and that he's got a dresser that belongs to Linnie Bradford."

Robert! I snatched up a towel and wiped the dough off my hands; then I hurried toward my parents' home. Halfway there I saw a rickety wagon with no drilling, pulled by a sad team of horses. The driver recognized me before I recognized him.

"Olive!" Robert Madison swung himself over the side of the wagon and rushed tome.

I held out both hands to him. "Oh, Robert, it's really wonderful to see you," I said, joy and excitement washing over me.

He gathered me in his arms and hugged tight. "Olive, I've been thinking about this moment ever since we said good-bye, back in the Wyoming territory."

We stared at each other long and wordlessly. He was thinner, but sunbrowned and clean-shaven, and his broad smile diffused a light over his entire face. When I smiled up at him, that light seemed to capture me too.

But we were sanding in the street. "Let's . . . let's go to my folks' house," I said, feeling my cheeks grow warm.

He helped me into the wagon. "Met your Ma and she told me where you lived. I'll have to find Linnie too, and give her the dresser."

I looked behind me and saw a huge object wrapped in

canvas. "Couldn't bring it without a wagon and team," Robert said, "but this rig was the best I could find. Traded my horse to get it."

"Linnie will be grateful," I answered, but my own heart swelled with gratitude and affection for a man kind enough to go to such trouble for a woman he knew so briefly.

Robert had no close family to fuss over him after his long years in the army, but when I renewed the story of all he had done for us, my own folks extended him a welcome almost the equal of my brother's.

"We want you to stay with us for as long as you're in Council Bluffs," Pa told him the next day after we'd all finished one of Ma's Sunday dinners.

"And you have to stay for the party we're planning," Ma said eagerly. "*Your* safety during the war is another reason we want to celebrate."

The children responded to him as quickly as they had before, and Ollie was soon calling him *"Tindy"* again. She was nearly eight, too old to use such a disrespectful address, but my chidings had no effect. An unpredictable blend of sugar and sass, Ollie smiled sweetly and said, "I'll call Tindy, *Mr*. Tindy if you want me to, Mama."

Robert roared with delight, and the rest of us laughed too.

Robert began making deliveries for me instead of Daniel, saying, "I might as well make myself useful."

He was amazed at the quantity of bread and rolls I turned out each day. "You can work harder than most men and still look as pretty as a picture fit to hang in the parlor," he told me.

It had been a long time since I'd seen such admiration in a man's eyes or been told I was pretty. I responded in spite of myself, feeling a happy, eager warmth, but I was determined not to give Robert any encouragement. He was a wonderful man, but I was a married woman. I was sealed to Percy for time and eternity, and even if I never saw him again, part of me would love him until I died.

"It is nice of you to help me while you're here, Robert," I told him, "but I daresay after Ma's party, you will continue on East."

On the ninth of June, one week before the party, Dorothy appeared at my door carrying a bundle she insisted was for me. I opened it, then stared wide-eyed at an exquisite length of amber-colored Oriental silk.

"Oh, Dorothy," I gasped. "I can't accept this."

"Of course you can," she said firmly. "I sent to California for it months and months ago, but until the war ended, shipments just weren't getting through."

She draped the silk around my shoulders, and I looked in the mirror. "Dorothy, it's beautiful," I murmured.

"Wait until you see *mine*," she said excitedly. "It's the lightest pink you ever saw. Caleb says when the dress is finished, I'll look like a big pearl."

We both laughed; then Dorothy asked if there was any possibility that I could have a dress finished in time for the party. "I'd love to see you in it," she said, "and I imagine that Sergeant Madison would too."

"It was lovely of you to get this for me," I said, ignoring her comment about Robert, "and I'll see if I can have a dress ready in time."

But I knew I wouldn't have time to sew, so late that afternoon I brought the silk to Linnie. When she saw me, she burst into happiness.

"Olive, it's a joy t'see you, and you got t'come look at my mother's dresser."

The dresser dominated the bedroom, the fine wood

so buffed and polished it shown like window glass.

"Linnie, it looks magnificent."

"Sure does," she agreed, "and Sergeant Madison was a powerful nice man t'bring it all that way for me. Fact is, Sergeant Madison is nice as Mr. Willis."

"Mr. Willis?" I questioned.

"Oh, Olive, him and me have come t'be real friends, and look at what he give me for my birthday."

She took a pretty brooch from the top drawer of the dresser. "He give me this and a whole, dressed hog. Ain't nobody ever give me such grand presents before."

She smiled. "He's comin' t'dinner tonight. He comes 'most every Friday, and I'm fixin' his favorite—squash stuffed with chicken."

I opened my parcel. "I've brought a fresh loaf of bread. Perhaps Mr. Willis will like that too, but I've really come to ask you to work for me."

We spread the silk out on Linnie's bed, and she was positive she could have a dress finished within a week. "For someone else, I couldn't be so sure, but for you, Olive, I know it'll get done, even if I have t'hurry Mr. Willis home a mite early."

Every time she mentioned Mr. Willis, her face lit up. She looked happy and pretty and excited, all the wonderful ways a woman looks when she's in love.

I touched her arm. "You and Mr. Willis—it's a romance, isn't it?"

Linnie blushed violently. "It ain't no such thing, Olive. You know it can't be when I'm married. But he's so sweet t'me and nice t'Nathan and Uriah—and well, he does say I'd sure make him a mighty fine wife . . . ."

Her voice faded, but then she added, "He's taking

me t'your folks' party. I hope people will think that's all right."

"Linnie, I think it's wonderful."

We were both silent for a moment, then I asked, "Do you ever hear from Stephen?"

She shook her head. "Never. Not one word. The boys fixed up a letter t'send him, a real good one, but he ain't never answered it. That puzzles me some, 'cause he seemed t'like the boys. Ain't no surprise that he never wrote a word t'me."

Her expression clouded, so I said, "Linnie, I'm certain you and Mr. Willis and your boys will have a good time at the party. With all my mother's planning, it's bound to be a success."

"And you'll be wearing a pretty silk dress. I'll get it done in time."

That night as I did my baking, I thought about her. She was happy and radiant in the love she'd always craved. I was thrilled for her, and I didn't think there was any good reason why she and Mr. Willis shouldn't get married if they wanted to. Stephen had never loved her, and she'd probably never see him again.

I pounded the dough with my hands, venting my feelings in the sticky mass. Their marriage hadn't been like Percy's and mine. We had loved each other once, deeply. But the only bonds between Linnie and Stephen could be dissolved by a bill of divorcement.

I thought about it for a long time. Divorcement was a drastic step, but sometimes it was justified. I sighed, wondering if Linnie could ever be pursuaded to consider it.

The following Saturday morning, the day of the party, Linnie brought the finished dress to my house. She was concerned that she hadn't marked the hem correctly, but when I tried it on, the dress fit beautifully. Linnie was as delighted as I was, and she told me she was going to wear a new dress too.

"It's blue," she added, "Mr. Willis's favorite color."

My sister Dorothy came over early in the afternoon. "Olive, let Val and Ollie go home with me," she said. "Val can help put the decorations up, and Ollie can play with Olive Ann while I get ready."

I consented, and Val and Ollie hurried to pack their party clothes.

"And I want you to wear these," Dorothy said, handing me a tiny box. I opened it and saw her diamond earbobs.

"Oh, Dorothy, I couldn't," I exclaimed.

"Olive, they're so beautiful, and I can't wear them," Dorothy said, refusing to take them back. "My dress looks like a pearl and I have to wear pearls with it, not diamonds. But they are much too pretty to leave in a box."

Robert stopped for a moment while Dorothy was trying to persuade me to wear the earbobs. I had agreed to let him take me to the party, but he wanted to warn me that he might be late.

"Don't worry," I told him. "I want to have all my baking done before I go, so I may be late myself."

After everyone left, I hurried through my baking, making over a dozen loaves of bread, then I concentrated on getting ready for the party. I bathed, washed my hair, and spent over an hour arranging it just right. I was twenty-eight years old, and the bouncy, girlish curls that had once annoyed me were not so unwelcome now.

Linnie had poured all her friendship for me into making the dress, and when I put it on, I was convinced it was the most beautiful garment I had ever owned. I had been sure I wouldn't, but at the last moment I put on Dorothy's earbobs.

I looked in the mirror. It had been a long time since I had dressed for a party, a long time since I had waited for a man to come to take me out. My reflection blushed with pleasure. For this one night, I would enjoy Robert's company. I would dance and laugh, greet old friends and have a wonderful time.

Someone was pounding the front door. Robert usually came to the side entrance, the way everyone in the family did, but this was a special occasion.

Smiling, I ran to the door and undid the heavy bolt and chain. The door was so rarely used, I had to tug a moment before it swung open.

There on the threshold, looking just as he did in my dreams, stood Percy.

Chapter 46

My legs threatened to give way. Percy reached out his hand to steady me, then his arms encircled me in an embrace.

"Olive, dearest Olive, it's been so long," he murmured, his mouth, his warm breath close to my ear.

He kissed me, but I was too numb to respond.

Setting his portmanteau inside, he closed the door. Then he held me at arm's length. He was real, and his radiant smile tugged my heart the way it always had.

I shook my head, not wanting it to happen, but an excitement, a glow, welled up inside me.

Percy! I stared at him, yearning to shout and cry and laugh, and then lose myself forever in the circle of his arms.

"You're lovely," he said, "more beautiful now than the first time I ever saw you."

Gently, he touched one of the sparkling earbobs; he looked down at my dress that shimmered in the evening light. "Olive, you had me worried when you didn't answer my letters," he said, his eyes hungrily searching my face, "but you were waiting for me, weren't you?"

Ecstatic, he hugged me again. "I arrived two days later than I said I would, but you kept yourself all prettied up until I got here."

My heart was pounding, but so was my head. I pulled away, trying to sort the thoughts that hammered through my mind. "I . . . I wasn't waiting for you, Percy. I had no idea you were coming."

"What?" he exclaimed. "Didn't you get my letters?"

I sat down to steady myself. "Three letters came, the third one less than two weeks ago, but I threw them all in the fire. I . . . I never read them."

Percy moaned. "Olive, my dearest, stubborn Olive."

I folded my hands on the table. "I'm dressed for a party my parents are giving at my sister's home, and Ollie and Val are already there. It's a celebration because my brother Ted has returned home safe from the war, and my whole family is together again."

Percy pulled up a chair next to mine. "That's one good thing that's come of all this. You've had a nice long visit with your family. I can't say you didn't deserve it, but Olive . . . Olive, going off the way you did. You have to admit it was childish."

He shook his head. "My own, unpredictable Olive, you're the same beautiful, reckless girl you were when you took those horses to the river on our wedding night."

I hadn't thought about that night in years. It was hardly the time for my mind to wander, but I found myself wondering what Robert would say if I told him about it. Somehow I knew he would grin and tell me what a wonder I was.

But Percy was concerned about Linnie. "The Bradford woman is not the kind to run off on her own," he said, looking reproachful. "Just think of how Stephen Bradford would have felt if he had returned to Deseret and found his second wife and their sons missing."

I was puzzled. "Are you saying that Stephen Bradford is still in the South Seas?"

Percy's beautiful, preaching voice boomed. "Brother Stephen lost his life bringing converts to the gathering. And his wife, under your influence . . . ."

Percy continued, but I didn't hear. *Stephen Bradford had been a good man, a high priest of the church. He had sent Linnie to my wagon to meet me. He . . . he was dead!*

An unwelcome smile tugged the corners of my mouth. I was sorry he was dead, but I couldn't help thinking that now Linnie could enjoy her romance with a free conscience. She could bask in Mr. Willis's affection and accept his proposals.

Suddenly Percy walked over to the sideboard. "What in the world are you going to do with all this bread?" he asked.

"I'm in business," I said proudly. "I run a bakery, and I earn enough money to support the children and me."

Percy groaned. "What a terrible thing for a wife of mine to be doing—working for other people like a servant."

He sat down by me again. "There were bank drafts in those letters you burned, money to take care of you and my children."

He clasped my hands in his. "My medical practice is established in San Francisco. I'm making money, and I've already raked in a fortune from good investments. I was ready to come for you last year, but during the war, travel was too risky. The moment the war ended, I began making arrangements to get away."

His grasp tightened. "Oh, Olive, it's a different country out there, a wonderful country. Gold is flowing, and when the transcontinental railroad is complete, there will be no limit to what San Francisco can become."

His touch, his presence sent shivers all through me, and as he talked, I could feel myself responding to his warmth and vitality. I closed my eyes, listening, and my body throbbed with longing.

"When Val is old enough, I'll send him to the best medical school in the country, and someday he'll come into my office. There's talk of running me for coroner, and if I go into public service, I'll want him to take over my practice."

He laughed and squeezed my hands again. "Olive, you won't believe it when you see some of my fashionable patients. And I'm going to get you a house right up there on Rincon Hill among them."

A breeze laden with summer fragrances stirred the room and seemed to blend with his voice, transporting me to the wonderful place he was describing. I could see myself in an elegant house, standing forever at Percy's side, watching our son grow to manhood and our daughter become a beautiful, young woman.

I opened my eyes and Percy looked jubilant. "Olive, I love you and I know you still love me—and now we'll be together again always."

"Yes, Percy," I murmured. "I still love you." I wanted to melt into the beautiful vision he held out to me, but there was an intruder, a pretty girl in a pink dress.

I jerked my hands free and stood up. "What about Emily?"

"She's fine," he said calmly. He tipped his chair back and fingered the gold nuggets on his watch chain. "She sent her greetings to you, and she's looking forward to our coming."

The breeze was chilly now. "You . . . you still have her as your wife?"

"Of course, Olive. I'm not the kind of man who

breaks his marriage vows.''

''And . . . and you expected to take me back as your wife too?''

''You *are* my wife, Olive. I love you and I want you with me.''

I shook my head, not speaking. There was nothing to say.

Percy stood up and put his hands on my shoulders, but his touch, his nearness did not affect me now. ''It was hard for you when I had to take Sophia to wife, but you got over it. You learned to love her, you know you did. You'll love Emily too. She's a wonderful person, completely docile and obedient, and there's a child now, a little boy.''

My voice was steady. ''Percy, I did learn to love Sophia, but after you took her, I wasn't your wife again until long after she died. I have to be the only wife, or I will not be a wife at all.''

''But, Olive, my marriage to Emily is an honorable one—the same as my marriage to you. I cannot forsake her. I'd always feel guilty knowing I'd wronged her.''

''But you wronged me, Percy. You promised me never to choose another wife, but when other wives were chosen for you, you married them without protest. You twisted words to destroy my happiness and your honor.''

I had turned my back to him, but I heard him catch his breath.

I looked out the window. Houses and trees loomed as shapes hardly visible in the increasing darkness. ''Percy, you should not have come.'' My voice was flat, without emotion.

''Oh, my God, Olive, you don't understand,'' he wailed. ''*Nothing* is right without you. Emily is a good girl, but something is wrong, something is missing.

Even when I take her to bed, I think of you. There's
something about you, even when you're being so will-
ful . . . ."

His voice faltered. "During the day, things happen
that I want to tell you about. At night, I wish you were
asleep at my side. And it doesn't get better. I miss you
more all the time."

He had come to stand close behind me, and I felt
crowded. I slipped past him. "It's impossible, Percy."

He sat down again, slumping low in the chair and
resting his arms on the table. "What if . . . what if I
keep Emily as a spiritual wife only? What if I promise
that no matter what happens—no matter what the
church orders me to do—I will never bed any woman
but you?"

"No, Percy," I sighed. "I couldn't do that to Emily.

With a muffled sob, he buried his face in his hands.
Suddenly I had to blink back my own tears; Percy was
all the things I had ever thought he was—loving, kind,
and intelligent. And he was still as handsome as any
man I'd ever seen. His graying hair and the lines on his
face added to his look of gentleness, and his eyes were
still as sparkling blue as they were the first time I ever
saw him.

And Percy was weak. How was it possible that
through all the years I had never realized it? He had
always acted so intense, so positive, but could he ever
have been sure of anything? Others had determined the
form of his thoughts, and during the night watches he
had never wondered or been baffled or made up his own
mind.

My poor darling! I put my arm around his shoulder
and lay my cheek against his hair. "Don't cry, Percy,"
I said. "Everything will be all right."

He raised his head and looked at me. "Do you mean

that, Olive? You and the children will go back to California with me, and everything will be all right?''

Gently I pressed my lips to his. I stroked his brow. "Percy," I said slowly, "I am going to stay here and get a bill of divorcement. You must go back to California and forget about me. Emily will take care of you. I'm sure she will.''

Percy groaned, a sound of anguish, and with all my heart I wished I could relieve his pain.

A light, familiar tap sounded and I pulled myself to my feet and opened the side door.

''I'm sorry I'm so late,'' Robert said, studying me from head to toe, ''but I had important business in Omaha.''

He wore a blue coat and satin vest—the first time I'd seen him dressed up—but his broad grin faded when he saw Percy. I touched his sleeve and led him into the room.

''Robert, this is my—this is Dr. Percival Terry.'' To Percy I said, ''Mr. Robert Madison.''

Percy shuffled to his feet and extended a hand. Robert hesitated, then touched Percy's hand without speaking.

''Go on to the party without me,'' I told him. ''Perhaps Percy and I will come later.''

''Olive, don't you know that . . . that . . . .'' Robert sounded angry, but he did not continue. He left abruptly, banging the door behind him.

''Is he a relative?'' Percy asked dully.

''No,'' I answered. ''Robert is the man I'm going to marry.''

The thought sent a refreshing happiness all through me, but Percy was incredulous.

''How . . . how can you marry another man? You are *my* wife.''

I shrugged. "You married another woman."

"But you . . . you belong to me," he said hoarsely.

"Percy," I said carefully. "I don't belong to you. I belong to myself."

He slumped forward, and for long silent minutes we stared at each other.

"I . . . I had better leave," Percy said at last. "There's a train due to leave Omaha early in the morning, and I'll be on it."

"But, Percy, the children—if we go to the party, Val and Ollie can see their father, at least for a little while."

I could tell by Percy's expression that he was willing to go, but then I remembered something. "But my father is there too. He's always said—well, that he'd like to get his hands on you."

Percy shuddered and turned his back on me. "I think I should go now, but I have things I would like to leave for the children."

He undid the straps of his portmanteau and took out gifts—a ball and bat for Val, an elegant doll for Ollie, and a blue velvet case that he handed to me.

"Mrs. Potter told me about the little one, so I didn't bring a gift for him." He shook his head sadly. "A little son I never saw."

"He looked just like you, Percy," I said softly. "And you would have seen him if you had stayed with me."

The case contained a heavy gold necklace. "Give it to Emily," I said, handing it back to him.

When we parted, he kissed my hand. Then I stood in the doorway and watched as he disappeared into the darkness, his head down, his feet moving heavily as his legs jerked forward. I felt a pain, but it was an old pain, one I was used to, one that would never go away.

Chapter 47

Only minutes after Percy left, Val bounded into the house. "Pa! Where's my Pa?" he screamed.

I went to him and put my hands on his shoulders. My words came with difficulty. "Your father is not here. You see—"

"But Sergeant Madison told us he *was* here. Said he'd seen him."

"That's true, Val." My eyes filled with tears as I looked at his desperately eager face.

Daniel and Ollie appeared in the doorway. "Val wanted to come home as soon as he heard his father was here," Daniel said. "Pa would have brought them, but he said he couldn't trust himself. If you want to go to the party, I have Caleb's carriage."

I shook my head. "You go back, Daniel. Tell Ma I'm sorry I couldn't come."

When Daniel left, I took Ollie by the hand and turned back to Val. He seemed to be peering into corners as if he expected to find his father hiding in the shadows.

"Your father came for us, just the way he promised he would. He loves you both very much, and Val, when you're older, he wants to send you to the best medical school in the country. He has a big medical practice in San Francisco, and someday you can work with him. He wants you very much."

"But where is he *now?*" Val demanded.

I sighed and felt the strength drain from my body.

"He's gone back to California. He has another wife there. He has had another wife all these years."

Val had rarely cried since the hungry winter of his babyhood, but now tears streamed down his cheek. "Uriah and Nate said he had another wife, but I never thought it was true."

"It's true, and Val, I don't want to be married to a man with another wife. You can understand that, can't you?"

Val nodded. Tears were still rolling, but he was eleven years old and he hadn't seen Percy since he was seven. He needed something more real, more immediate, than a shadowy memory.

"Val, Ollie, would you like Sergeant Madison to be your father?"

Ollie could hardly remember Percy. She had come home sleepy and disinterested, but now her eyes grew wide and alert. She clapped her hands. "Oh, Mama, if I could call him *Papa,* I wouldn't call him Tindy anymore."

Val was smiling too. "Sergeant Madison told me he'd like to be my pa. Said he was pretty sure it would work out that way someday."

It was my turn to smile. My refusals hadn't convinced Robert, and he was waiting for me to change my mind.

Before we went to bed, I gave the children their gifts. "Your father brought these things all the way from California for you."

Val picked up the bat and ran his hand along the smooth wood. "I never had a bat and ball before. Maybe Sergeant Madison will help me learn how to play."

Ollie was impressed with her doll. "Look, Mama. When you lay her down, her eyes close. When you pick her up, her eyes open. And they're blue, just like mine.''

She clutched the doll even after she was in bed. ''I'll name her Tindy, after my new papa.''

The next morning I was up earlier than usual, and I dressed with special care. I couldn't wear my silk dress; my good paisley would have to do. I arranged my hair in curls and hoped I looked as good by the light of morning as I had the evening before.

When I heard the wagon pull up, I ran outside, but it was Daniel, not Robert, in the driver's seat. I didn't pause to greet him.

''Where is Robert?'' I asked.

''I guess he's on his way by now,'' Daniel answered. ''Told me to say good-bye to you for him.''

I went cold. ''Where was he going?''

''Back East where he came from. Pennsylvania, I think. He was just about ready to leave when I came away.''

As Daniel hopped down, I pushed him aside and scrambled into the driver's seat. ''Oh, Daniel, I've got to hurry!'' I cried.

I cracked the whip to old Polly, and she started up, slow and easy. ''Hurry, Polly, hurry!'' It was like the night I had urged her and Mike to run for the river, but now Polly clopped along at her own pace, unmindful of my prodding.

A band tightened around my chest, and I could hardly breathe. *Robert is leaving because he thinks Percy and I are reconciled, and I'll have no way to get in touch with him.*

When I turned up the road that ran along Mosquito Creek, I saw Robert in the distance, astride his new horse, galloping off in the other direction.

''Robert!'' I screamed. ''Robert!''

I sighed with relief and joy when he reined his horse and looked back. I beckoned wildly, but he walked his horse toward me at an agonizingly slow pace. At the side of the wagon he stopped and leaned toward me.

"I'm glad to get a chance to say good-bye to you, Olive." He looked tired, his eyes refused to meet mine, and his smile was a real effort.

"Where are you going?" I asked, an idle question because I was determined that he wasn't going anywhere.

Robert looked down the road. "I'm heading back to Pennsylvania. I have a few people there—an aunt and some old friends."

"What was your important business in Omaha?"

He shook his head. "It's not important now, but I had been making arrangements to buy a general store. It's in a nice section of the city, and I thought that—well, with your bakery business and all, you and I might build it into something."

At last he looked at me, and now his smile was genuine. "I hope you'll be very happy, Olive. You deserve to be."

I nodded. "Oh, I'm sure I will be," I said eagerly. "And maybe we can have a small room next to the store where we serve the customers fresh bread and rolls with something to drink. But there would have to be windows. I won't work in a place that doesn't have nice, big windows."

Puzzled, he looked at me. "The store has a wide window that goes nearly clean to the ground," he said hesitantly, "but what about Percy?"

"He came to get us and take us to California. He said he'd give up Emily as a real wife if I'd go with him, but I sent him back alone. I told him I was going to obtain a bill of divorcement and marry you."

Robert let out a whoop that I'm sure was heard for miles. He dismounted and pulled me down from the wagon. Laughing, I put my arms around his neck. He kissed me, and I felt a great happiness surge, but then old memories tugged my heart. For a brief but painful moment I thought of Percy.

I pulled back a little, so I could look directly at him. "Robert, there's one thing I want you to know—something you must understand. I sent Percy away, but I'll never forget him."

Robert took me by the arm and pulled me into the shade of an elm tree in full, summer leaf. He kissed me again, and in the tightness of his embrace, I could feel his body pressing close to mine. I responded, completely giving myself to the rapture and love that soared through me.

When he finally released me, I pulled back, feeling myself blush like a young girl. I gasped for breath.

Robert put his hands on his hips. He was grinning broadly, and he looked remarkably pleased with himself.

"You'll forget him," he said.

There are a lot more
where this one came from!

Anne Maybury
Gothics

☐ **Falcon's Shadow** 22583-7 $2.25
The search for her true parents leads a young woman into a dangerous past.

☐ **Green Fire** 30284-X $2.25
The mysterious Orient held the terrifying secret of the "Green Fire."

☐ **The House Of Fand** 34408-9 $2.25
A young bride finds herself on a terrifying honeymoon of danger and deceit!

☐ **I Am Gabriella!** 35834-9 $2.25
Karen meets her long-lost cousin, only to have her vanish again—and reappear with a new identity!

☐ **Shadow Of A Stranger** 76024-4 $2.25
Tess senses that her husband is becoming a stranger to her. Then one day she overhears the words that are to change her life . . . if she lives long enough!

☐ **Someone Waiting** 77474-1 $2.25
A joyous reunion turns into a terrifying nightmare of evil —and murder.

Available wherever paperbacks are sold or use this coupon.

78c

More Fiction Bestsellers From Ace Books!